~ Praise from readers and reviewers for ~

𝒟𝒶𝓁𝑒'𝓈 𝒟𝑒𝓈𝒸𝑒𝓃𝓉

"With the addition of Dale's Descent the epic saga of The Master of Whitehall is quickly becoming THE vampire love story of the century!"

Little Red's Book Reviews

... a very nice surprise ... an "Old School" vampire story that was not only refreshing, it was written beautifully - bordering on old fashioned yet told through a modern voice.

The Indie Bookshelf

Dale's Descent is the PERFECT addition to the Master of Whitehall series. The author is unique in his style of writing. He personifies Dale as so realistic. As paranormal/vampire series go, you will NOT be disappointed!

Stephanie Beetham, Amazon Reader/Reviewer

I liked Dale when I met him in the first book, but fell in love with him in this one. He is quite charming, but can be extremely deadly to his prey. The author has written an intriguing series of love, friendship and emotional growth. His characters are all lifelike and likable.

Book Reviews by Lynn

A fantastic must read for vampire lovers ...

Young Adult and Teen Readers

The Epic Saga of
The Master of Whitehall

Continues with these
Other Titles
by
Rick H. Veal

Katelyn's Chronicles

Lexi's Legacy

Charlotte Ann's Coven

James' Journey

Other Works Include

Taylor's Tale

Jennifer's Ghost: A Tale of Ghostly Love

Hannah's Heartache

(A Master of Whitehall Novelette)

Veal's writing style is somewhat different in that he writes in a niche between Gothic horror and modern day vampire literature that no other author has delved into yet. He is one of only a small handful of authors who adhere to the classical, lethal vampire instead of the popular romanticized versions portrayed in current literature. His characters are not the modern whitewashed version of vampires but more of a cross between Bram Stoker's vampires and the ones found in present day paranormal literature. While they are likable they are *NOT* human and the body count that piles up is astounding even though the vast majority of the victims are criminals of the worst sort.

Douglas C. Meeks,
Amazon Top 200 Reviewer

Dale's Descent

A Journey Into Darkness

A Master of Whitehall Novel

Book Three

Rick H. Veal

Virgin Vampire Publishers

Published by Virgin Vampire

The Master of Whitehall: Dale's Descent
Copyright © 2014, 2017 by Rick H. Veal
Cover Art and Cover Layout by
Deborah Taylor, DCA Graphics, Inc.
www.dcagraphics.com
All other decorative art courtesy of
Karen Watson, The Graphics Fairy, LLC
www.graphicsfairy.blogspot.com
Body text set in Palatino 12 pt.
Library of Congress Control Number: 2014903888
ISBN: 0-9981044-2-6
ISBN 13: 978-0-9981044-2-3
Printed in the United States of America

Thank you for your purchase, for comments, or to obtain further copies, please find us on the web at www.themasterofwhitehall.com, on Face Book at The Master of Whitehall, or contact the author direct at author@prtcnet.com

Corrected and Expanded Edition
August 2021
10 9 8 7 6 5 4 3 2 1

~ Acknowledgements ~

I have been blessed and come to know so many new friends and readers through the first two books of The Epic Saga of The Master of Whitehall – "Katelyn's Chronicles" and "Lexi's Legacy". Your continued support has helped make this wonderful journey the resounding success that it has become and each of you holds a special place in my life. I wish I could name every one of you. However, to each one of you, named or not, I am very pleased to be able to call you my friend.

First, and most importantly, to the memory of my parents, Hoyt and Hazel, thank you for having been such great parents and for the Life Lessons you taught me; many of which I didn't realize the importance of until after you had departed this life. This work is lovingly dedicated to you!

I have the best crew of Beta Readers that any author could ever hope to have – Heather Alexander, Bree High, Angela Pratt, Kim Shaw and Samantha Truesdale. I offer my heartfelt special thanks to all of you. Each of you have made a special effort by taking the time out of your busy lives to proof read, make corrections and offer comments. You have all been so gracious in your help of promoting the series. Thank you so much for your friendship. You cannot imagine how much I appreciate everything you've done.

Yet again I offer my special gratitude to Debbie Taylor, friend and artist, for her many artistic talents in producing and designing the beautiful cover for Dale's Descent. You have once more produced a breath-taking work of art. It is sure to catch the reader's eye and ultimately draw them into the story.

I once again offer my debt of gratitude to my college English Professor, Dr. John Wright, for not only teaching me how to write, but to enjoy doing it, thank you, sir!

Chapter One

he small nightclub that I was sitting in was dimly lit but my eyesight allowed me to see everything in it as if it were lit with floodlights. There were only a couple of dozen people inside; it was still early evening, too soon for the late night crowd to have arrived yet. I had sat here in this same corner table every night for the last two weeks watching and waiting. My back was finally to the wall … and in more ways than just my choice of seats. I struggled yet again to fight back tears as I looked around at all the people who were enjoying their lives.

I saw that most of them were paired off into couples and all of them seemed to be having fun in the early evening. I didn't have fun anymore … I couldn't … in fact I had almost forgotten what it was like to have fun. I was all alone in this world with no one … and I was so very lonely. While I sat and watched all of them enjoying their lives … I was planning on ending mine … I was going to destroy myself ... and all I needed was just a little more courage to carry through with my plan. It shouldn't be too difficult a thing to do; after all, I was already dead. I had been attacked, killed and then brought back as a vampire on my sixteenth birthday.

That was certainly not the birthday present I had expected ... but it was one I'll never be able to forget either. But soon, I hope, this miserable existence will be over and I'll be free of the curse I've lived under for so many years. My only hope is that when I do end it, God will understand that I didn't choose this ... this curse ... that was so unexpectedly thrust upon me, it wasn't my fault. I would never intentionally have become what I am and done the things I've had to do to survive. I hope in His infinite wisdom that He will have mercy on me and not punish me any more than I have already suffered.

My name is Dale and for the last thirty five years I have been lost ... lost to myself, my family, and finally my maker when he destroyed himself, leaving me abandoned and all alone. I have spent the better part of the last two years traveling from place to place searching for and hoping to find others like me. I suppose that in the back of my mind I was intentionally coming to this place and for this purpose. I didn't want to live any longer ... at least not like this. I had been told by my maker that there were those who would destroy me if I ever came here ... and truthfully, the thought of someone else destroying me is easier to take than thinking about having to do it myself.

I had arrived in Charleston several weeks ago and after trying purposefully night after night still haven't found anyone like me. If there are any more vampires in this world, they are staying well-hidden and out of my sight. I'm really not sure how to locate others like me to begin with, but if there are others, they either don't want to be found or maybe they just don't want *me* to find them. Either way I am not going to continue like I am … I never wanted to be this way … I never wanted to have to kill to survive … but I had no choice in the matter. So I have made up my mind that if someone else doesn't come along and destroy me, I will do as my maker did … I will wait and watch for a burning building and then walk into the middle of the fire … I don't know of any other way to destroy myself … I just hope that it's quick and doesn't hurt too badly. I'm used to suffering, I've known nothing but hurt and suffering for too many years, but at this point I've had just about all I can stand.

So in the meantime I will sit here, hopefully watching and waiting for someone like me to show up. If no one shows up again tonight, then sometime before morning I will choose another victim and take their blood to quench the rising thirst in me. Afterwards I will return to my grave until tomorrow night when I will try once again.

Choosing the one I will take tonight shouldn't be too difficult. When I was turned into this … thing that I am … I was just at the point of losing that adolescent boyish prettiness and about to turn into a handsome young man. I have big brown eyes and my hair is a little long but curly so it looks shorter than it is. Although mentally I have matured over the years, I still have the body and looks of a teenage boy, something I have learned over the years to use to my advantage. Since I look pretty much like any other teenager, it's usually easy to find someone to take pity on a poor boy with nowhere to sleep. I've discovered over time that there are untold numbers of people, men and women, that's more than willing to take a pretty young teen home with them for the night. They always look forward to what they *think* is going to happen and I always look forward to what I *know* is going to happen.

I have killed thousands of times since that first awful night. Just like my maker ended my life so abruptly, killing my hopes and dreams, I too have killed a lot of hopes and dreams. In the beginning, I tried to keep count because I wanted to remember the face of every individual whose life I had taken. I wanted it to stay with me, to haunt me and remind me of what I had become and what I had done. I gave up that endeavor years ago. The bloodlust has controlled my every wakeful minute, taking away any preference for who I kill. It doesn't matter if they are young or old, male or female, rich or poor; all I want is to try to satisfy the driving thirst for blood that rages within me. I'm not a murderer, I don't think … at least I've convinced myself that I'm not. I only kill to take what I need to survive … to feed and continue my own existence. But maybe tonight's kill will be my last…. that's all I have left to hope for anymore.

I have spent the day like so many others, in a shallow grave that I had dug just before dawn and hid myself in the cool earth away from the burning sunlight. I rose earlier in the evening, just as the sun was setting and I haven't fed since. I know that I must find someone soon though … the thirst is getting stronger, my throat is burning with it … soon it will take over and control me again. The longer I sit here … the stronger the thirst becomes in me … I must feed … and soon. I can feel in myself that I am getting weak … and I have to be strong to do what I am planning … to end my cursed existence.

And so now, as I've done so many times before, I'll assume the role of some kind of blood-thirsty god reigning over his subjects and decide which life I shall end tonight. I settle into my role and begin searching the small club. I look at every girl and boy ... deciding ... wondering which one I should reach out and take when I'm suddenly startled by an unexpected voice.

"Hello young one ... you look as if you have lost all hope ... why are you downcast and appear so sad?"

The voice, calm and assured, floated gently through my mind. I quickly looked up from my hunt and all around me to see who had spoken to me. When I didn't see anyone after a quick search I realized that although I had heard the voice in my head, it had seemed to surround me, coming at me from all directions at once. I was unable to pinpoint exactly where it came from. That was something new, something I had never experienced before. I suppose it was some inner instinct, but I knew that it was the voice of another vampire, and unlike my maker this vampire was female ... and her voice was full of strength and authority. I smiled as an unexpected feeling of calm began to settle over me, realizing that I had finally found my executioner ... or more accurately, she had found me.

I couldn't believe it ... there really was someone else like me. I looked quickly all around the dimmed club again, searching every dark corner, every place that I would have concealed myself, trying to locate the source, I had to find her.

"There's no need to search for me young one," the voice continued in my head, *"you cannot see me unless and until I want you to see me. But for the time being, please understand that I mean you no harm, I only wish to speak privately with you."*

I quickly recognized the strong tone of authority her voice contained but underneath that I also sensed a gentle touch of kindness along with it. At the same time I also recognized the slight sound of disapproval that I had often heard in my own maker's voice. Fear began to slowly work its way through me as it had so many times when he had taken that same tone with me. I didn't know how to answer her so I did as I had always done with my maker … I slowly bowed my head in surrender and nodded to her … whoever, and wherever, she was.

"Please stand up young one and slowly walk outside … I will meet you there … and again, I mean you no harm … yet."

I stood up from my seat like she had instructed and began slowly walking toward the front door of the club and probably certain destruction. As I walked I began to think that whoever this vampire was, it was more than likely she would destroy me … or perhaps take me to another one that would. I smiled a little at the thought that either way, happily, I would soon be free of this terrible curse … and I wouldn't have to do it to myself … I had detested the thought of having to run into a burning building. I knew it would be quick but still the thought of the flames unnerved me every time.

The thought of what waited for me after I … what … ceased to exist … passed quickly through my mind. I had become a cursed creature, bearing as my maker had called it, the Mark of Cain upon my existence. I wondered what my future would be as I made my way to the door. I was sure I couldn't hope for the Heaven that my mama and grandmamma had taught me about. I was pretty sure God wouldn't allow me there after all the killings and deaths I was responsible for. If anything, I suppose I was probably bound for the flames of hell they had also taught me about.

I couldn't expect Heaven and I didn't want Hell, so I silently hoped that maybe, like they had told me so many times over, that God was merciful and He would find something between the two for me. But after the way I had existed for so many years … the darkness, the death, the loneliness ... I don't think anything could possibly be any worse.

I began to feel like a condemned man walking along death row toward the execution chamber as I continued my slow walk toward the front of the club, not daring to look around me for fear of what I might see. I pushed through the door, turned and headed toward the darkened alley alongside the building. If I was going to die, I would do it the way I had lived ... in the dark, where no one could see me. When I reached the alley I stepped into it, melting into its dark shadows and leaned back against the building. My shoulders slumped, and my hands snaked into the side pockets of the old army jacket I was wearing as a sign of complete surrender ... and I waited ...

Then without a sound or even a stirring of the air, she suddenly appeared in front of me, her eyes piercing into me, searching every part of me from my head to my feet. Her face was a blank mask, completely emotionless and stone cold. Her mouth was set in a straight line, neither smiling nor frowning, and her strong gaze sent a death-like chill throughout my body. She kept her silence, not speaking a word, as she stood closely studying me. I felt like she was looking through me ... into my soul – assuming I still had one – searching everything about me. I could feel her power as it flowed around and over me ... the shear strength of it pouring out of her and filling the air around me was horrifically terrifying.

All of a sudden I became aware that I was unable to move as she continued to stare into me. There was some unseen force, something physical, holding me tight against the wall I was leaning on. At the same time I felt the grip of invisible fingers wrapping around my throat. I understood at once that she was telling me if she so desired, she could force me to bow to my knees in front of her. There was no doubt in my mind that she was every bit a vampire ... a very powerful and dangerous one ... especially right at this moment ... a fact she was silently making known to me in no uncertain terms.

I tried to look back into her eyes as well, but I couldn't ... every time I tried, I had to lower my eyes in submission to the street. She radiated power and authority ... it flowed out of her like a mighty river ... and I slumped further against the wall, panic now roaring uncontrollably through me. An icy dread began slowly wrapping its tentacles around me, reaching callously toward my heart as we continued to stand there facing each other. Something inside me recognized that she was strong enough to destroy me in a flash of time if she wanted.

Then pulling on every bit of courage I had left in me, I looked back up at her, a little closer this time taking in every detail I could about her ... if she was to destroy me, I at least should know my executioner. She was smaller than me by several inches but maintained enough distance between us that she didn't have to raise her head to look at my face. Her hair was dark brown and hung around her shoulders, and like an executioner's hood it partially shielded her face from view. Her eyes were light brown and reflected the subdued light of the alleyway but held an intense sparkle to them. She was absolutely beautiful and like the Sirens of mythology, now that I had seen her, I couldn't take my eyes off of her. Unlike me, she was dressed nicely, and didn't look any different than any other ordinary girl, and had I not known, I would never have thought she was a vampire.

Suddenly and just as quietly as the first, two more of them appeared ... a man and another girl. They too had appeared out of nowhere, standing like guards on either side of my executioner. The man was well over six feet tall. He had long thick hair that sat just on his shoulders and he was big, built strong and muscular. His well-toned body was the exact opposite of my own teenaged body. His eyes were deep green, unblinkingly locked onto mine and again I recognized unquestioned authority flashing in them.

The girl that was standing on the other side was nearly as tall as the man. She was pretty and looked like some of the models I had seen in magazines. Her dark brunette hair was thick and long, almost to her waist, and it seemed to shimmer and move just so slightly in the gentle breeze. Her eyes were deep blue with an unknown depth to them and sparkled like the other two. She was also staring intently at me, showing no emotion at all. Although she was very pretty, she was also very frightening. I could sense the blood rage on her and knew that she had recently fed.

Together they made a very frightful threesome and I tried to shy away from them wishing I could blend further back into the brick wall at my back. Suddenly I found myself not wanting to be destroyed but to get away from these three. I really didn't mind being alone as much as I had thought. With the exception of the first night that I had been attacked and turned I couldn't ever remember being this terrified. The reality of having three such powerful vampires standing in front of me became too much for me to handle. I was scared and I didn't care who knew it.

I realized … now that I was actually facing final destruction … that I didn't really want to die … not as much as I thought I had … and again the fear of the unknown rolled unchecked through me. I slowly lifted my eyes back up and looked destruction in the face. When I did the thought of being destroyed was so terrible that I couldn't hold back the tears any longer. Unable to contain my anxiety

I began crying, shaking uncontrollably with apprehension. I broke down and cried like I hadn't cried since that first terrible night so long ago when I realized I was dead, but not dead. My tears, filled with blood ever since I had become this thing that I am, now flowed quick and free as they ran down my face and into my hands. I bowed my head again in defeat and covered my face with my hands so I couldn't see the end coming.

After what seemed like an eternity of waiting, finally realizing that she intended to make me watch as the end came, I slowly lifted my head back up, wiping my tears with the palms of my hands. I looked at the brown haired beauty still standing silently in front of me and with tears streaming down my face began to quietly plead with her, "Please, ma'am, I'm begging you, if you are going to destroy me, do it quickly. Please don't torture me anymore, just get it over with, I've had all the pain I can stand."

She continued to look intently at me for a few more seconds. I watched her closely as she took a step toward me and began to slowly reach out her hand to me. I knew that it would be the killing touch and I wondered what it would feel like. Would everything go dark … would I just cease to exist … I watched, filled with a terror like I had never known, as her hand came closer to me. I cringed, looking away in a last second desire to live, as she gently laid her fingers on my cheek. Her touch wasn't followed by pain and darkness as I had expected but instead by a calming wave that swept over and through me … something I hadn't felt in years … a feeling I had almost completely forgotten. I felt … love and compassion … flowing and spreading through me, covering and filling me. Her fingers and palm were soft and silky as she continued to rest them on my face; it was comforting and reminded me of my own mother's soft caressing of my face when I was child.

"Be calm young one," she spoke so quietly it was almost a whisper, "I told you we mean you no harm ... now what is your name fledgling ... and how did you come to be in Charleston?"

I knew my name but still I paused for a moment to think about it ... it had been so long since anyone had asked me what it was. For so many years I had been the only one to ever use it. My maker had always just called me either 'Boy' or 'Kid'. He had said that a name wasn't important and that since I was dead now, there was no real need to remember it any longer. But often times in the dark nights when I had a few minutes alone I would sit and quietly speak it out, to remind myself what it was, to keep it fresh in my memory. It was only a small thing, and I knew it would anger him to no end if he heard me doing it, but it was something I could do to spite him. Besides, if I had forgotten my own name it would have been the pinnacle of the terrible nightmare I had been living. I looked up at her, and meeting her soft brown eyes, I slowly began to speak.

"My name ... is Dale," I answered her slowly, trying to make a half-hearted attempt to smile at her, "Dale Krause ... at least that's what it used to be ... before I was turned into this ... this creature that I am now."

It felt good to hear my name spoken out without fear. I could almost taste it as it rolled off my tongue. Then something rose up inside me and I stood a little straighter, looking directly at her as I said it again and added, "I am Dale Krause and I'm here because I'm all alone now. I have been on my own for over two years. I'm lost and all I know to do is wander from place to place. I don't know what else I should do or where I should go."

With the three of them still looking intently at me she

spoke softly and easily to me again, "Then perhaps you should come with us Dale, we shall go back inside for a little while where the four of us can sit and talk. Depending on what you have to say, when we have finished our conversation, perchance we can help you find your way and instruct you in what to do."

I realized that I was now free to move, whatever force had been holding me had just as easily released me. I pushed hesitantly away from the wall I was leaning on and, now surrounded by three very intimidating vampires, began to walk back toward the doors of the night club. When we got back inside the noise level was beginning to rise and there were more people inside. I began to think that if they planned on destroying me, surely they wouldn't do it here, not in front of all these people. We returned to the corner table I had been sitting at, the three of them taking the seats that would place their backs to the walls.

"Please, take the seat on the outside," she gestured toward the empty chair, "we would like you to feel comfortable and not as if you are trapped in here." Then, for the first time since I saw her, she smiled at me. I took the offered seat and watched as she and the others settled into the remaining chairs.

I did appreciate the gesture of their giving me an open escape route. I had developed incredible speed and could have moved completely across the room so quickly that none of the people would have seen me. But I also knew there was no way I could move fast enough to get away from all three of them.

"Please tell us your story now Dale," she spoke, calmly but with an underlying threat in her tone, "how did you come to be here? Remember, the details are very important to us ... and ultimately to you ... so please don't leave any of them out."

I felt tears begin to once again well in my eyes, I shivered all over as fear flashed through me for a second time.

"Please try to hold your tears young one," she spoke softly, her voice becoming soothing and easy, "there are too many humans around us right at the moment. Although I can shield us from their view, I'd rather not, so please, if you wish to cry, wait until later."

"I don't know what to say," I began slowly, the tears still brimming on my eyes, "I don't know what you want to hear ... truthfully ... I don't. I'm not even sure how I got this way, it just happened one night."

"Then perhaps we should start at the beginning," she smiled, casually lifting one of her hands toward me in a calming manner, "now, how long ago did this happen to you child?"

I began allowing my memory to spiral backwards, I looked away, gathering my thoughts as I began, "I remember that it was 1978 ... and it was a Friday night, September twenty-second ... I remember the date clearly because it was my sixteenth birthday. I had just left the local pizza parlor where I had I had been celebrating with my girlfriend and some of our school friends."

"Your *sixteenth* birthday," she asked, quickly glancing at the other two.

"Yes ma'am, I had just turned sixteen that day," I continued, my memory of that awful night returning faster as I talked, "it was late, probably getting close to midnight, when we left. We stood around for a few minutes outside, talking and laughing with each other."

I couldn't help but stop and smile at the happy memories from so long ago before continuing, "We all split up to go back to our homes. While I was walking down the street toward my house this strange man stepped out from behind some trees along the sidewalk and asked me for directions. I began telling him what he wanted to know and then, I think he must have hit me, because everything just went black."

I almost cried again, my voice breaking at the terrible memory of that night.

"Please keep talking," she encouraged me.

"When I woke up again, I didn't know where I was … and … and I had been turned into … this," I said as I extended my arms and hands, palms up to show them what I meant.

"When you woke up, were you by yourself or was the man that you say attacked you still there with you," the male vampire asked me, raising his chin in a question as he spoke for the first time. He had a soft southern accent, speaking slowly and seriously as he gazed intently at me.

"Yes, sir," I nodded and answered politely, "he told me that he was a vampire … and that he had killed me and turned me into one, too. I thought that maybe I was having some kind of a nightmare … I just didn't know it was one I wouldn't wake up from. He told me that he wanted a companion because he was tired of living and hunting all alone. He told me that he had chosen me simply because I was young and he thought I was pretty. That's when I really began to get scared. I thought he was crazy, that maybe he was one of those perverts I had heard about on television … you know, the ones that like little boys."

"Did he … do things to you," the brown haired girl asked slowly, looking at me.

"Things …" I asked quizzically, then realizing what she meant quickly answered, "Oh … that … no ma'am he didn't ... but at first that's what I was afraid he wanted to do ... I even asked him if that's what he was going to do ... but he laughed and said that we were dead things now and even if he wanted to do that to me, the dead couldn't do such things anymore."

She ever so slightly smiled and nodded her head in reply.

"Where did this attack take place," the man asked, drawing my attention back to him.

"I lived in western Pennsylvania with my family," I answered, then added, "He carried me far away and told me that my life as I knew it was over now. He said that my family would never find me and that I had to obey him and do whatever he told me from now on. I knew that since I had no idea where I was or which way was even back home, I didn't have any choice but to stay with him. I did know, that besides being completely lost, I felt different and didn't know what else to do, so I went with him. He told me that we were creatures of the night, that we lived only at night, and that we died again each morning. I learned that I had to dig a new grave every morning before sunrise, cover myself, and sleep all day until dusk. He told me that I had to stay with him, and kill if I was to survive. I felt like a prisoner."

"What is this man's name," the brown haired girl asked me curiously, "and more importantly, what did you do to get away from him?"

"His name was Charles," I replied, "at least that's what he called himself. I got away from him because he destroyed himself, almost two years ago, in Boston ... I didn't even know he was planning on doing it. We were walking along the Mystic River late one night after we had hunted and killed when we came upon a building that was on fire. We stopped and watched it for a few minutes as the firefighters fought the flames. He turned to me while we stood there and casually said 'You have to take care of yourself now, boy, I'm finished' and then he ran straight into the flames. I stood shocked, not knowing what to do. I heard him scream once loudly when he first ran into the building. He was completely burned up and gone in less than a minute. I really wanted to follow him but after seeing what happened to him I was just too afraid to make the leap."

"After the fire was out I stood there ... suddenly realizing that I was all alone ... I didn't know of any other vampire ... or even if another one existed. I had been completely dependent on Charles for everything ... he wouldn't tell me anything about what we were and whenever I thought of something I wanted to ask he refused to answer my questions. I didn't know where to go or what to do next ... there was nobody to guide me now and I felt completely lost and abandoned ... so I just stood there, shocked at what I had seen him do, until the sun was almost up. I had to hurry that morning and ended up sleeping in the ground under an old abandoned building instead of in a proper grave."

"Later that evening, when I woke up, the memory of what Charles had done came rushing back to me. I knew I had to leave ... to get out of Boston ... I just didn't know where to go ... I had to find someone ... somewhere. I thought that surely we weren't the only two of our kind. So I began wandering from place to place every night. I spent the nights traveling ... usually after I would hunt and feed ... then close to dawn wherever I happened to find myself, I would locate an old cemetery to dig my new grave and sleep through the day. I repeated the process night after night moving further into the unknown. Whenever I needed new clothes I would either take them from my victims or find a fresh grave and strip the body of whatever I could use. As I continued to wander I began searching the night, calling out into the darkness hoping to find another one like me … but over and over nothing but silence and emptiness answered me. I was all alone and surrounded by darkness and loneliness … I decided I knew what hell must be like."

"So, when I finally arrived here, I determined that this was the end … I would stay here until I either found another vampire like me or until I built up the courage to destroy myself too. I was determined not to continue this existence all alone. I don't know how to do to someone else what was done to me … and even if I did, I wouldn't … nobody deserves this terrible curse I've lived under. And now, just as I was almost brave enough to destroy myself, suddenly all three of you show up out of nowhere."

"We didn't exactly come out of nowhere," the brown haired one spoke up, smiling easily at me now, "we've been aware of your presence for a couple of months … in fact, ever since the night you arrived here. I have been watching and observing you during that time, trying to decide just what to do about you the whole time."

"I don't know if that should make me feel relieved or not," I continued, "but I do know that for many years I've lived in darkness … I've known horror … and wretched loneliness. Then for the last two years I've lived in fear … I was afraid that I was the only one like me. Right now, looking at the three of you, I'm so afraid of what you will do to me. But my desire to be free of this curse is even greater than my fear of you … after all, that's why I came here … to be destroyed. I know that is why you are here … to destroy me … and I accept that … but when you do it, do it quickly … please make the end as painless as possible for me … I just don't want to hurt anymore."

Then the brown haired female, that I had now decided was the leader of this group, looked directly at me and her entire demeanor changed, her face grew softer and she tenderly smiled at me, "You have had every reason to think that your life was a cursed existence young one, but beginning tonight, we shall work on changing your thinking. You will soon discover that instead of being relegated to a 'cursed existence' as you refer to it, your maker, although unknown to you, actually bestowed upon you a truly wonderful and marvelous gift."

"You are innocent and bear no responsibility for your being or past actions. I do not understand how a maker could so callously lie to their fledgling, unless they didn't know anything themselves. However, one thing is certain … you shall not perish at our hands innocent one. My name is Charlotte Ann … this is James and his mate Katelyn. It is a pleasure to meet you Dale. Please come with us now and if you will stay with me as you stayed with your maker, I will teach you and train you in the ways of our immortal lives … and you have much to learn my child."

I felt a sudden thrill go through me like I had not felt in years when she smiled at me and used my real name … something I hadn't heard spoken by another being since that long ago night when I was attacked. She extended her hand to me and I cautiously reached out to allow her to take my hand in hers. Her touch was tender and reassuring … again, something I had almost forgotten.

Charlotte Ann turned toward the man and spoke quietly to him, "With your consent, I think perhaps we should return home now and begin Dale's introduction to immortal life."

He nodded slightly to her as I began to wonder where home was and what lay in store for me next. She lightly squeezed my hand in hers and I felt a rushing of wind surround me and suddenly we were no longer in the little night club. I felt myself moving through the night. I didn't know it at the time but my cursed existence had just come to an end and an entirely new life awaited me.

Chapter Two

 had grown up in the little mining town of Renton Junction, Pennsylvania, nestled in the foothills of the Allegany Mountains just a little east of Pittsburgh. My family was made up of my parents and two older sisters. Like most of the folks in the mining district then, my parents married young and started a family. By today's standards they weren't much more than children themselves when they got married. They were both only fifteen but my dad had already been working in the coal mines for two years. I'm pretty sure that I remember my parents being in their mid-thirties when I was attacked and taken away, changing all of our lives forever.

I was the youngest, born in 1962, when my parents were twenty. Since I was the baby and the only boy I grew up as the 'pick of the litter' for the entire family. My mom always called me her 'pretty boy' and petted me non-stop as I was growing up. My sisters thought that I was some kind of a live baby-doll that they could use to play dress-up with and show off to their friends. My dad taught me about work, both at home and in the mines. He spent what little spare time he had with me teaching me how to hunt and fish in the nearby woods and streams which became some of my most cherished memories.

He began teaching me how to fish when I was just a small child, and I became pretty good at it. Then for my tenth birthday, he gave me my first rifle, an old Remington single shot .22 caliber, and began teaching me to hunt. Soon after I began to supplement the family's meat supply with rabbits, squirrels, and other small game from the local woods and before long graduated up to take my first deer, a large buck, when I was thirteen using the German rifle my grandfather had captured in World War Two. Then when I was fifteen I shot and killed a huge wild boar using the same rifle ... after which my grandfather traded me the rifle and fifty rounds of ammo for ten pounds of meat from the hog.

My parents loved the three of us very much and took good care of us. I know that there had to be times when they would give up something they wanted just so we kids could have some good things too. Although we never had a lot we were very happy with the little we did have.

My mom worked at home, raising the family and my dad worked in the coal mines that surrounded the area making a meager living for us. We were never well off, and to some people we were poor, but we never went without either. We always had good, clean clothes to wear ... sometimes they had been purchased at the Salvation Army and more often than not they were homemade. However, mom always managed to save enough money to get the three of us a brand new pair of shoes and a new set of store bought clothes for the first day of school. That set of clothes then became our 'Sunday Best' for wear to church the rest of the year.

There was hot food on the table every day and we ate good. My mom always sent us out in the morning with a big breakfast under our belts. Then she would set a full supper every evening to finish the day off. My dad used to laugh and say that we should be happy because, unlike some folks, we at least had a varied menu. He said he could prove it because we would have beans, 'taters and biscuits one day and 'taters, beans and cornbread the next day.

We grew most of the food we ate. Every spring my dad would plow up the garden spot in our back yard and mom would raise a small garden so we had fresh vegetables and greens. She would can extra vegetables and make preserves out of fruit to last us over the winter. She also raised chickens so that we had fresh eggs to eat. She would gather the eggs we didn't need and use them in trade at the local grocery store. They were as good as money and provided us with butter, milk, and fresh, soft store-bought sliced white bread. Often times if we had one too many chickens it would end up on the table for Sunday dinner.

My dad helped out by always keeping a pig in a small pen at the back of our lot. Then when the weather got cold enough he would slaughter it so we would have meat through the winter. He made sure that we always had plenty of sausage, bacon, ham, pork chops and fatback. My dad used every part of that pig except the squeal, so that none of it went to waste. He even built a small smokehouse and a saltbox at the back of the house where he kept the meat after it had been prepared.

The memories of those years are of a good, healthy life and I enjoy thinking back about them. They have been the one anchor that has kept me and helped me deal with all that has happened in my life. Although I try desperately to hold on to those memories they sometimes tend to get a little fuzzy around the edges.

I knew that my life would likely take the same path as my dad's … just like his dad and his dad before him … I would grow up, go to work in the coal mines, marry, and have children. Then I would work until I was too old to work and I would die, most likely of the black lung. The only difference between my life plans and those of my family was that I was going to finish high school before I did any of that.

In fact, one part of my life's plan was already in place, and her name was Rebecca but I called her Becky. We had lived two streets apart and played together and gone to school together all our lives. But then in the eighth grade she began to look a little different to me and I also noticed that she talked and acted different toward me when we were together. We started spending more time with each other than with anybody else and by the time we were in the first year of high school we were officially 'boyfriend and girlfriend'.

I thought that she was the prettiest girl in the world. She was even prettier than Farrah Fawcett on 'Charlie's Angels', at least to me. Becky was my first and only love and it made me happy when I told everybody that she was my girlfriend. I saved whatever little money I could make working small jobs in our town and then I would take her to the movies every weekend on Saturday night, and spend everything I had on her. I bought her anything she wanted, whether it was sodas, popcorn, or candy. Then at the end of our date she would always give me a little kiss, usually on the cheek, but it still made me the happiest boy in town. We had already begun to talk about getting married just as soon as we finished school. I was so excited about spending the rest of my life with her.

Becky and I had been together the night that I was attacked. My parents had planned a special shopping trip in Pittsburgh the next morning for my birthday. I had already asked Becky to go with me and I was planning on using some money that I had saved up to buy her something special too. I loved her so much and I was so looking forward to spending the day with her ... but sadly that day never arrived for us. I sometimes wonder what happened to her ... if she still thinks about me and maybe wonders why I just disappeared and what ever happened to me.

The night I was attacked we had been at the local pizza place with a bunch of our friends for my birthday party. We had spent several hours there having pizza and playing a new arcade game called Space Invaders ... and I always let her beat me at it and win. Since the only customers that night were teenagers, the owners had turned up the music from the jukebox and when Becky wasn't beating me at Space Invaders she and I were dancing together.

Just at closing time, I went and put my last two dimes in the jukebox and selected our two favorite songs. I didn't know it at the time, but it would be the last time I got to dance with my dear Becky. It wasn't really a dance as much as it was just the two of us holding each other close and swaying to the melody of Olivia Newton John signing 'Hopelessly Devoted to You'. When the song ended Becky held on to me, putting her arms around my neck and looking into my eyes she breathed softly, "I am hopelessly devoted to you, Dale Krause."

"I love you so much, Becky Pittman," I replied with a huge smile.

"Happy Birthday, Dale," she whispered with a smile, "I have a special present just for you!"

Then she kissed me right there in front of God and everybody … and it wasn't a regular kiss either. She kissed me like she had never kissed me before. We clung tight to each other as everything and everybody around us disappeared, and her kiss became our kiss. She lingered in my arms and I felt her tongue slip into my mouth. Then she took my tongue in her mouth, gently sucking on it. That was my first real kiss and my body began to tingle in places that only she could make it tingle and I wanted that kiss to last forever. I slid my arms down her back and bravely rested my hands on her hips. I wrapped my arms tighter around her, pulling her closer, and I'm sure she could feel how much I enjoyed the kiss as she cuddled against me. I enjoyed the closeness of her body against me as we shared our own special kind of teenage love for each other. The love that we shared was real love and it was slowly working toward binding us together forever.

When it was over I walked her outside to where her mom was waiting to pick her up. Normally after one of our dates I would just walk her home but since our parents had agreed to allow us to stay out until midnight her mom had decided to meet us at the restaurant and pick her up. I have been so thankful, so many times since then that her mom made that decision and Becky was not with me when I was attacked.

"I'll see you in the morning," I whispered softly to her before she got in the car.

Her mom suddenly found something interesting on the other side of the parking lot to look closely at and turned her head away from us for a minute. I took Becky in my arms again and we shared a quick couple of pecks on the lips.

"I'm so excited about tomorrow," she whispered back to me, "do you think maybe we'll get to visit that big new Woolworth's store while we're in Pittsburgh? I would love to get to go in there and see all the pretty things they have."

"I'll ask my mom and dad," I answered her, "maybe they'll take us there."

"I hope so … and maybe I can find a new pattern there so I can make a special dress to wear just for you …"

"With lacy frills," I asked with a smile.

"Yes, with lots of lacy frills," she answered with her girlish giggle, "I can't wait to see you again … I love you so much, Dale."

"I love you too Becky," I answered her with one more quick kiss, "I'll see you first thing in the morning … good night!"

"Sweet dreams," she whispered with a final kiss.

Then she got in the car with her mom and I watched her ride away not knowing it would be the last time I ever saw her. I put on a huge grin and walked back over to my buddies in the parking lot who immediately starting laughing and picking at me about the kisses.

"Yeah, you guys just wish you had a girlfriend like Becky," I said, blushing at their laughter.

"C'mon Dale," one of my friends asked laughing, "tell us about it … I bet after a kiss like that you and Becky are going to 'do it' now … when's it gonna happen?"

"You know we can't do that," I laughed sheepishly, "we're not even married … yet … and anyway neither of our parents will allow us to be alone together in the house. Besides, what if we did do it and our parents found out about it? The only place they would ever let us go together again would be to church."

"Yeah, well at least the two of you would be smiling at church," one of them laughed, "unlike all those other folks."

We spent a few more minutes laughing and playing around with each other. Finally we all left in our separate directions, everybody heading home for the night. I walked through the town streets toward my house, thinking about Becky, our plans for the next day, and the kiss we had shared. I began to look forward to the next day and think about how much fun we would have in Pittsburgh. When I had gotten about two blocks from my house, a man that seemed to come out of nowhere surprised me, and interrupted my thoughts. I knew he wasn't from around Renton because he didn't sound like anybody I had ever heard.

"Hey kid," he spoke, "you got a Seven-Eleven around here ... how about show me where it's at?"

"Sure it's just down that street over there," I replied turning and pointing, "but it's already closed, they lock up at midnight," then when I turned back I realized that he was suddenly very close to me. I hadn't heard or felt him move but he was almost touching me.

"Yeah, kid, I know when they close," he said with a laugh and then he grabbed me and pulled me close to him. I struggled to get away but he was too strong for me and suddenly I felt liquid fire shoot through my body and everything went black ...

Chapter Three

hen I came to again, I couldn't open my eyes and my body felt strange, nothing at all like it had before the blackness covered me. I was tingling all over … it felt like little pin pricks covering my entire body and there was a dull ache moving through my limbs and joints. I wanted to move, but it seemed like my body had a mind of its own and wouldn't allow me to stir, so I stopped fighting it and just lay there, still and quite, wondering what had happened to me. I began to sense the details of my surroundings … even with my eyes still closed a picture started to build in my mind of where I was … somehow I knew that I was in a large building. I was lying on the floor and it was cold and hard beneath me. The air smelled moldy and damp … the strong scent of dirt filled the place and I heard the wind high above me somewhere. I knew that wherever I was it must have been abandoned.

I quickly became frightened because I didn't know

where I was … or how I got there … and I couldn't move … but at the same time I found I wasn't afraid of my surroundings. My emotions were flowing through me like a raging river, first one way, then another … I knew something was different but I just didn't know what it was. After a few minutes of silently listening to discover what was around me I suddenly became aware of a presence close to me. Something was watching me … I felt its eyes on me, and whatever it was, it was close, but just out of my reach … only a few feet away.

I gradually opened my eyes, then slowly and carefully turned my head in the direction of whatever was watching me. I knew that in this area it could easily have been a bear or a wolf. Instead, I saw the strange man who had attacked me. He was staring at me, his lips pressed tightly together not speaking a word. I could see him plainly in the darkness and began noting details about him that I hadn't seen back in town. He was crouching, just out of my reach, a few feet away from me, his eyes boring into me. They looked different now … bright in the darkness with a strange glimmer … they reflected the dim light, like a cat or opossum or some other kind of night animal did. Even squatting, I saw that he was taller than me. He was pale now but still looked very strong. He wasn't old … only in his twenties I thought … his hair was black and combed slick on the sides of his head. He was dressed in a pair of jeans and a flannel work shirt like many of the miner's I was used to seeing. I turned my head away from him and looked around the building in confusion. I tried to determine where I was and when I still didn't know, finally looked back at my kidnapper.

"I see you lived through it … at least you have the right kind of eyes," he spoke uncaringly and very noncommitted, "I was beginning to wonder if I had done it right or not."

"Done what right ... where am I," I started to ask, "and who are you, what have you done to me?"

"You are just so full of questions," he replied casually, bending to stoop next to me. I rose up on my elbows, my entire body still aching and tried to move away from him.

"Don't try to move yet, kid," he said, "you'll just hurt yourself more if you do."

"Please mister, whoever you are," I started to plead, "if you'll just let me go home I promise I'll forget about you and whatever you've already done ... I'll just pretend none of this ever happened."

"I can't just let you go kid," he answered, "and believe me, you'll never forget about me or this night ... because now you're like me ... I made you that way ... and, since you're like me, you're going to be my companion from now on. Besides, you are home ... at least your home for now ... but that tends to change, too."

"What do you mean I'm your companion," I asked in confusion, "are you one of those perverts ... please mister ... don't do that to me."

He laughed out loud at that ... a long, hollow, evil sound and replied, "No, kid, you don't have to worry about that ... at least not anymore. Even though you certainly are pretty enough to want to get you naked, and I suppose it would probably be fun ... at least for one of us ... but since I can't do what you're referring to anymore ... that means I'm not a pervert ... but only because I'm dead."

I looked at him stunned by his words ... I had been kidnapped by a lunatic.

"And since you're dead too," he continued with a laugh, "want to take a guess who else can't do it anymore either? In a way I actually hate that for you, too. But since you've never gotten laid, you don't know what you're missing so you'll never grieve for it anyway."

I continued to look at him in shock, beginning to try to figure out how to get away as he continued with a wink and a smile, "Although we're dead and can't have sex anymore ... we do still have the desire for it ... it's just that now we get our satisfaction in other ways."

"What do you mean 'dead'," I asked, trying to stop his rant, "I'm not dead ... I see you ... I'm sitting up ... I'm talking ... look I can move ... I can't be dead."

"Sure you are," he replied casually standing up, "I killed you back there in that little hick town in Pennsylvania. But don't worry about the being dead part ... I changed you when I did it ... I turned you into a vampire ... like me ... that's why you'll be staying with me from now on."

"A vampire," I started to ask, "mister are you some kind of nut case ..."

Before I could finish my thought he had leapt forward and wrapped his hand around my throat, lifting me to my feet and pulling me close to his face, his eyes glowing and piercing into me, his lips nearly touching mine as he whispered in a low menacing tone, "Don't you ever call me crazy, boy, or I will leave you where you stand to die in the morning sun."

I struggled to get away from him and he finally tossed me backwards to land with a hard thud on the floor. Then with a wicked smile opened his mouth and for the first time I saw he had fangs. I slid backwards across the floor to a near-by wall trying to get away from him. With my back against the wall I pulled my knees up to my chin and I started to cry, I was so scared of what I had just seen.

"Please God," I cried out, "don't let this happen to me

... I know I haven't prayed like I should ... but please help me now, get me out of here."

The man laughed out loud again, "They always call on God ... why is that, I wonder," he asked looking at me as I continued to cry, "but the thing is God can't help you now boy, you're already dead ... well ... mostly anyway ... you're almost a full-fledged vampire and will be by the time we rise next evening ... and by that time God won't have anything else to do with you because of it."

I looked at him in shock still not believing or fully understanding what he was talking about.

"Still think I'm lying to you," he almost smiled now, "reach up and wipe your face then take a look at those tears."

I did as he said, keeping my eyes on him, and slowly reached up and wiped my face with the back of my hand. When I took my hand away it was covered in blood.

"Oh God, please what's happening to me," I pleaded.

"There you go with that God thing again," he said, "look, kid, just accept it ... I'm dead, you're dead ... we're both vampires ... get over it."

"This can't be happening," I sobbed, "I'm just sixteen ... I just left my birthday party ... I don't know you, I've never even seen you ... why did you do this to me?"

"Alright, since you insist on asking so many questions ... let's back up and start with your first one," he said, standing back up and beginning to pace the floor of the building, "we are in an old warehouse ... it might be Ohio ... it might be West Virginia ... I'm not actually sure and it really doesn't matter because I wouldn't tell you exactly where if I did ... and I did this to you because I have been all alone for nearly fifty years. Actually I'm just tired of spending the nights all by myself so I decided to find a companion ... and there you were ... lucky you."

"But, you don't even know me ..." I whimpered again.

"Well, actually, I know more about you than you think ... you see, once I decided to take a companion I had to decide exactly what kind of companion I wanted. The more I thought about it the more I decided on a young boy ... only because you could keep up with me easier than some girl and you'd be simpler to dress. Then if we were seen together it wouldn't cause too much of a question. So after I made that choice, I decided that if I was going to take a boy, I at least wanted one that was pretty so I wouldn't mind looking at you. I also had to find one that probably wouldn't be missed too much. So I sought out the first small town I came across and started my hunt ... and then I saw you ... everything I had wanted ... a young, pretty boy that had few connections. So for the last couple of months I have been watching you, every night, making sure that you would be everything I wanted. The more I watched and followed you, the more my desire to have you grew. I just knew that you would be perfect ... everything I wanted in a companion."

I sat listening in stunned silence as he continued talking, telling me how he had followed me and watched me. He told me everything I had done for the past couple of months.

"Then finally, tonight I grew tired of stalking you, I decided it was time to do what I came for and leave the area. So I followed you all evening, watching and waiting for the right opportunity ... and then you made the mistake of walking all by yourself, completely alone on a dark street, so I took you. Your blood was so much sweeter than I could have hoped for ... and you're a virgin on top of it all. That made your blood all the more innocent and clean ... better than any I have had in many years. I almost hated to have to stop and give it back to you ... but since I wanted to keep you I had to control myself for once. But now that I think about it, it's really a pity you didn't get the opportunity to lose your virginity before I got to you ... you would have enjoyed it ... especially with that pretty little girlfriend of yours ... I almost took her too you know ... but decided at the last minute that she would be too much of a distraction for either one of us."

"But, my family," I said still crying, "what about my family, they'll miss me ... they'll hunt me, they'll find me ... I know they will."

"They may try kid," he laughed, low and slow, "but there're no signs of where you were or what could have happened to you ... no blood ... no clothing ... nothing ... just empty air ... it's like you just disappeared off the face of the earth. You can't ever go back anyway ... now that you're a vampire ... what do you think those God fearing, church going people would do if they caught a real live vampire ... especially one of their own? I'm sure they wouldn't stop with just you ... your family would be next ... after all they birthed you and raised you. What do you think they would do to your family ... your sisters ... your mom ... and finally your dad? Oh and don't forget about that sweet little girlfriend of yours ... just imagine what they would do to a girl who had bedded a vampire!"

"That's not true! We've never done that," I interjected.

"Boy let me tell you, in a case like that ... they don't care what's true and what isn't ... so now you need to think about those questions if you ever get ready to try to go back there on your own. And will you please stop all that crying, it's annoying and besides it's almost dawn, we have to go now ..."

"Go where?" I asked.

"Look boy, you're not stupid … I don't think … we have to find a grave to go to … we're vampires, remember … the sun will be up in an hour or so … we die each morning and then rise again each evening … now, get up, hurry, I feel the dawn coming quickly, we have to go."

He reached and pulled me to a standing position and tugged me behind him toward the door of the warehouse. We went outside and he pulled me close to himself and said, "Hold on, kid," and he threw me over his shoulder and started running with me like I was a sack of potatoes. In a few minutes we reached an old graveyard and, setting me back on my feet, he stood outside the fence looking over into it.

"I think this will do for today," he said looking it over, "there doesn't appear to be any fresh graves for somebody to come around and cry over during the day. We'll rest here through the day then begin our journey at sunset."

He grabbed my arm and I followed him inside as we moved toward the back of the place. He bent down on his knees and started digging with his hands, moving the dirt like he had a shovel. In a short time he had opened a large hole and putting one of his arms around me again pulled me into it with him.

"We'll wake up when the sun starts getting lower in the sky … at least I will … and I hope you do too … I'd hate to have to start my search all over again for another you," he said as he began pulling the dirt in on top of us.

"Wait," I almost shouted, "I can't breathe if you bury me!"

"You don't breathe anymore, boy, what part of 'dead' don't you understand?"

The terror of being buried alive filled me as I felt the dirt began to cover me. It was heavy at first and I tried to move but my captor held me tight with one arm wrapped solidly around me and with his free hand he began to pull the dirt in around us. The more dirt he pulled in on top of us the heavier it got … weighing on my legs and back. Then suddenly … it lost its heaviness and it smelled good to me … it felt good … almost as if I belonged to it … I felt myself becoming a part of it … fading into it … then it became light and cool as it completely covered my head and shoulders. I closed my eyes, the tears flowing freely down my face, and once again everything went black.

Chapter Four

 suddenly came awake and remembered where I was ... buried in a grave ... covered and surrounded by dirt ... with my kidnappers arm laying across my back holding me down. I struggled to get his arm from around me ... I had to get up ... I had to move ... I had to get out. I began pushing upward with my back and bracing with my arms. I was surprised at how easily the cool soil moved away from me. I felt the chill of the evening air as my head broke through the surface, and then I felt his arm fall away from around me as I pushed a little harder with my arms. Finally I broke free of my confines, sitting upright and looking around. I saw the top edge of the setting sun followed by the very last streaks of daylight still coloring the sky as I looked all around me to see where I was.

I stood up and stepped away from the partially open hole. I noted a large tree standing by the edge of the fence line and walked toward it to sit and think about what was suddenly happening in my life. I still felt like I was trapped in a nightmare. I had to come to grips with … with whatever I had become … I understood that I was different now … I just didn't have any idea how different. I took a seat on the ground and began to look around me. The first thing I noticed was that I could see into the thickening darkness as if it were full daylight, everything was sharp and clear. While I sat looking around I also noticed that I could hear … everything … no matter how quite it was … I could even pick out individual sounds.

I sat there for about half an hour, lost in thought, considering all the seemingly new things around me. My thoughts were interrupted by a soft rustle in the direction of the place I had been buried. I looked and saw the dirt begin to move just the tiniest bit. Then a hand popped out of the ground, quickly followed by an arm, then the head and shoulders of the man who had kidnapped me. He stood up, brushed himself off with his hands and turned all the way around once as he surveyed his surroundings.

The first thing I noticed as he stood there looking all around was that there was not a speck of dirt on him anywhere … his clothes … his hair … his skin … all were perfectly clean. He looked as if he had just stepped out of a bath. I looked down at myself in curiosity and realized that I was the same way … perfectly clean after sleeping in the ground all day long.

I caught the sharp sparkle of his hazel eyes in the early darkness as he searched for and found me. His gaze finally settled on me, peering into me, watching me as he stood there. Then he took a step and began walking toward me. Suddenly I felt the fear of him all over again and I tried to shrink down into the roots at the base of the tree where I was sitting.

"You're awake," he spoke, "how long?"

I quickly thought it best to not tell him everything so I just looked at him.

"I said 'how long' kid, you'd better answer me boy."

"Awhile," I shrugged, deciding not to lie and not knowing how far to stretch the truth, "probably about half an hour."

"You're lying," he spat out angrily, "a half hour ago it was still partial daylight. You can't wake up until its full dark."

Something inside whispered low to me that this was an advantage and to use it, so getting a little bravado I looked at him and said, "well maybe you can't, but I can ... I sat right here and watched the sun go down ... and the sky was beautiful too ... all streaked with reds and pinks ..."

He moved so fast I never saw him until I felt the sting of his hand across my face. He slapped me so hard and unexpectedly my head and upper body fell to one side.

"Liar," he spat at me, "you are a cursed and unholy dead thing ... you can't see the daylight ... the light of day is the reflection of God's glory and it will destroy you."

I continued to stare at him while I thought about that little exchange. I had no idea how long I was going to be tied to him but I knew I had to begin learning. I had to discover what I was ... everything I could about me ... him ... us ... and how to survive because I already planned to get away from him as soon as I could. So I tucked away that first small bit of information for future use. I knew I had to try to appease my captor ... he was the only one who could teach me what I needed to know.

"Alright," I lied to him, "I'm sorry, I won't do it again. You're right I climbed out just a minute before you did."

"That's what I thought," he smiled at me, "now do not lie to me again, I'll see that you are destroyed if you do."

"Yes sir," I almost whispered, "I'm really sorry."

"Good, now come on boy, it's time to go kill somebody and get our nightly drink," he said.

"I can't kill anybody," I protested, shocked as his words hit me, and then remembering his forceful slap I decided it was probably best to just shut up, watch, and listen.

"You can and you will … before long … just follow me … I can see the blood lust already rising in your eyes," he said.

We started walking together down the country road and I soon saw a small house in the distance.

"There," he said nodding towards it, "that's where we'll feed tonight. I've scouted this place several weeks ago, there's a woman and her daughter that lives there. I'll go inside and take the woman. When the daughter runs out, you take her … and be sure to drink every drop of her blood … whatever you do, don't ever leave someone alive … she must be dead when you finish with her."

I was shocked and torn at his words. One part of me wanted nothing more than to quickly run away … sickened by what he had said. But there was another part of me, something deep inside that was pulling me, drawing me closer to the house. I followed the man and he led me to the darkest side of the house, where he looked into the window.

"I'll go in now and take the mother," he began, "when the girl runs out be quick, take her before she can get far …"

"But … what am I supposed to do with her when I catch her," I asked.

"Don't worry about that kid you'll know exactly what to do when you get your hands on her."

Then before I could say another word he was gone. I heard a loud uproar from inside the house and pandemonium broke out in the large room. Suddenly a young girl, who looked to be my own age, burst through the front door and ran violently screaming into the yard. When I saw her running in fear something changed inside me … I could hear her screams of course … but suddenly I could also see, feel and smell the terror pouring out of her … and it excited something deep inside me … I had to chase her, I had to catch her.

I felt like I was losing control of myself as I took two long leaps and grabbed her from behind. She screamed again as I spun her toward me and she looked in my face. She struggled against me, thrashing about, her hands lashing out at me, trying to get away as I pulled her to the ground … and the more she fought me the more excited I became … I was quickly losing any control I still had over myself.

I felt a strange tingling along my upper gum and realized I had grown a set of fangs just like my attacker. I was almost shocked at the feel of the pointed tips of them touching against my lower lip. Then without thinking about it I opened my mouth and bit swiftly into her throat.

I tasted the salt from her tears that had run down her face and neck, her hair covered my lips, my fangs tore through her skin and the thick muscle in the side of her neck. I tasted the fear that was flowing throughout her … and it all tangled together as I bit into her. I felt the big artery in the side of her neck break as my fangs passed through, severing it. Her blood shot out of her ripped neck, quickly filling my mouth so full I had to swallow and then again and again. I couldn't believe how wonderful the hot blood flowing down my throat felt … it tasted metallic on my tongue ... coppery like the taste of a penny. It was rich and earthy ... like the dirt I had lain in all day ... but above all I tasted the terror that was filling her.

Then I heard her heart, beating rapidly in her chest as I continued pulling her blood out of her, completely lost now in the depth of her life, unable to stop myself. I shuddered uncontrollably as my body tingled all over with a new and unknown excitement. She began to go limp and I stopped and looked up at the sky, enjoying this astonishing new feeling coursing through my body. I felt her blood running in streams down my chin and dripping onto her face as I held her. I had never experienced anything that felt this incredible before.

Just as I was about to drop her to the ground, she groaned and her body quivered in my arms as the grip of death tightened its hold on her. When she trembled, another wave of terror rolled off of her, grabbing at me with unseen fingers, pulling me back to her. I looked at her throat and heard her heart again, still faintly beating, her neck glistening with a mixture of my saliva and her blood. Unable to control myself at the sight of it I again dropped my head to her neck, this time tearing into it, pulling and sucking every drop of blood I could out of her. I knew the moment she died ... I felt her body heave as life left her and came into me ... it moved throughout my body ... I felt so alive ... so fresh ... so new as I dropped her now lifeless body to the dirt.

I smiled as I took one last look at her then stood up and began to step away. She was wearing a light cotton gown that was now blood stained and torn in several places, hanging loosely on her body. She had lost one of her slippers as she tried to run away from me, the other now barely clinging to her foot. She looked to be about my age, no older than fifteen or sixteen, with long blond hair, and blue eyes that now stared lifelessly up at me. She was very pretty ... and now, I realized, because of me, she was very dead.

I stood there for another moment, looking at her pretty face, a mask of fright even in death. I couldn't believe what I had just done ... it was like it wasn't me but something inside me that had killed this pretty young girl. I couldn't stand to look at her anymore ... her blue eyes now clouding over with death kept staring back at me, accusing me of murder. I had to get away from her ... her voice was silent but still she loudly accused me ... I began to run ... I had to get away from what I had done ... as I ran I could hear her silent accusation 'Murderer!' ... 'Murderer!' following behind me as it floated across the still night air.

Soon, my kidnapper caught up to me and tackled me, pulling me to the ground.

"Where do you think you going, kid," he asked laughingly, "You can't run away from what you are ..."

"What I am is a murderer," I shouted back at him, "and you've done this thing to me!"

"Relax kid, its gets easier after the first time," he laughed, "soon you'll be killing with impunity just like I do."

"NO!" I shouted back at him, my voice roaring with a new strength I didn't know I possessed, "I won't ... I can't do that to anyone else ... ever!"

He threw back his head and laughed at me, his laughter loud and uproarious, ringing through the night.

"That's what you say now," he said looking at me, "but you can't help yourself, kid, you've got the Mark of Cain on you now ..."

"The what," I almost yelled at him, "what are you talking about ... what is the Mark of Cain?"

"Surely you recall the story of Cain and Able ... remember ... Cain killed his brother Able? Then God condemned him for it and marked him with a curse ... a scourge that proclaimed that he had chosen to spill his brother's blood and he would be persecuted by being made to drink his brother's blood ... he was sentenced to be a renegade and a drifter ... forced to wander the world in darkness ... other men would be unable to kill him ... and they would have nothing to do with him ... Cain became the first vampire."

"No!" I almost screamed again, "I won't be that ... I'll refuse to kill ..."

"Sure kid, whatever you say ... but just wait until tomorrow night ... then you'll kill again ... and again the night after that ... and the night after that ... for as long as you can imagine ... you will kill and drink the life blood of another human!"

I pulled myself free of his grip and ran to the edge of the woods along the road, wanting nothing more than to fade into the darkness there. I wanted to hide myself and what I had just done from everybody and everything. My conscience was tearing at me as I looked for and found a spot of thick darkness inside the tree line ... I settled into it, trying to hide, and I cried with the harsh realization of what I had just done ... I wept with bitter frustration at what I had become ... I sobbed for the young girl I had just killed ... how could I possibly live with the innocent blood of that little girl on my hands.

"Please God, I don't know if you hear me now, but if you do, please forgive me for what I've done ... for what I've become ... I didn't mean to ... I didn't ask for this ... this ... Mark of Cain ... I'm so sorry ... please show me a way out of this ... I don't want to have to kill again."

My prayer was met with a cold and still silence, the darkness seeming to close tighter around me, griping at me as I sat there. Finally, I looked up at the stars above me and in total defeat whispered softly, "I was taught to call you Father when I prayed because they said you cared for me and would hear me … you may not answer me now … or even care about me anymore, but dear God … Father, I promise I will never forget you or stop asking and pleading for a way out of this."

"I told you, it doesn't do any good to pray boy," my captor spoke as he stood leaning casually against a nearby tree looking down at me, "you're way too late for that now."

"Get away from me," I spoke low, almost whispering, "I hate you … I hate what you have done to me … I don't want to be anywhere near you!"

"Very well, if that's what you want …" he said nonchalantly, pushing away from the tree and speaking over his shoulder as he took a step back into the darkness, "you dig your own grave today and you'd better do it before dawn gets any closer. Sleep alone today … it's good for you to learn what 'alone' is all about … because without me, that's exactly what you will be … alone … with no one else. You'll wander the nights, kill and feed, then sleep in the ground all the day … welcome to your new life!"

I scrambled away from him, stumbling further into the dark woods. I fell on the ground, my face turned toward it as once more the pain and guilt of what I had just done ripped through me. I pushed myself up with my arms, snubbing as I felt the tears began to well up in my eyes again. I watched as one by one my tears, now filled with blood, the blood of that helpless and innocent young girl began to drip to the ground in front of me, pooling where they fell.

My fingers began to curl into the dirt, clutching, tearing and pulling at it, digging into it, deeper and quicker. I realized that I was quickly able to open a spot for myself ... that with just my hands I was able to tear a hole in the earth as easily as tearing a rag in two. I kept digging ... scratching at the earth ... I wanted to get away ... to hide myself from the awful truth of what I was ... a murderer ... and what I had done ... murdered a young and innocent girl. I wanted something that would match the depth and darkness of the abyss that now filled my body.

When I had burrowed out a hole large enough for myself I rolled into the dark earth and began pulling the dirt back in on top of me. Soon I was covered over, the welcoming feel of the cool earth drawing me into it, making me a part of it ... my last thought was that I must wake as soon as possible ... I had no idea why but I had to be up before my kidnapper ... and then I slept.

Chapter Five

hen I woke I did so with a start ... my eyes popped open and I automatically began reaching for the night. I broke through the surface and looked around me as I began brushing the loose dirt off of myself. I smiled as I realized that I could still see just the top ring of the setting sun. It hurt my eyes, burning them and I had to drop them toward the ground, but still it was just early twilight ... and I was up and fully awake. I smiled to myself that I had gotten up while it was still dusky light. I glanced back at the grave I had come out of and saw that I had barely disturbed the surface of the ground. There was almost no trace of where I had lain all day. I began to tuck away these little bits of information ... something to ponder on when I was alone ... pieces of a puzzle that I would assemble one night at a time.

I didn't know where my kidnapper had gone, but I was sure that he would show up in a few minutes. I set my mind to try to learn things from him about me and this ...

this creature ... that he had turned me into. The only thing I knew about vampires was what I had seen in horror movies ... the sunlight would destroy me ... I couldn't look at churches or crosses ... garlic was repulsive ... and I could never see my reflection in a mirror again. I'm sure there was more than that but if all of that was true then I had to try to remember every detail that I could ... I had to know more about this thing I had become. I also decided that I would not follow him and kill another innocent person tonight. I would not live that way ... I would rather ... what ... die ... but if as he said I was already dead ... then was it possible to die again?

While I thought about these things I suddenly remembered one of my Sunday School memory verses that said "It is appointed unto men once to die, but after this the judgement." So if I had died, was this creature I had become my judgement and if so, how long would it last?

I suddenly heard my kidnapper coming toward me and realized that while I had stood there thinking, the last bit of daylight had faded quickly away and it was now fully dark. I smiled knowing that I had had almost a full hour all to myself. I turned toward where I heard his steps in the darkness and waited for him to appear. Just as he was about to step into the little clearing where I stood I began brushing at my clothes with my hand to give the impression that I had just gotten up. I looked up, trying to appear surprised at his appearance.

"You came back." I began softly speaking, trying to sound humble, "you didn't leave me all alone like you said."

"I'm not going to walk away just yet, kid," he said with a snarl in his voice, "I turned you so that I would have someone like me to spend time with ... someone to talk to ... so I'll stay around for a while longer anyway. Just don't make me angry or I will leave you ... and you don't know anything about how to survive yet."

"Well, could you at least tell me your name," I asked, "so I'll know what to call you. My name is Dale in case you don't know."

"You're dead ... why should I need to remember your name," he said, "I'll just stick with 'kid' or 'boy' for the time being."

"Whatever suits you, I guess," I continued, with a bit of a snarky attitude showing through, "I can't call you 'pervert' for obvious reasons, so should I just call you 'attacker', or do you prefer 'kidnapper', that is unless you would like to tell me your name?"

"Watch your tone with me, kid, I can and will hurt you," he glowered at me, "but if you must know I just go by Charles, it's been good enough for a long time."

"Alright then ... Charles," I began warily, "are you going to tell me anything about what you've done to me ... about what you've turned me into?"

"Damn, boy, we can't talk all night," he spoke sharply, "we have to hunt and kill ... we can't wait and let the sun get too close to the sky."

"I don't think I'm going to do that again," I answered matter-of-factly, "I can't just randomly kill somebody."

"Sure you can, kid," he continued now grinning maliciously at me, "think about that pretty little girl last night ... her soft blonde hair and bright blue eyes ... recall how she struggled against you ... how she tried to fight you off and how that excited you in a way you had never been excited before."

"Think back of the smell of her fear, and the taste of her blood, filled with terror, as it shot into your mouth ... the sound of her heart beating loudly in your ears, pumping her life into you ... think how it sounded as it became slower and slower, struggling to live while you sucked the life right out of her ... how satisfied you were when she died ... while I know you don't have anything to compare it to, trust me boy, it's better than sex!"

"I'm even willing to bet that you didn't get that excited when you and your little virgin girlfriend played wrestle together in the yard. It's called the excitement of killing boy ... and you'll grow to love it! In fact, I bet that you are beginning to feel that dry burning thirst in the back of your throat ... that's what will make you feed ... that's what will make you kill ... and there's only one thing that will quench that thirst ... you know what it is ... and you know you can't fight it ... you have to give in and let it have its due."

I had felt the dryness and the desire to drink since I woke up, but I had no idea what was causing it. It had actually been something in the distance until Charles had pointed it out to me. Now, I felt it blaze up in me, calling out and I remembered clearly the taste of the blood I had taken last night. I didn't want to have to do that again ... I couldn't stand the feeling it left me with ... the knowing that I had murdered another human being ... but suddenly, I couldn't fight it and I knew inside me that I had to give in to it.

"Come along now, boy, we're going to a little beer joint I know just down the road a bit," he began, "then after we feed tonight we'll need to move on and put some distance between us and this place."

"Where are we going," I asked, "and how will we get there?"

"Don't worry about it," he snapped at me, "we may go south ... we may go north ... all that really matters is that we'll be far away from West Virginia when we next go to ground."

In a short time we walked through the doors of a weather beaten, broken down building that was trying desperately to pass itself off as a little social club. It was in reality just a backroad beer joint ... and it was crowded. There was a thick cloud of cigar and cigarette smoke clinging to the ceiling. It was hanging down, as if trying to make its way back to the merrymakers who put it there to begin with. There seemed to be at least one neon sign for every beer company known hanging on the walls – Bud, Schlitz, Old Milwaukee, Pabst, and some I didn't recognize. Some of them blazed brightly, others had dimmed and a couple of them flickered near last life. A pool table, surrounded by people sat off to one side, and a jukebox loudly blared the latest country tunes.

Putting aside the bright neon signs that now hurt my eyes, I quickly noticed even above the smell of the cigarette smoke and alcohol the scent of blood floated invitingly, beckoning me to it. I don't know how I knew that it was blood I smelled but I just did ... and it brought back the memory of the night before.

I stood still, looking around the inside of the bar. I could almost hear the whispered accusation from the night before floating on the air around me ... 'Murderer!' ... 'Murderer!' The now dead voice of the blond girl, my first victim – the one I would always remember – still condemned me. I felt the guilt begin to close in around me and I wanted to wrap myself in it and suffer. But before I could allow the guilt to settle too close on me though a girl walked up and put her arm around me, pulling close against me.

"Hello there pretty boy," she laughed looking up into my eyes and running her fingers through my hair, "aren't you just a little cutie pie … and what beautiful brown eyes you have, too!"

I looked back down at her as the scent of her blood filled my nostrils and the sound of her beating heart echoed loudly in my ears. She was pretty, and kind of sexy, too. She was probably in her early twenties, dressed in a flannel shirt that hung open over a snug tee shirt, a pair of short shorts made from an old pair of jeans and a pair of dusty old cowboy boots that came halfway to her knees. She had been drinking, in fact still was … she was holding a can of beer and a cigarette in her free hand and lightly rubbing my back with the other one as she smiled happily at me.

She continued to stare up at me, her eyes large and brown, full of life … and I felt the thing that I had become begin to stir inside me. I put one arm around her and pulled her closer against me, holding her …

"Oh, so you do like me," she laughed, "but do you talk … or perhaps you the strong silent type … but I'm betting you're just a little shy!"

I closed my eyes and breathed in the scent of her blood, knowing what was about to happen to her and that I was powerless to stop it. *"I need to get out of here … I need to go somewhere else,"* I silently thought to myself.

"I have an idea," she suddenly laughed, "let's get out of here and go somewhere else … we'll step outside for a while … around back where we can get some fresh air and get a little closer … you look so young and innocent … but I bet I can change that! I'll tell you what … if you'll promise to treat me to another beer when we come back inside, I'll treat you to something that I'm pretty sure you've never had!"

I wondered as she took my hand and began pulling me toward the door if I had sent that thought to her. She had spoken it so quickly and almost exactly as I had thought it.

Then the struggle began inside me all over again as we made our way to the back of the bar and a dark alley.

"Here pretty boy, you stand right here while I look around for something to cushion my knees on … I don't want to skin them up, you know."

When she gathered a pile of rags and laid them at my feet she put her arms around me, our bodies touching each other, and lightly kissed my cheek as she began to pull at the button of my jeans.

"Mmmm …" she whispered, "you're so young and so innocent."

"I'm not innocent … not anymore," I spoke softly to her, "I'm very, very guilty…"

"When I'm finished with you pretty boy you'll be even less innocent," she whispered with a big smile, "but let me see if I can make you feel better and maybe ease some of that guilt."

She raised herself up on her toes and kissed my lips. I tasted the tobacco and alcohol on her lips. It was a taste so foreign to me I almost gagged. Then a voice that was mine, but at the same time not mine, spoke out of me, "Don't get on your knees just yet, I want to hold you first."

"Oh, good … some tenderness from a tender, sweet little boy," she half giggled, cuddling closer against me and putting her arms around my neck, "I like that … yes, pretty boy, please hold me."

I closed my eyes again and tried to fight the roaring battle going on inside me … I felt my fangs began to grow, touching my lower lip as I nuzzled into her hair. I knew I was losing the struggle and I anxiously whispered into her ear, "Please forgive me for what I'm about to do."

"Oh sweetie you're supposed to wait until we after we finish before asking for forgiveness," she laughed, "let's have our fun first then we'll worry about asking the Good Lord for forgiveness."

"I wasn't asking God," I spoke slowly to her, brushing my lips against her neck, "I was asking you."

She stiffened in my arms as I sank my fangs into her neck, breaking the artery and releasing that wonderfully scented blood into my mouth. The creature that I had become now took over completely. I pulled her closer against me, lifting her completely off the ground and holding her tight against me, sucking at her neck. She didn't struggle against me, this was too easy, not nearly as exciting as last night, but I still enjoyed it. Her blood was different from the girl last night … it didn't taste of innocence … or even fear … instead it was strong and heady and filled me with a different kind of strength as I continued until, after about five or six minutes, I had drained her completely.

I heard her heart beating weaker, slowing and finally stopping when there was no more blood left to pump through it. Her arms fell from around my neck and her knees buckled under her as she took a final breath, exhaling slowly … I drew in a long breath as her life left her body … passing into me … and settling in my chest. I was suddenly filled with sorrow again as I stood there holding her now lifeless body … in spite of all … I had murdered yet again.

I wanted to cry, but knew it wouldn't do any good. I took her dead body and gently laid it down on the pile of rags she had laid at my feet so she wouldn't bloody her knees. I looked at her face, her big brown eyes now closed in death.

"I'm so sorry I did this to you," I whispered to her, "I never wanted it to happen this way … and you didn't deserve this kind of ending."

I straightened her hair, and brushed it away from her

face … I wanted to remember it … I wanted to remember each and every one that I did this to. Then as a final thought I took one of the rags and covered her face with it. I stood upright and quickly walked away, waiting to hear her whispered accusation of 'murderer!', and not daring to look back into that darkened alley.

y life continued much that same way ... I would kill ... the guilt filled me afterward ... I would cry about it ... and then I would hide myself in the ground ... and so it went, night after night ... the weeks soon became months and the months began turning into years. It was always the same routine ... rise out of a grave in the evening ... hunt and kill ... then back to another grave at the break of dawn. I hated it but I didn't know any other way to live now.

The only real difference as time went along was where we happened to find ourselves. We never stayed in one location too long, always moving from place to place. I was bound to Charles and I had to follow him everywhere he went and do what he said to do. I didn't know any other way to exist.

The only thing that varied much in my life ... or existence as I came to think about it ... was my victims. They ranged from young to old and everything in between. After a while it didn't matter to me if they happened to be male or female … I had no shame when I took a victim. I killed so often … at least once each night … until I became hardened to it. Killing didn't faze me any longer and I no longer bothered to try to remember the faces of those I killed. Soon there was no longer any sorrow or remorse in me for the lives I took. I had become an empty shell, a killing machine, with no feelings or compassion for those whose lives I ended. Still, every once in a while, especially when my victim was someone that was close to my own age I did have a twinge of conscience … but it quickly passed and was gone … just like their lives.

Charles and I seemed to travel constantly, mostly around the South and the East, from state to state. The one place we never returned to in all our travels was Pennsylvania, for reasons I grew to understand. Often times when we needed to travel quickly we would climb aboard a freight train just after dark and ride it all night, getting off to go to ground just before dawn.

Usually on those nights we found some drifters doing the same thing. Before the night was over, depending on how many shared our freight car, we would both take a victim. The first one never knew what was coming so was fortunate in their fate. The rest of them, once they knew what we were, lived their last few hours in fear, waiting on one of us to take them. When we were finished with them, we would carelessly toss their bodies out the open doors of the freight car as we traveled through the night.

We would usually hide on the outskirts of the larger cities, venturing into the darker and more dangerous sections to hunt and kill. Charles taught me that if we left a body in what he called 'the bad part of town' no one would care because those people were not important anyway.

When they were found they became just another dead body that wasn't claimed.

I left a trail of countless victims behind me as we wandered. Places like Memphis … Birmingham … Atlanta … Charlotte … Richmond … and an untold number of small towns in between … all received their visits from us. Finally, after a few years, we seemed to settle in and around New England … mostly in the Boston area, but sometimes going as far south as New York City and as far north as Bangor, Maine.

During those years we stayed mostly in the interior of the states, never traveling too close to the coast line. Charles made it very plain that under no circumstances were we ever to go south. We were never to get close to Charleston or Savannah, for any reason. He said that we must always stay away from those two cities especially, no matter what, because if we ever went there and were caught we stood a good chance of being destroyed.

Whenever I would mention either place or ask why we couldn't go there, Charles would only say that the southern coastal cities were not good for us. All he would say about it was there were some there who thought they were better than us … that they didn't appreciate him and wouldn't accept me. If I ever pressed the issue with him he would only repeat that we were not welcome in either place. I didn't understand his reasoning but I accepted his word … and quietly tucked that information away in the back of my mind for the future.

As a diversion to my existence I tried to keep up with my own age while I continued my spiraling descent into darkness. I wanted to know how old I would have been had I still been at home with my family … with my Becky. Soon my eighteenth birthday came and went … then my twentieth ... and my twenty-fifth did likewise. I stopped counting at my thirtieth ... I knew by then that I had too much blood on my hands to ever go home again. By that time I was certainly dead ... at least to my parents and my dear Becky ... and I grieved for my loss.

Time continued to move along and I moved with it. The further away I got from my human life the more the memory of my family began to fade. The pictures I had of them in my mind started to get a little fuzzy around the edges as I tried desperately to hold on to them. I looked at my own body, amazed that it never changed, I was still sixteen in appearance, and could not imagine my parents – and especially my Becky – as anything but the way I saw them last.

Finally in order to hold them closer to me, I began to make up stories of our lives together ... pretty pictures in my mind of what it would have been like to graduate high school ... to marry my dear love ... to have our first child together. Those imagined stories became the one tiny remaining speck of light in my life that I anchored to and that kept me from complete and total darkness.

Often times after we had hunted and killed, I would sit alone, as far away from Charles as I could get, and cry. I grieved for my family, for myself and, sometimes – just not often – for my victims. All those years I mourned the loss of my own life ... one that I would never get to live. My blood filled tears became a constant reminder to me of a life that I felt was stolen from me ... and as some kind of macabre punishment ... my judgement perhaps ... I had to live with the thief who had taken it. I became sullen and downcast most of the time, seldom smiling and never acting like the young teenager I appeared to be.

Charles still refused to teach me much of anything

about what I had become, only just the most necessary when it was needed. His standard answer to my questions was always, 'you're dead, you're a vampire, you kill people to stay alive ... and that's all you really need to know'. I felt trapped, stuck in a box that never opened or got any bigger. I looked at Charles as the one who had trapped me and held me there against my will. As a result my hatred for him grew stronger as the years passed us by ... he had stolen my life and my dreams and sentenced me to this prison I lived in. I absolutely loathed him and wished that I could die and be free of him. Anytime that I asked about dying all he would ever say was that there was only one way for a vampire to die ... and he refused to tell me more than that.

Although I didn't act like it, I was still Charles' companion during those years ... I hunted beside him ... I killed and fed with him ... but I continued to grow further and further away from him. Instead of becoming the companion he had wanted when he attacked me, I became distant, ignoring him whenever I could. I didn't speak to him unless I had to ... I never allowed a conversation to develop between us.

Charles still hadn't realized that I was awake before him and went to sleep after him. I slept as far away from him as I could ... and since he always went to ground an hour or more before me and rose up an hour or more after me, I had my choice of where I slept. I actually began to look forward to and enjoy that hour of freedom at the beginning and end of each night. It was a time I spent wandering in my mind with the memories of my human life, trying to keep them alive, trying to stay anchored to them no matter how far I drifted away in the darkness.

Only once during that time did I make a bid for my freedom. It was just after the turn of the twenty-first century probably about twenty-five years after he had taken me. I had acquired many of the vampire skills that I saw him exhibit. I could run fast … I could find and take my own prey … I knew how to find clothes and places to sleep. So one night I told him I wanted to go away from him … to go live and hunt on my own.

He exploded with a wrath like a white hot fire on me. He had slapped me around several times in the past when he was unhappy with me but this time he beat me severely. His swift blows landed on my head, my face and my chest. I doubled over in pain as he landed heavy punches to my stomach. When he had beat me to the ground he began to kick me brutally. I heard and felt one of my arms and several of my ribs break under his strong and rapid blows.

When his beating of me ended, I slowly crawled away from him, whimpering in pain, seeking shelter and somewhere to wait for the morning light. He continued to berate me as I drug myself at a snail's pace away from him. He reminded me that I was his and that I could not live without him. He told me that he had taken me to be his companion and that I would be his companion … and there would be no more discussion about it.

The one good thing that came out of that beating was that I discovered that my body healed quickly. When I went to ground that morning, my clothes still ripped and torn from his brutal beating, my body no longer showed any signs of the thrashing he had given me. The blood bruises that had risen on my arms and chest had disappeared, my arm and ribs had repaired themselves and I was amazed to find that I no longer had any pain where he had hit me. It was just one more thing to ponder on and tuck away in my mind for safekeeping.

When I opened my eyes the next night I decided that I

would see if I could stay in my grave and not rise. Perhaps that was the one way that I could die. So I lay there, wrapped in the cool, moist earth … it felt so good to be hidden away from everything … and I lay there all night, never once moving. I discovered something else new that night … I sensed when Charles came awake … then I heard him when he rose and left to begin his nightly hunt. Although I was fully aware of what was going on all around me, I felt like I was in a slumber. I heard the small night animals as they wandered around above me, a couple of them even walking across my grave. I heard Charles again when he returned, he even called out to me once but I stayed still and quiet. I was aware of the approach of the day, a tightening in my chest, and knew when the sun had risen and I slipped from a drowsy slumber into a deep sleep.

When I awoke at the end of the day, I again lay still, turning my thoughts inward to myself. If this was the way to die, I wondered how long it would take. My thirst, while there and noticeable, was not pushing me as strong as it had in the past, so I decided to spend another night in the ground. Charles might not allow me to get away from him and be free but nothing said I had to willingly join him every night. I knew that as long as there were no signs of me having risen up he wouldn't come for me. The one thing that he had taught me … perhaps for his own safety … was that you never, for any reason, disturbed the resting place of another vampire. So I decided to see just how long I could stay here … to find out if I could either die or if my thirst would force me out of the ground first.

I stayed in the grave for the next five nights, never moving, just listening to the world around me. Finally on the seventh evening when I woke my thirst was so severe that I could not ignore it any longer. As soon as my eyes opened I knew I had to give up my solitude and come out of the ground … I had to go and hunt, I had to feed. I slowly made my way out of the grave, taking my time because I was now severely weakened. When I stood up in the cool night air I felt the thirst, like long fingers of flame, burning through me and I suffered the pain of it in the back of my throat.

I had been sleeping in a wooded area not far from a rail hub so I began to make my way toward it. I knew that there would be some drifters camping in the area. When I got close I began to prowl around the outer edges of the camp and listen. There was absolutely no guilt in me by this time because I knew I was doing what I had to do to survive.

Soon I found one of the drifters who had walked away from the camp and I took him so fast he never even knew I was there. I was so thirsty that I literally ripped his throat out and drank every drop of his blood in record time. His life flowed into me and filled me. It rejuvenated me and my strength quickly returned to me. After I had finished the first of the hobos, the thirst was still burning like a wildfire in me, so I looked for another one. I spent the entire night circling the edge of the camp, taking one after another when they would wander off into the dark. I killed three times that night, drinking until I was bloated. When I returned to my hiding place at dawn I was completely restored and felt strong again.

I walked past Charles, never looking at him or speaking, and went directly to my resting place. I began moving away the dirt, clearing a place for myself. When I had opened my grave, I settled into it and began pulling the dirt back into place over me and slept.

That routine became my life for the next several years. I began to be able to spend more time in the earth. On the occasions when I had to go hunt and feed I would take several victims so that I would have the strength and endurance to remain hidden. Sometimes, after staying in the ground for a week or longer, I would rise and Charles would tell me we had to move. I followed him silently from one place to the next … and immediately went to ground again after killing and feeding.

I stayed in the ground until my thirst once again forced me out … I would hunt and kill until I was glutted … then back to the ground. I refused to acknowledge Charles in any way. If he was not going to allow me my freedom, then I wasn't going to allow him my companionship. I would live as close to on my own as I could with him still around. My hatred for him grew more and more intense … it became an all-consuming white hot fire inside me … my longing to be completely free from him, even if it meant destruction, became greater and greater.

We moved around several times during those years and the silence that surrounded me became almost unbearable at times, but I still refused to talk to Charles. Instead I turned inward to a world that I had created for myself. Sometimes, not often, I dreamed when I slept … always about my family … and Becky … and what a real life would have been like. I often wondered what it would be like to feel love again … that of my mother and that of Becky. I wanted so much to feel the touch of someone else, their arms around me, being a part of me. I was so tired of being alone, I wanted more than anything to be a part of something. But deep inside me I knew that would never happen … I was a vampire … a creature of the night … a loner marked with a curse … and that was the way I would have to exist until … until I didn't know exactly what or for how long.

One night just outside of Boston, I came out of the

ground to hunt and feed. But before I could get away and begin my hunt Charles stopped me. He grabbed my arm and held me tight and began to talk to me. I didn't have any choice but to stop long enough to listen to him ... I was too weak to fight him off ... but still determined to continue on my own way.

"Hey, kid, it's been a long time since we hunted together ... stay and hunt with me tonight ..." before I could say 'no' he quickly continued, "if you will go with me tonight, I've decided to show you something important about our life before the morning."

So my curiosity overtook my stubbornness and with a curt nod I agreed to go with him. It seemed like a fair trade off. If he was willing to show me something I didn't know then I was willing to spend one night hunting with him. During the night I only spoke just when I had to and then only to answer him. We found our prey quickly enough as we hunted and fed along the big railroad terminal on the north side of the Mystic river. Afterwards we continued our silent walk along the riverfront until he broke the quite.

"I gave you a new life kid, hoping that in return you would give me some companionship. But in reality I am just as much alone now as I was when I took you. You've made it clear enough over the last several years that you don't want anything else to do with me. So, I've decided to leave you alone, boy."

I looked at him in total shock unable to believe what he had just said to me. My years of simmering anger at him now boiled over and I began to tell him everything that I had felt since the night he had attacked me near my home.

"You gave me life," I sputtered, "what are you talking about ... you've given me nothing! All you've ever done was take away everything I had ... you took my life ... you took my family … you took my future! All you've given me in return is death and destruction … I die again every morning … I live in the night long enough to kill then return to another grave … you made me into a monster … now just like you did to me … I destroy lives … families and futures. Do you call that life? And in return for that you ask for companionship … I'll never be your companion … I hate you more and more as time passes … if I knew how, I would have killed you long ago for what you did to me … instead, night after night, I have to take my anger out on other innocent victims. No … you didn't give me life … you took it … all you ever gave me was misery … and then showed me how to pass that misery along to others."

"Do you hate me so deeply that you wish I were dead," he asked slowly.

"No, not just dead … you're already that … I wish for you to rot in the deepest pits of hell," I replied, my anger still running strong, "even that's too good for you … you can never imagine how much I hate you for what you've done to me."

"Then you shall have your wish," he began, speaking slowly, "this shall be the last night you spend with me. Before the sun rises, I'm going to set you free … you may go anywhere you wish and do anything you want … you may have your life all to yourself."

I smiled at the thought of freedom as a new hope blossomed out in me. We continued to walk together, neither of us speaking, along the docks and railroads of the waterfront. Not long afterward we turned a corner and there saw a building fully engulfed in flames just up the street. I had seen the glow of the fire in the night sky, smelled the smoke on the air and known that we were heading in the general direction of all the commotion surrounding such a large fire. We got as close as we could to it before the heat became unbearable, then we stopped, watching in silence as the flames licked toward the dark sky.

After a few minutes of standing there wordlessly watching, Charles looked at me and said, "Alright kid, this is where you get your wish ... you're free ... on your own now. I'm finished with you ... finished with me ... and finished with this life. Here's your final lesson from me ... so pay close attention because you may want to remember this one for the future ... this is how a vampire dies ..."

And with those words he took a step forward and then began running toward the building. He leaped high up into the air, turning, twisting and flipping as he did, and came down among the flames. I saw his figure for the barest fraction of a second as he was immersed in the fire. I heard him scream once, then he blazed up and just burst ... like some kind of skyrocket ... the sparks shooting out in every direction ... and just that quickly, he was gone.

I stood there shocked at what I had seen. I didn't know whether to believe it or if it was some kind of ruse. But as the truth of what he had done sank in to me I felt the weight of a heavy chain begin to unwind and fall from around me ... I was free of him and I could feel the freedom. But what was I to do with it ... I suddenly realized that I really was all alone now ... a man trapped in the body of a sixteen year old boy ... and another weight began to replace the one that had just fallen off.

I stood there silently watching for the next several hours as the fire burned itself out. When he didn't walk out of the flames as I almost expected, laughing at some cruel joke he had played on me, I finally accepted that I was free of him forever. I looked around and noted the sky beginning to lighten in the east and knew I had to go to ground and quickly. I didn't have time to find a proper grave so instead I found an abandoned building along the waterfront and crept silently inside it. I made my way into the depths of the basement and found a place to begin digging. The ground where I made my grave that morning was cold, wet, and stinking of rot. It perfectly reflected the way I felt inside as I pulled the last of the dirt in over me. Then as the sun began to rise on a new day, I closed my eyes and slept.

When I awoke I remembered what Charles had done … and that I was now all alone … I wasn't sure of what to do next. I didn't mind the idea of destruction myself … it meant freedom from the curse Charles had put me under. I just didn't have the nerve to do what I had watched him do … I could not envision myself running into a burning building. The most important thing I had to do on my first night of freedom was find new clothes. I had to replace the ones I wore to try to get the stench of the rotted earth off of me. I went into the night to hunt and feed … once again I would rob the living of their life … then when I was finished I would rob the dead of their clothing.

Afterward I found a quite spot along the riverfront and I sat there nearly the entire night watching the river flowing along in front of me, contemplating my new situation. I was free of Charles but I was alone and still didn't know much more than I had that first night so long ago … I really didn't know how to live and be free. I was like someone who had spent their entire life in prison, then was suddenly set out on the street and the prison doors slammed closed behind them. The world in front of me was strange and more frightening than ever before.

"Damn you Charles!" I yelled into the night, kicking my heels against the soft dirt of the riverbank, "You did this to me you bastard … you made me into a monster and condemned me to darkness … you robbed me of my humanity … you stole my life … you took me away from my family …" Then I bowed my head into my arms resting on my knees and sobbed in despair and hopelessness, my blood red tears dripping as I continued to whimper softly, "you took me out of my world and now you've left me all alone in your world with nothing and nobody to turn to … I hope if you did have a soul its chained in the deepest part of hell!"

While I sat there, beginning to take stock of the new freedom that had been thrust upon me and what I would do with it, an almost forgotten memory began to stir somewhere in the back of my mind. I remembered what Charles had told me about the southern coastal cities … that there were those there who not only would not welcome me, but would destroy me as well. I knew that Charleston was the closest to Boston and decided that would be my eventual destination. I stood up and began my journey toward Charleston, seeking an unknown executioner that would finally free me from my cursed existence. I moved in a southerly direction for the next several months, sometimes sidetracked, but always southward, always toward Charleston. Little did I know that when my journey came to an end in that small nightclub right outside of the city that it wasn't to be an ending at all … just another beginning.

Chapter Seven

 was amazed at the feeling of the air seeming to sweep and swirl around me as we moved through it. I had never traveled this way before … we weren't flying but we weren't walking or running either. It seemed that time was standing still as we just disappeared from one place and were moving unhindered through space toward another.

In a very short time we had stopped moving and were standing in the center of the largest, most elegant room I had ever seen. I looked around me, awed at the immenseness of it. It looked like everything I had always heard that a mansion would look like … the windows were tall, reaching from the floor almost to the ceiling, with thick drapes hanging on each side of them. The ceilings were sculpted in white plaster and blended into the walls with wide white moldings. There was a huge fireplace along one wall with a fire burning brightly in it and shelves of books stretching out from each side of it. Real paintings hung on the walls and the entire room was brightly lit with light coming from seemingly every direction. After a couple of minutes of just really gawking at the beauty that surrounded me I turned to Charlotte Ann and slowly asked in disbelief, "Where are we … is … is this … do you live here?"

She smiled at me and I was almost overtaken at how pretty this woman was, now bathed in light, as she answered me, "I suppose you could say this is my home away from home. I actually live in New York City, but spend some of my time here. This is James' and Katelyn's home, they have welcomed us in and have invited us to stay as long as we wish."

I turned and looked toward James, he offered me his hand, and with a friendly smile softly said, "Welcome to Whitehall Manor Dale, please make yourself at home."

"Thank you, sir," I replied remembering my manners. Then I looked over at Katelyn, her face had softened now and she was smiling at me but interestingly enough had not yet spoken to me. She continued to watch me with a keen interest, her eyes sparkling bright blue and a smile tugging at the corners of her mouth. I couldn't be sure if she was amused at me or just curious.

I suddenly began to feel out of place standing here … like the country cousin who had come to town. I looked down at myself and remembered how dirty and worn my clothes were and how perfect all three of them looked … and I began to get more than a little uncomfortable. Then I recalled that it had to be getting late, and wouldn't be long until dawn, so I would have the perfect excuse to leave soon.

I turned back to Charlotte Ann and slowly began, "It will be dawn soon … I will have to go to ground in a couple of hours … please, tell me where I can go to prepare a resting place."

She laughed happily and replied, "Child, the first lesson I think you will learn tonight is that you no longer have to sleep in the daylight ... that is one of the basic's that you should have been taught from the beginning."

"But, ma'am ..." I started and she stopped me with an upraised hand.

"Lesson number two," she said with a patient smile, "you are now a part of our family and we will be your family ... so please use our names ... Dale."

I was again nearly overwhelmed by some inner happiness when she addressed me using my given name. It was only a small thing, but it seemed so very important to me.

"But ... Charlotte Ann ..." I started over, slowly testing the sound of her name, "Charles always said that we were unholy dead things and the light of day was a reflection of God's glory and it would destroy us, it would make our blood boil and we would burn from the inside out. He said that we had to hide from it every morning."

"There's yet another thing that your maker lied to you about. You have a great deal to learn child. You no longer have to sleep, and you'll soon find that you don't need it any more. However, should you still wish to sleep, you shall be provided with a real bed in one of the upstairs rooms ... you may consider that your resting place and you shall not be disturbed there."

"Are you telling me the daylight won't destroy me," I asked again, still unsure of everything so suddenly happening around me, but still allowing my trust in her word to grow.

"Dale, you are not an unholy dead thing ... you are however an immortal being," she began to explain patiently, "one that will live forever. You are no longer human in any manner … and haven't been for a number of years … therefore, you have no need of human things … like sleep."

"Forever … I'll live forever … but Charles always told me that we only lived for maybe a hundred years and then we would crumble and die."

At this Charlotte Ann reached out her hand and lightly rubbed my arm as she smiled at me again, "I was born the first time in 1606, and then reborn to this life in 1628. I will soon celebrate my four hundredth year as an immortal … and while much of my vanity has disappeared many years ago, I still have enough to hope I don't look like I'm crumbling. Dale, you have just begun your journey through eternity … one that will go on and on … and on … forever."

I looked at her stunned at what she had just said, then with a smile she continued, "James was born in this very house in 1725, and is closing in on three hundred years himself … and Katelyn here … well, let's just say that Katelyn's bloodline is almost six hundred years long. There are other immortals that are older than all of us combined. In our world … your world, Dale … you are still a mere child at one hundred."

I stood in wonder, lost for a moment in my own thoughts as I considered what she had just told me. I looked at each of them in turn, and realized in astonishment that together the three of them had over thirteen hundred years of life experience. I was learning so much tonight and began to feel overwhelmed with all the new knowledge … I began to accept that everything had been a lie … all these years I had lived had been a lie … uselessly I had wasted so much.

"Dale, there are many things that we need to do to begin to reintroduce you to the daylight and the mortal world."

"The mortal world ..." I asked, now confused for sure.

"Yes," she relied with a patient smile, "you must be able to mingle and blend into the mortal world. You may not be a part of their world any longer but you still live in their world so you need to become comfortable around them. When you are able to conduct business with humans and not just feed from them it will make your life so much easier and more pleasant."

"I can actually mingle with real live people?"

"In time," she smiled again, "we will teach you how and the more you interact with them the more you'll feel comfortable around them again. But, the first and most pressing issue is that you need to feed ... I will take care of that for you. Then afterwards, and perhaps even more importantly, we need to take care of something a little more personal ... and please ... don't be offended Dale ... this is something you are not responsible for ... I know that you're clean ... but you stink ... your clothes, your body, everything about you has the smell of the grave all over it. So after you feed we will get you in a hot bath and wash that stench off of you."

I actually felt embarrassed that this pretty woman had told me that I stunk ... of course, I was sure I probably did, but I was just so used to it that I longer smelled it.

"I will go and find some different clothes," I said, still feeling embarrassed.

"There is no need for that, Dale," James spoke up, also smiling warmly at me, "Katelyn and I shall see that you have something to wear in the short term."

"Then tomorrow," Charlotte Ann continued with a new excitement, "I shall take you shopping ... you no longer have need to rob the dead of their clothes my child. You shall be outfitted with all the best … in no time at all you will look like a proper modern teenager should look. Then after you are clothed we shall go hunting together."

"Now *that* I know how to do," I said gaining a little self-confidence back.

"Perhaps, but if you will allow me to show you some things, maybe there is room for you to sharpen and hone your skills in that area, too," she smiled again, "But, for now, first things first … feeding and then the bath … come along with me, we shall begin."

I looked around me one more time and saw that Katelyn had moved closer to James and stood with her arm around him. Then for the first time since I saw her, she smiled a blindingly beautiful smile and spoke to me, soft and low, "Good day Dale, I hope that today will be a memorable one for you."

I smiled back, happy that she had finally spoken to me, "Good day Katelyn, and good day to you too James."

Then Charlotte Ann reached out and taking my hand lightly in hers, began to lead me out of the room we had been standing in. I followed her willingly toward a set of doors leading out into a huge hallway. Katelyn spoke again just as we were about to go through the doors and toward a magnificent grand stairway.

"I suspect you will probably be spending the rest of the day and probably early evening with Charlotte Ann. You should know Dale, that she is a wonderful teacher, and trust me, you can learn a lot from her …"

"I hope so," I replied with a huge grin, looking back at her, "but right now I'm really looking forward to that hot bath."

"I hope that you enjoy your bath … I'm sure it will make you feel different … more at home … and more like yourself again," she softly chuckled.

"I assure you Dale will be very different when you see him in the evening," Charlotte Ann said with a short laugh.

Then with a noticeable twinkle in her eye, Katelyn continued, "While you are busy with Charlotte Ann, James and I have something that we desperately need to take care of, too. Again, enjoy your day and I promise we'll be waiting here when you come back down in the evening."

 hen Charlotte Ann led me into the upstairs room, I paused and looked all around me, and just like when I had arrived in the room downstairs I was astonished at the enormity of it. There was a huge canopied bed that sat in the center of the room, taking up a large part of the space. It had white curtains, tired back on the four upright posts, just like the ones I had seen in books when I was growing up. There were two windows on one of the walls with heavy drapes covering them and hanging all the way to the floor.

But the most noticeable thing about the room was that it was calm and serene. It had the feel, although much nicer than what I was used to, of a place of rest. The lighting was dim, not nearly as bright as it had been downstairs, and it had an overall peaceful feeling. I felt as if I were secluded, completely cut off from the outside world and safe with Charlotte Ann standing by my side. Somehow I had a quiet reassurance that just as she had said, nothing would ever disturb us here. I sensed the storms that had raged inside me for so long began to break and an ever elusive but now calm peacefulness – that I didn't fully understand – slowly began to creep into and settle over me.

Charlotte Ann watched me for a moment with a smile while I took in all the new sights around me. She reached and gently took my hand in hers, and very softly spoke as she gently closed the door behind us, "Welcome home lost and wandering child, your journey through the long dark night has come to an end, the peace that you have sought for so long is right here, with me, in this room. You will find rest and comfort among your own kind … and there'll no longer be any need for tears of fear and sadness. This room, this house, will be your sanctuary and it's here that we will introduce you to the truly incredible life you've been given."

"Dale, my heart breaks for you child, you have had so much wrong done to you … you should never have been taken and turned at your age, it's just not right. I'm so sorry for you that you lost your human life without ever having the opportunity to live it. I cannot imagine the kind of life you have lived or the horrors you have experienced since being turned. And to compound the error of being turned as a youth your maker failed to teach you what it meant … what this life is all about and how good of a life it can be."

"But it's not too late to learn is it," I asked her seriously, "I was always a good learner in school, and always got my lessons fast. I promise that if you will teach me, I will pay attention to you and try my best to learn from you, please."

"You are very sweet Dale," she smiled at me as she still held my hand, "I will teach you and I have no doubt that you will learn. After tonight you will begin to see some marked changes in your life and the manner in which you live it. I cannot right all the wrongs and change them in one night … but we must begin somewhere."

"Unfortunately, the one thing that I cannot undo is your turning, and even if I could, you probably wouldn't want me to, and since you have been an immortal more than twice as long as you were a mortal, you probably wouldn't like it if I did. So let's you and I begin a new journey tonight, a voyage of discovery together. Trust me and I will walk with you, side by side, hand in hand, and step by step. I will lead you on a journey of exploration and you will learn exactly who and what you are."

"Then as you learn and grow into your new life, when you are ready, I will take you to the next level. But more importantly I will begin teaching you what it means to be an immortal … and not just a vampire … you seem to have already mastered that aspect of immortal life … and I will show you all that this life offers. Soon, you will come to fully understand what a wonderful gift you have been given and I can promise you that a newer, fuller and more rewarding experience awaits you from now on."

"I feel almost overwhelmed and lost," I commented.

"Dale, you are no longer a lost boy, you've been found and you're safe," she smiled reassuringly at me.

"That's more comforting than you can know," I answered her, and then looking around again, "but you said that you would take care of feeding for me. I haven't fed since I rose this evening and I'm beginning to feel it. Isn't it almost too late to go hunting … where do we need to go so that I can feed?"

"You will feed right here," she answered with a smile, "have you ever fed from another immortal?"

"Never," I answered, "the only other vampire I've ever known was Charles."

"Then that will be one of many firsts for you tonight. You will feed from me to begin ... and you will continue to feed from me over the next few days. For the time being you shall take your nourishment from me and it will take the place of human blood for you."

"Dale, there are other reasons you wouldn't understand now, but because of my age, my blood is very powerful. When you drink from me it will bring healing to you, your soul and spirit, and you will feel something new beginning to happen inside. During the course of the next week or so you will begin to notice that you are stronger, both mentally and physically. The more you drink from me, the stronger my blood will make you."

"Your thinking will become clearer, your reasoning skills sharper, you will become stronger physically, and your five senses will begin to change, too. My blood will activate gifts and powers that have been lying dormant in you since you were made. You have talents and capabilities that you have no idea you have. Your old existence is over and you are about to become more alive than you have ever been."

"But ... Charlotte Ann ... I don't know how to feed from you ... every time that I have fed I have always killed ... and I really don't want to hurt you."

"You have killed because you have only been feeding from humans ... and I'm not human. And trust me, you cannot hurt me ... besides you're only going to take a little bit at a time from me ... just enough to slake your thirst and start the change in you that should have been done a long time ago. Then at some point in the next day or so, after your system has had time to incorporate my blood, I will feed from you so we may strengthen our ties to each other. There's plenty of time for us to discuss all the new things you will soon be able to do ... but now ... we must begin," she said with a smile.

With that she took her hand and sliding it underneath her hair, shifted it off of her left shoulder exposing her neck for me and taking a step closer to me. I felt my fangs begin to descend and she laid her hand lightly on my chest, shook her head and whispered to me, "No fangs ... not this time ... with an immortal those are for something very special that you'll learn about later."

Then using her thumbnail she slid it across the base of her neck and opened the artery there. Her blood began to flow out and filled the room with its enticingly wonderful scent. She took a step closer to me, wrapped me in her arms, and with one hand resting on the back of my head gently guided me toward her neck. I quickly locked my lips to her and began to suck like a starved calf ... her blood was night and day different to any human blood that I had ever taken. I pulled mouthful after mouthful of the richest, best tasting blood I had ever drank. I wrapped my arms around her, greedily pulling her even closer to me ... I wanted it all ... I didn't want to stop.

Then as I drank her blood, enjoying the richness of it like it was a fine wine, I suddenly felt something different as it filled me ... I felt her inside me ... moving through me ... and I suddenly felt alive ... really alive like I had never experienced. While I continued sucking at her neck, I heard her soft voice speaking in my head as she had done earlier, *"Drink deep and be healed young one ... be strong and live ... know the love I freely offer you ... take my strength and gifts into yourself ... and live your new life to the fullest!"*

I began to sink deeper into her, losing myself in her. I felt our bodies wrapped together and the lines began to blur between us as if we were becoming one person instead of two. After several large gulps of her blood she gently raised my head away from her neck and whispered, "That's enough ... for now ... let it begin the healing process in you ... we have other things to do."

I didn't want to stop ... I felt like I was drinking from the proverbial Fountain of Youth ... I didn't think I could get enough. But I pulled myself away and watched in amazement as her neck wound closed and was completely healed in a matter of seconds.

"How do you feel," she smiled as she took a step backward, "is your thirst quenched now?"

"I've never felt anything like it before ..." I answered slowly, and looking at her with a smile covering my face, I added, "I feel ... so ... I don't know how to describe how I feel ... good ... different ... satisfied ... that's it ... finally satisfied and alive ... that's what I feel right now ... alive ... I had forgotten what it felt like," I finished saying, almost giddy with the rush of the new and powerful blood now moving swiftly through my veins.

"And that's just the beginning, fledgling," she smiled playfully at the use of the word, "you have so much to learn ... and learn you shall ... but the important thing now, is that we must get you in a bath."

Then reaching out to me she began to take my clothes off. She didn't bother to unbutton and remove them ... she just tore them apart at the seams. I was very surprised at her strength as she did that. When she had finished she gathered everything I had been wearing into a bundle.

"Oh, these things reek of death," she commented walking toward the big fireplace, "it makes me wonder just exactly what the embalmers are using these days."

She took everything I had been wearing, even my shoes, and put them into the fireplace. She took a step back and looking intently at the pile spoke quietly, "Burn."

I watched in amazement as the clothes I had been wearing suddenly burst into flames and disappeared up the chimney, leaving me feeling just a little exposed and uncomfortable as I stood, naked as the day I was born, in the center of the room. Although I was dead, she was still a girl, and I instinctively put my hands over myself, covering my most private parts.

She turned back to me and slowly looked me over from head to foot as if she were inspecting a new purchase. When she had finished her close scrutiny of me, she slowly smiled as if she were pleased with what she saw. Then she reached for my hand and took it in hers like I was a small child and led me through a door into the bathroom.

Inside the bathroom, sitting in the very center of the room, was the largest claw-footed bathtub I had ever seen. She filled it with hot water and then stepped away. With a smile on her face she silently pointed to me and then to it. Since it was the first time I had been in a bath since I was turned, I was unsure of what the water would do to me.

"Are you sure the water won't hurt me," I asked tentatively.

"Do you really think we would have anything in this house that would hurt any of us," she replied with a smile.

So reassured, and trying to keep my back turned to her to shield myself, I cautiously stepped over into the water. When I didn't notice anything different, I settled all the way to my shoulders and it actually felt so good, I think I moaned in pleasure.

"Alright Dale, you soak ..." Charlotte Ann said with a chuckle, "I'm going to change into something more comfortable and I'll be back to help you when you finish."

"I really don't have to go to ground anymore," I asked once again just to be sure.

"No Dale, all of that nonsense is behind you now," she replied, "you're about to discover that most of what you have thought about what you are, is nothing more than folklore and fantasy that's been perpetrated by immortals to protect us from humans."

"In that case, please take your time," I said as she started out the door and I settled even deeper into the hot water, "because this feels so good!"

"You haven't begun to experience feeling good," I heard her laugh as she disappeared through the door and back into the room we had come from.

I closed my eyes and enjoyed the warmth of the water like I had when I was at my home … when I was alive … I allowed my thoughts to wander as the hot water soothed my body. I was so lost in my thoughts that I didn't even hear Charlotte Ann come back in the room. I only felt a comforting presence cover me and I slowly opened my eyes to see her standing there.

She had changed from the clothes she had been wearing and was now wrapped in a beautiful blue silk robe that was tied at the waist and hung almost to the floor. It fit close to her body, clinging to her small frame. I allowed my eyes to wander over her body as she had done mine, slowly appraising her. I suddenly had the oddest thought about how pretty she looked … small and delicate … and such a pity that I was dead.

"Do you like what you see," she asked softly as she watched my eyes trace over her petite body.

"I'm sorry," I quickly answered, "I didn't mean to stare." Then I silently added to myself *"But I sure do wish I were still alive!"*

She chuckled softly, almost as if she were reading my thoughts and said, "Now, let's get the smell of the grave washed off you and discover what you really smell like."

She took a sponge that was lying there and pushing her sleeves up, she began to wash me. She started with my hair, then my face and shoulders, slowly but softly scrubbing at my skin ... and it felt wonderful ... I had never had anyone give me a bath. She continued rubbing and washing, working on each of my arms and hands. Then she moved to my back and finally to my chest and stomach. As she continued with the bath, her hands moving lower and lower on my body, I began to notice a tingling in the bottom of my stomach ... one that was far off in the distance ... a feeling that I barely remembered and was surprised at the thought that it could still be there. She smiled at me again and silently continued, moving to my legs ... and between them ... carefully washing everything.

When she had washed my entire body, she stood up and stepped away from the tub then said, "Now that you are clean, stand up, step out, and let's finish."

I did as she said and she took a large soft towel and began to dry me all over. As the towel, guided by her hands, moved over my body, I noticed the tingle in the pit of my stomach again, still light and far away, but there just the same. When she had dried my body completely, she wrapped the towel around my waist, then putting her arms around me, pulled me close to her and inhaled a deep breath.

"Ahhh ... there it is," she whispered as she held me close to her.

"There what is," I thought curiously to myself.

"Your immortal scent ... cinnamon and cloves ... and it's so fresh and clean smelling ... just like you," she answered right back in my head, taking a step backwards and smiling at me, "See, you can speak telepathically ... I knew you could we

just had to let it happen."

"How did I do that?" I asked shocked.

"It's a part of what you are Dale," she smiled happily, "just one of the many talents and powers that you will soon discover you possess."

"I wonder if it works like that all the time ... and did she hear my thoughts about her?" I thought silently to myself.

"Yes it does ... and yes I did," I heard her answer float softly through my head.

I looked in awe at her, again shocked by the words passing silently between us.

"Don't be too concerned about it," she spoke almost inaudibly to me, "the more you use it, the more you will learn how to control it and communicate using it."

Then taking my hand again, she led me silently back to the bedroom, while I concentrated on controlling my thoughts. She turned and casually took me in her arms again, this time pressing her body tight against me. When she did, it was my turn to notice ... the scent of her hair and body – lavender and lilac – rose gently off of her ... the softness of her silk robe against my bare chest ... the gentle way her hands were now slowly moving, lightly caressing my bare back ... and the tingle came rushing back ... stronger this time than it had been.

She slid her hands down my back and around my sides placing them on my waist, and looking curiously down at the towel wrapped around me she smiled, "Are you discovering something else new," she asked dropping her voice to a sultry whisper, looking at me with a knowing smile and raising one eyebrow in a quizzical gesture.

"I ... I ... I haven't felt this way since I died ... I didn't know ..." I began.

"Well, to begin with, you're not dead," she chuckled

softly, "but we can discuss the technicalities of that later ..."

Then she dropped her head a little allowing her hair to fall around her shoulders ... and slowly looked back up at me ... her brown eyes now soft, tender and inviting. She leaned in to me and very softly kissed me, her lips barely brushing mine. Her arms went around my back again and she pulled me close to her, deepening the kiss. I put my arms around her, and I felt her tongue slip into my mouth, exploring, searching, touching the tip of my tongue.

I hadn't been kissed that way since the last night of my human life. I enjoyed the feel of her arms around me, and I began to lose myself in her, returning her kiss in the same manner. Finally she broke the kiss for a moment and taking a small step away from me, opened her robe and let it fall at her feet.

I couldn't believe how amazingly beautiful she was ... her body was absolutely perfect ... her skin looked soft and creamy ... and I wanted more than anything to touch her and hold her. She reached out and taking my hand, placed it on one of her small breasts, then covered it with her own tiny hand, her delicate fingers wrapping softly around it.

She smiled at me and whispered softly, "I'm going to teach you many new things innocent one ... touch ... explore and discover ... take your time and learn."

She then reached down and slowly pulled the towel away from my waist and dropped it to floor. The tingle in the pit of my stomach suddenly dropped lower and exploded through my body with a new found forcefulness. I looked down and was shocked ... I saw something I hadn't seen since before I was attacked and turned ... I had a full, throbbing erection standing strongly up against my stomach.

She took a small step closer, winked and smiled at me

as she reached between my legs, her delicate hand gently cupping and holding me ... then ever so slowly she slid her hand all the way up my erection, wrapping it around the end. I had never been touched by anyone in such an intimate way ... her hand was as soft as silk ... and feelings I had never experienced shot through my entire body ... it felt so good I wasn't sure I could stand upright much longer.

"See ... you're not dead young one ... not dead at all," she chuckled low in her throat, winking at me and nodding her head downward at my erection, as she began gently stroking me again, wrapping her soft fingers tenderly around me.

She led me to the big bed and climbing into it pulled me down beside her. She put her arms around me and kissed me very passionately again and I cuddled close to her returning her kisses ... enjoying her soft, feminine touch on my skin. We slowly explored each other's body ... touching, stroking and petting as we lay there together. I experienced feelings and emotions that were all new to me. I groaned with happiness as I felt the excitement continuing to build in my body. I explored every inch of her small body, discovering and learning new things as I did. I lost track of time as little by little she taught me how to make love ... both how to give and take pleasure.

We continued our lovemaking throughout the remainder of the day and into the twilight hours. We passionately made love ... sometimes fast ... sometimes slow ... over and over again. I realized as we did that she was changing me, taking me from childhood innocence to manhood. She did things to me ... and showed me how to do things to her ... that I had never known or thought possible. I still could not believe that I was able to do the things I was doing but she guided me expertly until I relaxed and enjoyed every new experience.

When we had gone the full course and two bodies had joined together becoming one, I literally exhaled a slow breath. When it was over, and my newly discovered passion was completely spent, I felt that I kept a portion of her inside me, next to my heart. Although I would always have the body of a young teen, and the mind of an adult, I now possessed the experience of a fully mature and immortal man.

Charlotte Ann continued to hold me in her arms pulling me close against her. I had forgotten what it was to feel the simple touch of someone else. I didn't realize how much I had missed ... and how much I needed ... that touch, the companionship of another being. Her slow loving touch as we lay quietly together ... the softness of her small body against me ... an arm laying across my chest ... a leg intertwined, slowly caressing my own ... her delicate kisses to my neck and chest ... all anchored me to her, made me a part of her life, and gave me someone to love in return.

As we lay there cuddled together in each other's arms I became conscious of something else, too ... for the first time since that long ago night ... I felt like I was a part of someone else ... I felt loved. Her love continuously washed over me in wave after wave through the remainder of the day ... just as her hands had washed and cleansed my body ... her love now washed and cleansed my soul.

I continued to lay there in her arms, contented and happy, enjoying her soft caresses until I began to feel the familiar tug in my chest to find a hiding place. I realized that our day had turned into night, and was turning into day again. The sunrise was something I had seen and felt many times, even watching the top edge of the sun break the horizon, but I had never stayed above ground long enough to actually watch it rise completely. I felt a slow shudder move through my body and I struggled to stay still as the fear of the coming daylight began to fill me.

"It's difficult to break old habits," she whispered to me, barely tightening her arm around my shoulders, her other hand lightly stroking my chest and stomach, "but be assured that I will not allow any harm to come to you. While you may not be able to look at the sun until your eyes adjust more, you can at least enjoy the daylight … the drapes will keep out the brightest of the sun and help shield your eyes. Now be calm and enjoy the experience … stay here with me and watch as the night turns to day again … simply relax and allow your eyes to slowly adjust to the light. Before long you will complete your return to the daylight."

The room began to get progressively lighter, and a small touch of fear of the daylight ripped through me again, but my new found trust in her calmed me and began to push the terror away. Her whispered words, soft touch, and loving arms around me reassured me again and again that all was well. Soon, faster than I could ever remember it happening, daylight flooded the room, changing the appearance of everything.

"It's really daylight," I breathed out with a huge smile, "I know the sun is up … I can see the brightness through the drapes … and I'm not hurting or burning … this is so wonderful!"

"Welcome to immortal life … and your first real day of it," she smiled at me, her soft hand gently caressing my cheek, "you've walked a long, dark, and difficult road to get here, young one. You've been unduly wounded and hurt along the way … but soon, you will be completely healed – body, soul, and spirit – as you discover not just how to live, but how to love and to fully enjoy your new life."

Then as she kissed me again ... long and sensuously ... I was finally able to grasp that my long dark nightmare was really over ... my little lifesaver, now stretched out comfortably beside me had reached into my vampire world that was full of darkness and despair, and pulled me into her immortal world that was full of light and hope. She was leading me to the dawning of a new day ... in more ways than one ... the sun was going to shine in my life again ... and I looked forward to following her into this new life.

Chapter Nine

e continued to lie there together in the huge bed, watching and thoroughly enjoying each other's presence ... and in my case, although it was heavily shaded, wondering at the astonishing beauty of the daylight – something I had been unable to see in almost forty years. I shared some of what my life had been like up to this point ... the sadness, the loneliness ... and especially the hatred for my maker. Charlotte Ann in turn shared some of the finer points of what I could expect from my life as I matured. She assured me that there were going to be a huge amount of changes from what I was accustomed to taking place in my life. She again promised me that my life as an immortal would improve greatly and from now on I would begin to enjoy and be more appreciative of immortality.

"It's time for us to get up Dale," she whispered, softly kissing my lips again as she began to slowly untangle herself from me, "we need to get dressed and join the others now, there are a number of things we must do today."

"I can't imagine how much I have to learn," I said as I sat up on the side of the bed.

"We'll take it one step at a time," she smiled at me, "just like when you were growing up as a human you learned one thing at a time, now you will do the same. One of the most important things you must always remember as an immortal is that you can never just stay the same. While your body is stationary in time and will remain the same forever, the years and the centuries still continue to pass around you, and as they do you have to learn to adapt and change with them. You must always be a man of the times you currently live in, not the times you lived as a human, otherwise you draw too much attention to yourself. If you are to blend into the time you live in then you must look like the time you live in. We will start that process today by taking you shopping and buying you all new clothes."

"But I have no idea of what to buy ... or any money to buy with," I said as I watched her move around the room picking up a stack of clothes that were on a dresser.

"Dale, you have someone, an entire family to take care of you now, and until the time arrives that you become self-sufficient I will provide for you. Please, you mustn't worry about what you will wear or how to pay for it ... the store clerks will help you decide what to wear ... and I will take care of paying for whatever you may need," she answered me.

"I don't know what to say except thank you so much," I answered her with a smile as I reached and took the stack of folded clothes that she held out to me. I took them and began slipping on a pair of soft fleecy pants, then tugging a tee shirt over my head, pulling it down over my chest and adjusting it to fit.

"You're very welcome," she answered me, "and Dale, please don't feel like this is charity ... if you are to be family ... you shall be treated as family and you shall not go without."

I felt humbled at her words and I turned away from her so she wouldn't see the tears brimming in my eyes at her generosity. Taking a seat on the bed I pulled on a pair of socks that only came to my ankles. I looked wonderingly at them and thought that was certainly different, and then slid my feet into a pair of tennis shoes.

I stood up and Charlotte Ann looked at me and smiled, "Perfect, at least for the time being ... I'm so glad Katelyn kept some of her old clothes around."

"Katelyn," I asked slowly, "but ... Charlotte Ann, I don't want to wear girl's clothes."

"They're not just 'girl's clothes' anymore," she answered me with a little chuckle, "remember what I said about living in current times. They're called 'unisex' clothes now, and anybody can wear them. Step over here and take a look at yourself in the mirror and see how good you look."

I stood stock still, looking at her with a blank stare and slowly began, "Mirror ... but Charlotte Ann, I'm not allowed to look in a mirror ... and even if I do there's nothing to see ... I don't have a reflection in a mirror."

"Hum, is that so," she asked with a smile, "tell me why you wouldn't have a reflection in the mirror."

"Charles always said that because we didn't have a soul any longer there was nothing to reflect back," I answered her slowly.

"Well, let's dispense with yet another lie you were told," she said very seriously, "Dale, regardless of what anyone has told you, you do have a soul."

I looked at her, staggered at the thought of her words.

Before I could ask anything else she spoke up again.

"Allow me to ask you a question using his logic," she grinned at me, "does that chair, or the table over there, have a soul?"

"Of course not," I smiled at her, "they're furniture."

"Alright then," she continued, "can you see either one of those things in a mirror?"

"Of course you can, why wouldn't you," I continued, "they're real and solid and have something to reflect."

"You and I are real and solid, so why would we not cast a reflection in a mirror like anything else," she smiled back at me.

"Are you telling me that I can actually see myself in a mirror," I asked slowly, almost disbelievingly.

"You are real, and you are solid, so you must have something to reflect," she chuckled again, then quickly added, "that whole not being able to see a vampire in a mirror thing is part of the folklore that we immortals have passed down through the years to fool humans into thinking that we are just like them."

Then she reached out, took my hand and led me to a tall dressing mirror standing in the corner. I stood gazing intently into it fascinated at what I saw … the Dale that had looked at me the night I left home … the one that I thought had died nearly forty years ago … stood staring back at me. I felt myself begin to smile and he smiled back at me. I laughed out loud and tugging her close to me turned back to the mirror again and stood gazing at the two of us.

"Look, it is me …" I said happily, "I really can see my reflection, and I look just like I remember myself …" and my words began trialing off to nothing as realization quickly set in, "thirty-five years ago …"

"Dale, you will always look like the teenager you

were," she said with a smile slowly reaching up and patting my check with a reassuring touch, "the only changes that will take place are the maturing of your mind and thoughts. And in today's world, once we have you properly dressed, your young, nicely toned body will be a huge asset when it comes time to hunt, feed and should you wish, choosing a young human girl to play naughty games with under the sheets … and I will happily teach you how to be good at *that*, too!"

I turned my gaze back to the mirror to take in all of me this time. I slowly looked at myself from the top of my head all the way to my feet. I was wearing a dark gray-green shirt with an official looking seal and College of Charleston around it. I followed my eyes downward to my pants … they were loose fitting and made out of gray flannel. They were big and baggy and gathered tight around my ankles which made them look even bigger and baggier. They had the words "Old Navy" splashed on my left thigh. I supposed that since we were in Charleston they could very well be navy surplus, but either way they were comfortable. My tennis shoes were white with a few small scuff marks on the toe and had a big pink check mark on the sides.

"Well, what do you think," Charlotte Ann asked, smiling at me, "will those work until we can get you more?"

"They feel good, and fit pretty good too," I answered, "and except for those pink check marks I guess they don't look too girlie after all."

Then she put her arms around me, smiling and looking into my eyes drew me to her. Our lips met and a gentle kiss quickly turned into a deeply passionate kiss full of longing and desire.

"I'm glad you like the outfit," she said with a laugh, slowly breaking the kiss, "now let's go downstairs, we'll have plenty of time to get carried away and play some of our own naughty games later, right now the others are waiting for us."

She took my hand and we literally disappeared from the room and in the next second were standing in the huge parlor I had first seen last night when we came here. James was standing at the bookshelves next to the huge fireplace, looking at a book when we appeared in the room. I looked around again at the majesty and splendor of the enormous house as he continued to concentrate on the book. I couldn't stop thinking how odd it seemed, after all I had been taught, that a vampire could not only have a mate, but could actually live in a house like this surrounded by wealth and light.

"Good morning, Dale," James spoke quietly, drawing my attention to him as he slowly closed the book and slid it back into a space on one of the shelves, "I hope that you had a pleasant evening."

"It was ... very enlightening," I answered him slowly.

He chuckled slowly then continued, "Once again, welcome to our home, Whitehall shall always be open to you ... you may consider it a second home if you wish and you are welcome to come and go as you please, anytime you please, and stay for as long as you wish."

"Thank you," I said humbly, "you are very kind to allow me to be here."

"Oh, and Dale, just amongst ourselves," he added with a knowing smile, "we much prefer the term 'immortal' to 'vampire' ... that term is just a vulgar human word and holds such negative connotations."

"I ... I'm sorry ..." I began as I realized that he had read my earlier thoughts.

"It's alright, it's only a matter of semantics," he

continued with a smile, "and I apologize for listening in on your thoughts I will not do so again, we all deserve our privacy, but in the supernatural world we are known as immortals. It's the humans in the natural world that call us vampires."

Just then Katelyn came into the room and she certainly looked different to the way she had when I first saw her last night. My initial impression of her had been that she was hard as nails and dangerous as strychnine, and I'm sure that as an immortal she certainly could be ... but now ... she was absolutely beaming with happiness ... she was absolutely breathtakingly beautiful ... and looked extremely sexy, too. Her dark brown hair seemed to flow in the air around her as she appeared to glide silently into the room joining us. She was still barefooted and wearing a pair of light pink satin looking pajama bottoms that was clinging loosely to her hips and long legs. They were topped with a white, lacy tee shirt that had no sleeves, barely covered her chest and left a lot of her slender body fully revealed.

"Good morning Dale and Charlotte Ann," she said cheerily as she joined James, sliding her arm around him, smiling happily and lightly kissing his lips, "and good morning to you my love!"

I looked back at Charlotte Ann with her own beautiful brown hair, sparkling brown eyes and sultry smile. My memory flashed back to last night, then to the recently shared kiss, and I had to fight the now all too familiar tingle in the bottom of my stomach. I couldn't help but think to myself that all three of them, in addition to having untold wealth, were all so perfectly beautiful.

"*And you're perfectly beautiful too,*" Charlotte Ann winked and whispered softly in my thoughts, "*just you wait and see.*"

"Dale," James spoke up again, "please have a seat, I think we all need to talk and decide the next steps to pursue in order for you to have a successful reintroduction back to the mortal world."

I glanced warily at the morning sunbeams angling into and filling the parlor. I eased as far away from the direct light as I could and took a seat in a chair that was situated in partial shadow away from the big windows.

"Don't be too concerned with the sun, Dale, it may sting your eyes just a little until they adjust and you get used to it again but it won't hurt you," and to prove her point she stepped ideally into the full sun coming through the huge window.

I was surprised at her voice, especially after the tough as nails first impression I had gotten of her. She of course spoke with a soft and very feminine tone, but I could hear it was full of compassion and understanding for me. It was very much like the tone of Charlotte Ann's voice when she talked to me.

"I'm beginning to form some ideas as to *my* next course of action with Dale," Charlotte Ann began as we settled into our seats.

"Seriously Charlotte Ann," Katelyn suddenly burst out laughing as she took a seat beside James, "and does it consist of more of last night's course of action?"

"It seems that Dale and I both have some catching up to do," Charlotte Ann answered her with a shrug and a soft laugh, "I haven't had a steady immortal lover in nearly half a century since leaving London, so I'm sure there will be plenty more of last night's 'course of action' to come."

"It definitely sounded like you made a lot of progress last night towards catching up," Katelyn said still chuckling.

"Oh not nearly enough," Charlotte Ann winked at

her, "but Dale is ... shall we say a quick learner ... and he is able to demonstrate his lessons in a very satisfying manner ... he's also pretty adventuresome, too. So, yes, we shall both be making up a lot of lost time in the near future."

"Then we must compare notes," Katelyn laughed again.

"Oh we will ... and soon," Charlotte Ann laughed with a mischievous sparkle lighting her eyes, "besides, it seems that Dale and I weren't the only ones having fun and first experiences last night ... how was yours ... did you enjoy your evening, too?"

"Oh yes I did ..." Katelyn giggled back at her, "and just as much as you did. Human sex with an immortal is great, but immortal sex with an immortal is ... wow ... I didn't know sex could be that good ... it was beyond great ... and well worth that four week wait, too!"

"I'll say you certainly sounded like you were enjoying yourself ..." Charlotte Ann snickered, "you sounded like you got a little more than happy once or twice didn't you?"

"Let's just say I'm going to have to buy some new sheets to replace the ones I ripped up," she laughed again.

Both of them broke up in gales of laughter at her comment. I slid uneasily down in my seat and looked away, uncomfortable at being the topic of their conversation. The subject of sex was not something that we had openly talked about in our home when I was human. I shyly looked over at James, perplexed at the sudden turn of the conversation. He slowly shook his head at me with a rueful smile.

"They're girls ... and I assure you they will speak as if we aren't present ... often," he spoke silently to my mind, *"it's something you just have to get used to."*

"Do you two think we could return to the issue at hand," James quietly interjected.

"Oh James, we're not embarrassing you now are we," Charlotte Ann looked at him with a wink and a knowing smile.

"Of course not," he answered with a smile, "I'm merely concerned with Dale's comfort."

"Sure you are," Charlotte Ann grinned playfully, then half turning in her chair continued, "Katelyn, you and I can continue our girlie talk later … it seems the guys want to return to our main conversation."

"Yes we will," Katelyn snickered, "I have plenty of questions for you … did you know, I found out there was no recovery time needed … I mean, how cool is that!"

Then looking back to me, Charlotte Ann began, "I think the first thing we need to take care of is that you really must have a larger selection of clothing. So let's start at the mall, and work our way through the young adult clothing stores. In the process we can work on getting you comfortable around humans again. Katelyn, since you need new sheets, would you like to go to the mall with us and help get Dale fitted with a new wardrobe?"

"I would love to go," she laughed and quickly added, "you know I'm always good for a shopping trip with you … besides, for some reason I seemed to have used a lot of energy last night and I really do need to feed."

"Yeah so did I and it has left me a bit thirsty," Charlotte Ann chuckled, "and Dale, I think that with Katelyn and me on each side of you we can gently ease you back into society."

"I'll try whatever you think I need to do," I answered uncertainly.

"You just need to be aware that when we get to the mall you will be surrounded by literally hundreds of humans, many of which will likely bump into you or rub against you as we shop. You shall have to practice some constraint on your part but we will do our best to help protect you from your own nature. We can always make a swift exit if necessary."

"It will also probably be a good idea for you to feed while we are there. Which of course brings up another small detail ... do you know how to feed by taking only a little from your victim, or is that something we should practice?"

"I've killed every time, Charlotte Ann," I answered, "that's all I know how to do."

"Then perhaps we can use this trip as a learning experience for you, too," she mused.

"Dale, I have an idea," Katelyn spoke up, looking directly at me now, "I want you to think for a moment and remember back to when you were a human ... and tell me what you enjoyed eating more than anything else."

"That shouldn't take long," I smiled, "my favorite food was my mom's homemade chocolate cake."

"Oh, that is a good choice, my mom used to make good cakes too, and I always enjoyed them," she continued with a smile, "but when your mom made cake for you, did you eat the whole thing at once or only a slice at a time."

"I tried to eat only small bites of the slice," I smiled at the memory, "it was so good I wanted it to last forever."

"That's exactly what I wanted to hear ..." she answered with a chuckle.

"What are you getting at, Katelyn," James asked.

"I think I have an idea ... just watch what I'm about to do," she answered him.

Then looking at Charlotte Ann she continued, "Please help me out if I need it ... and you ..." she said glancing over at me, "*you* be careful!"

I looked questioningly at her and she just smiled and

continued, "I want you to feed from me Dale ... but when you do, I want you to think about your mom's chocolate cake ... take only a little bit ... then stop."

"Katelyn, that is ingenious," Charlotte Ann said, and looking at me asked, "Do you think you want to try that?"

"I guess so," I answered slowly.

With that Katelyn stood and motioned me to come to her. I stood and walked across the room to her and she put one arm around me. She smiled and looked into my eyes as she drew me closer to her. I was amazed at how easily she mesmerized me with her thrall and I felt my own will bend and break to hers. I immediately felt myself sinking into her magnificently bright blue eyes, losing myself as I sank deeper into their swirling depths. I was overwhelmed at the love I saw in them and began to relax as I felt that love flowing out of her and into me. I watched as she slowly drew her thumbnail across the base of her neck, leaving a trail of dark red blood behind, and then she closed her arms around me enveloping me in her presence. I put my arms around her and tilted my head to her neck as I melted into her seemingly becoming a part of her.

"Remember mama's chocolate cake," I heard her voice float softly through my mind.

The taste of her immortal blood was rich ... it was very similar in taste but still distinct from Charlotte Ann's ... and both tasted so unlike any human blood I had ever drank. I began to suck at her neck pulling hard and steady, my nature quickly rising up. I closed my eyes in pure happiness as I continued to lose myself deeper into her. Her blood filled my mouth ... and she filled my body as I swallowed.

I felt her step softly into my mind, looking and touching, roaming through my memories, taking some and examining them, while others she left completely alone. Then she allowed me to look back into her thoughts. I saw flashes of her memory … a young school girl … then in dance class … walking elegantly down a fashion runway … and finally dressed as a cheerleader – leaping, jumping and twirling. I also saw a couple of what appeared to be solid wood doors … and I knew there were memories behind those that she did not intend to share with me. When I stepped back and retreated from her mind, I felt her hands lightly caressing my back, pulling me closer to her as I began filling my mouth once again.

"Remember, Dale, slowly now … drink slowly … and try to stop on your own after you take this mouthful," I heard her whisper in my mind, lightly reminding me try to stop on my own.

When I had filled my mouth a second time I forcefully pulled myself away from her. I opened my eyes again, no longer locked in her thrall, and saw that her graceful neck was badly bruised and blackened where I had sucked so hard pulling the succulent blood out of her.

"Katelyn … you're horribly bruised," I stammered, "I'm so sorry … I didn't realize I was so rough with you."

"Don't worry about it Dale, I'll be alright in a moment."

Then to my utter amazement, the bruising began to disappear right before my eyes. It flowed backwards into the wound she had opened as it too began to close in on itself, leaving her neck as smooth and unblemished as it had been when I started.

"Very good, Dale," she smiled at me, still holding me and looking into my eyes, "do you think you can do the same thing with a human … at the mall today?"

"I can try," I answered her slowly.

"But remember, unlike with an immortal, you will be using your fangs, and so will have to close the wounds on a human or else they will soon bleed out and die. When you finish taking a little sip from a human, if you will lick the wounds left by your fangs, they will close on their own, leaving only a light bruise no larger than a small passion mark as the only evidence of your bite."

"And I promise I won't get too jealous if you leave some hickeys behind today," Charlotte Ann laughed, "but also keep in mind that you are only taking a small drink so you need to be careful. When you bite, do it slowly and carefully so that your fangs only puncture your victim's artery and not sever it. We can deal with the hickeys your bite will leave behind but bodies at the mall are a little bit tougher."

"Charlotte Ann and I will both be there to help you if we think you're going too far," Katelyn promised, "so now that you've fed it's time to go shopping ... I'll be right back, I need to change into some real clothes."

She disappeared up the stairs, running like she was in a hurry. In just a few moments she joined us again in the parlor, now dressed in a pair of tight fitting, faded jeans and a tee.

"I'm ready now," she laughed, "let the shopping begin!"

Charlotte Ann reached out taking my hand in hers and the three of us disappeared.

Chapter Ten

hen we settled again I looked all around and was taken aback at what surrounded me. I had seen modern shopping malls ... but only from the outside ... at a distance ... and only late at night ... I had never been inside one. I was suddenly hit from every direction with smells and noises of all kinds, many I couldn't identify. There were so many, and from so many directions, that my sense of hearing and smell was nearly overwhelmed. I was dazzled by all the flashing lights and colorful signs and posters everywhere I looked.

But the one scent that stood out among all of them was the blood, there was so much of it and it filled the air. There were humans everywhere I looked. Some were constantly walking and looking in store windows as they did. I saw some that were standing and talking to each other. Many sat casually on benches and watched others passing them by.

While we stood there three teenage girls jostled us,

literally pushing us out of their way as they made their way through the crowd. All three of them were looking down at a phone in their hand, laughing and not paying any attention to what was going on around them. I heard their hearts beating loudly, and the smell of their blood blossomed up in my face, calling out to me.

I had to fight the sudden rising of the bloodlust with everything in me. My body tensed and I prepared to lunge in their direction. Their hot blood was calling so loudly that it nearly blocked out everything else. Suddenly I felt Charlotte Ann and Katelyn both grab my hands in theirs just as I was about to leap.

"Fight the urge," I heard Charlotte Ann whisper, "they're children … just the same as you were … control your nature, don't let your nature control you."

"You'll be alright … you can do this," Katelyn added leaning closer to me, "we're both here to help."

I closed my eyes and squeezed their hands in mine. The three girls moved on disappearing into the crowd, laughing and talking with each other and not one of them even realized their very close brush with death.

Being surrounded and jostled by humans was something new and unexpected, but if Charlotte Ann and Katelyn could endure it, I could learn how to do it, too. I slowly opened my eyes and making a strong effort to block the scent of all the blood, I looked around me again. I was amazed at all the wonderful things that surrounded me. For a moment I felt like Rip Van Winkle after he had awakened from his twenty year sleep.

"Where are we," I asked slowly as I continued looking all around.

"We're just outside Charleston, at The Citadel Mall," Charlotte Ann answered me.

"And we're less than twenty miles from Whitehall," Katelyn added, "I shop here all the time. I especially like New York & Company down at the far end of the mall. I buy some of my more stylish clothes there, and James just loves Victoria's Secret and the selections they carry."

"Well, I'm sure I would like it if it's one of James' favorites," I began, "do you think maybe we should start there looking for my new clothes?"

"Probably not, Dale," Charlotte Ann smiled putting her arm around me and pulling me into a hug, "Vickie's is definitely 'girl's clothes', although I'm sure that you will grow to like it as much as James does."

"There are still plenty of other stores here just for you Dale," Katelyn began, "we're going to visit American Eagle, Hollister, and Abercrombie for your things," then pointing to the pants I was wearing, "and we'll try to work in a visit to Old Navy while we're here."

"You'll enjoy yourself and get more clothes than you know what to do with," Charlotte Ann added with a laugh, "but first lets you and I disappear and watch while Katelyn shops and feeds. She's a good actress so learn from her hunting skills and watch as she interacts with her victim. Then when you feel like you're ready you can give it a try too."

She and I dropped back a couple of steps and followed Katelyn into one of the many stores along the side of the mall. She began to wander around the things on display, casually picking up first one item then another, looking at each and then laying it aside. All the while I could see her quietly looking around, searching for her victim. I noted how she looked at every person in the store, without being noticed, sizing them up then continuing her search. It didn't take long though before she was singled out … by a sales clerk. I would have guessed he was a college student. She smiled prettily at him as he came up to her and asked if he could help.

"I'm pretty sure you can ..." Katelyn replied, smiling suggestively at him. I watched as she looked right into his eyes and I'm positive she was reading his thoughts.

"I'm planning a trip to the islands in a couple of weeks ... and I'm looking for a new bikini ... do you have anything special that you can show me?"

"We just received all of the newest selections for this season from the New York show," he replied, his eyes wandering lustfully over her lithe body, "if you'll just follow me, we have them displayed over here. I'm sure we can find something that would look perfect on you!"

"Oh that's wonderful," she added with a flirtatious giggle, catching his eyes and holding them just an extra second, "I prefer yellow ... and the smaller the better ... I like to show off all my ... shall we say ... assets."

"You certainly have some nice, mmm, assets to show off," he smiled hugely, his eyes going back to her legs and the tight jeans she was wearing, "I think I might have just what you want ... right over here."

"I'm pretty certain you have exactly what I want," she added suggestively as she followed right behind him.

In a few minutes she had selected a bikini that was more strings than anything else and holding it up asked him, "I really like this one ... but can I ask a big favor ... do you think I could try it on ... just to be sure."

"I'm sorry, I'm not supposed to allow you to try on swimwear," he said shaking his head.

"I'll model it for you ... privately in the dressing room if you'll let me try it on," she smiled and winked at him.

The clerk looked her over again and said, "Well, for

you, and just this once, I think I can make an exception."

"Oh thank you so much ... I'll just take me a minute to change," she giggled at him, and allowed him to lead her toward the dressing room.

She then disappeared into a dressing room while the clerk waited outside on her. In just a minute she opened the door a little and stuck her head out and whispered seductively, "Come on in, I'm ready for you now ..."

He looked all around as if he couldn't believe what she was doing. After making sure no one was watching, and with a huge smile at his unforeseen luck, he quickly stepped inside the dressing room with her. After a few minutes the two of them came back out. The little bikini was still attached to its hanger and the sales clerk now looked a little dazed as Katelyn turned to him, licked her lips and said, "Thank you so much ... and I commend you on your excellent taste ... so I think I'll take this one ... it's perfect."

The next store we went into I watched as Charlotte Ann repeated Katelyn's performance, except that she guided her victim towards the back corner of the store where it wasn't as brightly lit. I stood back with Katelyn and was suddenly surprised when Charlotte Ann and the sales clerk she was about to feed from just vanished ... nowhere to be seen.

"What happened," I asked Katelyn, "where did they go?"

"They're standing right where they were," she replied, looking at me with a knowing smile, "Charlotte Ann's just shielding them from sight while she feeds."

I continued to watch where they had been standing and in a few minutes, they reappeared again, chatting as if nothing had happened. I had just discovered something else new in my rapidly expanding world.

Charlotte Ann quickly rejoined me and Katelyn and, with a satisfied smile and a twinkle in her eye, the three of us walked back out into the center section of the mall. Each one of them took up a place on either side of me as we walked along together. I was silent in my thoughts as I mulled over the fact that I had just watched both of them feed … in public and in the daytime. I was also amazed that although they left their victims somewhat dazed afterward, they didn't kill them. A thought that not too long ago would have been utterly foreign to me … but now it seemed to be entirely plausible.

"Would you like to try to feed now," Charlotte Ann asked, interrupting my thoughts while we walked, "do you think you can only take a little like you saw us do?"

"I think so … but can I do what you just did," I asked curiously, "the disappearing thing?"

"Probably not just yet," she smiled at me, "however, I'm sure that's a talent you will develop over time. But until then why not follow Katelyn's example and use a dressing room, it offers the privacy you need."

"Will you please stay close to me just in case," I asked.

"We'll both be close by you, in fact, we'll even set it up for you," she smiled and looked over at Katelyn.

The three of us walked into a store called 'Hollister' and I immediately liked it. The lighting was dim, they were playing loud music, and it was closely packed with tables and racks of clothes everywhere. I stood silently looking around appraising my surroundings as any predator would. I was back in my own environment now, the hunt, and I felt very comfortable and at home as I watched for my prey, the blood lust beginning to rise up strongly in me. Everything about this place combined perfectly and I felt myself easily slip into the hunt.

While we stood there looking around at the various clothing tables a teenage girl, probably no older than what I had been, came winding her way through the displays, smiling hugely and bouncing up to me. She was as tall as I am, easily able to look me eye to eye, with curly sandy blond hair, big green eyes and a wide smile. She was dressed in short shorts and a tight tee shirt with 'Cheerleader' printed across the chest and a name tag just below her right shoulder. She had her hair pulled back in a ponytail and her neck was fully exposed. Her skin was flawlessly clear and I could plainly see the dark blue line of her carotid artery running up the side of her neck … and I smiled. My mouth watered at the thought of biting into her young, tender neck and my natural habits took over … my eyes narrowed and my fangs begin to tingle … it was feeding time.

"Not yet," Charlotte Ann whispered in my mind, *"not here, wait just a little longer until you can get her alone."*

"Hi, there!" the girl smiled at me, and I watched as her eyes traveled all the way down my body, then with a girlish giggle she said, "Welcome to Hollister, what can *I* do for *you*?" She completely ignored Charlotte Ann and Katelyn standing on either side of me.

"This is our little brother, Dale," Katelyn spoke up, drawing the girl's attention away for a moment.

"And he's just moving to Charleston to live with us," Charlotte Ann added, "so we are going to buy him some new outfits to celebrate his new home."

"That's so cool Dale, welcome to Charleston," she said as she reached and laid her hand on my arm and began lightly rubbing it. Her touch was soft and extremely sexy, sending powerful tingles up my arm. I was further shocked to realize that with her hand on my arm I could hear her thoughts as plain as if she were speaking directly to me.

"*Oh my God, he is so HOT … I can't believe how awesome he looks … when I finish with him he'll look like he belongs on a runway … and I've got to get his number before he gets out of here … then maybe I'll undress him rather than dress him!*"

"I'm so happy you're here now, Dale … it's nice to meet you … my name's Maddy," she giggled again her words now gushing out of her as she continued looking into my eyes, and I realized that she was flirting with me, "well actually it's Maddison … my name that is … but I mean … really … who would go by that?"

"That's really a very pretty name … it's different," I smiled back in a feeble attempt to flirt with her, too.

"C'mon, let's get started and find you some really cool stuff," she continued giggling nervously, "we can have so much fun getting you in all the right things … and I go on break in less than an hour … I would love to show you around the mall while your sisters shop … and I would so love to hear all about where you're from," she added with a huge smile, her eyes sparkling brightly. Then she grabbed my hand and began pulling me towards some hanging racks, away from Charlotte Ann and Katelyn.

I smiled back at the two of them as they followed a few steps behind.

"*You go boy … work your magic,*" I heard Charlotte Ann speak softly to my mind.

"*I would say be safe, but in your case, I'll just go with be careful,*" Katelyn added a silent chuckle, "*enjoy your meal …*"

I wasn't exactly sure what she meant by that safe part, but I would be careful and I would enjoy my meal. I followed Maddy around the store as she picked out several shirts and pants and showed me how to mix and match them to look good together. She took several of them and held them up to me to see if they would fit and show me how they looked. She kept laughing and giggling as she picked out different clothes, often allowing her hand to brush my arm or side, even the top of my leg a couple of times. Each time she touched me the blood lust roared through me, stronger and stronger all the time. I needed to feed and the way this girl was fawning over me I wouldn't be able to restrain myself much longer.

When she had picked out a small armload of clothes, Charlotte Ann stepped in and with a smile, locked eyes with her and slowly suggested, "Maddy, why don't you help Dale in the fitting room with some of these ..."

"Oh, yes ... you horny little thing, please do ... before you rape him right here in the middle of the store," I heard Katelyn silently snicker.

"We want to make sure they are a perfect fit ... and I'm sure he wouldn't mind the help."

"Thank you Charlotte Ann," I sent a thought her way.

"Just be careful, please try to stop," I heard her come right back.

"Chocolate cake ..." Katelyn reminded me with a chuckle, *"or in this case red hot chili pepper cake!"*

"Yeah, that's a really cool idea, I'd love to help him get dressed, you've got a lot of stuff so let's use the large dressing room down at the end, besides there's more room to move around in it," Maddy said looking me over again as she grabbed my hand and led me into the dressing room and closed the door behind us. I was finally alone and secluded, now I could feed.

"Let's start with getting you out of your shirt," Maddy giggled at me and began to pull my tee up and off my chest allowing her fingers to trace up my stomach and across my chest.

I smiled back at her, looking right into her eyes. She stopped, frozen in place, looking into my eyes and I sensed the exact moment she lost control and became mine. The back of my throat felt like it was on fire, burning with desire. I could hear her heart beating quickly, the scent of her hot blood filling the enclosed space. I breathed it in, knowing this was not going to be easy. Her blood smelled so delicious, and for the first time ever I had to think about not killing.

"Do you know how much I want you right now, Maddy," I spoke softly to her holding her eyes with mine.

"Show me," she whispered back, and pressing her body against me she put her arms around my waist. Her will was now completely intertwined with mine as she willingly offered herself to me.

"I want to take all that you have to offer ... but I will make myself stop ... I promise." Then I put my arms around her, pulling her even closer to me. I felt my fangs come down as I bent my head to her neck, the scent of her skin and blood overpowering the soft perfume she was wearing. She moaned quietly in my arms as I quickly, but carefully, bit into the soft spot just below her ear. I was careful not to sever the artery as my fangs easily broke into it, opening it like a fountain and I quickly retracted them. Her blood shot forcefully into my mouth, hot, fresh and with just the tiniest touch of remaining innocence. Her heart was strong and pumped hard as sudden fear from the sting of my bite rushed through her body. I tightened my arms around her and drank slowly, making sure to take my time with her. She never struggled or said a word as I held her locked in my grip, sucking gently at her throat.

The first taste of blood from a victim was always erotic to me and for years was how I had gotten my satisfaction. After the first mouthful of Maddy's luscious blood, I raised my head and closed my eyes basking in the pure pleasure of her freshness as it began to flow into me. I opened my eyes and looked back down, into her green eyes now lightly glazed over. She looked a little confused, unsure of what was happening, as I lowered my head to her soft neck once again. I sucked hard, pulling her close against my chest as I filled my mouth a second time and slowly swallowed, savoring the wholesomeness of her young life.

Then with every bit of self-control I could muster I forced myself to stop. I raised my head from her neck for a moment, and still possessed by the sensuality of the blood lust I looked back down at her ... young, pretty, and full of life ... then I saw her blood ... rich, earthy and bright red ... still flowing from the open wounds in her neck and again I lowered my head to it. This time, instead of putting my lips to it and filling my mouth, I closed my eyes and slid my tongue over the two small holes I had made. Then I began slowly and carefully to lick her neck, gently lapping up the remaining blood around the small wound in her neck. When I raised my head again I was amazed to see that the wounds had indeed closed, she wasn't bleeding anymore, and only a tiny bruise, the size of the tip of my thumb, remained behind where I had fed.

When we rejoined Katelyn and Charlotte Ann, Maddy was having a difficult time standing up. I hadn't taken much, but she was small and even the pint or so that I had taken was enough to leave her weakened.

"Sweetie, you look a little frail, maybe you should take the rest of the day off," Charlotte Ann began.

"I do suddenly feel very faint," she almost whined, "and I don't know why ..."

"Do you think maybe you could be just a tiny bit

anemic," Katelyn asked with a knowing smile.

"I don't think so," Maddy replied looking at her, "but maybe I should go home and rest anyway."

"I'm sure some rest will make you feel much better. I think for all of your trouble we'll just take all of these," Charlotte Ann said, and then tucking a fifty dollar bill into the top of her shorts pocket, added, "and give you a little something extra for your time and excellent service. Thank you for all you've provided today!"

The three of us walked quickly out of the store and started down the mall in the other direction. I tingled all over with the fresh blood I had taken, enjoying the thrill as it worked its way into and through me.

"You did very good Dale," Charlotte Ann said when we had gotten a few doors away.

"That's the first time I've ever been able to – or known – that I could feed that way," I replied, "it was a little difficult at first but I'm so happy that I was able to take only what I needed. It feels good knowing I didn't kill that pretty little girl and that she will go home to her family tonight."

"It will get easier the more times you do it," Katelyn said and then with a laugh added, "but as horny as she was acting over you the least you could have done was plant the idea of a roaring orgasm in her mind … you know you can give her a little pleasure in return for the pleasure she gave you."

"I didn't know I could do that," I said in wonder, looking over at her.

"It's a learned art," she replied with a grin, "you'll soon find that there are all kinds of games you can play with the human mind. My college boy back there had to go change his underwear after I left and he'll be having some pretty erotic dreams for the next week about what he thinks happened in that dressing room today."

"I suppose I could always go back and try again," I added with a huge smile.

"Ah, Dale …" Charlotte Ann spoke up, "over here …"

I quickly turned my attention back toward her.

"There's only one girl you're going to be giving orgasms to in the foreseeable future … and it had better not be with mind games either," she laughed and cuddled against me as we walked.

For the next several hours we continued to shop, continuing our sibling act in every store we visited. I was actually pretty comfortable having two 'sisters' playing dress up with me again. Before the day ended though, I had fed from three more girls in the stores we visited … and it did get easier each time. I even tried some of the things Katelyn had told me about planting ideas and the last girl I had fed from … well … she enjoyed herself as much as I did … and she was still smiling hugely when we left her store.

Finally, the last place we visited was Victoria's Secret. After the three of us walked in and I had a quick look around it didn't take me long to figure out the secret Victoria had and what it was about this place that James liked so well. I stayed very close to Charlotte Ann and Katelyn while the two of them shopped. I'm sure the amazement at what I saw on display was plenty evident on my face.

When they had finished their shopping and we stood back outside in the center of the mall, Charlotte Ann looked at me with a grin and said, "Let's go home now, you've had a good first day out, you've certainly fed well, and now you have all new clothes … and I have a few new things to show off to you."

"Yeah, and I picked up a cute little silk goody for James' enjoyment, too," Katelyn smiled and winked at

Charlotte Ann, "and I even have new silk sheets to go with it!"

"Then we can be assured of having a couple of very happy men with our trip today," Charlotte Ann added and the two of them laughed happily, grabbed my hands and we disappeared from the front of the store.

Chapter Eleven

hen we reappeared I looked around to find that I was back in the parlor at Whitehall and James was standing patiently by the huge fireplace seemingly waiting for us as if he had sensed us coming. I was simply amazed at this new way of moving from one place to another and doing it so quickly. Charlotte Ann had called it 'traveling' and Katelyn had said that it was a form of teleportation. I didn't know all the details of how it worked but still I was in awe that we could seemingly appear and disappear at will.

"Katelyn, you said that we were nearly twenty miles from here," I asked, "how do we do that … the whole moving from one place to another … and so quickly, too … we were there … and suddenly we are here."

"Dale, you must understand that as immortals time and distance has no constraints on us," she began to explain, "and because time doesn't affect us, it only seems to stand still when we move from one location to another."

"We don't truly move through time," Charlotte Ann took up the explanation, "we simply use the power of our minds and will ourselves to be somewhere else. That's why it seems to you as if we disappear from one place and reappear in another in a matter of seconds."

"Although the Change took place in you, most of the powers of 'The Gift' have been neglected and laid dormant in you. Now that it is being awakened it will begin a renewed work in you. Soon you will develop the same ability and be able to travel anywhere you would like on your own."

"You will notice the ability growing stronger in you as you use it," James continued my latest lesson, "in the beginning you will only be able to travel short distances. I think if you were to try, you will find that you are already able to move easily around the house and surrounding property by yourself. Then as you become more comfortable with it, and learn to control it, you will move faster and in further distances."

"Hummm … well all things considered," I mused slowly, "I suppose it does beat having to hobo a train to get around."

The three of them laughed uproariously at my comment but this was certainly another part of my thinking that had to change. I had discovered so much in the last day that my mind was boggled. Until last night I would never have thought that this life was possible in these surroundings … it went against everything I had ever been told … and the way I had lived. Although I was still amazed at the enormity of Whitehall and all of its beauty, the most astounding thing of all was the feeling of family and home that went with it. James, Katelyn, and Charlotte Ann looked and acted like any human family. I could easily feel their love for each other, but most importantly, now that they were adopting me as a part of their family, I was beginning to feel that same love for me, too.

While I considered that amazing bit of knowledge I looked around and noticed that Charlotte Ann and Katelyn had both vanished, leaving only James and me standing in the parlor. I remained still and concentrated on them for a moment and realized I could easily sense their presence in the upstairs rooms. I remained silent and began listening intently. I recognized that although I couldn't actually hear the two of them moving around in the rooms above us, I did hear the gentle sliding of drawers and the soft click of closets opening and closing. I smiled because I knew exactly where they were and what they were doing.

"You found them," James noted softly.

"I can *feel* their presence but I can't *hear* them," I answered, "what I do hear is the drawers and doors opening and closing so I know where they are and what they are doing."

"I hear their steps and their conversation with each other," he smiled back at me, "your senses are developing better and you are learning very quickly. Soon you will not only be able to hear them but any other supernatural creature anywhere around you. It's a part of your protection. But in the meantime, while we wait on them to finish, would you care to join me on the veranda? Perhaps their busying themselves upstairs putting away your clothes is intended to give you and me an opportunity to talk. I'm sure you still have a few questions that you would like to have answered. You may ask me about anything you wish and I will try to answer it to your satisfaction."

Charlotte Ann and I had disappeared to the upper level of the house to give James and Dale a chance to talk. It also gave me the opportunity to discuss some things with her that had been on my mind. There was so much that I had seen in Dale's mind when he had drank from me and much of it bothered me, but one item in particular more so than any others. I had been dwelling on it and was actually excited about where my thoughts had taken me. Dale and I might actually have something in common that I hadn't considered.

"Charlotte Ann," I began while we put away Dale's new clothes, "I would like to try to do something special for Dale."

"I thought I had already done 'something special' for him," she winked and grinned hugely.

"Not that you saucy little minx," I laughed at her.

"Okay then," she laughed, continuing to busily put his new clothes away, "but what exactly *do* you have in mind for him Katelyn?"

"When I looked in his mind earlier today, while he was feeding from me, I saw a lot of old hurts remaining. I think if we can address some of them, it might help him more easily grow into this life and provide him a way to leave the old one behind."

"I think that's a good idea," she answered with a grin, "do you have anything specific you would like to do?"

"Charlotte Ann," I began slowly, "is it possible to take him back to his human home for a visit?"

She stood there, silently thinking for a moment, turning over in her mind my extraordinary request.

"It's certainly not impossible, but it is highly unusual for an immortal to return to their home, especially while any human family remains alive. Even though he has been gone for a long time there still remains a lot of danger in someone possibly seeing and recognizing him," she mused thoughtfully, "but why do you ask?"

"I lost my parents, suddenly and tragically," I began to explain, "so I know the pain and hurt of that. But I know how I lost them, and, thanks in large part to James' help, that wrong has been partially righted, and I've been able to begin a healing process. Dale in effect lost his parents much the same as I did but in addition they lost him too, and neither of them really knows how or why. He is still grieving for them and there is a deep longing in him to see them. He only wishes that he could let them know he is alright."

"It's interesting that you noted that," she continued slowly, "like you, I have explored his mind and memories when he has fed from me. During those times, and since, I've come to know more about him, and have sensed a great deal of sadness in him. That is never good for one so young to harbor so much sadness. Often the sadness completely takes over and they destroy themselves. I would so hate to see that happen to Dale."

"We both know that if he really is going to be successful in this life," I continued, "there has to be a clean break with the old one. Can we at least attempt it?"

"This is obviously something that you feel very strongly about," she said, and then with a quick smile added, "so I suppose we should decide how to implement it and begin planning our trip to Pennsylvania."

"Thank you for understanding," I smiled and hugged her, "here's what I was thinking ..."

I quickly outlined what I had in mind and she actually agreed with me on most of the points, even adding one small detail that I had not even considered.

James led the way to the veranda doors and smiled as he opened them wide and walked out on the spacious rear porch. I hesitated at the sight of the bright sunlight covering the porch, then trusting fully in him I stepped out and into the full daylight for the first time since I had been attacked. I cringed as the brightness of the afternoon sun struck my eyes and I had to close them for a moment and lean against the wall.

"Owww ... that hurts," I breathed out, covering my eyes with my hands and looking away from the brightness, "I guess I'm still not as used to the daylight as I thought."

"Considering that you haven't directly seen the sun in almost thirty-five years, I think you are doing very good," James said as he took my arm and led the way to the far end of the porch that was thickly covered with climbing vines and colorful flowers. The entire area was washed in a dim ... and comfortable ... shade.

We took our seats in a couple of lounge chairs and, fully covered in shade, I settled into the deep cushions with my hands still shielding my eyes. I began to slowly reopen them, peeking warily between my fingers. I sat quietly thinking about what he had just said as I tried to open my eyes again. I slowly raised them toward the outside, to look across the rear of the property. I quickly had to drop my head again as my eyes were once again burned with a stabbing pain.

"Do it more slowly and remove your hands as you feel comfortable," James spoke, now sitting beside me, "your eyes must adapt and become accustomed to the light again. The change that took place in you when you became an immortal greatly affected your eyesight and causes your eyes to be extremely sensitive to light. However, since you have only lived in darkness since then, they haven't had the opportunity to regulate. They can and will adjust to the sunlight in the next day or two and then the stinging will go away completely."

"How long will it be until I can walk comfortably in the sun like you do," I asked.

"I think if you shield your eyes with dark glasses, probably another day or two, then in about a week you should be able to walk about at ease without the added protection."

I settled further into my chair and quickly began to notice the warmth of the indirect sun as it penetrated my body. It felt good to sit in the daylight and experience the warm air on my body again. I had almost forgotten how good natural warmth could be. I slowly took in a deep breath, smelling the surrounding flowers and greenery of the back gardens, and smiled as I exhaled. Then I sat bolt upright and looked at James, astonished as I realized what I had just done.

"My lungs… James … they work … I can breathe," I exclaimed, "I just took in a deep breath and exhaled."

James smiled back at me and answered, "Yes, you can breathe … your lungs work fine … as does all the remainder of your internal organs. It's just that you no longer need as much oxygen as you did when you were a human. So even though they work, you rarely use them."

I closed my eyes and took in another deep breath, enjoying the sensation of my lungs filling with air … and I smiled.

I heard James softly chuckle as he sat in the chair beside me so I slowly opened my eyes and asked, "Did I do something funny?"

"Not at all," he answered still smiling, "it's just that it has been many years since I have been around a basically newborn immortal ... and therefore I tend to take for granted many of the things that you are just beginning to discover ... such as the breathing. Although I suspect you have been doing so for a long while – albeit unconsciously. In a sense, you are rediscovering life – and all that it has to offer – and I have to say that I find your innocence to be quite refreshing."

Unsure of how to answer his thoroughly honest answer, I continued to sit in silence for a few minutes, still breathing in deeply and exhaling, testing my lungs, using them like a new found toy.

"This is so wonderful James," I finally slowly spoke up, "all these years I have thought that I was nothing more than a walking dead man. I'm actually starting to believe that I may really be alive."

"I assure you, Dale," James spoke softly, "you are very much alive, more so now than you ever were as a human and you will be forever."

I thought about what he had just said, rolling it over in my mind. Forever – time without end – was still an enormous concept for me to completely grasp but I was trying.

"I feel like I'm starting all over again ... there's so much I don't understand ... and I have so many questions," I breathed out softly and slowly, "it feels like I'm waking up from a bad dream. I was told ... and I believed ... that I was dead. It's like I have been lost ... cut off from life ... and suddenly here is this whole new and wonderful world opening up in front of me. I don't know anything about what I really am. Charles always said that he had killed me and brought me back as a vampire ... I mean ... immortal.

You see, even the name of what I thought I was has suddenly changed and I have to get used to that."

"Yes, to a certain extent, it has and you do. However, you are now and will forever be a Vampire ... it's just that being a vampire is only a small portion of being an immortal."

"I'm not sure I understand," I answered.

"I suppose that simply put, a vampire is what you are, an immortal is how you live. Take for example a human, they are, for the most part carnivores – which defines their diet, how they survive if you will – yet no one generally refers to them as carnivores, they are called mortals."

"Okay, I think I'm following you," I grinned, "so being a vampire defines my diet – how I survive – and being an immortal defines my lifespan ... forever."

"Absolutely correct," he smiled, "but you have to admit that calling yourself immortal is much better than calling yourself a vampire."

"Yeah, you're right," I agreed, "and I know there is so much more I have to learn ... and I feel more than a little overwhelmed at the thought of it."

"In a sense you are starting over Dale," he smiled at me, "but there's no need to feel overcome, because this time you will have plenty of assistance to adapt to this life."

We sat quietly for several minutes while I thought about this wonderful new world and life that was opening up to me.

"James," I finally spoke up, breaking the silence that had surrounded us, "we're not the only immortals in this world ... are we?"

"There are indeed many more of us," he answered, then adding a smile, "although there's not as many as some mortals would like to think. In the preternatural world, our kind … vampires as mortals prefer to call us … are the only true immortals because we never die. There are others in the preternatural world with various talents … shifters, weres, and in some instances casters and seers … and because of their unusually long lifespans, and abilities, they are called supernatural beings."

"But are the three of you like the most powerful immortals in the world?"

"I very much appreciate that Dale," he chuckled low, "and while we may not be the most powerful, we are among the oldest, and do wield some authority."

"I suppose what I'm trying to ask, is our world organized like the human world, is there someone … somewhere … in charge and making the rules," I asked slowly.

"In the sense of someone being 'in charge' we really have no such structure in our world," he continued, "the hierarchy of the supernatural world comes more as an acknowledgement of age and abilities by others. As immortals, most of us live individually. There are some cases of covens, but even then they are loosely bound, their members being free to come and go whenever they please. In our case, we are more a family than a coven … Katelyn and I are mates and Whitehall is our home. Charlotte Ann visits whenever she wishes and remains as long as she wishes. Of course you are also welcome as long as you wish. While we may live under one roof, we are all individuals and come and go as we please. Although we appear to be a family, none of us have authority over the other."

I sat and thought about what he had said, trying to sort out everything before I continued. I had certainly experienced a taste of Charlotte Ann's ability outside that club when she had pinned me to the wall. I had never felt anything that strong, that powerful or that terrifying in my life.

"Then is Charlotte Ann the most powerful in our world," I asked.

"When it comes to controlling and using supernatural powers," he continued patiently, "Charlotte Ann is one of the most powerful and her age is certainly a factor in that. She and I are both numbered among the elders, although neither of us ranks among the ancients."

"What are the ancients," I asked curiously.

"An ancient is an immortal that has lived over at least one millennium, there are very few of them, and by virtue of such long life they have gained extraordinary powers and abilities," he explained.

"Although not an ancient, Charlotte Ann does carry pure ancient blood in her, which gives her nearly the same powers and abilities of an ancient, and that alone demands an entire other level of respect," he commented.

I had no idea what he meant by that but it sounded important.

"When Charlotte Ann is at home in England," he continued, "she is the oldest immortal that was a natural born English subject. As a result any other immortal in the United Kingdom recognizes and respects her authority."

"I understand that," I answered, "but this is America."

"You are correct, and in the entire North American continent I am the oldest natural born American, having been a colonist when I was turned …" the cutting his eyes toward me, smiled, "by Charlotte Ann."

I was stunned at his admission and had to let that sink in before I could reply, "You mean that Charlotte Ann … is your maker … and she lives with you?"

"You may find this difficult to believe," he said smiling, "and it's a very long story, but she and I loved each other dearly when she turned me. Although she spends as much time as she wishes at Whitehall, she does maintain her own home. While I claim the right of rule, such as it is in this country, I defer to her out of respect for her both as my maker and her wisdom gained through the ages."

I sat shocked at all he had just told me but then I saw the opportunity to have my largest question answered.

"You said that Charlotte Ann turned you," I spoke up looking at him seriously, "can you explain to me how she did that because I still don't fully know how I became an immortal. All I remember is being attacked and then waking up like I am now, filled with all these new urges and desires. What happened to me and why didn't I die ... I would at least like to understand that."

"The changing from mortal to immortal is a complicated process," he began slowly, "and something we will discuss in detail later, as you continue to acclimate yourself. But for now I will give you a simple version so as not to inundate you with too much information."

"When you were attacked, your maker drained all of your human blood out of you. When that happened it caused every organ in your body to suddenly and completely shut down causing your body to go into deep shock. He saved your life by giving you his immortal blood, however weak and diluted it was, in return. You never died, regardless of what you were told. You were only unconscious for several hours while your body and organs became acclimated to the new blood and began to function once again. When his immortal blood began to work its way through you it retained enough of its original strength to revitalize all of your organs and began a complete genetic makeover in you."

"The vampiric gene that is contained in our blood completely destroys the human body and nature. In its place it creates a new preternatural body and nature. As an individual you are actually made up of three different parts … a body that contains a soul that has a spirit. It is your soul and spirit that make you who you are, your personality if you will, and those did not change. The only thing that changed was the physical part of you, your body and internal organs. For all practical purposes you are still the same Dale that you have always been with the exception of no longer having a human body or a human nature."

I sat back and quietly considered the things he had just told me. Although I still had questions, I was beginning to understand what I was, how I became what I am now, and that I am living a real life. I had discovered more in thirty-five minutes because of James' patience and understanding than I had learned in thirty-five years. I knew there would be much more to follow … a discovery of a new life and a new way of living it. I smiled contentedly as I relished the thought that now I had someone to guide me. There was finally someone who knew what it was all about. Someone bigger than life, who would teach me all the things I didn't know.

The afternoon sun began to sink lower in the sky, the daylight giving way to dusk and finally to darkness as night covered us while I continued to sit there, now at ease, with James sitting quietly beside me giving me time to think about all we had discussed. Charlotte Ann and Katelyn slipped silently through the doors and joined us. They were my family now and we sat together just as any family would in the cool evening air. Finally, after so many years, I felt the closeness of family again. While I still missed my parents, my sisters … and most of all my Becky, I knew that I had a new family now. This immortal family loved me and would take care of me just the same as my mortal family had done.

After a few minutes of sitting quietly in the darkness, everyone tuned in to the sounds of the night around us and seemingly lost in our own thoughts, James softly broke the silence, "I trust everyone had a good day and fed well."

"It was a good day for all of us," Charlotte Ann answered him slowly, "I think we all learned from it … and there's a good chance the day's lessons aren't over yet."

I quickly noticed a distinct and lingering look exchanged between James and Charlotte Ann.

"Is that so … that could indeed prove very beneficial," James mused softly and I knew that something had been communicated silently between them.

"Dale, you should know that immortality looks good on you and you wear it well," James commented turning his look back toward me, "and though you may not fully realize it or fully appreciate it just yet, you were indeed fortunate to have been given second life. The immortal aura is so strong in you that it is almost radiant. That is a sure sign of strength and latent power waiting to be called on."

"Thank you," I replied with a happy smile, "but I have to credit that new look to Charlotte Ann and Katelyn. The one thing that has tormented me over the years was that I had to kill. I had to take innocent lives and tear apart families just to survive. I didn't know any better, but today they taught me a different way to hunt and feed. I am happy to know that after today I can feed and I don't have to kill to do it. We actually had a very successful hunt this afternoon."

Then beginning with our arrival at the mall I related the entire afternoon to him. I told him about the different stores I had discovered. I talked about shopping and described all the new and different clothes Charlotte Ann had bought for me. I told him that now I would be able to blend in with humans when I hunted. Finally, I told him about the four girls I had fed from and how each of my experiences had been different. At some point in my story I realized that I sounded like an excited kid talking about something new but still noted that he continued to listen intently with a patient smile.

When I had finished my story about the day, Charlotte Ann reached out and with a smile took my hand in hers.

"Dale," she began quietly, "while Katelyn and I were upstairs this evening we were discussing you and some things that have affected your life. A large part of becoming an immortal is that you must have a final and complete break with your human life. That's something that has never happened for you and it's something that you need if you are to be completely happy in this life."

"I … I don't think I understand what you're talking about," I began hesitantly, caution filling me.

"The three of us want nothing more than for your transition to this life to be full and complete. Due to the manner in which you were taken and brought into this life, many things have been left undone. Call them loose ends if you wish but they are things that need to be corrected. What I'm saying is that you need and must have closure toward your human family and the life that you once lived."

"How am I supposed to do that," I asked, again cautiously, a light touch of fear beginning to take hold in me.

"You can't, not by yourself at least," she continued, "but with our help you can. We have agreed, Katelyn and I, to take you back to your human home for a visit. It will only be a short visit, just long enough for you to be able to see your family, tell them you are alright, and say the good-byes you were never given the chance to do. Then before the night is over you shall have the healing and closure that you so desperately need."

I sat in shocked silence as her words sank in to me. I had lost my family ... they had lost me ... and now she was offering me the chance to go back to them ... to finally say good-bye. I wondered to myself if that would open or close old wounds ... what would I say ... how would I say it? I had often wished that I could see them again but now that it was a reality and about to happen I began to feel more than a touch of fear in me. I had been told that I could never go back ... and what the consequences of that would be if I did. There was also the fear of how my family would react to my sudden reappearance.

"Is that even possible ... I didn't think I could ever go home again," I slowly asked, looking at Charlotte Ann and feeling the sudden pain of the loss of my family tear through me once again.

"Normally, you can't," she replied, "but in your case a grave error was committed and we all think it would be helpful for you. You have to be able to put your human life in your past and leave it there. There must be closure to this issue so that you can move on with your immortal life and be happy."

"Dale, you weren't much more than a child when you were taken and our kind should never change a child. The error was then compounded when you were lied to and never taught. One of the wrongs, having been turned against your will, we can never do anything about, the other, we can correct by teaching you."

"However, to be successful in this life, one has to make a clean break between the mortal and immortal lives. Unfortunately, you were never given the opportunity for that to take place. You still look longingly back at your human life. There are still some doors that need closing."

I glanced quickly at Katelyn as I remembered the solid doors I had seen in her memories. She smiled at me and slowly nodded knowingly at me.

"Katelyn and I have talked," Charlotte Ann continued, "about doing this, and we think that in your case, with the circumstances when and how you were changed, that a visit may be advantageous for you."

"How and when can we do that," I asked.

"Right now, tonight," she replied with a beautiful smile, "go with us, trust us the same as you have so far … and allow us to make further changes in your life."

Each one of them reached and took one of my hands in theirs. I felt both of them lightly squeeze and then felt the stirring of the air around me. We traveled through space as once again I felt time stand still … and I knew that we were moving toward a small mining town in western Pennsylvania.

Chapter Twelve

 s the air began to slow around us, I looked and saw some very familiar sights but now they were very different to what I was used to seeing. Instead of the big veranda of Whitehall where I had been only a moment ago, I was now standing on a cracked and broken sidewalk beside a darkened street about two blocks from my house … very nearly the exact same spot that I had been all those years ago when I was attacked and taken.

I looked around at where I stood and was assaulted all over again by the memory of that terrible night. I saw the trees where Charles had stepped out of the shadows. I heard his questions and felt his grip as he attacked … and this time I felt his fangs sink into my neck … the blazing fire of his bite roaring through me … and the strong pull as he began sucking the life out of me. I cringed, taking a step backward at the awful recollections of the end of my human life and the beginning of the long torturous nightmare.

"This is where it happened," I slowly whispered to Charlotte Ann, "this is where I was attacked ... the memories are so clear ... just like it was yesterday ... it's just as fresh ... I didn't want this part of it."

"We all had our individual experiences when we were born to second life," she answered, "some good, some not so good, some confusing ... but nothing will ever hurt you again ... put aside the fear of the past and face the memories of that night full on. Look them in the eye and know that you were completely innocent ... there was nothing you did to provoke the attack and nothing you could have done to prevent it."

I stood silently for a few minutes replaying the events of that first night with Charles and everything he had said to me. Then slowly I began to speak, recalling the events of that night, "He told me that he had chosen me ... that he had stalked me for over two months ... and that he had decided to take me that night ... there really was nothing I could have done differently to prevent what happened was there?"

"Not a thing," she shook her head, "when a rogue decides to take a human ... only they can change their minds and unless they do ... it's done ... and their victim has no choice in the matter."

I felt a tiny bit of relief roll though me with the knowledge that I was only the victim and could not have stopped what happened. I looked around one more time and slowly nodded my head.

"What's done is done," I echoed her, "can we continue on now ... I don't want to remain here any longer ... I would like to finish the walk that I started that night ..."

Charlotte Ann reached and took my hand, intertwining our fingers together and we began walking down the street with Katelyn a close step behind us. It was late, probably about two in the morning, and like three shadows, we made our way silently down the narrow street toward where I had once called home. The three of us talked low as we continued walking toward my house. Charlotte Ann and Katelyn began detailing how they had planned to make this visit successful.

The small town, Renton Junction, where I had lived was like so many typical mining towns in the shadows of the Allegany Mountains. It was small but everyone here took care of and was proud of what they had. I was surrounded by memories and the late night sounds and smells from the neighborhood. I smelled the wood smoke from any number of fireplaces and stoves. I saw remnants of the smoke as it lay in layers in the night sky above the community. I listened and heard dogs barking and even some early roosters crowing as we passed. They were sounds that reached deep and stirred old memories ... sounds that had once meant home.

The only human sounds I heard were those of people sleeping soundly in the near-by houses. I knew that in another couple of hours or so the silence would begin to give way to the start of a new day. The first miners and their wives would begin to rise and soon the smell of a new day's breakfast – bacon, eggs, ham, and biscuits – would fill the air. The memories continued to flood me as I stopped and stood for a few minutes looking around ... so much had changed in my life and yet in this little community so much had remained the same over all the years since I had been gone.

It seemed strange to be finally finishing the walk that I had started so many years ago. I felt time begin to unwind. The newly found light in my life began to spiral quickly backward, across the years of darkness that had enveloped me. Suddenly I was a sixteen year old boy again, coming home after his birthday party.

"Let's begin our visit at your parent's house," Katelyn spoke up, taking a step to come back even with us, "you can spend as much time as you would like to with them. They still live right here, in the same house you grew up in. They are alone now, your dad is retired, and your sisters no longer live in the area. They both married and moved to other states several years ago."

I stood quietly at the bottom step of what had been my home, looking up at the front door and reflecting on all that had happened. I recalled the warnings that my attacker had given me about what would happen should I ever come back here. I bowed my head and closed my eyes, thinking about my sisters and knowing they, at least, were safe. When I raised my head I looked at Charlotte Ann and slowly asked, "If I go through that door ... if I do this ... will my parents be safe ... I mean they won't be hurt by others will they?"

"Dale, no one outside of your parents will ever know that we've been here," she answered me with a smile.

"When you go inside," Katelyn began, "your parents are probably going to think they are dreaming at first. We would like the visit to be over before daylight and since there's still a few hours before dawn, you can talk to them until you are ready to leave. However, keep in mind that because of your slower heartbeat, your touch is going to feel very cool to them."

"And don't forget," Charlotte Ann added, "you look exactly like you did the night you left home ... they are going to see their sixteen year old boy ... nothing about you that they can see has changed. But Dale, they have changed ... your parents are now in their early seventies so you must be prepared for that. Your time with them may get very emotional but try not to cry in front of them. They wouldn't understand and you wouldn't want to have to explain why you cry tears of blood."

"Can we leave in a hurry if we have to," I asked.

"All you have to do is say so and we'll be gone," Charlotte Ann reassured me.

"Dale, this visit is for you and no one else," Katelyn added, "and if at any time you're not comfortable, we can end it and leave. This is to help you put aside the past. We all have to have some kind of closure with our human lives so we can continue with our immortal lives. But also after this night your parents will never worry about you again. They will always be at peace concerning you."

"Let's go inside then," I said slowly, nodding my head in understanding.

When we had stepped through the door I stopped and looked around at our living room. It seemed smaller than I remembered it being and the furniture had changed but not much else. I noticed several pictures hanging on one of the walls and I stepped over to examine them. There was only one of me ... I was smiling and happy in my last school picture ... and the frame was draped in black crepe. I reached out and touched it, letting it slide between my fingers. It was there to signify someone who had died ... but I wasn't dead, they just didn't know it. So I reached and carefully removed the mourning cloth from around my picture, gently folded it, and slipped it into my back pocket.

The rest of the pictures, all surrounding mine in the center, were of my sisters and depicted their continued lives. I closely studied them, following the course of their lives ... all the things I had missed ... graduation ... weddings ... births ... I saw the years' progress as they aged and changed.

They looked happy ... they had families ... children ... and I had to assume by now probably grandchildren. I smiled silently as I realized that somewhere I had nieces and nephews ... I was an Uncle ... something I had never considered. Then pulling my eyes away I turned and moved wordlessly on through the house.

We silently glided down the small hallway and into the kitchen where I had eaten so many wonderful home cooked meals. Charlotte Ann and Katelyn followed close behind me as I looked all around the tiny kitchen taking in memories ... the small table, now with only two chairs instead of five ... the sink with dishes stacked for drying ... the stove with a dishcloth draped over the handle to dry. I inhaled the smells of my mother's cooking that still lingered in the air.

While I slowly turned in place still continuing to survey the area I suddenly froze in place ... there, sitting on the counter was one of my mom's fresh homemade chocolate cakes. I walked slowly over to look closer at it ... I couldn't believe what I was seeing. There was a handwritten card lying beside it that read, 'Happy 52nd Birthday to my Pretty Boy – Wherever he is!' I read the note as I stood there and could not restrain myself any longer as a couple of red tinged tears began to roll down my face.

"It's my birthday ... and I didn't even realize what day it was," I almost whispered, "I can't believe that I would really be that old."

"Go ahead and take a piece of your cake," Charlotte Ann said to me smiling, "that will be their evidence that you were actually here – they'll know they weren't dreaming. It will be a huge comfort to them when we're gone."

I looked for and found a knife in one of the close by drawers and cut out a modest sized piece of cake.

"I will actually try to eat it after a while," I smiled, with a tear still on my face as I carefully began to wrap it in a napkin.

"Why not eat it now," Charlotte Ann asked softly, "it is your birthday and she did make for you."

"Can I really do that," I asked wonderingly.

"Just like anything else take it in small bites," she answered with a wink, "savor and enjoy the taste of your mother's love."

I hesitantly broke off a small piece and cautiously raised it to my mouth. It felt foreign when the chocolate icing touched my lips but there was no other immediate physical reaction. I smiled and popped the piece into my mouth. I closed my eyes in pure ecstasy as the taste of my mama's homemade chocolate cake filled my mouth and coated my tongue. The memories of the many times I had eaten it burst forth from some long hidden place in my mind … and I groaned in happiness. I delighted in the taste, making that little taste last as long as I could before finally swallowing it … then I felt it disappear into nothingness as soon as it hit my stomach.

"I did it … I really ate a bite of cake," I said excitedly, "I can't believe that I really did it!"

Then I looked down in wonder at the small piece of cake I held in my hand. Suddenly the significance of that little piece of cake, just a small part of the whole, and what it really meant dawned in my mind. I was awed as the full impact of a new truth settled in my mind. I couldn't help but be astounded that such a minor thing could illustrate so many realities.

"This life is all about learning and growing," Charlotte Ann answered me with a smile and gently put her arm around me.

I looked and saw Katelyn standing behind her. She was smiling too but I also saw a tear brimming in her eye. I turned my attention back to the remaining piece of cake in my hand and slowly, purposefully, took another bite ... and then another. I continued one bite at a time, savoring each one until the piece was completely gone.

"See, I did it," I said with a huge grin, turning toward Katelyn, "small bites of a small piece and, although it's more difficult than you can possibly imagine, I'm going to leave the rest of the cake."

"Yes, Dale, you did it," Katelyn beamed back at me, "and I knew you could if you tried."

I turned back to the counter and picked up the note that my mom had so lovingly written and reread it again. I smiled as an idea formed and I began to look around for something to write with. I found an ink pen in a drawer and then on the bottom of the card I wrote, 'Thank you for remembering me, the cake was as delicious as always, I love you both – Your Pretty Boy', then dipping my finger lightly into the chocolate icing on top of the cake I pressed it to the note.

I silently stood it up inside the little slot where I had taken my piece of cake before continuing through the house. Charlotte Ann and Katelyn's reassuring presence stayed with me as I walked down the small hallway toward my Mom and Dad's bedroom. The three of us stepped through the open door and into their bedroom ... I looked behind me when I suddenly couldn't feel their presence anymore. I knew when I didn't see them that Charlotte Ann was shielding herself and Katelyn so it would appear to my parents that I was all alone.

I turned back and stood silently watching both my parents sleep peacefully as again the memories of my life flooded my mind. The passing of the years was made very real to me as I watched them. They had aged so much since the last time I had seen them. I knew they both had to be getting close to seventy-five but in my mind's eye I had remembered them the way they were. They still looked like my parents but now they looked old and frail. I'm sure that was due in large part to a life of hard work. I almost turned and walked away but something inside kept me there. I owed them … and me … this moment. I slowly moved to the end of the bed on my mother's side and quietly spoke.

"Mom … Dad … wake up … it's me … I've come home again."

They both stirred and quickly sat up, realizing there was someone standing in their room. Their sleep was quickly replaced by astonishment as they realized exactly who that someone was … their lost boy. They both stared at me in shock and disbelief, knowing that what they were seeing couldn't be real. I had been missing and assumed dead for so long and now I stood smiling at them just like I had never left. As the shock of seeing me began to wear off my mom was the first to speak.

"Oh, look … it's my baby … I can't believe it … he's finally come home to me!"

She quickly threw off the blankets covering her, got out of bed and started toward me. I saw tears forming in her eyes and spilling over, running down her cheeks.

"Oh, Dale … my pretty, pretty little boy … is it really you … I'm so happy that you've come home … I've missed you so much and thought about you every day since you disappeared."

I took half a step backward, held my hand up, and softly said, "Mom, please wait for just a moment before you try to hug me. I know that I still look like you remember me

... but I'm different now ... I'm not the same little boy that left so many years ago ... everything about me has changed."

She stopped in her tracks and took a second look at me as the sudden realization dawned on her that I did indeed look just like I did all those years ago. I saw a flash of confusion cross her face as she asked, "How can you possibly be the same after so long?"

"When I was a child you used to tell me that the good things never change," I answered her with a smile, "it looks like you were right."

"What happened to you baby ... where did you go ... what did you do," she asked, then looking at me almost frightfully continued, "oh no ... no ... no ... did you die baby ... Dale, were you all alone and scared?"

"No mom, I didn't really die," I smiled at her, "at least not in the same sense that you would think of dying ... I only moved from one world to another ... I'm very much alive ... just different now ... with a different nature. When you hug me, I'm going to feel different to you ... my skin will feel cooler than you remember, but that's only because my heart beats slower now than it did ... but other than that I'm still pretty much me."

"I don't care about all that," she said, still crying and taking another step forward and opening her arms to me, "I just want to hug my little lost boy ... to feel you in my arms again ... I want to hold you close and protect you ... please?"

I couldn't tell her 'No' so I stepped forward and opened my arms. We met and I felt my mom's arms go around me and her love began to flow through me like a tangible force. I realized that a mother's love is a real, physical entity as it surrounded me. I put my arms around her and as I held her I felt all the hurt and pain of missing her evaporate, lifting like a heavy blanket away from me.

"I love you mom and I've missed you so much," I said as I held her close to me.

She stepped away and slowly reached her hand up, laying it on my cheek, patting it softly and stroking my face. She looked up into my eyes, her own eyes now watery with age and tears. Her hand felt soft and cool on my face, the years had made us almost the same temperature. She smiled as she continued looking into my eyes, "Nothing's changed, it's really you and you still feel like my little boy ... and now you're home, right where you belong. I'm so happy to have you back."

I turned my head toward my dad and softly spoke to him, "Dad, you shouldn't worry about me any more either, please take care of mom for me ... and enjoy your retirement. I hope you both live long and now much happier lives. It's been a lot of years ... and a long journey for me since I left ... but I finally made it back home again to let you both know that I'm alright. I never had the chance to tell you good-bye and that I loved you. I wanted both of you to know that I wasn't dead ... just different ... I'm more alive than either of you can ever imagine me being ... and I have a better life than ever before ... I won't ever die so please don't grieve for me anymore," I smiled at them.

"Does that mean you're leaving again," he asked as tears began to form in his eyes.

"I have to dad," I answered him, "I live in another world now ... and I have to go back where I live. But before I go, I want you to do something special for me ..."

"Just ask, you know I'll do anything I can son," he replied.

"I saw all the pictures in the living room," I

continued, "would you please call both my 'sissies' for me and tell them that I love them and miss them, too … I wish that I could have been here to know their families and be a part of their lives."

"I will call them first thing in the morning as soon as they wake up," he replied shaking his head, "but they'll never believe me."

"Dad, it doesn't matter if they believe you or not," I answered him, "what's important is that you and mom both know that I'm alright … that I didn't die … I've waited and wished for so long to be here with you again … and I have enjoyed our visit … but I have to go now … I don't have much time."

"Baby, do you really have to go … can you please stay for a little while longer," Mom asked hopefully, "It's almost morning and I'll cook your favorite breakfast for you."

"Thank you mom …" I grinned at her, "but I already took a piece of cake from the kitchen … I didn't think you'd mind too much … and thank you both for remembering my birthday … but I really do need to go now."

Then as I turned to leave I thought about my picture.

"Wait, there's one more thing," I said turning back to them and taking the streamer of black crepe that had hung over my picture out of my pocket. I took her hand in mine, placed it there, and then put her other hand on top of it.

"Put this away for me after I leave," I smiled, "there's no need for you to mourn any longer. I'm not dead so it doesn't belong on my picture any more. Please remember that I'll always love you … good-bye mom … good-bye dad."

Suddenly I felt Charlotte Ann and Katelyn's presence around me and I knew that she had extended her shield to cover me. I watched as my parents stood looking around at what they thought was an empty room.

My dad moved over to mom and took her gently in his arms and holding her close I heard him softly say, "Our son came home tonight … he came to give us peace … and to assure us that he wasn't dead after all."

"No, my baby's not dead … he's just … gone," I heard her whisper as she stood looking at the spot where I had been standing, holding the black crepe and lovingly rubbing it in her hands.

The three of us turned and silently made our way back through the house and out to the street. I took one last look at my childhood home and couldn't hold back any longer as several tears trailed down my face.

"It hurts having to leave again," I slowly said, "but it also feels good knowing I had the opportunity to say good-bye this time."

"I know it hurts," Charlotte Ann said as she took me in her arms and held me, "but with the pain comes healing and with the healing comes a new freedom to live."

I could feel the healing already beginning as I stood there in her arms. I felt her love, and it too was a physical thing, flowing through me. She comforted me and helped ease the pain I had carried for so long.

"Now Dale, there's one other place, a very special place, that we want to take you before we return to Whitehall," she whispered as she stepped back from me. I looked questioningly at them and saw her and Katelyn both were grinning happily.

"This next part of your visit will be just as special as home, too," Katelyn said with a big smile, "I think you'll like it!"

The three of us moved quickly through the darkness

to the other side of town and stood silently in front of another house. It looked almost like the one we had just left. The tiny front yard was well kept with small shrubs and flowers planted around it. I looked inquisitively at Charlotte Ann.

"This is where Becky lives," she answered my look with a smile.

I stared back at the house in silence not knowing what to possibly say. I clearly recalled Becky's face and I was once more flooded with emotions. The memories of my first love came rushing back to me. That night so long ago suddenly became last night once again. I pictured us standing in the restaurant, our bodies crushed together, as we slowly danced. I felt her arms around my waist, I recalled the scent of her hair, and I heard her whispering that she loved me.

"We thought you would like to visit her too," Katelyn spoke softly, "before leaving once again."

"Is she ... alright," I asked hesitantly, not really wanting to know if she was married.

"She's well," Katelyn replied, "she's a widow now ... she married a few years after you were taken. Her husband was killed in a mining accident not long after and she never remarried. She had one child from her marriage ... a son that she named Dale."

I looked at her, shocked but happy, that Becky had remembered and honored me in such a way.

"Her son is twenty-five now and very successful," Katelyn continued, "he lives and works in Los Angeles. He comes to visit a couple of times a year and sometimes has her fly out to visit him for two or three weeks at a time. He takes good care of her, providing anything that she needs."

"When you see her," Charlotte Ann added, "keep in mind that she is the same age you would have been had you remained here. Although she has had a good life, and the years have been easy on her, she still has changed and is not the same little girl you may remember."

"I still want to see her," I said, "even if just for a few minutes."

We made our way into the house and toward where she was sleeping. I sensed her presence and her remembered scent filled the house, washing over me. I entered her room and stood there silently watching her sleep. I smiled as the remembrances of first love raced unchecked through me. The memory of our closeness the last time we were together filled me like it had only been yesterday.

This girl ... this woman ... who except for a cruel intervention of fate, would have been my wife and the mother of my children, was peacefully sleeping in front of me. I thought about the years that had passed, realizing that she would soon be approaching her fifty-second birthday also. I smiled as I continued looking at her. Her curly brown hair was still there ... though not as long and not as brown ... a few strands of gray now curled through it. Her face was no longer that of an innocent teenage girl ... but had matured to that of a beautiful woman. I again recalled the first time she had told me that she loved me as my eyes wandered across her delicate body, covered only with a sheet. I smiled at the slight stirring in the pit of my stomach as I discovered that I still found her to be just as desirable as the last time I had held her in my arms.

"Becky ..." I spoke softly, "my sweet little Becky ... please wake up darling ... it's me ... Dale."

She stirred and came suddenly awake. Then realizing there was someone standing beside her bed she quickly pulled the sheet up to her throat and held it there as she looked at me. I heard fear beginning to creep into her voice as she spoke, "Who are you … why are you in my bedroom … what do you want," she asked as she continued to look at me.

"It's just me Becky," I spoke softly, "please don't be frightened of me … you know I would never hurt you … but I've wanted so much to see you again."

Her sleep clouded eyes instantly cleared as recognition lit her features and she realized exactly who it was that had awakened her from her dreams.

"Dale … Dale Krause … but how … where did you come from," she asked in confusion. Then she closed her eyes, shook her head, and reopened them to look right at my smiling face.

"It's been a long time Becky," I said looking directly into her eyes, "I've missed you so much and wanted to see you again so many times."

"But it's … it's been thirty-five years Dale … what happened … where have you been," she asked, "and … and … and you look just like you did the last night I saw you! Are you real … am I dreaming?"

"No Becky, darling, you're not dreaming," I answered her, "I'm very real … I just wasn't able to come home to you."

"But Dale … you just disappeared … we searched for months for you and when we never heard anything from or about you … we all thought you had died … what happened … where did you go?"

"It's a long story my love … a horror story that you wouldn't believe if I told you. I was attacked and kidnapped Becky … I was taken a long way away and I became something different … so different that I couldn't come back to you," I said as I reached and slowly laid my fingers on her cheek, cupping her face in my hand.

"Your hands are so cold," she said involuntarily wincing away.

"You know the old folks say that cold hands mean a warm heart," I answered her, as I reached and took her hand in mine, "come to me Becky … I don't have long to stay … and I want to be close to you … to share a dance with you … one more time … please."

She slid out of her bed and took a step toward me. She put her arms around my neck and I wrapped mine around her waist. As I held her looking into her eyes, the years began to unfold, further and faster, moving backward until we were just two teenagers in love, holding each other close. I looked past her eyes and into her mind where I saw her still fresh memory of us together on that last night. I continued to hold her there, our bodies close and touching again, as we swayed, dancing together one more time.

"I have been through and endured so much since the last time we saw each other," I whispered softly in her ear, "and across all the years, you were what anchored me to reality. During all that time you've never been far from my thoughts and through everything I've suffered, I have remained 'Hopelessly Devoted to You' Becky Pittman."

Then I kissed her … just a light peck on the lips … exactly like the last time I saw her. She cuddled into me when I did and whispered back, "I've missed you so much Dale … please don't leave me again."

"I have to Becky," I sighed, "I'm no longer a part of the world you live in … and unfortunately I haven't been since the last night I saw you. I have to go back to my world now … back to the place where I live and belong."

"What are you Dale," she asked looking into my eyes, "you said that you became something different … can you tell me what … I know you're real … I can touch you … so you're not a dream or a ghost ..."

"Becky ..." I started to say, "I'm a ..."

"No Dale, you mustn't tell her that," I heard Charlotte Ann softly whisper in my thoughts, *"if you really want her to know, she must figure it out on her own."*

"I'm just different Becky ... I can't tell you what I am," I continued, "that is a question that only you can answer. But if you will remember everything, every detail, of what happened here tonight ... my touch ... my words ... remember my eyes and how I look at you. Then when I am gone, begin to search out your thoughts, your heart and soul, and you will soon discover the answer to your question of what I am. I can tell you this, you and I still share the same world, we just live in separate realms of that world now, I can cross into yours, but you can't cross into mine. In my world I'm immortal, and as long as you keep me in your thoughts I'll remain a part of your mortal world, too."

"I've had you in my heart ever since we were children, Dale," she whispered, a tear rolling down her face now, "and I intend to keep you there as long as I live."

"Before I leave I want you to know that I loved you more than anything in this world Becky. I was looking forward to us spending our lives together and I believe that we would have had a wonderful life, but that opportunity was taken away from us by events that neither of us could have predicted or prevented. Just say a prayer of thanks that you didn't walk home with me that night. Please don't forget me Becky ... and when you do think of me in the future ... rest assured that you still 'Light Up My Life'."

I took a step away from her, letting my hands trail down her arms. Taking her soft hands in mine I held them another moment looking into her eyes again. I slightly turned my head toward where I knew Charlotte Ann and

Katelyn would be standing and barely nodded. I turned Becky's hands loose and stepped away. I now felt and saw Charlotte Ann standing beside me and I knew that I was in her shield and that Becky could no longer see me. She looked around her now empty room, the tears streaming down her face. Then speaking into the emptiness she whispered softly, "I will never forget you Dale Krause ... and don't you forget about me either ... I still love you ... come back for me when we can be together for eternity."

"I'm finished here ... take me back home now ... please," I asked as I turned to Charlotte Ann. She smiled her own pretty smile and took my hand. I felt the air stir around us and knew that we were moving, returning to Charleston as time once again stood still for me. In what seemed to be only a moment I looked around and recognized the surroundings of the big parlor at Whitehall.

I took a seat on one of the antique love seats spotted around the room. My emotions at what had just happened were running wild through me. I was happy that I had visited my family and even more so that I had spent time with Becky, but now I felt like I wanted to be alone and cry.

Old wounds had been reopened and memories came rushing back as I thought about how many people's hopes, dreams and lives had been torn apart because I had been snatched away from them. I knew this had to be a part of the healing even if it did hurt right now.

Charlotte Ann came over, sat down beside me and putting her arm around my shoulders drew me close to her. It felt good to have someone to comfort me, to understand what I was feeling. She held me close and petted me for a few minutes.

"I will leave you with your thoughts for a little while … you need some time alone to work through them … but I'll be here for you when you are ready," she softly whispered as she brushed her lips lightly against my ear.

Then she stood and joined James and Katelyn at the far side of the big room. I looked down at the polished wooden floor and began to retrace my night. For the next two hours I sat in silence, replaying the scene with my parents, thinking about my sisters, their families and all that I had missed. I thought about Becky and I replayed not only our relationship but our final hour together. I frequently shed a tear as I completed each of the individual journeys through my mind. I quietly took each recollection and slipped it neatly into a special place in my heart. A place where I could take it out and examine it any time I wanted … or maybe share them with someone in the future.

When I was fully satisfied that I had dealt with each memory I looked up at Charlotte Ann and smiled at her. I felt light and new … all of my past was now cleaned up and put away. She and I both knew that my human life was at long last closed and safely tucked away behind me … never to be mourned over again. Now I looked forward to the immortal life that lay in front of me … it was brighter and more inviting … beckoning me to leave the old life behind and begin a new journey.

Chapter Thirteen

 spent the remainder of the night with Charlotte Ann wandering together around the surrounding grounds of Whitehall. Sometimes we talked quietly and other times we just walked, enjoying the cool night air and the sounds of the local wildlife that filled the woods and marshes around us. We could have easily passed for two young lovers to any casual observer as we walked together slowly strolling and holding hands. Finally, in the late darkness, just a couple of hours before dawn we sat down at the base of an old oak tree. The roots surrounded us like a natural chair. I put my arm around her and she cuddled in close to me.

"I'm happy that you're here with me," I said softly to her, "thank you for tonight … I needed that visit more than I ever thought … and I needed you to help me through it … you saved my life when you found me … and now you've helped me leave the old one behind and look forward to a bright new one."

"The first time I saw you and talked to you I knew there was something deep inside you," she replied, "on the surface I saw a lost and lonely child, one that had been hurt and abandoned ... but below the surface – inside – where it really counts ... I saw a strength and depth of character ... and I knew that you were worth saving ..."

"Is that why you didn't destroy me that night," I asked softly.

"Truthfully, that was a part of it," she answered me candidly, "but an even larger part was the inner strength that I sensed you carried deep inside you ... a strength of character ... that helped you survive all these years as an untrained immortal. It was that deeper something that kept you and supported you until fate could bring our paths together. It's unfair that you have had to live the way you have since you were turned but in the long run it has made you a much stronger immortal. I saw that you needed a companion in your life ... someone to teach you and train you ... but more than that, you needed a friend."

"You've certainly been that in the last few days," I smiled, "I came to Charleston wanting to be destroyed ... I'm glad now that you looked and were able to see below the surface ... thank you for your mercy and now showing me a better way to live."

"Dale, none of us can live alone, we all must have some contact with someone to make us complete. I want to be more than just your friend and lover," she said, "I want to prepare you for eternity. There is so much I can teach you from my own experience about this life if you will allow me to be your teacher and mentor. You must remember that Fate brought our paths together and one day it could just as easily take them in separate directions again. If that day comes and we separate to our own lives once more, you will know more than just how to survive ... you will know how to live, love and be successful."

I sat there silently now as I let her words sink in, frightened at the thought of someday being all alone again.

"I hope that day doesn't come any time soon," I said slowly, "I don't think I could go back to living alone again."

"If and when that day does come Dale, there will be someone for you," she replied, "it could be another lover ... or perhaps even an eternal mate ... but Fate will not abandon you to be by yourself."

I sat there without a sound as I looked at this beautiful woman that had saved my life and thought about the possibility of not being with her forever. My mind was already swirling with the thoughts of my past and my present ... now the future struggled for a place too. I kissed her hair as I decided to deal with the past and the present ... I had eternity to contemplate the future.

"Charlotte Ann, I have to ask something that has been bothering me," I began slowly, "in the last few days you've taught me how to feel good about what I am ... how to feed and survive without killing ... and you've helped me close old wounds where my family is concerned. But what about the rest of my past ... I have been responsible for destroying the lives and dreams of countless victims and their families ... am I supposed to make amends for that in some way?"

She sat quietly for a moment before beginning, "It speaks volumes about your personality and moral framework that you would ask that. But the past is something that cannot be changed. Humans are our natural prey Dale, and we are very dangerous to them. We live among them and act like them ... we even share their world with them. But, in the end, we are what we are ... predators."

"However, like any other predator, to ensure our survival, we have evolved and changed as the world around us has evolved and changed. In the modern world we have adapted to taking only what we need and not killing as often. That change has enabled us to live in the open and not draw attention to ourselves. But it has not always been that way."

"When I was made in the early seventeenth century, we killed our prey and had no concerns about them. Can you imagine how many thousands of human lives over nearly four centuries that I have been responsible for ending … or James … or even my maker before me?"

"So then are you saying that I shouldn't be concerned with my past victims," I asked wonderingly.

"In nature there is an endless succession of life and death, one leads to the other and you can't have one without the other. Some call it the circle of life but for that circle to be complete it must have two parts … predator and prey … and neither survives without the other. In your past, you fulfilled your part of the role of predator in the only manner that you knew how … now, in the present and the future, you are and will continue to fulfill that role of predator … it's just that you have learned a different and better method of doing so. We call ourselves immortals, because we are, but when it's all said and done, we are still vampires and killing is a part of our nature. It is a nature that we can and often times do choose to control … but ultimately it's up to each one of us when we attack whether or not to stop short of a kill."

I sat there in silence as I pondered her words. My past was my past … I was not a murderer … I was a predator and what I did was a part of my nature, and it came to me naturally. Now for the first time, I saw and understood a new way to survive, and I could easily see an endless and less troubled life in front of me. I wondered what things Fate held in store for me. While I thought about all we had talked about I began to feel the slight tug in my chest of the coming dawn and the accompanying anxiousness of needing to find a resting place.

"I feel the night changing," I commented softly, pulling her protectively closer to me, "the dawn isn't far away. I can already sense the sky beginning to lighten."

"The sun will rise just over there," she pointed off to our left, "right between those two stands of trees."

"I think I would like to go back inside now," I said, "I'm not too sure my eyes are ready for the full brightness of the morning sun just yet."

We stood and started walking back toward the big house together. As we did she put her arm around me and rested her head on my shoulder. I thought once more about how fate had suddenly brought this wonderful woman, born over three hundred and fifty years before me, into my life to teach me how to live again.

"Thank you again Charlotte Ann," I whispered as I kissed the top of her head, "for being here … for being you … for everything."

We went inside and up the stairs to the room that we were using as ours. I was slowly conquering my fear of the day but for the time being I wanted to stay hidden away, with her beside me, until after the sun was up. I had noticed since my first day that there was less pain in my eyes now and what was there was more of a discomfort than anything else. Still, I felt comfortable, safe and protected, behind the heavy drapes where my eyes had time to adjust slowly to the brightness as daylight filled the room.

While we waited for my eyes to continue their adjustment we resumed our talk. I listened with rapt attention as Charlotte Ann told me about her human home in London and her current home in New York City. She talked about the English countryside where she had grown up and promised to take me there someday for a visit. She described the Manor House that her father had built in the last quarter of the sixteenth century. She related the story to me of how she had purchased it from an elderly couple in 1753, nearly a century and a quarter after she had been turned. Then she began to describe to me the penthouse apartment she had purchased in the Waldorf when she came to this country in the middle of the last century. It took up an entire upper floor of the famous hotel.

"Perhaps we should go there," she mused, "you are already comfortable with the Northeast and New England. I think that it would be a good place to continue teaching you how to live and become more comfortable around mortals again. There are plenty of them there for us to feed from and if you happen to have an accident and kill one then it's easy enough to dispose of a body."

"I've already been to the city a couple of times," I answered, "but just to the outer edges, never into the city itself. Charles always held back and wouldn't ever go inside. He said it was another area where we wouldn't be welcomed."

She chuckled slowly at my comments and replied, "I can assure you that had he shown up with you at his side he would not have been met with the red carpet."

I wasn't sure what she meant by that so I filed it away to talk about at a later time, then continued on, "I'm much more familiar with Boston and its surrounding area ... we could go there if you would like ... if you think I won't be welcomed in New York either."

"I can guarantee that now you will be perfectly

welcome in New York. Besides, I think it's probably best if you don't return to Boston for a few decades ... or maybe even a couple of centuries," she smiled, "let yourself heal and allow the bad memories of that place to fade away before you go back."

"There are certainly a few memories I wouldn't mind fading completely away," I replied.

"Then let's start making some new and good memories of our own ..." she smiled as she put her arms around me. Her eyes twinkled happily in the early dawn and I felt the now familiar stirring in the bottom of my stomach as she leaned in and kissed me ... very passionately, "together ... you and I ... right now... today."

Charlotte Ann and I made our final decision to leave for New York and we were going to tell James and Katelyn about our plans. While it was still early she and I went downstairs to the parlor to meet them and say our farewells.

"I think that Dale and I are going to be leaving this morning," Charlotte Ann began when we had all gathered, "we have talked it over and decided it's best if we go up to the city for a while. It's so much larger than Charleston, we will have more room to hunt and we can mingle in better with the people there."

"I'm already comfortable in the Northeast since I've spent a large part of my immortal life there," I picked up the conversation, "and I need to practice my skills of taking a small drink. If I need to, I'm also very good at hiding bodies in the bigger cities ... in case I get carried away and take more than just a small drink."

"Of course you know that we will be disappointed to see you leave," James began, "I have enjoyed having company in the house again … it doesn't seem as large and empty as it was."

"Well you and Katelyn are still on your honeymoon," Charlotte Ann laughed, "I'm certain that you can find something to do to occupy your time and fill up all this empty space."

"I don't think we're the only ones honeymooning right now," Katelyn added with a soft chuckle.

"Exactly," Charlotte Ann agreed, "and while the two of you chase each other through this big old house, Dale and I will be chasing each other through my apartment."

"You both know that Whitehall's doors are open to either of you at any time," James said looking at both of us, "you are always welcome here."

Then looking at Charlotte Ann he continued, "Do you wish to travel or would you like me to call the pilot and have him prepare the plane."

"Please, if you don't mind I think we'll fly up," she answered him, "we can go into LaGuardia, it's smaller and closer to downtown."

"I shall have him file the flight plan," he said in return.

"And would you also please ask the pilot to arrange to have a driver waiting when we arrive," she asked.

"Consider it done," James answered with a smile.

"Dale, when you come back to Charleston," Katelyn began as she stepped over to me and gave me a hug, "I want you to take me for a nice long walk in the sunshine."

"I promise," I smiled as I returned her hug, "we'll do a long stroll … and I won't wear sunglasses either."

"James, will we see the two of you at the Ball next month," Charlotte Ann asked with a huge smile,

"I wouldn't miss it for anything," he answered

smiling and putting his arm around Katelyn's waist, "especially this year ... I have a very special presentation to make!"

"I wouldn't want to miss that moment," Charlotte Ann chuckled, "but Katelyn, you really must have an exclusive dress for the occasion. So, if you will come up to the city a week or so before, you and I shall find the perfect dress for you."

"Am I to finally get a 'little black dress'," Katelyn smiled happily, "for special occasions?"

"I'm afraid not dear," Charlotte Ann continued, "while you do have long beautiful legs and shapely knees, we will not be showcasing them at this event. This celebration will be one of the most special junctures of your integration into the immortal world – so you will get a full length, perfectly tailored, black ball gown for the evening. We can go back and find you a little black dress – probably at Vickie's – some other time."

"Any excuse to go shopping, right," Katelyn laughed.

"Call it what you will," Charlotte Ann chuckled, "although I've never known us to need an excuse!"

"While we are there," James interjected, "I shall pay a visit to Weismann's for her accessories."

"Well I wouldn't want to miss that either," Charlotte Ann laughed, and with a mischievous grin added, "and will you be making this special introduction in drag again this year?"

"Probably ... that's the one time of year I almost have to do that," he started and that's where Katelyn broke into the conversation.

"Whoa ... y'all just stop right there ... what are the two of you talking about this time ..." and looking at James she asked pointedly, "and what does Charlotte Ann mean about you being in drag?"

"Oh, I'm sorry Katelyn, she's referring to the annual 'All Hallows Eve Ball' at The Palace. They bill it as a Halloween party. It's a formal event and one of the biggest social occurrences of the year in our world. There's usually several hundred immortals from around the world in attendance.

"Yeah, that sounds good ... but Drag ..." she asked with interest, tilting her head and raising her eyebrows.

"It's not exactly the kind of drag you are thinking about," he smiled, his eyes sparkling, "I call it 'Vampire Drag', but it's really just formal wear. It's the only time of year that I go all out with the traditional black tux, opera cape, top hat, gloves, and cane," he explained with a smile.

"Alrighty then," she laughed, suddenly relieved, "I think I can deal with vampire drag!"

"Then it's settled, we will see both of you in a few weeks," Charlotte Ann said happily.

"By all means," James answered, his arm around Katelyn and smiling big.

Chapter Fourteen

hen we arrived in the city we went straight to Charlotte Ann's home in the Waldorf. Like Whitehall the Waldorf was huge and very plush. She showed me around the residence and how and where to enter and exit the building depending on whether or not I wanted to be seen. In no time I began to settle in and feel comfortable knowing that her home was my home. This was a place that she and I could be alone ... a place for me to continue to learn and mature. I wanted to spend hours and days with her asking questions about my life. There was so much that I still didn't know. I also wanted to go see the city but more importantly, right now, I needed to hunt and feed. I could feel the slow burn of thirst building in the back of my throat. The two of us soon went out together to find a victim to feed from.

"When I'm in the city I mostly hunt in and around Central Park, down into Times Square, and Greenwich Village" Charlotte Ann said as we left the building and began walking down Fifth Avenue, "there's always a varied selection in any of those places to choose from. The park is a place where you would probably enjoy hunting on your own rather than together but I'll take you there during the day and show you around. I think tonight that we should begin down in the village. There's an ever changing variety of nightclubs down there and we can find anything we want."

"I almost feel as if I'm back to my old self," I commented as we walked along, "I'm surrounded by darkness, it's crowded and I'm hunting. Still, I will do my best though to practice the 'no-kill' skills you and Katelyn have taught me."

"Dale, you are a predator and killing is in your nature, but it's a nature you can control … you just have to want to," then with a short laugh added, "and wanting to control it makes living among all these deliciously smelling humans so much easier."

Although I had seen the city from a distance in the past, it was so different being in the middle of it. I looked all around as we continued walking and to anyone who happened to see us they would have thought I was just another tourist gawking at the tall buildings of the downtown area. We soon found ourselves transitioning from the bright lights and busy avenues to a darker, seedier part of the city. I began to become even more comfortable and as I walked I could feel myself fading into the darkness and blending in with the shadows. I felt the blood lust rising stronger in me as I quickly evolved further into the hunt. The smell of blood filled the air around me as we continued walking. The slight burning that had been in the back of my throat became more intense and I began to look forward to quenching it.

We continued moving along the busy streets. I noticed the further we moved into the village the younger the crowd became. They were going about their usual nightly lives, meeting and going from place to place, looking for entertainment. I started searching to see if perhaps there was one I could pick out for myself. We went deeper into the district and turned down a street that was laced with nightclubs and I smiled to myself. It didn't matter whether it was a big city or a small town, the clubs and bars were always the same ... and they were excellent hunting grounds.

Some of the clubs had hawkers standing outside the doors calling to us to come inside and have some fun. We passed most of those up and continued our walk. Soon we spotted a place that had a long line waiting outside and wrapping around the side of the building. The hawker was calling to everyone to come inside for an unforgettable adventure. The entire front of the building was painted black and on each side of the door bright white lettering in a circle with a coffin in the center proclaimed the name, 'The Dark Side, A Gothic Vampire Club'.

Charlotte Ann laid her hand on my arm as we continued to survey the building and listen to the loud music coming from inside. Then with a little chuckle spoke softly, "Well that's new since I was here ... and it does look interesting ... I think we may have just found exactly what we have been looking for."

We took a couple of inquisitive steps closer to the man that was guarding the front door and letting people in and out. He was about my height and had long blondish hair that hung almost to his waist. Even though it was full dark he was wearing dark round sunglasses and dressed all in black. He wore a gold necklace that had a bat with its wings spread wide hanging from his throat. His nails were sharply pointed and as he continued talking to the passers-by I could see that he had a set of fangs. I almost laughed.

Charlotte Ann stepped up to the man and smiling hugely she said in a playful manner, "Goood Eve-va-ning".

"No madam, for the vampire it is morning," he replied looking at her and flashing his fangs.

"Do you have some real live vampires in there," I asked, looking curiously past him and into the club.

"Why not go inside and see for yourself kid," he said and with a flourish opened his hand toward the door, "please enter freely and of your own will ... but beware of what lies inside."

"That sounds like fun," Charlotte Ann laughed and turning toward me said, "I think I would like to go inside and see what's there."

"Oh yes, by all means little lady, please do, and have your first drink free," he answered as he handed us both a ticket. I looked at it and printed on it was "One Free Blood Cocktail".

"Mmmm ... a blood cocktail ... sounds just like what I had in mind," Charlotte Ann laughed again, "this looks like it's going to be fun."

"Please enjoy yourselves but be careful," the doorman said with a final warning laugh, stepping aside and allowing us to enter, "a pretty young girl like you might very well become the free drink ... don't let the vampires bite."

She reached and lightly stroked the side of his face with her fingertips as we stepped past him, through the door.

"Oh darling, I would so love to see one of your vampires try to bite me," she laughed out loud, "they might find out that this 'pretty young girl' is just full of all kinds of surprises!"

The two of us laughed at her joke as we walked into the dimly lit club and looked all around us. It was actually much larger than it appeared from the outside and very overcrowded. We always attempt to blend into a crowd, but this was one horde that had anybody taken the time to notice, she and I would have been the ones that definitely stood out as different because of our dress. All of those I saw around me had really bought into the Goth lifestyle. I wondered if it was because it made them feel special or if they just needed to be different to feel alive. They didn't realize what a game they were playing or that their lives were the stakes of the game.

We continued our scrutiny of the club to see who or what may have been in there with us.

"With the exception of the caster standing by the bar and the shifter over in the far corner, it appears that we are the only immortals in here right now," Charlotte Ann said after a second quick evaluation of the room, "but the night is still young and there's no telling who might wander in. I'm going to feed while we still have our pick … just call out if you need me … otherwise I shall meet you after dinner."

She turned one way and disappeared into the throng leaving me standing there alone. I took another quick look around and noted that the humans looked like a sea of black leather and chrome piercings. The ones that were closest to me appeared to have everything pierced that could be pierced … and I almost shuddered to think what couldn't be seen. They were jam-packed together in a moving mass that was supposed to be a dance.

I went the opposite direction that Charlotte Ann had disappeared in and began my hunt in earnest. I made my way slowly through the club looking at everyone, something

I had done an untold number of times in the past. I felt the blood lust begin to tingle through me as I was deciding which one to choose. I needed to find someone that was alone but didn't stand out as different from the rest of the herd. I moved slowly through the room, continuing my round about circle as I did ... searching ... looking for just the right one. I smiled to myself when I spotted her. She was standing all alone, close to a wall, trying to cover herself in the dark shadows.

She was small and waifish in appearance. Her hair was dyed jet black with red and purple streaks and cropped short easily exposing her neck. Her face was made up with white powder, her eyes lined with heavy black mascara and surrounded by red shadow. Her lips were painted black and shone in the low light of the club.

She was dressed all in Goth black, wearing a small leather vest that was decorated with silver skulls and coffins on top of a lacy camisole. She was proudly displaying a strip of pale mid riff between the camisole and the top of her shorts. Her bare arms showed several tattoos that, from the shine, I could see were nothing more than temporary decals. The tips of her fingers, with black painted nails, protruded through a pair of netted half finger gloves with hand bones printed on top. Her shorts, complete with garter straps hanging loosely from them, were tight and very short. They emphasized her small hips and thin legs which were covered with fishnet stockings disappearing into the tops of heavy black boots with thick soles giving her a couple inches of extra height. She was attempting to look the part of a vampire ... and I was about to give her a lesson in exactly what that meant.

Although she was trying desperately to appear to fit in, to be something she wasn't ... she didn't ... and I sensed her discomfort and insecurity … making her that much more of a target. I watched her for a short time standing quietly all alone holding a drink and only sipping on it. She looked uncertainly around the crowd as if hoping to find someone she knew. I decided she would be perfect and like the predator I am I began to close in on her, staying just out of her sight until I was standing right next to her. She jumped a little at my unexpected closeness, the fragrance of her blood leaping out at me from her sudden scare. When I spoke to her, she smiled, looking me over and forgetting her sudden fear.

I took in every detail of her as I remembered the thousands of others like her across the years. The biggest difference between her and them was that none of them had survived their meeting with me. Although she was supposed to survive, in these surroundings I still wasn't sure whether or not she would … it would be just as easy to drain her and leave her small body slumped in a dark corner. I reached out gently touching her face, knowing my fingers would be cool to her skin. I saw a shiver run through her body as I let my fingers slide down her cheek to just under her ear. I moved them toward her throat slowly tracing the large artery in the side of her neck, noting the rapid beat of her heart. I smiled at her as I rested my finger on the tip of her chin, tilting her face up to look directly into my eyes.

She looked back at me with golden amber eyes that quickly betrayed the look she was trying to present. They were soft and deep, the color of honey. They were actually very pretty. The dim light made them almost sparkle as I gazed into them, holding her captive and beginning to bend her will.

"I'll trade you … a drink for a drink," I said to her with a grin, and tucked my free drink coupon into the front pocket of her shorts. After a few more exchanged words I took her elbow in my hand, guiding her toward an even darker corner in the back of the room. When I had her where I wanted her I gently turned her so that she faced away from the crowd and pulled her to me. I put my arms around her and, lost in the depths of my thrall, she easily folded into my grasp. She cuddled against me, her body soft and tender, putting her arms around my waist. Anyone who happened to walk by would have thought we were only making out.

I breathed in the smell of her blood, strongly intriguing and sensuous, and tightened my hold on her. She moaned in pleasure as I nuzzled into her hair, whispering softly into her ear, "You smell wonderful ... so tender and delicious ..."

I lightly kissed her neck, my fangs came down and I quickly and easily bit into her, piercing the artery and holding them in place for a few seconds. She stiffened in my arms and I pulled her closer, muffling her soft cry as the pain of my bite exploded through her body. Her blood shot powerfully into my mouth ... hot, rich ... and surprisingly ... purely innocent ... she was anything but what she appeared. I suddenly found myself unexpectedly aroused as I held her against me and began to slowly drink from her.

I closed my eyes in unforeseen ecstasy as I filled my mouth with the pure untainted innocence of her life, taking it into me. I swallowed and felt its warmth begin to spread into my chest. I shuddered throughout myself hating the thought of having to stop ... her blood was so wonderfully chaste and innocent ... I wanted it all. She tightened her hold on me and again moaned softly against me, unable to move in my embrace. I continued to drink, slow and easy, being careful not to drain her too quickly. I was going to thoroughly enjoy every drop of her delectably perfect blood.

I casually looked through her mind, picking at what was there, as I took a second drink. I saw that she really didn't belong here in this place. She was only playing a role ... trying hard to be something she wasn't ... she wanted desperately to fit in somewhere. Her name was Stacy ... she was from a small town in the mid-west ... and barely nineteen years old. Her life in the 'Big City' wasn't what she thought it would be and she hated the way she was living but was afraid her parents wouldn't allow her to return home.

I raised my head from her neck and looked into her face. Her eyes locked to mine, now filled with the blood lust. Terror filled her face when she saw my extended fangs. Her eyes grew huge, tears filling them and spilling down her cheeks as she fully realized what was happening to her. She whimpered low, almost to herself, "You're a ... a ... real vampire ... and you've bitten me!"

"Imagine that Stacy ... a real vampire ... in a vampire club," I laughed at her, "what did you expect ... a werewolf?"

She sighed, her tiny body shaking in terror as she gave up and collapsed against me. I heard her thoughts streaking through her mind as I filled my mouth and swallowed once again, "*I'm going to die ... but this is only a game ... I'm not supposed to die ... I'm just playing a role ... I don't want to die, not really ... not here ... not now ... I'm too young!*"

I could hear her heart thundering in her small chest pumping her life into me. I saw her blood pouring in a stream down her neck, forced from the wounds I had made there by her now wildly beating heart. I lowered my face back to her neck, and began filling my mouth again with her luscious blood. I smelled the sudden despair and fear of dying as it rose off of her like steam while I continued to suck the life from her. I felt sorry for her but I needed to fulfill the thirst now driven in me by the bloodlust. As I did I spoke silently to her mind again, *"You should be more careful the roles you play ... you might find yourself an enticing little morsel to something that you really didn't want to attract in the first place."*

When I sensed her fear of dying again pass through my soul, compassion overcame me. I forced the bloodlust away from me and quickly passed my tongue over the wounds I had made, closing them and stopping the blood flow. I began licking away the remaining bloody streams on her neck leaving it clean and spotless except for a tiny bruise. I nestled into her short hair, still holding her small body close to me, breathing in her scent, and spoke softly in her ear, "I'm not going to kill you Stacy ... this time ... I've only taken a couple of pints ... just enough to satisfy me and leave you very weak. I've closed the wounds in your neck ... and you won't die from my bite."

I began to pet her, slowly stroking her hair, my hands wandering down her back. Her fearful tremors began to subside as I held her close in a gentle hug. I realized now that having destroyed so many families, I was being given a choice and an opportunity to restore one. After a few moments I raised my head and looked into her eyes again. I smiled at her, still flashing fang, as I said, "But in return for your life you must do something for me."

"Anything," she answered fearfully, beginning to tremble again, "just please don't kill me ... I don't want to die."

"Go home Stacy ... to your parents ... you've had your adventure in the big city ... and because you had it with me, you survived. I stopped feeding, even though your virgin blood was sweet and delicious to me … I'm giving you another chance at life. Please Stacy, don't be lost to your family the way I was to mine … call them … now, tonight … I promise you they will welcome you home."

"I don't usually allow my prey to escape Stacy. So you can rest assured that I'm going to be following you until you leave for your home. So go now, to your parents, to your home, and live your life, stop trying to be something you're not just to please others … be what you are … be who you are … and be happy with it. But take the memory of me with you and know how close you came to death. And should I see you anywhere in the city after tonight you will not be so fortunate next time. I hope for your sake that you may never cross paths with another of my kind again."

I took my arms from around her, and once again looked deeply into her eyes. I leaned toward her, very lightly kissed her forehead and whispered, "Remember what I said," and stepped away from her walking resolutely toward the front door of the club and the cool night. I began walking down the street and had gone about half a block when suddenly Charlotte Ann appeared and began walking next to me. She slid her arm around my waist and together we walked silently for a couple of blocks. The taste of the sweetness and innocence of the girl I had just taken filled me with long forgotten memories of my first victim.

"You demonstrated great maturity and self-control back there, Dale. You found a little lost girl … you fed well … left her alive … and then gave her back her life and family … I'm very proud of you," she commented softly, finally breaking the silence of our walk.

"You watched me feed," I asked, "I thought you were hunting also?"

"I was … I just have more experience than you do so

it doesn't take me as long. I found two young fellows who just thought they were vampires," then with a low laugh added, "you should have seen and heard the pictures and thoughts of vampires that I planted in their minds. When they get home they'll remove those fake plastic fang caps from their teeth and never wear them again!"

"What exactly did you do," I asked as we walked on.

"I bit them," she answered bluntly, "they wanted to play vampire so I went along with their silly game ... I just showed them how it was done."

I tried to keep from laughing at her story but then with a mischievous grin and a twinkle in her eyes she added, "And that second one actually tasted pretty good ... I wasn't sure I wanted to stop. But once he realized he had crossed paths with a real immortal ... well, suffice it to say he ruined the ambiance of the moment by doing something very nasty on himself!"

I roared with laughter at her description of what had happened.

"It was probably a good thing though because I really wanted to get away and keep an eye on you ... it was your first time being away from me. I wanted to watch you hunt and feed ... just to see if you would be able to control the bloodlust and stop on your own," then looking at me with a devilish smile added, "old feeding habits are sometimes hard to break."

"Would you have stopped me if I hadn't," I asked, looking seriously at her.

"No, I wouldn't," she replied gravely, and then looking up at me continued, "that girl was your catch ... your quarry ... it wasn't my place to interrupt you while you fed. Her life was in your hands at that point ... it was your decision whether or not she lived or died ... and I would have supported your choice either way."

We walked along in silence for several blocks as I quietly contemplated what she had just told me, realizing that there really was no changing what I was ... only maintaining control over it.

The remainder of the night was spent walking the streets of Lower Manhattan as she showed me several places of interest. We both fed again in the early hours of the morning before finally making our way to a pier in the Lower East End. We cuddled together like two lovers and sat back to watch the sun rise above the East River. Before the sun rose fully above the skyline and the waterfront could get too busy we left and returned to the apartment. We changed from our nighttime hunting clothes into some regular street clothes and departed for another day in the crowded shopping district.

Chapter Fifteen

uring the next couple of weeks I continued to explore New York with Charlotte Ann and quickly became comfortable with the city and its surroundings. In the beginning we went out more in the mornings and afternoons to walk and shop in the downtown areas and I began committing the various streets and avenues to memory. In a matter of just a few days I knew where and how far away I was at any given time in relation to the apartment. We spent many hours walking along the sidewalks and in the various stores of the shopping district. We hunted further and further away from the apartment as I became more familiar with the city.

I continued getting used to the sun and the normal activities of living in the human world. It didn't take long for my eyes to make the full adjustment to the bright sun and I was soon able to walk around without my dark glasses. I quickly adapted to the daylight, and was as much at ease in the full sun as I was at night in the moonlight. I suppose that being able to go anywhere, anytime was the most enjoyable part of discovering what my life was supposed to be like. Charlotte Ann made a huge a difference in my life ... I was happy ... I smiled more than ever and soon I felt right at home living around mortals. Charlotte Ann took care of me too, paying for anything I needed and most things I wanted. She enjoyed shopping for clothes so she ensured that I had a wide selection to choose from when it came time to go out.

While the days were spent learning my surroundings and shopping, we reserved the nights to hunt and feed. Charlotte Ann and I didn't hunt every night, often skipping a night or two. I was surprised to learn from her that as we age we actually need less to renew ourselves. She would often go a week or more without feeding. Of course I still needed to feed on a regular basis so she would accompany me every time I went out. The more I fed, the stronger I became and I began to notice several 'gifts' that I didn't know were present in me begun to show up in my life.

It seemed that in addition to these gifts developing and manifesting, my mind also changed along with them. It was almost as if someone had lifted a blanket from around me. My preternatural abilities ... the five senses ... became stronger than ever. My eyesight sharpened to a point that I could see things clearer and in more detail than ever before. My hearing became so acute that I could listen in to conversations over a quarter mile away.

The most astounding thing that came about though, was that as we walked the various areas of the city I came to be able to understand and speak all of the different languages I heard around me. I found that after being in someone's presence for only a few minutes I could pick up their language and speak it without flaw.

When I asked Charlotte Ann about all the changes in

me she explained that 'The Gift' had been in me all along. It was actually waiting for me to use it, to grow into it and become truly immortal. She told me that it had not had the opportunity to show itself because of my lack of exposure to the human world.

My hunting and stalking abilities also increased dramatically after we arrived in the city because there was more opportunity to use them. Charlotte Ann had been correct about hunting in Central Park and I did enjoy all the time I was able to practice and improve my hunting and feeding skills there. It gave me the opportunity to become more adapt at feeding by taking only a small drink and not killing. There were some nights when I would feed three and even four times. As it turned out those three or four small drinks were just as satisfying and easily the equivalent that a single kill had been in the past. Charlotte Ann kept up her assistance in helping me to hone my hunting talents. In no time at all I started to feel at ease and began to develop and perfect my own style of hunting.

Charlotte Ann demonstrated being a good teacher and was very patient as I learned. While we do enjoy another's company, immortals are by nature lone wolves, especially so when hunting. However, she and I did continue to hunt together until I became more familiar with the area. The only time that we would separate in a hunt was when we had both located our prey and we went to feed. Although we treasure each other's company, even when we are hunting, once we locate our prey we both still prefer to feed in private.

I knew that soon I would be ready to hunt on my own again. I actually looked forward to venturing out alone, to find and take my prey again. So after the first month or so Charlotte Ann and I began to hunt separately. She preferred to hunt at night, in the various clubs where a young pretty girl could more easily allow herself to be picked up by a man. I found that I preferred to feed in the malls and shopping areas, probably because of my first hunt at the mall in Charleston. I felt at ease there because there were more mortals that looked like me and I could melt into the crowd not drawing any unwanted attention.

The various malls and theaters proved to be successful for me on any given evening but especially on Friday and Saturday evenings. There were always crowds filling the food courts, the theaters and the surrounding stores. Choosing my prey was simple. I quickly discovered that there was some good that came from having been turned when I was so young. I was pleased to realize that combined with my youthful looks and the preternatural draw I was very attractive to humans. I quickly discovered that I could have any girl I chose, and while they're not my first choice, a few of the guys, with just a quick glance or a friendly word.

Depending on the clothes I chose to wear I was able to pass myself off as anything from a high school student, a college student, or even a new college graduate. If I were hunting in the mornings, I pretended to be a student at one of the local colleges. I chose my prey in the snack areas – no pun intended – and then quite often found myself in some girl's dorm room where I discovered that sex with mortals – while not nearly as satisfying as immortal sex – wasn't such a bad thing either and made a good way to pass away an afternoon.

When I was hunting later in the day or early evening, I became a recent college graduate working in the city. I dressed the part of a successful, and for my age wealthy, young executive, and again I had my choice of any and all of the girls in their early twenties. The same was true of the tourists if I happened to be in the downtown shopping district in the mid-afternoons.

In the early evenings and weekends I dressed and acted like the teenager I appeared to be and I didn't have to try too hard to make others believe that I was just a youth. For all intents and purposes I was just another high school student … although one with plenty of money … hanging out at the mall.

I quickly came to understand that many of the modern teen girls are very materialistic so I always wore the latest, most expensive and sought after young adult styles while I was seeking my next victim. My hunting cover in and around the malls was that I was new to the city, having just arrived from out of town and I was visiting my big sister. I found that there was no shortage of girls willing to show a new, sharply dressed boy around. Then when it came time to feed, there was always a trendy new movie playing for me to take my new friend to see. I especially enjoyed the irony of all the newly released teenage vampire movies that they seemed to love so well. Of course, once we were seated in the darkened back rows of the theater, she and I became the star of our own teenage vampire movie and I always fed extremely well.

The most important part of evolving into my newly discovered life during this time was that I grew closer to Charlotte Ann and our relationship became stronger. There was no doubt that she was my teacher and my mentor but just as importantly she was also my lover. I spent as much time learning from her both the finer aspects of making love, and increasing my hunting skills.

Since I had never known that I was able to have sex I had a lot more to learn in that area than I did hunting and she gladly shared her knowledge with me. We would often spend an entire day in the apartment as she taught me and led me in new adventures as we continued to learn each other's body. She showed me how to please her and in turn she pleased me to no end. Many times we held each other, quaking together in mutual orgasms, as we continued to learn new things about the other.

One afternoon, after we had spent the morning playing like a couple of young heartthrobs, we lay together in the bed, cuddling, as I held her in my arms. I lay there silently watching her, happily looking at her contented smile.

"Can I ask you something," I softly spoke in the dimness of the room.

"Only if you promise to do *'that thing'* you do so well again," she laughed softly and snuggled closer to me and lightly kissed my lips, "I'll answer anything you ask me."

Of course I knew that *'that thing'* could be any number of orgasm inducing skills that she had taught me to give her pleasure so I replied, "If you answer my questions I promise to not only do *'that thing'* again but a whole lot of other *'that things'* too and for as long as you want."

"Then you better start asking," she purred at me, "because I'm ready for some more of *'that thing'*."

I took her in my arms and kissed her slowly and passionately then looking at her with a huge smile I said, "There's the down payment on *'that thing'*!"

"Mmmm ... I can't wait for full payment," she giggled, "now, what do you want to know ... and do hurry, please."

"There's still so much I don't understand about this life," I began, trying to get serious, "but I do understand that you have become a big part of my life. Can you explain 'us' to me … what we have … our relationship … what we have become?"

"I'll answer that with a question for you," she smiled at me, "what do *you* think we have … what do *you* think our relationship is?"

"Charlotte Ann, I love you … and, if it's possible, I believe that I love you more each day," I answered smiling, "you saved my life … you've taught me not only how to live but how to enjoy my life … how to love someone else … and how not to kill. That's something I never experienced until you came into my life."

"And you want to know if this is forever," she smiled knowingly.

"I do, because the only other things I have to base my life on are the experiences I had with my maker," I continued, "he told me that I was his… that he was my master … and I was bound to him and had to obey him. Is that how this life works … when you found me did you become my master … am I bound to you now … and to obey you … am I just a piece of property that can be passed from one master to another?"

"You do realize that with both of us lying in bed with absolutely no clothes on is probably the wrong place to ask that question," she giggled as she kissed me again, "and while we will discuss that 'Master' question later, you are not 'bound' to do my bidding … at least not for a few more minutes anyway. In our world, because we are predators and by nature treasure our independence, we are never truly bound to another. Our freedom and individualism, the ability to live our own life as we wish, is a very important aspect of our lives."

"So, then … are we mates now … like James and Katelyn," I asked.

"Dale, I love you very much," she continued explaining, "you are special and you are very sweet ... not to mention you are getting pretty good in the skill of lovemaking ... but our relationship is one of lovers, not mates."

"There's a difference," I asked.

"Oh yes ... a big difference. In our world, you may have many different lovers and be together for years, but when you mate it is for eternity, there is no such thing as divorce."

I thought for a moment about what she had just said then asked, "You've lived for so long ... nearly four centuries ... why don't you have a mate?"

"I do have a mate," she answered me nonchalantly.

"You have a mate," I asked slowly, uncertainty spreading through me.

"I am mated to my maker, Ferdinand," she answered, "we were deeply in love when he turned me and we immediately became mates. We lived together for one hundred and twenty two years from September of 1628 until the summer of 1750. However, when you spend that much time with someone you begin to get tired, and start to desire some time for yourself. It's like growing up and maturing, you need to be separate and live your own life for a while."

"I needed time away, to return to England and explore life on my own and he needed time away to live his life alone for a while, so we agreed to go our separate ways and meet again later. We had initially hoped to meet again in Paris in forty or fifty years. However by that time the French Revolution was in full swing and precluded our reunion. We have been apart since then, although over the years I have felt his presence in passing and even heard his voice in the far distance. I know that he is still out there ...

and someday … when both of us are ready, fate will bring us together again to continue our shared lives."

"But, what would he think of you and me as lovers," I asked, "wouldn't he be … angry … at you … and especially me?"

"You're thinking in human terms," she smiled at me, "a mated relationship in the preternatural world is different to a marriage in humans primarily because we have eternity. Mates in our world may spend several lifetimes together then mutually agree to live apart for a time, often several centuries or more, and then come back together again. While we are apart and living our lives we often take other companions, and knowing him as I do, I would venture to say he has had many more lovers than I have while we have been apart. Even so there is never anything as strong as the bond of a mate."

"How will I know if or when I meet my mate," I asked, now curious about my own life.

"You really don't … at least not until it happens," she said, "your mate could be a human that you bring over …"

"My mate will never be a human that I bring over," I interjected quietly, "although you have shown me what a good life this can be and taught me many things, I will never do to a mortal what was done to me."

"Never say never my love," she continued, "and while turning a mortal might not be your first choice, Fate still has a vote in who, what, how, and when … besides, your mate could already be an immortal. If she were an immortal, she could be someone that is many years younger or older than you; likewise if she is human, it's possible that she, her parents or even grandparents have not even been born yet. When you meet her, you will begin to develop feelings toward her. She will also begin to feel something special for you. Neither of you may understand what it is at the time, but then one day, everything suddenly clicks in place and both of you know that you love each other, have for some time, and are meant to be mates. When that happens, there is nothing that can keep the two of you apart."

"But what about us," I asked, "when … or if … that happens, do we just walk away from each other?"

"You and I will always have something special, but not always physical, over the years our relationship will continue to grow and deepen to a far greater depth than just lovers could ever have. But for the time being," she smiled as she kissed me again, "we are lovers, so let's act like it … I want you to do *'that thing'* again!"

I pulled her closer to me and she kissed me deeply, her hand wandering across my chest and stomach. When she reached the bottom of my stomach she began to gently stroke me, her soft hand gliding slowly around me.

"I think now would be a good time for us to discuss that 'Master' part you asked about," she said as she continued her gentle caresses and continued to kiss me, "for now, you be the master and I will be bound to you … you can tell me to stop anytime you wish and I will do as you say."

She continued to kiss my lips, and then she moved to my neck, tenderly kissing me several times. Then I felt the tip of her tongue as it traced the path of the large artery in the side of my neck. She lightly traced around the edge of my ear with her tongue and with her soft little girlish giggle she whispered against my ear, "Do you want me to stop now?"

"Nun-uh," I replied, the pleasure beginning to quickly build in me and spreading throughout my body.

Then she moved a little further and placed her soft kisses on my chest, then nipped at each of my nipples, and gently sucked on them.

"How about now," she asked looking up at me smiling.

Unable to speak I just groaned my response to her. She continued kissing her way down my body until she slipped completely under the sheet. Suddenly I felt something like never before … and the pleasure that ripped through my body was so unbelievable I had to lift the sheet to be sure that what I thought was happening was really happening.

She stopped what she was doing for a moment, looked up at me with a smile, licked her lips, winked and asked, "Do you want me to stop now?"

"Noooo …" I replied breathlessly, "please don't stop … that feels so fantastic … you can do that forever!" I dropped the sheet back over us and let my head fall back against the pillow, enjoying the most intense pleasure I had ever felt.

After what seemed like a very short few minutes of her loving, she moved back up, covering my body with hers. She kissed me again, her tongue probing into my mouth. I kissed her back just as passionately, after what she had just done, I couldn't get enough of her. She slid downward again and taking me inside her, she sat up on me, her hands on my arms. I felt her knees tighten against my sides as she began to rock. We quickly found our rhythm, moving together, and becoming one being.

She leaned forward, never breaking her tempo, to kiss me again and whispered into my mouth, "Don't … you … dare … say … stop … right … now!"

"I promise, I won't …" I answered her breathlessly,

"and don't you stop either ..."

Suddenly she sat bolt upright on me, and I felt her inner muscles grip me with a powerful strength, as she began to rock harder against me. I picked up the pace, thrusting harder into her and suddenly she just breathed out, "Oh Dale ... oh yes ... yes ... yes ..." and she fell forward against me, her lips searching and finding mine, kissing me strongly as her small body quaked in my arms, shaking throughout as her orgasm overtook her.

I reached my own point of no return and I wrapped my arms around her as I continued thrusting harder and faster into her. When I couldn't hold myself back any longer, and holding her close to me, I rolled with her. Now on top, I thrust one last time as deep and hard into her as I could, releasing my passion and emptying myself into her. Now it was her turn to hold me against her as my own orgasm rushed through me over and over again. I felt her legs circle my back and pull me into her, holding me tight against her, our mouths hungrily seeking each other as we slowed our sensual dance and finished our lovemaking.

Afterwards we lay quietly in each other's arms, no words necessary. For several hours we continued petting, touching and gently kissing, often broken with fits of silly giggling like two kids at the wonder of our love.

Finally Charlotte Ann cuddled in close to me and whispered softly against my ear, "Next time we switch roles and I'll be master for a while."

"Mmmm ... I think I might like that ... Master," I replied softly as we held closely to each other.

he next afternoon Charlotte Ann and I left the apartment and began walking along Fifth Avenue. After about three or four blocks Charlotte Ann casually looked at me and said, "Would you mind going with me down to the Financial District … I have some business that needs attending to today … I need to call upon my agent?"

"You have a financial agent," I asked in astonishment.

"Of course," she answered, "in my time we used agents, now called investment brokers, to handle our monies and investments. The agents only made money if we made money so that made them much more reliable than bankers who, as the old saying goes, would 'steal the pennies off a dead man's eyes'. The bankers haven't changed much in four hundred years and aren't likely to in the next four hundred. So over the years I have continued to use the brokers. The current agency, now based here in New York, was originally established in Southampton in the middle of the sixteenth century and my father used it for his shipping business. They now have offices around the world, mostly in the larger cities ... London, Paris, Rome and recently Moscow ... that enables me to have access to an agent should I find myself anywhere close to those places."

I was stunned at her answer. I knew that since we had been together wherever we had gone and whatever we had done Charlotte Ann had always had plenty of money, but the thought of her having a financial agent was just amazing to me. I wondered how anyone could ever have so much money that they needed someone else to handle it for them. I continued turning those thoughts over in my mind as we walked along until she spoke up again.

"I know what you are wondering about," she began again, "but Dale you have to consider that when one has lived as long as I have the opportunities to amass great amounts of wealth often present themselves. Your first opportunity will present itself today ... I'm going to set up an account for you so that in the future you will have some of those same opportunities. I can assure you that if you trust my agents and allow them to take care of your accounts, they will make you more money than you could ever imagine ... you will never be able to spend it all ... and you will have forever for it to continue to increase."

When we arrived at the big office building Charlotte Ann spoke quietly to the receptionist and we were quickly led past others who were sitting in the waiting room, into a private elevator and ushered into an office on the top floor.

I was nearly overcome with the sweet, succulent blood scent of the young lady who opened the door to us. I had never encountered such a mouthwatering delicious aroma from anyone.

"Ms. Erickson," the lady in the office said as she met

us at the door with a huge smile, "it's such a pleasure to finally meet you, my name is Colleen Stoddard. I have just recently taken over your accounts after Mrs. Johnson retired."

"It's my pleasure Colleen," Charlotte Ann replied as she took the young lady's hand in a gentle shake, "I do hope that Sandra is well and enjoying her retirement."

While they continued their small talk I looked around at the opulent surroundings of the huge office. It was brightly lit with one entire wall of windows looking out over the city providing a beautiful view. The other walls were paneled with light oak and backlit with several paintings of various country scenes hanging on them. The furniture was all very modern and the carpet was thick and soft, even to my step. It all combined to make a very welcoming and comfortable place.

When I looked at Colleen she appeared to be the quintessential successful New York business woman. I also saw a remarkably young woman for the position she filled. She was very pretty, tall, nicely built ... and young ... only in her early twenties. Her brown hair hung easily around her shoulders with just a slight curl at the ends. She was wearing a stylish dress that ended just above her knees with a pair of matching high heels. I noted that her legs were long and perfectly shaped as my eyes traveled over her body.

I again caught just the lightest scent of her blood and heard a strong and steady heartbeat as I stood there. I began to feel a little tingle in the back of my throat as the blood lust stirred to life in the center of my chest. My thoughts were interrupted suddenly by Charlotte Ann softly placing her hand on my arm, breaking the spell as she spoke, "Colleen, I would like you to meet Dale, he is my dear friend and new protégé, and he is the reason I'm here today."

"It's so nice to meet you Dale," Colleen spoke, flashing a quick smile and revealing perfect white teeth. She reached out to shake my hand and I saw that her fingers, like her legs, were long and perfectly shaped with impeccably manicured nails. Her touch was warm, her skin soft and smooth when I took her hand in mine and smiled at her. She looked at me with gray eyes, the color of clouds, soft and deep with an almost preternatural light dancing around in them. I watched as she tried to sneak a quick look down my body, taking in every detail. I grinned at her quick scrutiny of me. While she may have been all business on one hand, her thoughts on the other were all woman. When she looked back up, I smiled knowingly at her, capturing her eyes with mine and holding them. I looked past her eyes as I silently whispered into her mind, *"I hope you enjoy what you see as much as I do."*

Her cheeks colored a deep red at the sudden thought that her inspection of me had been caught. Her heart sped up by several beats and the smell of her blood, fresh and hot, blossomed out filling my nostrils as her temperature suddenly shot up a couple of degrees. The temptation to strike right then was so strong that I had to force myself to push it to the back of my mind. But at the same time I continued to imagine how enjoyable it would be to drink from her ... the scent of her blood was enticing ... singing its own song as it called out to me. I decided then that given the opportunity I would take her ... I knew that she would taste as delightful as she looked.

"Good afternoon Colleen," I answered with a smile and a sparkle in my eyes, "I assure you it's my pleasure to meet you."

I saw her shudder almost imperceptibly as somewhere deep inside she suddenly felt an unexplained danger. I released her from my gaze, and she spoke, her voice just a little too high, almost if she had been shaken, "Very well then, shall we get down to business," she asked moving toward her chair and instinctively putting her desk between us.

Charlotte Ann and I took a seat in front of the huge desk as Colleen took her seat behind it and with a few keystrokes of her computer had brought up all of Charlotte Ann's information and began to quickly scan it.

"You have a very large and impressive portfolio, Ms. Erickson," she began, "although I did glance briefly at it when I took the accounts over, this is the first time I have actually looked in depth at it."

"Thank you, it contains some very old investments that have been in my family for centuries," Charlotte Ann replied smiling, "and please Colleen, I insist that you call me Charlotte Ann … my mother was Mrs. Erickson."

"Very well, Charlotte Ann," she smiled back at her, beginning to relax again, "and how exactly can I assist you today?"

"I would like for you to pull some assets, at your discretion, from each of the various accounts and set up a separate account for Dale … of course you will continue to oversee and manage that account as well, I assume."

"Yes, I can do that," she smiled even bigger, knowing she had just picked up another account, "and how much would you like to establish the new account with?"

Charlotte Ann took a piece of paper off the desk and wrote a number on it, folded it and slid it across to Colleen.

I plainly heard her thoughts as she took the slip of paper and opened it, raising her eyebrows slightly, "*Oh my goodness … that's more money than I could possibly make in several lifetimes … I wish I could be her protégé,*" she glanced up slowly at me, *"he looks like just a kid ... but he must be pretty awesome in bed ..."*

She quickly regained control of her thoughts and turned back to Charlotte Ann, "Should I also place your name on the account as a signatory as well?"

"No, I think that Dale is mature enough to have total control of it," Charlotte Ann answered her with a sly smile.

"Yeah, he's definitely more than awesome in bed ... wouldn't I just love to know exactly what he does to make her so happy," Colleen thought quickly.

"You can only imagine," I heard Charlotte speak telepathically to her, *"multiple and powerful orgasms, again and again ... several times a day ... perhaps you may wish to sample him soon."*

"I'm sure that with your expertise you can see to it that his account multiplies," Charlotte Ann continued smiling sweetly as if nothing had passed between them, "of course he will also need a separate account to draw cash from whenever he needs it for his own personal use."

"I will set up both accounts immediately for you," she said still looking at Charlotte Ann. Then turning to face me she smiled hugely, "Dale, you should be able to live very comfortably on the proceeds of these investments."

"Very good then, I shall leave the two of you to finish any necessary paperwork. Since both of you will be working closely financially perhaps you can get to know each other a little better," Charlotte Ann smiled again as she stood to go.

"Thank you Charlotte Ann and I will certainly do all in my power to see that your trust in me is well placed," Colleen continued as she accompanied her to the door.

"Thank you for your time today Colleen, I do hope that you have a pleasant and enjoyable afternoon," she said with a large smile and a final nod to Colleen. Then looking directly at me before closing the door behind her she whispered quietly to my mind, *"She is very special and smells so utterly delightful … but she is exceptional in more ways than you know right now, with many hidden talents … so satisfy your thirst … you will enjoy feeding from her like none other… but be very careful with this one and don't kill her … she is going to make you a very wealthy man."*

After Charlotte Ann left the office I turned back to Colleen, captured her eyes with mine and suggested to her mind that we sit on the sofa. Then with my most disarming smile I asked her what else she needed me to do … because I knew that I needed to get a little closer to her before I struck.

"Why don't we take a seat on the sofa," she asked, echoing my thoughts, "we can do all the paperwork and get your signatures there."

It took us about ten minutes to finish the final details during which time I continually made eye contact every time she looked up. I felt her will beginning to weaken as I drew her in, closer and closer. After the final signature was in place I again looked in her eyes and this time I didn't mean to let her go. I felt when she surrendered her last bit of will and I moved against her, putting an arm around her and drawing her into my embrace.

"I don't understand what's happening to me … why I'm feeling this way," she whispered softly as she leaned in closer, lost in the depths of my stare, "but I want more than anything to kiss you … right now … and for you to kiss me."

I took her in my arms and we kissed long and deep, my hands moving across and down her back tightening my hold on her. She moaned softly in pleasure as our kiss lingered. Then in a fleeting moment of self-control she recovered her will, looked at me and slowly said, "I ... I ... I'm so sorry Dale ... I don't understand what I'm doing ... I ... I've never acted this way with a client before ... but I just can't seem to help myself."

I smiled at her as I gazed into her eyes once again and spoke very low and soothing, "You are a very strong willed woman Colleen, just let go for a few moments ... do what you know you shouldn't ... take the moment ... Carpe Diem ... and I promise I'll make this afternoon more pleasurable for you than you could ever think possible."

I leaned in and tasted her lips again and she locked her arms around me. We kissed passionately for several minutes during which time I searched her mind. Soon I found the hidden thoughts I was looking for ... her most lustful fantasy ... a dark desire that she had possessed since she had first discovered sex as a young teen. It was a craving that in her mind, she thought it to be so vulgar and so dirty, that she had always been too afraid to pursue it, afraid of what someone else might think if she did, so instead she had hidden it away, buried, she thought, in the deepest recesses of her mind.

Although it was hidden away she had never been able to leave it there, she had taken it out many times during her moments of private intimate fantasy, lovingly petting it, building on it, wanting it ... wishing it into reality ... desiring it more than life itself.

I took the fantasy that she unknowingly offered up and began to turn it and implant it back into her mind. Suddenly she found herself experiencing her long sought for castle in the sky ... complete with all the anticipated emotions and sensations she had expected. She willingly surrendered herself to it pushing all of her inhibitions completely away.

I gently guided her body backward to lie on the sofa, folding her in my embrace and covering her body with mine. I kissed her lips, then her chin and finally down the front of her throat. Now engrossed in her own fantasy, she was completely under my control. Her body writhed in expectation of the untold pleasure that she could see coming in her mind's eye, it was everything and more that she had always wanted.

I momentarily closed my eyes in anticipation of my own pleasure, very nearly losing control of myself as the scent of her body and her luscious blood floated around me. I knew I had to be very careful with her as I brushed her hair aside, exposing her long slender neck. I breathed against her ear and kissed the side of her neck, looking, searching for that one special spot. I quickly found it and felt the strong pulse of her blood moving through the artery there ... I again heard her heart beating strong and loud in her chest. I couldn't hold back my own eager desires any longer ... there was something different about her, something I couldn't explain and I wanted her ... I wanted to taste her blood on my lips ... flowing across my tongue ... filling my mouth and running down my throat ... and I wanted her more than I had ever wanted anyone.

My fangs extended and I bit into her soft neck ... a quick stabbing bite ... just enough to open the artery and set her blood flowing freely. When my fangs penetrated her neck, and the sudden shock of my bite tore through her body, she cried out in pleasure and arched her body strongly against me as the first beginnings of an orgasm overtook her body. Her blood filled my mouth, her heart pumping it strong and fast ... it was wonderfully delicious ... sweeter and better than any I had ever tasted ... including the young virgin girl at the Vampire Club ... just as I knew it would be.

I sucked at her neck, drinking deeply from her as I pulled several mouthfuls of her hot luscious blood into me. I swallowed again and again and found myself not wanting to stop … and I recalled the chocolate cake … still it took every ounce of determination I had to pull away from her neck. I passed my tongue slowly over the two small holes, closing them and stopping the blood flow. I began to leisurely lick away the last remnants of blood from her neck, lapping away every tiny stain, leaving it clean and enjoying every last taste I could get.

Before I retreated from her thoughts I took the final piece of her dark fantasy and set it safely back into her mind now for her own enjoyment. When I placed it back where it came from she lost the last remnant of her self-control, and began twisting and turning under me like something wild, her dark fantasy now becoming more real for her than reality itself.

"Oh God … oh yes, yes … oh my God don't stop … it's so good … it's everything and more I've ever dreamed it would be … my God I've never felt anything so wonderful … please don't stop … keep doing it … again and again!"

She groaned loudly in rapturous delight as an unseen lover performed the acts of her deepest yearnings on her. She whimpered like a small child, entranced in pure ecstasy. Heightened purely by her own expectations she quickly became enveloped in the throes of the most intense orgasm she had ever experienced. She thrashed about uncontrollably, her body shaking violently as orgasm after orgasm washed over her until her fantasy had carried itself out to a final finish.

I lifted my head from her neck and looked back into her eyes again. She was continuing to enjoy that special place in her mind. Her imagination was still running wild …

her body still convulsing with pleasure. I smiled at her and softly spoke, "I promised pleasure … I hope you enjoyed it as much as I did … you were more wonderful than I imagined … thank you so much Colleen."

She smiled wistfully at me, her eyes now glazed over with the passion of untold satisfaction. I knew she was unable to speak just now … she had to be incredibly weak from the loss of blood … I had taken more than I should have … but it had tasted so incredibly delicious. I continued to hold her in my arms, her supple body molded tightly to mine, relishing in the satisfaction she had provided for me.

I slowly disentangled from her and stood from the couch, still quietly admiring her beauty. I leaned in and lightly kissed her lips again, then covered her eyes with my hand and softly whispered, "Sleep now dear Colleen … rest peacefully and regain your strength. When you wake again, remember and enjoy your fulfilled fantasy … mortal life is short and fleeting … only a moment in time, many times it's often over before you can live and enjoy it … so don't ever be afraid to let yourself go and delight in whatever fantasy you wish to revel in."

I stood there, watching her for a few more minutes as she now slept serenely, her head turned slightly to the side. I reached and gently brushed the hair away from her face, exposing her long beautiful neck to me once again. I saw the tiny purple bruise just under her ear where my fangs had penetrated … the incredibly sweet taste of her blood still filling my mouth … and the bloodlust began to rise up in me again, threatening to take over. I knew I had to leave because she would not survive another attack. I would have to wait for another day to return for a repeat visit to her luscious fountain … a visit that would also include a night in her bed. Her succulent blood had served only to whet my appetite and I wanted more … it wasn't enough … I had to feed again. But I would have to find it somewhere else … and soon.

fter I left the office and the memory of Colleen's delightful blood behind me, I spent the remainder of the afternoon and evening hunting and feeding in Central Park. I circled slowly through the park a number of times, taking my leisure and lingering around the darkest areas. I fed several more times during the night … none of them as slowly or sensuously as I had in Colleen's office. There had been something different about her and her blood that was unexplainable … she and it was like none I had ever had … both were absolutely delightful.

Over the years I had learned how to prowl … to be a predator … how to find my prey … and I was good at it. Only now, after having fed from Colleen, I was so caught up in the bloodlust I didn't play with them, each time I located my prey and closed in on them, I snatched them into a quiet place and fed quickly, drinking deeply before leaving them to recover on their own. Finally in the early morning hours just before dawn, with the bloodlust finally sated in me, I returned to the apartment and Charlotte Ann.

She strolled casually into the living room, barefooted and wearing one of my fleecy College of Charleston shirts that Katelyn had donated when I first arrived at Whitehall. She was still flush from her own feeding; her dark brown hair and eyes sparkled with a preternatural shine. She looked beautiful … every inch a young and very desirable girl … small and extremely sexy showing off in a shirt … and I suspected nothing else … that barely covered the tops of her thighs. She was at ease, completely relaxed, and I couldn't help but appreciate the sight of her. I felt a slow stirring desire for her begin in the bottom of my stomach. There was no doubt that if her preternatural draw was that intense on me, I couldn't imagine the effect it had on her human prey. They would be completely helpless and under her control.

"Welcome home," she whispered seductively as she lightly kissed me, the lingering taste of blood from her feeding still on her lips. I pulled her close to me, pressing our bodies together, enjoying the feel of her small frame against me. I returned her kiss with a prolonged warm greeting of my own, letting her know what I had in mind.

"Stop that," she said with another laugh, "before I throw you on the floor and take you right now!"

"You don't have to throw me … for you … I'll lie down willingly, besides, it's your turn to be the master," I chuckled.

"In time my liege … in time," she smiled as she patted my cheek, "I trust you had a very delightful afternoon and were able to get better acquainted with our new agent after I left?"

"She and I became … very familiar," I replied with a

smile, "and I also discovered that she has some deeply buried but very alluring fantasies."

"I'm certain she does ... and you made all of them come true," she asked with an expressive smile.

"Well let's just say that I ensured she had a very pleasurable afternoon, and one that she won't soon forget," I answered and then added, "in fact, I suspect that's probably the most fun she's ever had with her clothes on ... or off."

"Please tell me she tasted as good as she smelled," she asked with an evocative smile.

"She was better than she smelled," I answered her, "I don't know what it was about her but I have never been affected by and so strongly drawn to another mortal as I was by her. It wasn't just the scent of her blood but the scent of her skin and her body too ... it was almost overpowering to me ... when I bit her and began to drink, her blood was unlike any I had ever tasted and I found it very difficult to stop."

"I know exactly why," she laughed, her eyes sparkling happily, "I haven't had her kind in a couple of centuries ... and had you not been with me, I would have taken a good long drink of her myself."

"You said 'her kind', what do you mean by that, is she a member of the supernatural world," I asked quizzically knowing that she was about to reveal some heretofore untold secret about this life that I had no idea about.

"You found her so attractive and she had such a pull on you because she is part Fae and carries Fae blood in her body."

"Fae ..." I asked curiously, "as in a fairy ... do you mean they really exist?"

"Of course they do, they're just another of the many

beings in our world," she said, "I was quite surprised when we entered her office and I caught the scent of it. I would say that she probably doesn't even know that she is part Fae, but I would wager she has a relatively close ancestor, probably a great grandfather that was full Fae …"

"Really … a fairy … I fed from a fairy," I mused almost unbelievably.

"Yes, you fed from a Fae … an extraordinary occurrence to be sure because the Fae are rarely seen in this realm. They tend to stay in their world but occasionally do cross into ours. When they do they are like the sirens of old, sensuous, alluring, and irresistible to humans, which would explain her Fae ancestry."

"I guess that would explain my … mmm … unusually strong attraction to her … feeding from her was especially enjoyable … but Charlotte Ann, I wanted her … badly … I wanted to bed her … to hear her scream with enjoyment!"

"I'm sure the Fae attraction is exactly what caused your strong desires", she laughed, "and when you return for a second drink, since you fulfilled her fantasies this time, take her to bed and fulfill your fantasies with her … or better yet, combine hers and yours together for a really memorable time."

"I believe I shall do exactly that," I smiled.

"Oh and by the way, although fairy is an acceptable term, it's probably not a nice term to use when you're in close proximity to one of them, if you get the opportunity to use it … it's much like referring to an immortal as a bloodsucker. The Fae are fierce and mighty warriors in their kingdom, but when they enter our realm, they are frightened of us because we are the only being in this world that can kill them. After yesterday I assure you that you will never forget the scent or desirability of Fae blood. It is intoxicating

... far more so than that of an innocent child. I applaud you for being strong enough to stop when you did."

"The effect of the Fae on immortals is the draw you felt ... their blood sings a song to us, pulling us to them. Think for a moment about the pull that Colleen and her, probably only one eighth, Fae blood had on you ... then imagine that draw multiplied ten times over. If you ever get close to a full Fae, your nature takes over and you immediately attack, draining and killing them."

"A Fairy ... I mean Fae ... now that's astounding," I said with a smile as I put my arms around her and lightly kissed her lips, "now *that* gives me a couple of new fantasies of my own!"

"Really Dale," she said with a smile and a wrinkle of her nose, "you're acting like the sixteen year old that you look like and not the fifty year old you are ... one would think you've discovered a new toy or something."

"Well, I have discovered something new ... thanks to you ... and I do have almost thirty-five years to make up for," I answered with a hopeful grin.

"Yes you do ... and all eternity to do it in ... and you're going to need it too, because you have a long way to go to be able to keep up with me," she laughed back.

"Then now's a good time to start," I said as I took her in my arms and kissed her again. She passionately returned my kiss then slowly broke away from me.

"There'll be plenty of time for us to play ... I promise," she said with a final kiss, "but in the meantime we have some plans to make. I received a call earlier this morning just after I returned from hunting. We'll be having company this weekend."

"That sounds exciting ... who," I asked.

"Katelyn is coming up for the weekend ..."

"That's wonderful news ... I'll be sure to thank her for showing me how to use fantasies for my prey's enjoyment ... do you think that we can all go hunting together," I asked hopefully.

"Actually, you and I are going to stay in the background most of the weekend ... it's going to be our duty to protect her," she continued.

"I thought she was pretty self-reliant and didn't need protection," I laughed.

"She is normally," Charlotte Ann continued, "but she is bringing her best friend, Lexi ... a human ... with her. I suppose that we will be protecting Lexi more than we will Katelyn. Although we want both of them to have a carefree weekend, not worrying about what may or may not be going on around them."

"A human," I asked slowly, "is it even possible to be friends with humans?"

"It is," she began, "but it is often very difficult. Our nature can quickly take over so if we do have human friends that we are close to we must maintain a strict control over it."

"But why does Katelyn have a human friend? I would have thought that being as old as she is she would see humans only for feeding," I said.

"Dale, you may find this difficult to believe, but Katelyn is younger ... much younger ... than you are," she answered me.

"But you said she was almost six hundred years old."

"I said that her *bloodline* was almost six hundred years old," she gently corrected me with a smile, "you really must learn to listen and not just hear. You had been an immortal for well over a decade when Katelyn was born the first time to her human parents. In fact, the night we found you she had just returned from her first hunt."

I was flabbergasted to learn that Katelyn was a new fledgling and even younger than I was ... she seemed so mature and experienced.

"Well, I suppose that explains her friendship with a human then," I commented.

"It does," she responded, "and I'm sure that Katelyn will be happy to tell you her story when she's ready. But the short version is that her and Lexi were roommates in college and became best friends. Then Katelyn met James and they soon fell in love. After James allowed her to discover that he was an immortal and offered her 'The Gift', she accepted it, and joined him in this life as his mate. Since Katelyn and Lexi were so close, James made arrangements for Lexi to go to Europe to teach in the university at Berlin while Katelyn made the transition. After she was brought over I was there to teach her and help bring her along when you came into the picture."

"Just wait until I see Katelyn," I laughed, "now that I know we are both learning this life!"

"You will be nice," she chuckled.

"Of course I will, but now we have something more in common to talk about," I said, and then changed the topic as a new concern came to me, "can she stay with us ... I mean since she has a human with her?"

"No, they won't be staying with us but they will be close by," she answered with a smile, "James owns the suite just above us. He purchased it in 1893 when the hotel first opened so he would have a place to stay when he was away from Whitehall. He is responsible for me buying this suite. When it came up for sale in the middle of the last century, he contacted me and suggested that I purchase it. That's when I moved from London to America."

"Then what do we have to do this weekend," I asked.

"Just enjoy ourselves and have a fun weekend," she answered, "we will go wherever they go but stay hidden in the background. I need to learn a little about her human friend, so I will meet them when they arrive but I would prefer that you stay out of sight, at least for the time being. Lexi has no idea that Katelyn has turned since she saw her last and there are no plans to tell her. So, the fewer of us around her, the better, and the less chance of her discovering something she shouldn't. After I meet them and spend a few hours together I will drop out of sight too. Then for the remainder of the weekend we will only step in if needed. I hope that we are not needed, but we are not the only immortals in the city. I can assure you a young, fresh immortal like Katelyn coming to town, especially bringing an innocent human companion with her, will likely draw some of their attention. Fortunately, they all defer to my authority."

I silently remembered the talk I had had with James and what he had said about her being considered an elder. I really wanted to ask her to tell me more but didn't feel like now was the time to go into it. Besides, I was sure that she would explain it all to me when she was ready.

When Thursday afternoon arrived, so did Katelyn and her human friend. Charlotte Ann met them at the airport and helped them settle in to their suite. Afterwards the three of them left for a shopping trip along Fifth Avenue while I returned to Central Park to hunt and feed in the early evening. While I hunted I thought about Charlotte Ann's comment that there were other immortals in the city and found it strange that I had never seen or sensed the presence of another one anywhere close.

While I pondered on that I recalled she had also said they deferred to her authority which made me recall the events of our first meeting. I remembered well the cold fingers around my throat and the invisible force that held me tight against the wall that night. I thought about the pressure that had pulled at my shoulders letting me know she could have put me on my knees had she wanted. I began to realize that there was still much I didn't know about Charlotte Ann and what a powerful immortal she really was. I began to wonder about her position in our world and just what she could be capable of doing. If she was able to protect not only myself and Katelyn ... but also a human friend ... from other immortals with just her presence alone ... what kind of a place of authority did she occupy? There was so much more I had to learn about the workings of the supernatural world and my own immortal place in it.

I filed my thoughts away as I became more involved in the hunt, I could think about them later. Right now, however, if I was going to be spending any time at all close to a human ... especially one that I couldn't take ... I had to feed and be well satisfied. I had learned over the years that just as a hunter selects different game for their needs, a vampire also chooses different prey for whatever their needs are. In this case I needed strength and stamina so I went in search of joggers ... those who looked the strongest and most vigorous. Over the course of the afternoon and early evening I took several victims, all out for a run, and all very strong, before I returned to the apartment.

The next morning I got my first look at Katelyn's human friend. Charlotte Ann and I left the apartment to follow them as they shopped and enjoyed the sights of the city. We took up our positions close to them. Charlotte Ann was a few yards to the front and one side, and I was about the same distance to the rear and the other side of them.

I watched as they strolled along carefree, completely relaxed and not paying attention to anyone or anything going on around them. Katelyn knew she was protected and didn't have to worry about her surroundings. I could see they were having fun and understood why Charlotte Ann and I were watching over them.

I smiled as I sent my thoughts toward Katelyn, just a simple greeting, as the two of them continued their walk, *"Good morning Katelyn … it's good to see you again."*

I saw her look up and around, trying to locate where I was as she smiled in recognition. Just as quickly her own thoughts filled my mind with a happy greeting in return, *"Hello Dale … I can't see you but I can feel you and hear you so I know you're close by. I'm so happy that you are here with us … thank you for helping watch over my friend … and don't forget about our walk in the sunshine either … soon!"*

I smiled at her reminder and wondered when, or even if, Charlotte Ann and I would return to Whitehall. Then I turned my attention toward her friend. She seemed to be very bubbly and happy, almost dancing as she walked. There was no hiding the fact that she was thrilled to be close to Katelyn. She was beaming with happiness and was displaying an almost hero worship at just being together with her friend.

I continued to watch, carefully appraising her. She was very pretty, and was actually similar to Charlotte Ann in height and appearance. That, of course, made her appear to be the complete opposite of Katelyn who was tall, and had such a striking beauty that she seemed almost unapproachable.

Her hair was much lighter than Charlotte Ann's, being a combination of light brown mixed with blonde. It just touched her shoulders and moved easily as she walked. Her eyes matched her hair and were a soft pastel brown and the light dancing around in them easily reflected her bright and cheerful smile.

She may have been a couple of inches taller than Charlotte Ann but still my overall first impression of her was that she was tiny, almost elfish in her looks with a fresh child-like innocence about her. I smiled to myself as I realized that she was the embodiment of everything 'The Girl Next Door' was supposed to be and look like. There was no doubt that she was thoroughly human, through and through … and that made her all the more appealing to my immortal nature.

I listened closely while the two of them chatted as they walked along. Her voice was tiny and almost childish, like her. It tinkled like a wind chime as she spoke, and even with preternatural hearing I had to listen close because of the softness of it. When she laughed it was bright and happy, sounding pleasant, more of a gleeful giggle than a sharp laugh.

I lifted my nose to pick up and fix her scent and smiled when I did. I noted that it was velvety smooth and very feminine. I breathed it in again, savoring it and thinking to myself that it was soft and fresh, much like an expensive bath powder would be. I was immediately impressed with Katelyn's own inner strength knowing that she would be sharing a suite with this delectable little morsel of a human.

I allowed my eyes to slowly wander over her again as I felt the first tingling of the bloodlust begin to stir deep in my chest. Her childish innocence, radiant aura, and delicate scent all combined to become a powerful drawing force pulling at my nature. There was no doubt her glowing personality would quickly draw the interest of any other immortal that happened to see her … it had certainly gotten my attention … quickly titillating the immortal in me.

Quickly recovering and reminding myself that I was charged with her protection, I pushed away my instinctive feelings, and looked at her once again … this time not with the eyes of a predator, instead I looked at her through the eyes of a protector. I smiled to myself as I suddenly felt an unusually strong sense of protectiveness begin to rise up in me and surge outward toward her. Now with the gaze of a guardian and not a huntsman, I understood that for some unknown reason I couldn't fully explain – I credited it to her being Katelyn's best friend – there was indeed something about her that seemed important, something needful and worth protecting.

Still, I felt that there was something else about her too, something very unsettling, that I wasn't fully seeing. The longer I concentrated on her, the more my senses tingled as I tried to determine exactly what it was I was feeling. In spite of that uneasiness I realized that she seemed to be a very likable girl. I determined to do all in my power to ensure that she remained safe until she and Katelyn departed for Charleston once again.

The rest of the day was nothing out of the ordinary, Charlotte Ann and I stayed close to the two of them while they shopped and generally acted like tourists. During the afternoon and early evening I stayed close by them while Charlotte Ann went off to hunt and feed. Finally around midnight, Katelyn and Lexi returned to their suite for the night. I knew that once inside they would be safe for the remainder of the night. So, ensuring they were safely inside I left for Central Park to get in some late night hunting of my own and prepare for the next day's activities.

When I returned to the apartment just after dawn, Charlotte Ann and I discussed the previous day, like the two bodyguards we had become, and how smoothly it seemed to have gone. There had been no issues at all and after my morning greeting neither one of us had interfered with the two of them as they shopped. I did mention to Charlotte Ann my concern about the feelings I had picked up from Lexi.

"What exactly did you feel from her," she asked me curiously.

"I'm not sure," I began as I thought back about it, "but there is something unsettling about her ... it's almost like there's a supernatural buzz of some kind around her."

"Do you think what you're feeling is evidence of some latent powers she may have? I do know, at least according to Katelyn," she mused, "that Lexi has absolutely no idea about the supernatural world."

"Maybe not, but still, there's something there," I continued, "it's almost as if whatever it is, it's off in the distance and I can just barely pick it up."

"I'm curious as to what you are feeling, Dale ... do you think Lexi is dangerous to us," Charlotte Ann asked.

"I don't think *Lexi* is so much dangerous to us as it's something that is, or will be, dangerous to *Lexi*," I answered.

"That's very interesting that you should say that. Perhaps we should just watch her more closely until they depart," she continued, "I'm interested to see if you can identify what exactly it is that you're feeling."

Dale's Descent

The remainder of the weekend was untroubled with the exception of one incident on Friday night when I got to see firsthand a display of Charlotte Ann's power and authority. While Katelyn and Lexi were shopping in the afternoon they had decided to go dancing after dark. They had chosen a club in the center of mid-town that looked interesting and they decided to go. Charlotte Ann and I slipped into the club right behind them and picked a spot across the room where we could dance when we wanted and still keep an eye on them. The club was modeled after one of the 1980's Discos complete with the twirling flashing lights and the loud music. I loved it … and the music … probably because I had spent most of the '80's either hiding in the dark or buried in a grave.

Katelyn and Lexi both were good dancers and over the course of the evening they spent more time on the dance floor than at their table. I knew that Katelyn was able to take care of herself and found it amusing as I watched her feed several times during the evening from the guys she was dancing with. After a couple of hours they returned to their table and I watched as Lexi quickly pulled Katelyn back out on the floor.

They were both laughing loudly and enjoying themselves tremendously as they ran together back out to the floor and began to dance with each other. I watched as they continued to dance, glancing questioningly at Charlotte Ann as their dance quickly went from mildly entertaining to seductive and finally … just down right erotically provocative. I didn't know that two girls would dance together like that … at least not in public … but they certainly put on quite a show for the crowd who had made way for them leaving them surrounded by a circle of other dancers all laughing and clapping right along with them. While I continued to watch their dance, Charlotte Ann softly laid her hand on my arm and with a big smile said, "They're just playing and letting the men know they can dance ... keep watching and see what happens."

I continued to watch, still stunned at their performance, but sure enough just as the song ended they were each picked off by a different man and continued to dance. I watched as Katelyn once again fed from her partner while they danced. Then she returned to her seat and began to quickly scan the club. I let my own awareness lag for a moment turning my interest instead toward Katelyn as she carefully watched Lexi while she danced. I could see in her eyes and her smile there was no doubt that she loved Lexi as she would have loved her own sister, and was very protective of her, very much like a mother watching over her child.

I knew that she was keeping an eye on her when she suddenly sat bolt upright and glared in Lexi's direction. I followed her line of sight and saw that Lexi was wrapped in the arms of another immortal. I immediately saw that she had been enthralled in his gaze and that she was dancing too close for her own good. I knew exactly what was about to happen as I watched him. There had been too many times when it had been me guiding a victim towards the edge of the dance floor and a darkened corner.

"The human girl you are dancing with is mine," I heard Katelyn's telepathic voice cut so strongly across the huge room that anyone sensitive to it would have heard it, *"and I would appreciate it if you would release her and allow her to return to me."*

I suddenly felt like a spectator in an old western

movie as he lifted his head and looked around the room finally locating Katelyn. I watched curiously as Charlotte Ann crossed her arms, one finger lightly tapping her lips as she set her gaze on this unknown immortal, waiting and listening for his answer ... an answer that came laughingly, and full of contempt in the same telepathic voice, *"I think what you meant to say is that she was yours, young one ... and I must commend you on your excellent taste in humans ... she smells so incredibly delicious ... but I believe I shall enjoy this one tonight ... and thank you so much for providing her ... now run along ... there's plenty more in here for you to choose from ... you can find another one for yourself."*

"If you don't release her and return her to me this instant, I will burn you where you stand," Katelyn spoke again, her tone now low and very threatening.

"Oh, I'm so very frightened of you ... but you really don't want to pick this fight ... fledgling ... I'm much older and stronger than you ... now please don't make me hurt a pretty little girl like yourself ... especially over a human," he answered her, drawing Lexi tighter into his immortal embrace, *"just run along now so I can feed and everything will be alright."*

I saw Katelyn stand up and fire flashed in her eyes as she raised her hand in his direction. Before she could say or do anything else Charlotte Ann spoke calmly and quietly across the scene, *"Perhaps you should be more careful who you call a fledgling ... and the question is actually are you absolutely certain that you are the one who wants to pick this fight ... young one?"*

His eyes shifted from Katelyn, moving toward the direction of Charlotte Ann's voice. He looked intently trying to determine who was speaking to him now as he searched the crowd. I felt her shield fall away, revealing herself to him, as she continued to speak, *"My blood flows in her veins ...*

and I can assure you she is plenty strong enough to light you up with no problem ... you know who I am ... novice ... do you also wish to find out who she is ... or perhaps you would prefer a demonstration from her ... now show the deference due to both of us and I'll allow you to leave – without the girl of course – but anger me further newcomer ... and you know I can and will eliminate you."

"*Charlotte Ann,*" he spoke her name in complete surprise, "*please forgive my indiscretion ... I didn't realize you had returned to the city ... or had extended your protection to a human.*"

The air around me literally crackled with energy. I involuntarily recoiled away from her, my skin tingling at the feel of raw power contained in her words as she angrily cut him off in mid-sentence, "*It doesn't matter to you to whom or when I extend my protection to any being, whether they are mortal or immortal. It would do you well fledgling to always pay attention to who or what is in your immediate surrounding ... never assume that I am not here ... you may consider that your lesson for the evening ... now go ... hunt and feed elsewhere with my blessing ... but do so before I grow weary of playing games and become really angry with you.*"

This uninvited immortal, whoever he was, dropped his hold on Lexi and in a flash was gone. I looked across at Lexi, now appearing a little perplexed but no longer enthralled, as she looked around in confusion. Her face showed a touch of fear as she realized she was standing alone and didn't know or remember how she had gotten to the far side of the room.

Katelyn was instantly at her side, an arm around her waist and led her back to their table. I continued to watch as they talked quietly for a few moments. I knew that Katelyn was wiping her memory and replacing it with something else. Lexi took a final sip of her drink and laughing happily with Katelyn they stood and started hurriedly for the exit. Once outside they turned toward the Waldorf and safety.

Except for the circumstances it could have been almost comical ... one tiny, innocent, almost childlike little human, unaware of precisely how close she had just come to death, now surrounded and protected by three very strong and powerful immortals ... one seen and two unseen ... making their way through the crowded streets of the city.

Chapter Eighteen

he remainder of the weekend passed, thankfully, with no other incidents involving either Lexi or any other immortals. Then on Saturday night, Charlotte Ann and I, still unseen of course, accompanied her and Katelyn to The Met for a show. They both wore long, formal black dresses and were wearing the most diamonds and jewels I had ever seen. The two of them sat in James' private box just to the right of the stage and, although Katelyn was much more alert to her surroundings after the incident at the disco, both of them were happy and fully enjoyed their evening. After the show, we saw them safely back to the apartment where they remained until the next morning when Charlotte Ann escorted them to the airport and they departed for Charleston.

The weekend had certainly been a different kind of experience for me. I had enjoyed it, especially being able to see Katelyn again because she kind of felt like family to me.

However, I was glad when it ended because watching over and protecting a human, even though she was Katelyn's friend, was just not something I was accustomed to doing.

I hoped that perhaps now Charlotte Ann and I could get back to our regular routines. I was enjoying living in the city and was beginning to settle into a comfortable life. It was the first time I had ever been able to live a somewhat normal life since I had been attacked. The idea of living unnoticed in the human world had been a completely strange concept to me, but one I was quickly learning to enjoy.

Charlotte Ann was more than ever my teacher, guide and lover … she was everything to me that a Maker should have been. But more than that … she was my friend and my companion … and I quickly grew to love her dearly too. She had saved my life … taught me how to live again and shared so much with me. But in the back of my mind I remembered her words that we were lovers and not mates. Although I didn't want to hear it, she would sometimes remind me that one day in the future I would find my mate. When that happened, though I couldn't understand it now, it would be a much deeper relationship than what the two of us currently had … but I just could not imagine loving anyone more than I loved her.

I continued to spend the days with Charlotte Ann systematically teaching me things I needed to know to become stronger and more proficient as an immortal. Under her guiding hand I soon came to the conclusion that this immortal life was better than I had ever imagined it could be. She helped me discover new skills and abilities that I didn't know I had. Then she would allow me to demonstrate how to use those new found talents and instruct me how to hone them for better control. I never had any idea that I possessed such supernatural powers and I found them to be more than amazing.

She also concentrated on teaching me to be a good lover. She maintained that as long as we were lovers, our bodies belonged to each other and were for passion and pleasure. Due to my inexperience as a human teen and then my, supposedly, inability as an immortal, we spent many hours and days being intimate. Often times we would spend the entire day for just that purpose. Our lovemaking was intense and I enjoyed every moment of it with her. She enjoyed sex and delighted in watching me learn what it was all about ... something that made it even more special. She taught me that lovemaking was not reserved just for the bedroom but for anywhere and anytime. She taught me how to make love to a woman in every way imaginable ... how to take her to the very heights of pleasure ... and in return she pleased me in every way imaginable ... often in ways that I had never even considered possible.

Every evening after the day's lessons – whether they were practical or amorous – I would venture out into the streets to hunt and feed. Although I had been an accomplished hunter before Charlotte Ann entered my life, she helped me to fine tune those skills and become even better at taking my prey. I quickly perfected the art of taking only a small drink. The fact that I no longer had to kill greatly improved my social skills and made hunting even more enjoyable for me. I soon changed from just stalking and feeding to actually spending time with my victims. I often would walk through the Park where I would meet some girl and strike up a conversation with her. I then casually spent time talking with her, getting to know her, and finally inviting her to a movie. I still preferred to feed in a dark and secluded place so the back rows of the theater were perfectly suited for that purpose. The times that we would spend 'petting' in the theater were rewarding for both ... I fed and my victim experienced her darkest fantasies ... a definite win/win for both of us.

Early one morning, just after dawn, I returned to the apartment after a night of hunting in Central Park. I had fed several times during the night and was looking forward to a leisurely day with Charlotte Ann. She was waiting for me when I came in and greeted me with a deeply passionate kiss.

"Good morning lover boy," she murmured clinging to me between kisses, "I hope you had a successful night."

"Not nearly as good as the morning appears to be," I said as I folded her in my arms and returned her kiss.

I began to look forward to a day of romantic playing and carried the kiss a little further. Then she broke the kiss and looked into my eyes as we continued to hold each other.

"That'll have to do you for now," she smiled and winked, "just a little tease to keep you on your toes. We'll continue and finish this later, but before we do we need to take a trip."

"Where are we going," I asked curiously, disappointed at the sudden turn of events.

"Back to Charleston," she began, "we must go back to Whitehall for a while ... something unexpected has come up."

"Whatever it is, good ... that means I can take Katelyn for that walk in the sunshine I promised her," I grinned.

"You may have to postpone that for a bit too," she said, looking at me seriously and then continued, "we are going back to lend our assistance with an unanticipated issue."

"Our assistance … what's the matter," I asked, my own curiosity beginning to rise, "is everything there alright?"

"It will be," she smiled and slowly added, "it's just that we must help with some unforeseen circumstances. I know how you feel about what I going to tell you, but nevertheless, it is what is … a couple of days ago … Katelyn turned Lexi."

I was speechless as I stared at her in shock. I couldn't believe what I had just heard. I turned away to try to process what she had just told me. I closed my eyes and recalled a mental picture of Lexi … her easy smile, her tiny soft voice … and saw how happy she had been that weekend with Katelyn. I felt tears of sadness begin to well up in my eyes for Lexi and I slowly began to speak, my teeth clenched and my jaw tight, carefully measuring each word, using all of my restraint to control my quickly rising anger.

"How … could she do that … and to her best friend … I hated my maker with everything in me and I didn't even know him. I can't imagine what Lexi must feel toward someone she *thought* was her best friend doing this to her."

"Dale …"

"No … Charlotte Ann … just … no … you're not supposed to do this to someone you love and care about!"

"Dale … sometimes the gift is given because you love and care," she almost whispered trying to console me.

"I knew she couldn't be friends with a mortal … why did she even try … that poor innocent, sweet girl … she has – had – family and friends that loved her. I know because I heard her talking about them to Katelyn."

"We will become Lexi's family now," she started to say.

"What was Katelyn thinking when she turned her," I interrupted again.

"Dale … please turn around and look at me," she said softly, but sternly this time.

I turned back and looked right into her eyes … and was shocked to see her own blood red tears brimming in her eyes.

"Katelyn loves and cares for Lexi and that's why she turned her … she wanted to save her life … to prevent her from dying … and she had Lexi's consent to do so."

"What do you mean to save her life," I asked, "what happened to her?"

"Do you remember the feeling you had of something supernatural about Lexi," she asked.

"Yes … it was something odd … something out of place," I answered.

"You commented that you thought whatever it was, it was more a danger to her than she was to us," she continued.

"Yes, but what does all that have to do with turning her to save her life," I asked still confused.

"When you got close to Lexi, you felt a supernatural presence, and it caused you to be concerned and uneasy. You had just enough of my blood in you to trigger a warning that something was wrong … that something about her was just not right. But what you didn't have, was enough experience to know exactly what you were feeling so you were unable to recognize what it was," she continued patiently, "that's why I was so interested in your feelings when you mentioned it to me. Dale, the thing that you sensed but couldn't identify was that Lexi had cancer. I detected it in her the moment we met … and I understood right away what it was. Although neither she nor Katelyn knew it at the time ... I knew then that Lexi was dying and had very little time left."

"Cancer ... but she looked perfectly healthy," I protested.

"Some things don't show on the outside, but when you have lived in the supernatural as long as I have you are able to sense when something evil is present. Especially if that something evil is such an insidious and hateful killer as the one that had infected Lexi," she answered.

"And Lexi gave Katelyn her permission to turn her," I asked again slowly just to reassure myself.

"Yes she did, and she also knew exactly what was going to happen when she turned. Katelyn and James both talked in depth and explained to her, prior to turning her, exactly what Katelyn would do, how she would do it, what Lexi would become, and how she would live afterward."

I was absolutely stunned and unsure of just what to say.

"Dale, you must consider Katelyn and how she felt about this for a moment too," she continued slowly, "the news of Lexi's cancer and impending death was devastating to her. You must remember that Katelyn is still very young herself and she recently lost both of her parents. She is still in many ways getting used to leaving behind her own human life and becoming an immortal with everything that entails. Then suddenly, on top of all that, she was facing the death of her best friend, too. All of it combined was overwhelming to her. So when James explained to her that she had the ability to turn Lexi, to save her life, and prevent her from dying, it was an easy decision for her to make. Think for a moment how you would have felt if that had been you."

"I suppose that if it were my best friend, and I had the ability to save their life, I would do the same thing," I said thoughtfully.

"I know you would," she smiled at me, "because you are a kind and caring person."

I put my arms back around her and held on to her for several minutes like some kind of life preserver. Finally, with my cheek resting lightly on the top of her head I began to speak again, "I'm so sorry I over reacted Charlotte Ann," I said slowly, "it's just ..."

"I know," she said as she cuddled closer against me, "and I understand your reaction based on your experiences."

"Tell me what we need to do," I asked, "how can I help?"

"Lexi will need us to be there for her," she said, "it's that simple. We will open our arms and lives to her, the same as we did with you, and welcome her into the family. We will begin to teach her all the things she needs to know to survive in her new world ... and Dale ... all of us ... including you ... has something to offer her as she learns and becomes comfortable with her new life."

"The first month is always the most difficult for a new fledgling. They are at their weakest during that time. She will need help in fully understanding the transition from mortal to immortal. We must help her learn how to hunt and feed; again we all have something to offer her. She must rest often, especially after feeding, while the change completes itself in her. She must also become comfortable that while she rests, we will all be there to protect her."

"While the change works in her, she will begin to see the world around her in a completely different light. She must become accustomed to and understand the differences as she looks at it through her new eyes. She must be prepared to live as an immortal in a mortal world, the same as you did. Then, when the time is right we will slowly introduce her back into the human world."

"Finally, I suspect, due to the special relationship that exists between a maker and their child, Katelyn may also need and appreciate our guidance. The next few weeks are going to be a time of transition and learning for all of us."

With that she tightened her grip on me and I felt us begin to move. The air swirled around us as we left New York and moved toward Charleston and Whitehall. This was the first time I had traveled supernaturally over such a long distance. Although I was aware of moving through space, time was standing still … in more ways than one. I closed my eyes and held tightly to Charlotte Ann.

Chapter Nineteen

hen I opened my eyes again we were standing just inside the huge front doorway of Whitehall looking down the long, wide hallway that led into the rest of the house. I stood quietly next to Charlotte Ann and listened. The house as always was nearly silent, the high ceilings and thick walls quickly absorbing any stray sound.

I smiled to myself when I heard Lexi's barely audible wind-chime voice. It was coming from the direction of the parlor and tinkling softly in the air. I began to listen in and noted that she was having a conversation with James and Katelyn about her new life and new self. She was questioning what all the changes meant to her. I smiled and absently nodded as I stood there listening, fully understanding her desire to know everything that was happening in her new life.

"I think we should make our presence known," Charlotte Ann spoke silently to me with a smile.

I followed her down the long hall and to the entrance of the parlor, still listening to Lexi pose questions to the two of them about her transition. James was patiently explaining what being an immortal meant and some of the things she could expect to enjoy from her new life. I dropped back and continued to listen while Charlotte Ann turned the corner and stepped unannounced into the parlor.

"Good morning, everyone," she began with a cheery laugh, "sorry I'm a little late, but I got here as soon as I could and I do hope I haven't missed anything important."

There was a sudden silence as Lexi stopped talking. After a long moment during which no one spoke, Lexi finally broke the silence, her already tinkling voice rising a full octave, and very slowly asking in a tone of sheer unbelief, "Charlotte Ann … wha … what are you doing … here … and … and you … you … you're a …"

"A what sweetie … vampire," Charlotte Ann finished for her, and then laughingly added, "yeah, I suppose I am … but now that you mention it, it looks like I'm not the only one … you look like you've done a little … uh … 'changing' since I saw you last, too!"

"Yeah … I … I know that," Lexi continued slowly, "but I didn't expect … I mean James and Katelyn … but I didn't know there were …"

"Others," Charlotte Ann laughed again, "Oh my innocent little newborn … that's so sweet … but please tell me you didn't honestly think that the three of you had a lock on this gig … did you?"

"Actually," she continued, sounding somewhat dismayed, "until four days ago … I really hadn't considered the existence of a supernatural world … let alone that I would become a part of it … so … there are four of us now?"

"Well, actually there's at least five of us," I spoke up

as I stepped through the door chuckling, unable to stay back any longer.

"Dale!" Katelyn shouted, and in a flash she was up and across the room. She wrapped her arms around me in a hug, kissed my cheek, and laughingly said, "I'm so happy to see you … you owe me a walk in the sunshine!"

"It's good to see you again, too, and I'm ready for that walk anytime you are," I answered and kissed her cheek lightly, then stepping aside and looking over her shoulder I added, "And hello to you too Lexi, it's nice to finally meet you in person."

Lexi stood there, loosely surrounded by the three of us, biting her lower lip and looking very perplexed. She looked so pitiful standing there, her face reflecting the confusion that was suddenly filling her. I actually felt sorry for her and was afraid that she was about to burst into tears. I saw that she was completely overcome with the sudden appearance of me and Charlotte Ann as she silently stared, first at me and then Charlotte Ann, and finally back to Katelyn again.

"Lexi, I'm so sorry we upset you young one," Charlotte Ann said opening her arms toward her, "perhaps we should have made ourselves known in a little different manner and not have suddenly surprised you." She put her arms around Lexi in a reassuring hug for a few moments then stepped back and with a big grin added, "But you should have seen the look on your face when you realized I was an immortal … now *that* was priceless!"

I turned to her and opened my arms to offer her a hug too. She stepped slowly into my arms and I looked into her soft brown eyes and said, "Welcome to immortality little sister it looks like your new family just doubled in size."

She folded easily into my arms and I could hear and

feel her heart beating at the slow immortal rhythm as she stood there. Her now familiar scent, still soft and fresh as it had been, filled my nostrils. I inhaled again, firmly setting the scent of immortality in my memory. I recalled how I had thought it reminded me of an expensive bath powder and now realized that her scent was like rose petals.

I opened my arms and she stepped away looking back up into my eyes for a moment. I heard her unguarded thoughts racing through her mind as she stood there. I smiled at her and in a near whisper I answered her silent question, "I saw you in the City ... I was with Charlotte Ann watching over and protecting you and Katelyn the entire weekend ... that's how I knew you."

Finally, when Lexi had gotten over her shock of our unannounced entrance she looked around with an uncertain smile and asked, "Are there just the five of us ... or is there any others I need to know about or meet?"

"I can think of several others just off the top of my head, Lexi," Charlotte Ann answered her, "and in years to come I'm sure that you shall meet some or all of them. But for now, until you get fully accustomed to your new life, it's just us."

Over the course of the next couple of hours Lexi began to get more comfortable with Charlotte Ann and me. We also had the opportunity to get better acquainted with her as the five of us talked and laughed having a mini reunion of sorts. She was soon relaxed and at ease again joining us in the conversation.

After a while Charlotte Ann spoke up, "Lexi, perhaps you should know the reason I'm here. I did come to welcome you into the family, but more importantly I am here to assist you ... as I did Katelyn ... and James before her ... in making a successful transition to immortality. You are the newest member of our family and I can already see that you are going to be a strong and very powerful immortal."

"I know I have a lot to learn Charlotte Ann … but right now … I don't feel very strong or very powerful," she answered her, "this has been the most unique five days of my life and actually I feel pretty weak and confused by all that's going on around me and in my life."

"As you should, remember you are not even a week old yet," Charlotte Ann began seriously, "but I can assure you Lexi, you have a reserve of strength and power residing within you that you have no idea of how strong it is. You do not get chosen for this life … even by your best friend … or survive the transition to this life without the innermost resilience and determination to do so."

"I just wanted so badly to live and not have to die," she answered her.

"That's exactly what I'm talking about," Charlotte Ann smiled reassuringly, "and now it is time for you to live, to enjoy your new life and to begin growing into it. Are you ready for your first hunt?"

"Oh but I've already had my first hunt … and kill," she answered her excitedly, a big smile covering her face, "Katelyn took me out a couple of days ago and I actually chased, tackled and took a big deer … all by myself!"

I bit my lower lip trying my best not to laugh out loud knowing that Lexi was still a new born and so had no idea what Charlotte Ann was talking about.

"That's good practice …" Charlotte Ann smiled back at her, "but it's not exactly what I was talking about. You're the real thing now sweetie, and this isn't a movie, you don't live off the blood of animals. I was asking if you were ready to hunt and take your first human."

At that point James spoke up and looking towards me

asked, "Dale, why don't we give the ladies a little 'girl time' alone. I'm sure they need to take care of some of their own affairs. I think perhaps now would be a good time for you and me to go and do some hunting of our own. Would you care to accompany me downtown?"

"I would love to go hunting with you," I answered, feeling honored that he would ask me to go along with him, "I don't know very much about Charleston, but when I'm in the City, I like to hunt in Central Park. Is there some place similar to that here?"

"Yes, there is," he answered, "it's known as The Battery and White Point Gardens. We shall go down there and see what we can find. While it's not Central Park, it does have trees, grass and walking paths, so we should do very well there. There are usually plenty of tourists in the area. Afterwards we can work our way up East Bay to the Market, and from there it's only a short walk up Meeting to Calhoun and the college. There are numbers of college students that fill the little coffee shops and study areas there. I can assure you we shall fully satisfy our thirst before returning."

When the two of us arrived at White Point Gardens I looked around and immediately liked what I saw. The streets closest to the two rivers were brightly lit but the park area of the garden itself was bathed in darkness. The old oaks that lined the walking paths and outer edges cast their overlapping shadows into the center of the park, providing a shadowy and perfect place to hunt. James and I began to stroll from the upper end of the park toward a large gazebo in the center.

I surveyed the park, familiarizing myself with my surroundings. I noted that there were only four main paths in and out of the park. I scanned the area, pinpointing the different benches and monuments, the location of the dim foot lamps placed along the paths, and finally the two large cannon at the far end of the park still looking out across the harbor, standing their silent vigil over the city.

We had gone about a quarter of the way down the center path when I spotted a girl standing beside one of the small lamps next to a park bench and holding what appeared to be a map. She was mostly covered in the shadows cast by one of the huge trees and was having a difficult time reading it. I smiled as I watched her continue to concentrate on the paper she held, oblivious to anything around her.

"I believe I see someone I know," I smiled at James, "please excuse me for a moment while I go over and say hello. I'll meet you down by the guns when we finish our tour of the park."

Then I stepped into the shadows, moving silently from one to the other, allowing the darkness to cover me as I quickly slipped back into my old habits of the hunt. I scanned the area in front of and to each side of me, watching to make sure nothing came between me and my intended prey.

I walked up to the young tourist and stepping out of the shadows, I spoke a quiet greeting, "Hey there, you look lost, can I help you find your way?"

She turned, looked at me with a smile and said, "Thank you so much but I'm not really lost, just waiting for one of the carriages to come back around and take me to my hotel."

She glanced back down at her map as I continued to stand there. She slowly began to raise her head to look at me again. I locked her eyes to mine when she did and I smiled.

"Oh …" she whispered, suddenly confused but enthralled in my stare … "of course."

I moved closer to her and swiftly took her in my arms, closing them around her and drawing her close against my chest. In the blink of an eye I had bitten into her neck and began to take a long drink of her blood. It was hot and strong as it flowed down my throat, filling me. I began to take a second, longer pull from her neck. I swallowed it quickly and licked the two punctures I had made, closing them back and stopping the blood flow.

I released her and took a step back, smiled again and still looking in her eyes spoke softly, "Thank you so much for the directions, I believe I can find my way now."

"You're welcome," she slowly answered, shaking her head once trying to clear the confusion, "I'm glad I could help, I think, I hope you have a good evening."

Then I was gone as quickly as I had appeared leaving her confused and wondering what had just happened.

The burn in the back of my throat was now just a dull ache, only enough to let me know that I would soon have to find another drink. I moved quickly to the far end of the park and took a seat on one of the benches there. I spread my arms wide along the back of the bench and casually crossed my legs at the ankles, relishing the feel of the fresh blood I had just taken as it began to work its way through me.

I sat back to admire the area while I waited for James, and even in the darkness I could plainly see Fort Sumter, sitting out at the entrance to the harbor. In a short time I felt James' presence and looked over to find him standing beside one of the massive siege guns that was pointing across the harbor and watching me closely. I noticed the light sheen on his lips and the warmth in his cheeks and I knew that he had fed too.

"I admire your hunting style," he commented, "the manner in which you take your prey quickly, cleanly and then move on is commendable."

"Thank you sir," I answered him and with a soft chuckle added, "it is a skill I have been practicing since I was the tender age of sixteen and have now very nearly raised it to the level of an art form … with the exception of that part in which I now leave them alive. That happens to be a new and rather refreshing addition to my repertoire of skills."

James laughed out loud at my perfect imitation of his old world gentlemanly English, "Ah and yet another skill reveals itself."

I realized what I had just done and quickly said, "James, I'm so sorry … I don't know where that came from … I really didn't mean to sound like I was mocking you, please forgive me."

"I assure you Dale, there was no offense taken," he continued chuckling, "You will discover that having the ability to sound like someone else is a skill that will serve you well in the future. Besides it has been said that imitation is the highest form of flattery … I shall therefore consider myself flattered."

He leaned casually against one of the huge cannon next to me and pointing up the street to our left, chuckled softly and looking at me with a smile said, "This is East Bay, let's continue our walk and see if we run into any other acquaintances."

I was surprised to hear a perfect imitation of my own voice coming out of him.

During the next hour and a half we continued our trek through the historic district of the old city and both of us fed numerous times. It was still early enough in the evening that finding plenty of prey on the streets and in the small alleys was no problem at all. We made our way up to and around the Market, then began to walk up Meeting Street. We were both very nearly satisfied by the time we walked through the gates of a small courtyard café that James mentioned he often frequented when he was hunting.

The little area was fully enclosed with a passageway on the far end leading through to the next street over. It was crowded with small round tables and wrought iron chairs. The outer side of the courtyard was lined with tropical plants and several small trees. The inner side, leading into the restaurant itself had a promenade that was supported by ten white columns that looked like smaller versions of those on the front of Whitehall. There was a three tiered fountain in the center of the courtyard that quietly bubbled adding an air of relaxation to the area.

We chose a place and took a seat at one of the small tables. It was crowded with tourists and even a few college students. Everyone was engaged in their own little world ... the tourists were having dinner and drinks while the students were mostly laughing and playing around. The air was filled with the smell of fresh brewed coffee, baking bread and fresh cookies the restaurant offered. It had a homey feel and I could see how it would be a good place to hunt or relax after a hunt as we were doing now.

A young pretty waitress, obviously one of the local college students herself, made her way through the crowd and stepped up to our table. I was nearly overcome by her scent which wafted through the air and settled around me like a shroud. It was wonderfully mouthwatering, so much so that I felt the tingle of my fangs ready to extend. I looked her over and quickly took in everything about her. She had shoulder length black hair with a reddish tint, large green eyes and a big friendly smile. She was wearing a tight white tee shirt that accented her small breasts and thin waist, tucked into a pair of black short shorts that revealed long pretty legs.

"Good evening Mr. DuBois, it's good to see you again … how are you tonight … and who's your friend," she asked happily, smiling brightly and then looking at me, her eyes wandering across me as I sat with my legs casually crossed.

"Hello Taylor," James replied flashing his brilliant smile, "I'm very well, thank you … and this is Dale Krause … a cousin of mine from up in Pennsylvania."

I tried to overcome my shock and surprise that he had given her my name and where I was from.

"He's new in town and I'm showing him some of the sights. It's been a rather pleasant day … how about yours?"

"Pretty good," she grinned, "but I'll be better in another hour and a half … I'll be on my way home then."

"You won't be walking alone in the dark will you," he asked still smiling at her.

"Yeah, but it's only about three or four blocks now that I'm back in the dorms. My roommate graduated and left, so I couldn't afford the apartment by myself anymore."

"Then I hope you have a pleasant and safe walk," he said, "but if you would like an escort, just say so."

"Thank you, I'll be careful," she smiled, "can I get you anything tonight?"

"Please, would you mind bringing us a beer?"

"Sure thing," she said, smiling back at him and then looking toward me, "but you know I'm going to have to check ID on your friend."

I saw him gaze into her eyes, holding her there for a moment. She stood perfectly still, her eyes wide and looking into his like she was lost. I saw James' eyes flare and I knew he had spoken to her mind.

"Oh, that's alright," she smiled, "I'll take your word if you say he's old enough."

"I assure you Taylor, he's older than he looks," he laughed as she turned and disappeared toward the bar.

"She knows you," I asked incredulously, "and you told her my name?"

"Of course she knows me ... I'm a regular here," he answered me laughing, "and the beer and the tip will ensure we can take our time, talk as long as we like, and not be interrupted by anyone else. We still have a while before the girls finish their evening out."

"How does she know ..." I started to ask.

"Wait ... just a moment," he said holding up his hand, "Taylor is on her way back."

Just then she twisted her way through the crowd and set two glasses and two bottles on the table in front of us.

"There you go," she said smiling as she filled each glass, then turning to go, she quickly asked, "by the way, where's Katelyn tonight?"

"She's out with a couple of friends," he answered easily, "her best friend and roommate from college just moved back from Germany and came to live with us ... and you remember Charlotte Ann, from New York ... she came down for a visit this afternoon so the three of them went for a meal and a girl's night out."

"Now *that's* a girl's night out I'd like to be a part of," Taylor laughed, "I know that with Katelyn and Charlotte Ann involved they're having a blast! How about tell them I said 'hey' and I hope they had a good time."

"Thank you Taylor, I will ... here take the beer out of this and keep the rest," James said and handed her two twenty dollar bills, adding, "can you see to it that Dale and I are not disturbed again."

"Yes sir, Mr. DuBois and thank you," she beamed, looking at the money, "I hope you have a great evening!"

I watched as she turned and began making her way back through the crowded patio. I was flabbergasted by what I had just heard and seen take place … a human had known James' name and even asked about Katelyn and Charlotte Ann. I could understand him being a regular but was still stunned at their exchange.

"Does she … know," I began.

"She has no idea," he answered me chuckling, "she only knows that Katelyn and I are lovers and that we come here regularly."

"But have you …" I started to ask.

"Yes, Katelyn and I have both taken a drink from her in the past … she's very delectable … much more so than her scent would lead you to think … in fact, she is one of the few that I have returned to for a second drink … perhaps you shall soon have the opportunity to sample a taste for yourself … and maybe even spend the night in her bed … she's as delightful and talented there as she is delicious. She knows us well enough to be comfortable around us, and she would be completely at ease spending an evening alone with either one of us as she would with Katelyn or Charlotte Ann."

I sat there still unsure what to say when I looked up and saw Taylor making her way quickly back toward our table.

"Mr. Dubois, I'm so sorry … I know you asked not to be disturbed," she began as she came up to our table. Instead of her smile and inviting scent, she looked utterly terrified and I caught the smell of absolute fear pouring off of her.

"What is it Taylor … you look upset," James asked

looking up at her.

"I know you said that if I ever needed help to just let you know," she took out her pad and pen as if she were taking an order and dropped her voice to just above a whisper as she continued, "but you see the man sitting directly behind me, the one in the far corner?"

"The one in running gear," he asked, cutting his eyes just enough to look around her.

"That's him, " she answered, still speaking low and now her voice beginning to tremble, "he's been following me for the last four days … first around campus … then I saw him when I was walking home last night … he ducked behind some trees when he saw me looking at him … and now he's here. That's my table and I'm afraid to go over and take his order."

"Taylor, I want you to do exactly as I say," James began, then taking her hand in his he continued, "be calm, just be your natural happy self …"

I watched as she completely relaxed under his thrall, the smell of her fear quickly dissipating.

"Walk over to him and take his order just as if he were any other customer," he continued soothingly, "then taking your time, casually go put it in … and when you come back he will be gone, I promise," he finished with a genuine smile and released her hand.

I watched as she did exactly as James had instructed her, and then when she had disappeared into the restaurant, he said, "Wait here on me while I go take care of her little problem."

James stood up and walked slowly over to the man, leaned over and spoke like he knew him. The two of them shook hands, the newcomer stood and I watched as James led him out of the courtyard and back out onto Meeting

Street. About fifteen minutes later, James returned, alone, smiled at me and took his seat as if nothing had happened.

"It's a very fortunate thing for Taylor that we happened to be here this evening," he said looking around for her, "he had some very nasty plans in store for our young friend. If he had had the opportunity to carry through with them, I'm afraid we would not have seen her again after tonight, and that would have been such a waste of a young life and a good person. But she won't have to worry about him now … he's resting peacefully in a dumpster several blocks away."

Just then Taylor walked uncertainly up to our table, glancing around questioningly for the stranger.

"Hi Taylor, I spoke with the man you pointed out … he has agreed to go away and never brother you again," James began, and reaching into his pocket he pulled out a one hundred dollar bill and smiling brilliantly at her, handed it over, "he asked me to give you this and to say that he is very sorry he frightened you. He insisted that you have this to cover his order and give you a large tip since he had to leave so hurriedly before it arrived."

"Thank you so much Mr. Dubois, I don't know what I would have done had you not been here," she beamed, putting the bill into her pocket, the relief literally covering her as she turned to walk away.

"Spoils of the hunt," I asked smiling when she was out of earshot.

"She might as well get some use out of it," he chuckled, "he no longer has any need for it."

We sat there, silently for a little while longer until James asked, "Do you understand what tonight and, with the exception of the unexpected interruption, the little exchange with Taylor has been all about?"

"I'm not real sure," I answered still trying to sort everything out in my head.

"I wanted to bring you out with me in order to demonstrate that it is not only possible but necessary for an immortal to socially interact with humans. Preferably you should find a location where both you and the mortals surrounding you feel comfortable, someplace that's public. A large part of maintaining your inconspicuousness is being able to carry on a simple conversation in a relaxed environment with a mortal. While Taylor thinks she knows me and considers me her friend, the only thing she really knows about me is that I am a regular customer and I have a girlfriend, still she feels relaxed enough in my presence that she does not see me as a threat to her. She has learned that I will chat with her and that I'm a good tipper. Beyond that, she doesn't suspect – or remember – anything more."

"I would never have believed what I just witnessed tonight would be possible," I began, "how do you do it?"

"It comes with age and practice," he assured me, "and the more you practice, the easier it becomes. It is a skill that you will master as you learn to assimilate and become more comfortable in the mortal world. Remember that you must change as the times change around you and that includes more than just dress and speech. Part of that changing is that you must learn to interact with them, study them and know how to imitate them. If you neglect to do so then you will begin to stand out as different ... and humans notice and remember someone that is different to them. When you and I leave here this evening none of these people will remember either one of us which means that we have successfully blended in with them."

We spent the next hour sitting comfortably in that little courtyard watching those around us and talking quietly. I watched James as much as the people that came and went, milling about the area, comparing his actions to theirs. I saw that he would occasionally pick up his glass and take a quick drink. He would move in his chair, leaning back, and crossing his legs. Other times he would lean forward as if we were in deep conversation. He pointed out different groups and how they behaved. I began to note mannerisms, both his and theirs, and commit them to memory for the next time.

Finally, James stood and speaking quietly to me said, "I think you have learned enough for one evening. The girls should be back from their hunting trip now, so I suppose that we should return too."

"Good night Mr. Dubois ... and thank you again," Taylor said with a warm smile glancing up from a table she was wiping, "and the same to you too Dale Krause ... I hope to see you again soon too."

"Thank you and good night, Taylor," I replied with a happy smile.

"I hope you have a good evening Taylor," James answered with a knowing grin, "we'll see you next time."

he next few days passed quickly and I began to get accustomed to being at Whitehall again. Still Charlotte Ann and I began to make plans for returning to the city in order to continue with some of the things I still needed to 'catch up' on. We had returned from an early hunt in the tourist district one afternoon and, relaxing on the veranda talking about what we would do when we returned to the city. I noticed James and Katelyn slowly approaching while we talked. I quickly become aware of Katelyn standing very close beside James, with her arm around his waist, and grinning happily.

"I get the distinct feeling that we are about to be ambushed," Charlotte Ann chuckled softly, nodding her head toward them.

"Charlotte Ann, it's such a pleasure to have you and Dale with us again," James began, "Katelyn and I have been talking and we would like to ask a favor ... how would the two of you feel about remaining at Whitehall for the foreseeable future? You know there is plenty of room for you."

"Dale and I have already begun making plans and talking about returning to the city but you know that if you need me I will try to do anything you ask ..." Charlotte Ann replied looking at both of them with a knowing smile, "of course Dale will have to decide for himself, whether or not he wishes to stay. Is there an issue or a problem?"

"Oh none at all," Katelyn added with a happy smile, "but you know that I'm still pretty new to this life ..."

"Yes you are ... *little sister*," I interjected with a laugh, "and I just found out that tiny tidbit right before we left to come down and help out with Lexie."

"Maybe ... but I'm still prettier than you are," she laughed and playfully stuck her tongue out at me before returning her attention to Charlotte Ann, "and you know there's a lot I still have to learn ..."

"Yes," Charlotte Ann said, her smile beginning to grow, "and ..."

"Well, although Lexi is adapting incredibly to immortality," Katelyn continued, "she is still sleeping after every hunt ... and I can't possibly teach her everything she needs to know either ... and there's so much more for her to discover and learn about."

"I'm sure there is," Charlotte Ann continued smiling.

"I believe that the four of us, with our combined knowledge, would be able to assist Lexi in making an even quicker and easier transition," James spoke up now smiling.

"I'm sure we have a wealth of sharable information," Charlotte Ann agreed, and then looking at me asked, "Dale, what do you think, would you be amendable to remaining here and assisting?"

"I'm going to stay wherever you are Charlotte Ann,

and if you think I have something more to offer Lexi, I'll be happy to do whatever I can. Besides," I looked at Katelyn and added a grin, "it probably wouldn't be right for us to abandon James with *two* newborn fledglings on his hands would it?"

"That's awesome," Katelyn nearly shouted laughingly, "I mean … it's just that … well you know … maybe with more of us around Lexi will become more comfortable in her immortality."

"Yes … and I'm sure it has absolutely nothing to do with the two of you just wishing to have us stay here," Charlotte Ann asked smiling and looking right at Katelyn.

I looked at James who had now stepped back and was barely able to contain a smile.

"There might be just a little bit of that, too," Katelyn said finally cracking and laughing.

"Then it's decided," Charlotte Ann chuckled, "we shall remain here for as long as you need us."

The following days quickly turned into weeks and as they did the five of us began to blend into a family. Then over the next few weeks Lexi began to become a real life lesson for me too. I paid close attention to her, observing with interest as she continued to grow into the immortal life. It amazed me the way the three of them closed ranks around her, protecting and teaching her as she began to mature. I saw them do things for her that I didn't realize a maker should do in assisting a newborn to adjust to this life … things that made it easier … things that I never experienced with my maker … and it made me want to help her as much as I could too.

Lexi spent most of her time over the next few weeks

with Charlotte Ann and Katelyn practicing at becoming comfortable as an immortal in the mortal world. The two of them sheltered her, never being more than an arms-length away. Often they would spend entire days together and go down into the historic district on 'self-guided' walking tours that more often than not turned into hunting trips.

Then when Lexi began to feel more and more comfortable among mortals again, James would go out with her. He taught her, the same as he did me, how to become more confident and blend into a crowd. When they were together he would allow her to venture a little further away from him, much the same as he did with me. It was sometimes like training two children at once. Lexi was comfortable knowing he was close by and often walked as much as a block or two in front of him. As a result, her comfort and confidence levels soared and very soon she was living happily and comfortably among mortals again.

Her hunting skills began to improve quickly and soon she developed her own style by taking a little from each of the talents we all had to offer. When she went hunting all four of us took turns going out with her. Since hunting was one of my better skills, and that was because of nature and not nurture, I felt like I finally had something substantial that I could offer her.

I can hunt during the day but I prefer to do my hunting and feeding at night, it's just the way I learned it from the beginning. So when it was my turn to go out with Lexi we always began our trips just after full darkness. I shared with her all the little knacks I had learned over the years. I showed her how to blend into the shadows and to silently approach her prey staying just out of their sight. I taught her about the different phases of the moon and had her watch to see how each had its individual effect on humans. She was amazed to learn that the moon actually did effect the behavior of mortals.

Lexi preferred to hunt during the full moon and I suspect that was because her first hunt with Katelyn and Charlotte Ann was under a full moon. However, my favorite time to hunt was during the new moon, the dark of the moon as some call it, when the nights are at their blackest. It was during those dark nights that I taught her how to stalk her prey, to suddenly appear out of the darkness, grab them, feed and disappear back into the darkness again.

I enjoyed our trips out as Lexi continued to learn more and become a better hunter … and I soon noticed a subtle change taking place in me, too. The more time I spent with her and everyone else the more I began to feel like a part of them. I no longer thought of 'me' and 'them', I thought of 'us' … I thought of family. I soon felt that as a part of the family I was actually contributing something and helping another member of the family to succeed. I experienced a happiness that I hadn't had in decades.

I soon moved our hunting lessons from the outside to the inside. I instructed her in the things I had learned in the city about the shopping malls and attracting prey there. We talked about the theaters and using the back rows as a place to feed. She had already taken some of Katelyn's acting skills and Charlotte Ann's alluring sex appeal combining them into a deadly blend. When she added in the techniques I offered, and interspersed them with the skills James had taught her, she became a very dangerous predator … not to mention a real pleasure to hunt with.

She and I would often go to one of the local malls and spend an entire afternoon there. We looked like any other young couple hanging out, laughing, talking and playing our way through the mall. While the casual observer would have thought that we were young lovers, we were actually picking out and discussing the pros and cons of various mortals as prey. I think because we were both young and, in our own way, still learning, it made our time together that much more enjoyable and I began to look forward to our hunting trips. Lexi became a real delight to watch when she would venture out into the crowd and use her newly learned skills to feed. I was proud of her accomplishments and told her as much.

The first huge milestone that Lexi had to overcome in her immortal development came a little over a month after Charlotte Ann and I had decided to stay in Charleston. Lexi's parents had been informed that she had died while undergoing medical treatment for the cancer. They of course planned a funeral and memorial service for her. They had invited Katelyn and James to attend and both had agreed to be there. Lexi made it known that if it was possible she also would like to attend. It surprised me that she would want to be present at her own funeral, but Charlotte Ann told her that if that was what she wanted, she could make it possible.

Charlotte Ann continued to talk at length with her over the next couple of days about her decision. She wanted to prepare her for what she would see there. She told her that while it would help provide the needed clean break with her mortal life, it would also likely be a painful and emotional experience for her, one she needed to seriously consider before making a commitment to attend. Lexi would not relent saying that she felt like it was something she had to do for herself.

The day that we were to attend Lexi's funeral was almost surreal for me. When I was a human I had never attended many funerals and certainly not my own. When we arrived at the cemetery in Savannah there was already a large crowd of at least a couple hundred people gathered at the gravesite. James and Katelyn had arrived before us and were sitting quietly in the last row of chairs. Charlotte Ann hid the three of us in her shield and we stood at the front of the gathering and watched.

Just after the beginning of the memorial service Lexi put her arm around me and clung to me for the remainder of the service. I put my arm around her shoulders and held her, trying to comfort and reassure her through it all. It was difficult enough for me, and I know it had to be for her, to watch as her parents wept openly for their little girl. I wondered if my parents had done the same for me all those years ago.

I felt the waves of intense sorrow flooding through her as she stood next to me, my arm wrapped protectively around her. We listened while her parents and friends spoke about her life and how she had touched each one of them. A couple of times during the service, it became too much for her to endure and she hid her face in my chest, her blood red tears flowing freely. When she did I tightened my hold on her, wishing I could shield her completely from what was happening, instead I tried the best I knew how to console her.

When the service had ended she watched without a sound, her tears still flowing silently down her cheeks, as her parents and others slowly departed again to their mortal lives. When there was only the three of us left standing on the windswept hilltop, she stepped forward and stood, her head bowed, silently crying and looking at the gravestone with her name on it. Then she quietly stooped down, her tears slowly dripping on the ground, and silently traced out her name engraved in the marker. After a few moments she stood and turned, looked at Charlotte Ann and bravely said, "I think I'm finished here … my human life is over … this represents who I was … not who I am … please take me home now."

When we returned to Whitehall after the funeral I went and sought out a quiet place at the back of the property next to a slowly moving stream. I sat there uninterrupted and thought about what had happened today … the things I had seen and felt … the more I thought about the day the more I noticed there was a strange stirring inside me that I didn't understand. The funeral had touched something deep inside me and my emotions were in a stormy turmoil.

Lexi's despair at what was happening had awakened feelings in me that I thought were long gone. I recalled the feelings of hurt and sorrow that were pouring off of her, sobbing as she clung closely to me. They tore through me, making me feel what I thought were long lost human emotions again. But strangest of all, while I had stood there trying to comfort Lexi, my thoughts kept returning to … Becky.

I continued to sit there next to the stream for some time, watching the water slowly flowing by, lost in my thoughts and feelings. I was trying desperately to sort out what had happened today, what I had experienced, when I felt Charlotte Ann's hands on my shoulders. I looked up at her and smiled as she stepped around in front of me and stooped down. She reached out to me, taking one of my hands in hers, the other soft hand gently caressing the side of my face.

"Lexi wasn't the only one deeply affected by today's

events," she spoke softly in the cool evening air, "I watched the expressions on your face and felt your emotions throughout the memorial. I thought perhaps after a little quiet time alone you would like to have someone to talk to about today, too."

I looked at her and again saw my little lifesaver. Her eyes, sparkling brightly, were fixed intently on me and she had a caring smile playing at the corners of her mouth.

"Thank you for coming … I'm glad you're here," I replied, "I was just sitting and thinking."

"I've been watching you today Dale," she spoke slowly and softly, "I know that the events of this afternoon had a huge impact on you. It wasn't just Lexi that had a life changing experience today … you did as well … something touched your soul … but it didn't stop there, it kept going further down and settled very deep inside you … something good that you probably don't recognize yet … but I do and I'm so very happy for you."

I was puzzled at her words but quickly pushed them away as she turned and took a seat on the ground beside me. I put my arm around her and pulled her close against me. I nuzzled into her thick hair and softly breathed in her ear, "I love you Charlotte Ann … so very much."

"I know you do … and I love you, too," she whispered back.

We sat there, silently wrapped in each other's arms, for the remainder of the afternoon and into the early darkness of the evening. Finally, she stood and extending a hand to me said, "Come on Dale, the night is young, the moon is out … go with me … lets you and I go down to the port facility and hunt."

We spent the remainder of the night around the docks and shipping terminals. As it turned out we both had a successful night and when it was over I had put aside the strange feeling that had flooded me the day before. Finally, in the early morning hours, just after daylight, Charlotte Ann and I returned to Whitehall, our thirst fully satisfied and ready to face another day.

Chapter Twenty~One

he longer I remained in Charleston, the more I began to like it. I began to feel like more than just a guest at Whitehall. I was making memories there – good ones – and so soon came to realize that it was home; I lived there and belonged there. I became more comfortable with the surroundings, began to settle in, and soon Whitehall became as much a part of me as I was a part of it.

I soon decided that staying in Charleston might not be a problem for me. It was smaller than the city and it was warmer which made it nice. The weather, hot or cold, doesn't have any effect on me, but now that I was able to be in the daylight, the blue skies and sunshine, certainly did. The historic district also offered a more comfortable atmosphere for hunting and feeding because the various clubs and bars were smaller and more intimate. So considering all that and given my choice, I would be staying in Charleston.

One night a few days after Lexi's 'funeral' all of us went out for a night of hunting. We decided that Charlotte Ann and I would hunt together and Lexi would join Katelyn for the night. James, unless he's hunting with Katelyn, really prefers to hunt alone, so he went his own direction.

The four of us began about half way down King Street a couple of hours before midnight. We paired off as agreed, Katelyn and Lexi would be going back up the street, Charlotte Ann and I, were going down the street. We were dressed as college students because this late most of the tourists were gone for the night.

I watched as Katelyn and Lexi began walking up King Street laughing and chatting like two close friends and I was reminded of the first time they had come to New York for a weekend. So much had changed since then and I smiled to myself as I observed both of them comfortably slip into their hunting routines.

They were having a good time together as they concentrated on looking for a place to hunt although both had already agreed that they were going to The Silver Dollar. It was a well-known college bar and hangout, so both of them felt comfortable there surrounded by partying students. Just before they turned to go into The Silver Dollar, Katelyn looked back over her shoulder at me, and her voice floated softly across the distance, "Hey Dale … just so you know, I've already claimed your morning, so please don't make any plans … have a great night and feed well … I'll see you after the hunt!"

"Yeah sure, thanks … and you have a good hunt too," I laughed back wondering what she could possibly have in mind for the next day.

Then beginning our own trek out into the historic district, Charlotte Ann and I casually walked further down

King. We walked close, our hands intertwined, laughing and chatting together and looking like a couple of love struck students out for an evening stroll, quickly putting some distance between us and the other end of the street. We crossed into Marion Square and the two of us separated, agreeing to meet on the other side. I stood back and continued to watch Charlotte Ann as she made her way through the park.

It wasn't long until I saw a man walk up to her and start talking. She had found her first prey and, guiding him to a darkened area under some trees, she took him. I thought how much they looked like two lovers, sitting together on a park bench, as she drank slowly from him. When she was finished she stood up and slowly walked away leaving him sitting on the bench.

We met up again on the far side of the park and continued our hunt, strolling easily down Meeting Street, turning on Broad Street and walking toward The Blind Tiger Pub. They were hosting a large party and the crowd was spilling out of the main building and into the street. We quickly made our way inside and found that both sides of the club and the rear courtyard were just as crowded. The music was loud, the lights were dim, and it was the perfect place to hunt.

We separated once indoors, each of us taking a side, and quickly blended into the youthful crowd. We stayed there, mingling with the partiers until just before closing. Both of us fed several times as we worked our way through the crowd. I was particularly successful in the back courtyard where it was easy to get my prey into the shadows. I took anything from a single mouthful to a couple of pints from each of my chosen victims and when we left no one even knew we had been there. It still amazed me that two immortals could go into a building full of humans, work our way through it, feeding as we went with no one paying us the least bit of attention.

Early the next morning after returning to Whitehall, James and I were sitting comfortably in the parlor where I was relating to him the activities of my previous night's hunt. James still had a fresh glow to his skin from his own hunt so I knew that Charlotte Ann and I were not the only ones who had had a good hunt together and fed well.

While we were talking Katelyn walked quietly into the parlor and took a seat in James' lap. She placed one arm around his neck, and kissed him lightly on the lips, "Good morning lover, I see you had a good hunt last night," she said with a happy smile.

"It appears that I'm not the only one either," James answered, giving her a look of pure adoration as she cuddled close to him while waiting politely for us to finish our conversation.

I smiled when I saw that her skin was richly tanned and I knew that she had fed extremely good last night. When she had been a human she had a natural medium tan, and now when she fed well it manifested by returning her skin nearly to the same tanned tone she had then.

"So anyway, Charlotte Ann and I had a very smooth and productive hunt last night," I continued, happily turning my attention back to James, "we were in the lower end of the district, at several of the bars and eateries. She and I both had a veritable smorgasbord of various delights! I found it to be a little heavy on the blondes but I did manage to sprinkle in a few brunettes, and finally, just for variety, tossed in a couple of redheads and all of us had a good time."

"Dale! You are so awful," Katelyn laughed at my description of the night.

"Even so, I fed well, and the important thing is that, thanks to you and Charlotte Ann, I left none of them any the worse for wear," I smiled, continuing as I glanced at her, "I fed until I couldn't feed anymore."

"I do know that Dale here is a very talented hunter," James added with a chuckle, "he seems to be very attractive to the girls. They actually come to him ... of course that does take a little of the fun out of the hunt."

"Yeah," I added with a big grin and a pretended air of superiority, "and in addition, I got a handful of names and phone numbers, too! I guess when you got it, you got it!"

Katelyn looked at James with a laugh and said, "You men are all the same, you never change do you?"

"Never," he answered her with a smile and a light kiss on her lips, "were it not for you ladies we would all be absolutely incorrigible!"

"Hum, guess that means I probably shouldn't use those names and numbers, huh?" I added with a slow innocent grin.

Katelyn burst out laughing, "Yeah, you think? It probably wouldn't make the Top Ten List of good ideas Dale! I believe if I were you I would put them in the fireplace and forget all about them. After all, Charlotte Ann's not ready to share you just yet, and I know you wouldn't want her get jealous now would you?"

"I concur wholeheartedly with Katelyn," James said smiling and chuckling, "I've seen Charlotte Ann get jealous and it's not a pretty sight."

"Well, now that we have that taken care of," Katelyn smiled happily as she slid off James' lap, stood, and extended her hand toward me, "it's such a beautiful day out Dale ... and if you're not too busy to take a pretty girl for a stroll, I'd like to collect that walk in the sunshine you promised me."

I looked at James and he chuckled and said, "Please go with her ... if you haven't already learned from Charlotte Ann, it's probably best just to do whatever they want ... I hope you enjoy your morning."

Katelyn hooked her arm in mine and we started toward the front door. We stepped out onto the porch, passed between two of the huge white columns, down the steps, and started toward the fountain in the drive. It was still early and there were a few scudding clouds partially covering the sun, still the warmth felt good and I smiled happily.

I was almost giddy that after so many years I was able to be in the daylight ... and with Katelyn. She and I had not spent a lot of time together since my adoption. In fact, I had spent more time with Lexi while she learned to hunt than I had with Katelyn. Which also meant that I didn't know her as well as I did James and Charlotte Ann. Katelyn was the only one of the family that I had never hunted with ... and I knew that she would make an interesting hunting partner. In the meantime, I was looking forward to our walk and an opportunity for both of us getting to know each other even better.

Suddenly, with no warning, the clouds parted, and the sun broke through bathing us in brilliant morning sunbeams. Katelyn looked over at me and with a laugh said, "Look Dale you're in the sunshine ... and you don't sparkle!"

I wasn't real sure what she meant by that but I laughed with her and answered, "Yeah and I'm not exploding into flames, either!"

Although I had been regularly going out in the daylight it still astonished me every time I did that I could actually walk in the full sun. I had been told for so many years that I had to stay hidden in the darkness or else I would burn from the inside out.

"So just take a look at you," Katelyn laughed happily again, "bright sunshine and no sunglasses either! And to think not too long ago you thought you'd never see the sun again!"

"Or walk along with a pretty girl that I wasn't about to kill," I answered her with a wink and a laugh.

"Yeah, I guess there was that part too," she replied softly, "I'm sorry I didn't mean to bring back bad memories."

"Don't be … it was all I knew … but now, thanks to you, when I look at some girl, I see chocolate cake to be sampled instead of a rare steak to be devoured," I laughed out loud, "but seriously Katelyn, it was nice to learn that I wasn't as bad as I thought I was … although, to be totally honest, I do still enjoy the occasions when I can devour the steak instead of tasting the chocolate …"

"That's alright," she replied smiling, "we all have to enjoy a steak every once in a while … it keeps our life interesting."

"Even so, discovering that I really am alive … and most importantly that I have a family again … has made my life more than interesting."

"I'm glad you became a part of our family too," she said smiling, "you're fun … kind of like having a little brother around."

Then she stopped and turned toward me and continued, "But Dale, I have to tell you, that first night I met you, you were so scary ... and I was so frightened of you," she confessed.

"Me," I asked shocked, "why?"

"Yes, you ... because you were so different to us ... I was still a newborn, only about two weeks old ... I was comfortable with James and Charlotte Ann ... like you, they were all I knew ... but you ... you were the epitome of what I had always envisioned a vampire to be like."

"You're kidding right," I chuckled slowly, "that is so funny Katelyn, because if you had only known how terrified I was of you that night ... I was literally shaking inside ... so much so that if you had jumped at me and said 'Boo!' I would have ran away and never looked back. I was so relieved when Charlotte Ann finally got me out of the same room with you ... especially after she mentioned that your bloodline was almost six hundred years long ..."

"Yeah but I bet she was able to make you forget all your fear of me wasn't she," she interjected with a laugh.

"In short order and in ways I never thought possible," I agreed chuckling, "still, at the time, I thought you were probably the oldest and most powerful vampire in the world. I didn't know until much later that you were only a couple of weeks old and had just returned from your first hunt."

Katelyn turned and looked at me, her eyes got wide and with an evil smile she showed her fangs and started wiggling her fingers at me and said, "Oooo ... I'm going to chase you my little pretty and when I catch you I shall suck the marrow out of your bones ..."

Then before she could continue we both broke out in wild laughter at her acting.

"Well, I suppose that's a lesson for both of us not to judge our own kind ... especially by how we look or sound," she said.

We continued to walk on for a little while skirting the edge of the shadowed allee and across the front lawn. I was enjoying the feel of the sun's warmth on my face. When we approached a small tree, I noticed a dark shadow flutter across her face for a brief moment. She nodded toward the tree and said, "There's where I had my first supernatural experience, although I didn't know it at the time."

"What happened," I asked.

"I was bitten by a big snake and almost died."

"You were still human?"

"Yes, that was before I even began to think that James was anything except the most astonishing man in the world and I was the luckiest girl alive to have him."

"Why didn't you die?"

"The most astonishing man in the world saved my life," she smiled at the memory, "I was delirious from the venom by the time he got to me, but still coherent enough to know I was dying. I could feel the darkness closing in all around me. He held my head up and poured a cup of anti-venom down my throat. I didn't find out until much later that he had given me his blood to drink. It killed the poison and saved my life."

"Is that when you were changed," I questioned curiously.

"No, that came later, after I discovered his true nature and asked him to turn me."

"You wanted to be like this," I asked almost shocked.

"Dale, you have to understand what my situation was like at that time. My life was a complete wreck ... my parents had been murdered ... I had been forced to sell our home and our business ... then I had to pack up what little I had left and move away ... and on top of all of that the court system later dropped all charges and released the two men who had killed my parents."

"Oh, that had to hurt to see them escape justice that way," I commented.

"They didn't get away," she smiled hugely at me, "James located them and they became my first hunt and kill … I got both of them the same night."

"I'm glad for you that they didn't get away, I hope you played with your dinner a little before you ate it," I laughed.

"Let's just say that my parents never had time to be frightened before they died," she commented seriously, and then adding a grin continued, "but I made sure those two did … you know, a vengeful vampire can be a terrifying thing. And then to add insult to injury, I placed both of their nude bodies in bed together, all wrapped up in each other's arms as a parting gift for their families."

"Now that's funny," I laughed, "I love the way you think!"

"So anyway," she continued her story chuckling softly, "the only family I had remaining after the robbery and murder was my aunt and uncle who gladly took me in and tried to help me readjust. With their help, I was trying to put the shambles of my life back together again when I suddenly met this magnificent man."

"The very first time I met James, he touched something deep inside my soul, and I soon fell in love with him. It seemed like something good was finally coming out of all the bad that had happened to me. I felt protected when I was around him and I wanted to spend the rest of my life with him. Of course, I was shocked when I finally put all the pieces together and found out he was an immortal, but nevertheless, I still loved him and I wanted to be *like* him so I could be *with* him. Now we have more than just a single lifetime to spend together … we have eternity."

"It's easy to see that you and James have a very special kind of love for each other," I replied.

"Yes we do, Dale, we are each a part of the other … we know what each other thinks, feels, and is about to do … although we are two separate individuals, we really are one … and I think that is what being mates is all about. The decision I made, to give up one life and accept the life he offered me, is one that I will never regret."

"Charlotte Ann has told me that one day I'll find my mate," I said slowly, "and when I do I hope that we share that same kind of special love that you and James have."

"When you find that one unique person Dale, it's the most wonderful love in the world," she assured me with a happy smile, "and it's so much more than just physical – although that part's pretty great too … it's a much deeper kind of love. The best way I know how to explain it to you is that Fate finally brings two halves together to make a whole."

We spent the next couple of hours together as we continued our walk around the grounds with the sun shining and both of us happily talking and sharing stories of things that happened in our lives … human and immortal. She shared with me what it had been like growing up in Atlanta. She talked about the hopelessness of being alone when her parents died. She told about the thrill of meeting James and what it was like for her when she turned. She confessed how broken she had been when she learned of Lexi's cancer. She related her happiness when she found out she could offer Lexi 'The Gift' and how it delighted her when she accepted.

In turn I told her about my life in a small mining

town, all about my parents and sisters, and how I never realized that we were poor. She already knew about the attack and my turning. I saw red tears filling her eyes when I told her about my first kill and how I had felt afterward. I finished with how fortunate I was to have been found and adopted by all of them.

When our walk was over and we returned to the house I knew that mine and Katelyn's relationship had changed. We had transformed from two immortals sharing a house and became a brother and sister sharing a home. She no longer just *felt* like family, she had *become* family. I loved her and would have protected her just the same as I would have my human sisters. Once again I became aware of the loneliness that I had lived with for the last thirty five years and that it was fading further into the past as I was drawn deeper into a proper family relationship.

here were still many lessons remaining for me to learn while I continued the 'fitting in' process with my new family. Most of the time, I found myself on the receiving end of the instructions regarding immortal life and how it should be lived. Due to my very patient teachers, my level of maturity greatly increased as they trained me in a life that I had been living for nearly forty years but knew next to nothing about. Occasionally though, I did get the opportunity to pass along some guidance of my own.

Lexi had decided, some several months after she had been turned, that she was lonely and wanted to begin searching for a mate of her own. Then one afternoon while she was at the mall hunting, she had met Mikey … a human. She had been enamored of him from the time she saw him. They soon began seeing each other and had dated almost continuously since. I had my own views on mortal and immortal liaisons and so I quickly developed a fear of where her relationship might be going and how it might end. Nevertheless, since she appeared to be happy with the situation I kept my thoughts to myself. I did however, watch the situation closely. I would do all in my power to see that he remained a mortal. However, if he tried to hurt her, she was family and family comes first, therefore I had no qualms about killing him if it became necessary. He was after all just another human as far as I was concerned.

I had accepted the necessity of Katelyn turning Lexi to save her life, and in the same situation I can't say I wouldn't have done the same thing. Even so, due to my own experience, I was still vehemently opposed to bringing a human over and especially just to have a companion. So when I learned of Lexi's intent to turn Mikey, I decided that she and I probably needed to have a serious talk about the situation.

The opportunity came late one night when she had returned from a date with him. I stood in the shadows without a sound and watched her as she sat quietly on the rear porch happily lost in her thoughts. Finally I stepped out of the darkness and soundlessly joined her. I sat with her for a while casually chatting and waiting for her to turn the topic to Mikey, which of course didn't take long because he had become her favorite subject to talk about. When she began her chatter, I continued to listen intently to her as she talked about him. There was no doubt that she was a young girl – and one that was deeply in love.

"Oh, Dale, it would be so wonderful for me if I could bring Mikey over," she said, "we would be so happy and together forever."

"Lexi, please, don't turn a human," I almost begged her, "and especially not if it's just to have a companion."

"Dale, I was alone most of my human life and didn't

have many opportunities for relationships," she continued, "and now that I'm an immortal, although I have all of y'all, I sometimes feel more alone than ever."

While we continued to talk I silently reached out and put my arm around her shoulders, drawing her against me. She cuddled in close to me, putting her arm around my waist and resting her head on my shoulder. I breathed in her soft rose petal scent and my heart began to break for her as she continued.

"Please try to understand why I want a companion. I was an only child and I didn't get to date much when I was a teenager. I looked like a little girl until my last year of high school … and nobody wanted to take a date to the prom that looked like a twelve year old. When I went to college, I only dated one or two guys and never anything seriously or long term. I realize that I have all of you and you're my family, but that's a different kind of love to that of a companion or a mate."

"Lexi," I began slowly, trying to explain without hurting her, "please let me be Mikey's advocate and plead his case for him. I'm begging for his life. I understand why you were brought over, and I don't have a problem with that. But I want you to understand why I am so adamantly against just turning a mortal. I hated my maker with everything in me because of what he did to me. I promise you there was anything but love for him on my part. I would not want you to have that same kind of hatred directed toward you by Mikey."

"But there's a difference for me and Mikey," she said hopefully, "we know and love each other already. If I bring him over, we will have each other forever and our love will never die."

"Lexi, it's called 'The Change' for a reason," I replied,

"because everything changes, and if you turn a human just to have a companion, you take the chance of being more alone and less loved by that person than you've ever been. Lil sis, I'm an immortal because somebody wanted a companion … and they chose me … and there was nothing I could do about it. It sounds like you have chosen Mikey and if you have, there is nothing he can do about it either. You are the only one that still has a choice in the matter … and only you can still choose to do something about it and not allow it to happen."

"Yeah, but Dale you have Charlotte Ann and Katelyn has James," she whispered slowly, trying to hold back her tears, "and I just want to be like all of you … I want a companion too."

"Lexi, while it's true that James and Katelyn are mates – and that's forever – but please remember, Charlotte Ann and I are just lovers – and that's only temporary. I know and understand that if her mate, Ferdinand, were to come back into her life, I would have to step aside because they *are* mates. If that were to ever happen, then, like you I would be alone too. But Charlotte Ann has reassured me that should that day ever come, Fate will not leave me alone but will direct my life until my mate enters it. I think that I can say the same to you, trust Fate Lexi – it gave you a second chance at life and brought you to where you are now – and I don't think it will ever leave you alone. You just have to wait for Fate's own time."

I decided that the best way for her to understand what I was trying to say and the possibilities she faced was to show her. She needed to see what I had endured before she made an irreversible decision. So as I held her small body snuggled close to me I laid my head on top of hers and opened my mind and my thoughts to her.

I began to play for her the horror movie that had been my life. I allowed her to see the hurt and the confusion I had lived with in the beginning. She saw the memories I held of my first kill and how terrified I was of what I had done and what I had become. But most of all I let her see the hatred I had for my maker. I showed her the abuse I had endured from him. I laid bare everything about me and who I was, not holding anything back from her. I permitted her to see more about me than I had ever revealed to anyone, including during my most private conversations with Charlotte Ann. I was trying desperately to save a human's life.

When it was over she clung to me and softly whispered, "Thank you for sharing your life with me. I knew that you had had a difficult time. But Dale I had no idea it had been so terrible for you ... you've suffered so much ... our experiences of being born into our new lives, and how we were brought into this world, are as different as night and day."

"That's because you had someone that loved you, Lexi," I began, "and when you were brought over it was done out of love and necessity to save your life. Every day since you've been brought over you have been surrounded by love and taken care of by those around you ... none of that ever happened for me."

"Dale, I'm so sorry you had such a terrible experience," she whispered. Then I felt her tighten her arm around my waist and she cuddled a little closer against me as she now tried to comfort me. We sat there silently no words necessary, until after the sun broke the horizon and began its daily trip across the sky.

Lexi stayed away from me, and Mikey, for the next couple of days but I knew her mind was already made up. For good or bad, she was going to offer him immortality. I sadly stood aside and silently watched her go early one afternoon. She had gone to his house with the intent of proposing that she turn him so they could be together forever. Later that evening when she returned there was a flurry of activity in the big parlor. I didn't go to investigate, but judging from the sudden heaviness and unexpected discomfort I felt settling in my chest, I could easily assume that her trip had not turned out the way she had hoped.

James and I walked to the front porch and took up positions across from each other, each of us leaning against one of the huge columns and silently stood there waiting for the tempest to pass. Suddenly the two screen doors that covered the massive front entrance exploded outward and Katelyn abruptly came thundering out through them.

"Where're you going," I asked her, "and is Lexi alright?"

"No, she isn't alright ... and I'm going into town to see Michael," she hissed, "he's about to find out what being a monster really all about."

"Perhaps I should go with you," I volunteered with a smile, "I do have a little more experience at killing than you do."

"I'm not going to kill him ... I can't," she said with a clenched jaw, "but only because I promised Charlotte Ann I wouldn't ... and at this point, that's the only thing saving his lousy life!"

"I didn't make any kind of promise," I said grimly.

"No, Dale, thank you for the offer, but this has to be between me and him," she answered, "but trust ... after what he said to Lexi and the names he called her, if I were going to kill him, I wouldn't need any help. Right now, I would love nothing more than to sink my fangs into his neck. Instead, I'm only going to make him extremely uncomfortable ... but only because I promised not to kill him ... still he will get a small taste of exactly what a monster really can be."

And then she was gone, disappeared just that quickly. I smiled at her reaction but remembering my initial fear of her, was glad at the same time it wasn't me on the receiving end of her wrath. I decided that I should go inside and see what had happened. I went to the parlor and saw Charlotte Ann standing at one of the windows, her telephone in her hand, talking softly to someone. The room was full of Lexi's scent but also filled with the smell of immortal blood which I hoped, for Mikey's sake, had only come from her tears. Because if he had drawn blood from her in any manner, promise or not, he was a dead man walking.

When Charlotte Ann had finished and put her phone away she turned to me with a smile.

"Charlotte Ann ..." I asked slowly looking around, "where's Lexi?"

"She's gone to rest," she answered, nodding toward the book shelves, "in there."

I knew about the little hidden room behind the massive shelves and what it contained. I also knew what Lexi was trying to do ... I too had tried to escape the pain by going to sleep ... and it didn't work. I continued to stand there for a few minutes considering the situation. When I felt Charlotte Ann pass behind me as she left the room, I made up my mind and decided what I was going to do.

I stepped over and slid my hand behind some of the books and threw the lock that secured the shelves. They opened and I stepped through into the unlighted space inside. I could sense Lexi's presence but at the same time was nearly overcome with the sensation of heavy sadness and utter despair that permeated the room. The anguish I felt was so extreme and bore down on me so hard that I thought it would make me cry ... the hopelessness she had carried with her covered me like a blanket.

I knew that even in the near death like sleep Lexi could still sense my presence in the room so I stepped cautiously over to her coffin so that she would not think I was disturbing her resting place and become alarmed. I stood quietly beside it for a moment then reached out and gently laid my hands on the polished lid. When I did I literally felt her grief and despondency from Mikey's rejection move up and through my arms settling heavily in my chest. I stood there, both hands resting lightly on her coffin and wishing there was some way that I could alleviate her misery.

I looked and saw the silver plate embedded in the top and spoke the words as I traced the heavy engraving with my finger ... 'Little Lexi', it read, 'Friends Forever' ... and I sensed her relax at my presence while at the same time she continued her descent deeper into the immortal sleep ... and her absence washed through me.

"Lexi," I quietly whispered into the darkness, my head bowed over her coffin, "I know that you can hear me ... I've done what you are doing ... I know the pain you are feeling right now ... I've felt my own and I feel yours now ... I've experienced the bleakness ... the hopelessness ... but what you are doing doesn't help, it doesn't make it go away. Please Lexi, you're my family ... my little sister ... wake up and come back to us ... I'll help you face whatever you need to face to heal and move on into the future."

I continued to stand there for a few more minutes

before turning to leave. When I did, I saw Charlotte Ann framed in the opening, leaning against one side and intently watching me. I saw the sparkle in her eyes from the dimly reflected light of the little hidden room. With an understanding smile she opened her arms to me. I stepped into her embrace and felt a tear run down my face as she held me.

"I tried Charlotte Ann ..." I began, "I tried so hard to talk her out of going to Mikey ... I knew she would get hurt and I didn't want to see that happen and now she's gone away."

"She'll come back soon," she assured me as we stood there together. She looked up at me and I was pulled into her eyes by her smile, both were dazzling in the brightly lit outer room. I couldn't help but think how beautiful she was, as she leaned against me. Then, our arms still around each other, we turned to walk away, and the big shelves began closing silently behind us.

"Your soul is filled with tenderness and goodness ... so much that you are able to feel her pain Dale ... when she hurts, you hurt with her ... and that's a good thing," she whispered softly as we walked out together.

The atmosphere seemed to be heavy throughout the house after Lexi retreated to her coffin to sleep, almost as if there had been an actual death in our family. The house itself reflected the destitute sadness that we were all feeling – a sense of helplessness for one of our own. I knew that Lexi would come back, in time, but Lexi had to be ready to come back. I also remembered that when this life had gotten to be too much for me, I had spent the greater part a decade lying in a grave. I hoped that Lexi wouldn't be gone for that long.

Later that evening, the heaviness seemed to lift just a bit after Katelyn's return from Mikey's house. We all seemed to get somewhat of a pick-me-up when she related her encounter with him to all of us. I still wanted to kill him for hurting Lexi, but Katelyn explained that at the very least he was now fully acquainted with the concept of exactly what a monster was or was not. He was also certain of the fact that Lexi did in no manner fill that description. She detailed that Lexi's revenge had been set up and was in place … but it would have to be Lexi's decision whether or not to serve it.

Chapter Twenty~Three

 few weeks passed after that and Lexi did wake, but just after she rejoined us she announced that she had decided she was going to leave Whitehall and the family. Her hurt was still deep and very painful and she didn't wish to remain in or around Charleston and the bad memories it now held. She needed time to heal, to be alone and to think through it all. She told us that she thought the best place for her to heal would be Savannah. It was a place she knew and was comfortable with. Although no longer a human she was going to return to her human home and her parents. While she was there she was going to attempt to live as close to a human life as possible.

None of us wanted to see her leave the family, but our natural sense of independence being what it is we wouldn't attempt to stop her either. We supported her decision regardless of our personal wishes. We all gathered around her to see her off, each of us saying a heartfelt good-bye and wishing her well. When it came my turn I stepped up and opened my arms to her.

"Dale, thank you so much," she whispered to me as I hugged her close in my arms, "I knew when you came in to me and I heard your words … and each time I would float up toward consciousness, I remembered them … they gave me peace before I sank back into the comforting darkness again."

We lingered there an extra moment holding each other close. I felt her inner strength but at the same time I suddenly realized how small she felt … how she seemed to belong right where she was … close to me … and I had a sudden desire to protect her just as I had when she was a human. When she stepped back I held her hands in front of me and looked into her soft brown eyes.

The world around us suddenly disappeared, there was nothing but the two of us and our eyes locked on each other. Something inside me shifted and I was shaken to the very innermost part of my being. For just a split second I saw Lexi like I had never seen her before … I saw me – alone, confused and hurt – then it was gone as fast as it had happened … and she was just Lexi again.

Shortly afterwards she took her leave and I was left to wonder about what had happened in that shared moment of time. Later in the day I was quietly walking through the back gardens when I was joined by Charlotte Ann. She took my hand in hers interlacing our fingers as we continued to walk.

"You seem awfully quiet and withdrawn," she said after a while.

"I suppose I was just lost in my own thoughts," I answered softly.

"What are you thinking about," she asked.

"I was thinking about Lexi and her leaving us," I replied.

"Is that all," she asked with a knowing smile.

"I suppose that I'm a little frightened," I began slowly, "just when I get a new family and begin to feel like a part of it, all of a sudden it seems like it is being torn apart. I don't want to lose any of it, it's too important and means too much to me."

"Dale, all families everywhere, whether they are mortal or immortal, go through changes," she said trying to sooth me, "members leave and go their own way and often others come and become a new part of the family. It's called growth."

"It still doesn't feel right," I mused, "it's almost as if a part of our family … us … a part of me … is missing now."

"Are you sure it's just about a missing family member … or is there something else, something deeper that you're feeling," she continued slowly probing my thoughts, "perhaps something you are trying but are unable to identify?"

"I don't know," I answered her slowly, "I saw something today, Charlotte Ann … when I hugged Lexi … I saw her, but I also saw me … the way you found me – alone, confused, and in pain … it was something different … something that I've only felt one other time … when we were at her funeral … and I'm not sure I know what it is."

"I think you do," she smiled happily, her eyes twinkling in the early morning sun, "look inside yourself Dale … to the very center of all that you are … that's where the answer lies. If you'll take the time to think and remember all that's happened since you joined this family … all that you and I have talked about … all the things I've taught you … then you'll find the answer to what you're feeling, and when you do … you'll know exactly what you saw and how that look of loneliness, confusion, and pain relates to your life."

Chapter Twenty~Four

 everal weeks after Lexi had left for Savannah, life at Whitehall began to settle again and return to a normal daily routine. All of us just accepted that she was gone and would, hopefully, one day come back and be part of the family again. Until then we would continue to carry on with our lives much the same as any other family would.

Although we do mingle freely with the humans in the area, we try very hard to maintain a low profile in order not to make any undue memorable impressions on the local people. It would be very disastrous for a mortal to discover our true nature and raise an alarm. Such an event would only lead to an unprecedented blood bath for the locals and a permanent relocation for us ... and since we like the Low Country, we would prefer to remain unknown and unnoticed.

We do on occasion attend some local events and festivals, usually the bigger the better. We intermingle some in the community to keep up a presentable façade, but still keep a comfortable distance. We hunt and feed when we need to, but even then we make every attempt to do so outside the area of our home. We travel whenever and wherever we wish, but for the most part we remain close to the Charleston area.

I'm really sorry to make our existence sound so exciting but most informal observers would think that we were a typical family living on an old family home place and our lives were pretty boring. Contrary to the way the lives of immortals are portrayed in books and movies we do live an ordinarily routine life. We don't face huge obstacles and there's not a constant uproar in the supernatural world. In fact there's more upheaval in the mortal world than there ever is in the preternatural world. While it's true that there are many other supernatural beings ... other immortals like us ... as well as Shifters, Lycans, Casters, and Seers ... we all maintain a respectful distance and as much as possible we live peaceably with each other.

The extent of our family is contained within the property boundaries of Whitehall ... there's just us ... James and Charlotte Ann have absolutely no connections left to any mortal family. I've had no further contact with my mortal family ... and I really don't care to either ... since my visit to see them. I've said my 'good-byes' to them, I'm at peace with my past and ready to face my future, and in another quarter century or less I'll be like James and Charlotte Ann with no human connections remaining. Katelyn's only surviving human relatives are her aunt and uncle but they live on the other side of the country in Oregon. The only contact she has with them is either the internet or telephone.

Regardless of just how mundane our lives appear, the

important thing is that among ourselves we are a tight knit family and have each other. If one of us needs something, no matter the reason, we close ranks and are there to do whatever is needed. The one thing that we have in abundance for each other is love, just like in any regular family, for whichever one of us is hurt or needs it. It seems that most of the time the source of the hurt comes as a result of ties to the mortal world. Lexi was a perfect example of how we supported and helped our own. Another opportunity presented itself a couple of months after Lexi had departed. This time it was Katelyn that needed us to stand strong with her after her aunt was involved in an automobile accident.

It all began one morning when Katelyn's soft Georgia voice floated through the house to each of us, "James … Charlotte Ann … Dale … I need you … please meet me in the parlor."

We immediately answered her call. She was visibly upset and although there were no sign of tears I knew from the look on her face that they weren't far beneath the surface.

"I have to go to Portland," Katelyn began, "Uncle John just called and told me that aunt 'Chele was involved in an auto accident last night … and it doesn't look good."

"Then I shall accompany you," James answered her, putting his arms around her and pulling her close to him. That's when the dam holding back the tears broke and they came full force.

"Oh James," she burst into tears and threw her arms around him, cuddling closer to him, "Aunt 'Chele is the only blood ties I have to my human family … she can't die … she just can't … not yet … and certainly not this way."

"Where is she," he asked her softly, holding and

petting her while she continued to weep.

"Uncle John said that she was at the Providence Medical Center in Portland," she answered slowly, "and they have her on life support!"

I watched as Charlotte Ann stepped up and gently took Katelyn's arms from around James, replacing his arms with hers, "Please James, allow me … I'm a woman … Katelyn and I need to be alone for a few minutes … I'll take care of this … you and Dale go make the necessary travel preparations."

The last thing I heard Charlotte Ann say as we left the parlor was "Cry all you want Katelyn … even the strong have their moments of weakness. When we get to Portland though, you must be strong again … you cannot afford to be weak for your family so let your tears out now … while you are here with me … you won't be able to cry when we get to Portland."

In less than an hour the four of us were aboard the jet and flying toward Oregon. James had instructed the pilots that we needed to get there as quickly as possible. We landed in Portland in just under four hours, a car and driver met us, and we went directly to the hospital. It was less than six hours from the time Katelyn received the phone call from her uncle until she was walking into the intensive care unit at Providence, protectively surrounded by the three of us.

We made our way past the waiting room and through the big double doors someone had buzzed open on the other side. I immediately noticed the change in the feel of the air once inside the intensive care unit proper. The atmosphere of the waiting room and the people outside had been one of subdued hope, but here in the hallway leading to the nurse's station, the air was filled with despair and hopelessness. I glanced in some of the rooms as we walked past and noted that all were darkened and there was no sound or movement except that of the medical equipment inside. I was suddenly struck with the thought that the four of us, often representing Death itself, now walking silently in the center of the wide hallway, was the physical embodiment of what most of these patients were waiting for ... and I hoped for their sake they wouldn't have long to wait.

Katelyn's Uncle and one of the nurses met us before going to her Aunt's room. She stepped into his arms and they hugged silently for several moments.

"Katelyn, it's so good to see you again," her uncle began, his voice breaking with emotion, "I'm so sorry it had to be like this ... I wish there was something I could do."

"How is she Uncle John ..." Katelyn asked hugging him closer to her, "and where is she?"

"Miss Corbin," the nurse spoke up softly in the quiet hallway, "my name is Julie and I'm your aunt's attending nurse this evening. Please understand that we are doing all we can to make her comfortable. Your uncle has told me that they are your only remaining family."

"I want to see her ... now," Katelyn spoke sharply, then quickly added, "I'm sorry Julie ... I don't mean to sound short with you ... it was a long flight and I'm worried about her ... please forgive my tone, but can I please see Aunt 'Chele now?"

"I'll allow you to go inside in a moment but your uncle has asked that I advise you of her condition ... before you see her. I'm very sorry Miss Corbin ... but she is in a terminal condition. She only survived the accident by some remarkable inner strength. She has extensive internal injuries ... and at the doctor's suggestion, and with your uncle's consent, we removed the life support earlier today, and in the last two hours have begun withholding any life sustaining drugs."

I saw Katelyn reach out and put her arm around James, pulling close to him.

Then looking at a chart she was holding the nurse continued, "Your aunt sustained six broken ribs, four cracked ribs and a broken breast bone. Her right lung and spleen have been ruptured and her liver lacerated. The internal bleeding has slowed but only due to a dropping blood pressure. Currently her heart rate is about thirty to forty beats a minute and her blood pressure is holding around sixty over thirty. She is breathing on her own but it's sporadic, only about six to ten times per minute. Miss Corbin, your aunt is barely hanging on and could expire at any moment."

All three of us were watching Katelyn's reaction as she took in the nurse's words. She stood silent and tight lipped, then slowly asked, "How did the accident happen … was anyone else hurt?"

"There was one other vehicle involved," the nurse answered.

"What about the people in the other car," Katelyn continued, "were they hurt also?"

"The other driver was falling down drunk," her uncle spoke up, his voice full of bitterness, "he drove through the intersection against the traffic light at over ninety miles an hour and hit 'Chele broadside on. He was driving under suspension for another DUI, he had no insurance and he walked away from the wreck with a small cut to his forehead and arm."

I felt rather than heard a low growl roll through Katelyn at his words.

"He won't be walking for long," I heard Charlotte Ann speak silently, *"I will see that that situation is taken care of before we return to Charleston."*

Katelyn turned and looked at her, then slowly nodded her head once in answer, silently passing sentence on him.

"Miss Corbin," the nurse spoke up, "your aunt is in this room but you'll have to see her alone ... I'm sorry but I'm only supposed to allow immediate family in ..."

"Julie, I believe you can allow us in," James spoke with a smile, looking into the nurse's eyes, "we are all immediate family."

"I think, bearing in mind the medical situation, perhaps I could make an exception in this case," she agreed, looking back at James, her eyes glazed from his thrall.

The four of us walked slowly into the room followed by the nurse and Katelyn's uncle ... the blinds were closed and it was dimly lit ... the machines surrounding Katelyn's aunt were beeping and humming. She only had one line still connected to her hand, she was very pale and her face was badly bruised. Katelyn reached and took the other hand in hers and held it.

I saw Charlotte Ann silently and slowly look around the room.

"She's still here, Katelyn," I heard her whisper softly in a tone that only the four of us could hear, "she's fighting hard and Death hasn't been able to make his claim yet ... but he isn't far away."

At that Katelyn looked up and with a smile spoke softly, "Uncle John ... can I have a few minutes alone with her ... you've been here for a while, why don't you take a break ... I promise she'll be alright while you're gone."

Then turning to the nurse continued, "Julie, would

you please go with him to the cafeteria and see that he has something to eat and drink?"

The two of them turned and walked out of the room leaving us alone.

When the nurse and her uncle had left the room, Katelyn turned to James and said, "I am not going to allow her to die … not here … not in this way … and certainly not this young …"

"Katelyn …" I began slowly and carefully, "please … not what I think you are thinking."

"I'm not going to change her Dale, but I am going to save her life," she answered me with a reassuring smile, then turning back to James, she continued, "James, you saved my life once by giving me your blood to drink … how much of my blood will it require to do that same thing for her?"

"Since you have both mine and Charlotte Ann's blood in you," James answered thoughtfully, "probably less than a pint to repair the internal damage."

"If you do this Katelyn, it'll happen fast …" Charlotte Ann added, "and there'll be no medical explanation for it."

"At this point, I don't care about medical explanations, Charlotte Ann … the doctors and nurses can explain it or not however they wish. But aunt 'Chele was there for me when I needed her most … now I'm here for her when she needs me most. If you will please shield us and block the door."

Then turning back to her aunt she began speaking in a low tone, "Aunt 'Chele … it's Katelyn and I know that you can hear me … I love you very much and you're not going to die today … I'm not going to allow it. I'm going to do something that will save your life … you won't understand it, but please don't be afraid, you know I won't do anything to hurt you. I'm going to fill your mouth with a liquid and when I do I need you to swallow. It won't hurt, I promise, and you're going to be strong afterwards."

This was something I had never seen so I watched her with intent interest as she opened her wrist and held it just above her aunt's lips. The blood began as a slow drip, falling on her lips and then running into her mouth. It quickly picked up speed and was soon pouring from Katelyn's wrist and filling her aunt's mouth. I was amazed that when her mouth filled she swallowed and it began to fill again ... and again ... over and over as the blood now gushed out of Katelyn's open wrist.

Then suddenly, out of nowhere, a soft lady's voice spoke, *"I'm so proud of you and what you're doing Katelyn."*

Katelyn looked up, smiled and answered, "Thank you mother ... I love you and miss you, but I'm just not ready to let her go yet."

"That's enough, Katelyn," Charlotte Ann spoke up as Katelyn continued to allow her blood to drip into her aunt's mouth, "I think she has had enough to repair the internal damage ... you don't want to give her too much ... you wouldn't want the side effects to be too long lasting and become discomforting for her."

"James, how long will it take," Katelyn asked carefully as she quickly licked the deep gash in her wrist and stopped the flow of blood she had opened there.

"At her current heart rate, it should take about ten to fifteen minutes to work its way through her system the first time," he answered, "after that you will begin to see a steady and continual change in her condition."

"Well, now that everything seems to be under control here," Charlotte Ann said with a smile, "if you will excuse me, I need to go and locate some information about someone that lives in Portland."

"Dale and I shall join you momentarily, Charlotte Ann," James spoke up, "as soon as the healing power of the gift begins to work in her. After that Katelyn will probably need to be alone with her aunt for a while."

Charlotte Ann turned and walked quickly out of the room and disappeared down the long hallway. In less than half an hour Katelyn's aunt began to stir and groan. Her heart rate, breathing and blood pressure all began to climb steadily.

"It's working now," James spoke softly to Katelyn, "I think it best if Dale and I leave you alone with her. You should be the first one she sees when she opens her eyes again. She will continue to mend rapidly. The nurses will come at once as soon as they see a change in her monitors. If it gets to be too much for you to handle summon me and I will come immediately."

James and I disappeared around midnight to join Charlotte Ann to hunt and feed. Katelyn remained at the hospital the rest of the night and all the next day for some family time with her aunt and uncle.

I had been with Charlotte Ann many times and watched her hunt and feed, but that night she displayed a ruthless savagery the likes of which I had never seen before. She caught the man she was looking for coming out of a small bar and grabbed his arm literally dragging him down the street and into a dark alley. She pinned him against a wall like she had done me the first night except this time she was flashing her fangs.

"Stay back, this one is all mine," she instructed James and me as we started to follow her down the alley, and then turning back to the frightened man she almost growled as she continued, "You are responsible for causing a great deal of pain and distress in the life of someone that I love and care deeply about ... that said, you owe me a blood debt ... and I'm here for payment!"

When she attacked him, she literally began ripping his throat out a bite at a time. Although he was the only one to die that night, he met a slow and agonizing death. When she had finished her attack, his body was so mauled that when it was found it would be blamed on a vicious animal attack.

We remained in Portland until the next evening by which time Katelyn's aunt had made an astonishing recovery. She was awake and although still weak, she was lively, talking and occasionally laughing a little with her husband and Katelyn. Much to the bewilderment of the doctors and staff, all of her vital signs had returned to normal and her bones seemed to be healing at an astonishing rate.

The medical team, unable to explain what had happened, finally just admitted that there were some things medical technology just cannot rationalize. In the end they decided that they must have misdiagnosed some of the internal injuries and credited her recovery to the same inner strength that had helped her survive the initial accident.

The four of us returned the following afternoon to the airport and boarded the plane back to Charleston and our rather mundane and ordinary lives.

fter several months of living in Charleston, and learning to be part of a family again, I looked back at all that had happened to me – the many changes that had taken place both in my life and in me as a person – and found them all to be good. I compared the helpless, hopeless condition I had been forced to live with for so many years and discovered that I had made a marvelous transition from what I called a miserable existence to a full, happy and rewarding life.

When I had first arrived in Charleston, I was searching for an executioner. Instead, I had found a family of immortals who adopted me and gave me a new life. There was no doubt that life as I knew it had taken a serious turn, and for the better. The last few months of my life had been more fulfilling than any since the disaster of my sixteenth birthday party.

When I was first attacked and changed by Charles, my life … or the nightmare that I called my life … consisted of two things and only two things – killing for blood and sleeping in a grave – nothing more, nothing less. But since the night that Charlotte Ann found me … rescued me I believe would be a better term … so much good has happened for me. Between her, James and Katelyn, each and every one of them have welcomed me in as a part of the family and taken a real interest in me, teaching me things I never knew.

Since the night I had been attacked and all the years following, I had thought that I was only an empty shell of a walking dead man. I had felt condemned to a life of darkness, a life of killing others so that I could survive. Charlotte Ann had begun my new education by showing me that I wasn't at all what I thought. Katelyn, by using a very simple illustration, had shown me that it was possible to take only a small drink from my prey. Then the two of them had taken me out into the mortal world to practice that particular skill. I watched and learned from both of them how to successfully hunt, feed and not kill when I did. James had spent time with me going over the more scientific explanations of what it meant to be an immortal and what had happened to make me that way.

When I had been in the city with Charlotte Ann, I had learned how to spend time with my prey before feeding, often talking to them. But James had taught me how to take that skill to an entirely new level … how to be comfortable in the presence of humans. I could now sit in a restaurant or street side café and carry on a conversation with anyone. He had also pointed out that since Charleston was predominately a tourist and college town the act of remaining unknown was much easier. The tourists were constantly changing and every four to five years, the entire student populace of the local colleges turned over completely.

It seemed that my world was growing bigger and my life getting more interesting by the day. Still there was something wrong. I felt incomplete and empty on the inside regardless of how much time I spent with everyone. There was something happening inside me, something I had never experienced and I just couldn't put my finger on it. I finally decided the best thing to do would be to talk to Charlotte Ann, tell her what I was feeling, and ask her to explain to me what was happening.

Before I could have that conversation though Lexi returned home from Savannah, but only for a couple of weeks. She was on her way to Europe with Gale, who, it turned out was one of the ancients and a longtime friend of Charlotte Ann's. Gale had watched over and protected Lexi at Charlotte Ann's request while she was in Savannah. Then when the time was right Gale had stepped forward, befriended her and helped guide her through to a complete and total healing from the wounds that Mikey had inflicted upon her.

I didn't want to see Lexi leave again but she had been in love with Europe since she was a small child and was so happy about getting to return. She planned to visit some of the places she had not seen while she was teaching in Berlin. She was exhibiting her usual child-like happiness and exhilaration about the trip and I wanted to see her happy so I wished her well.

I did however note that something seemed to be different about her since her return. She had changed while she was in Savannah ... she seemed to have suddenly matured well beyond her years – she was so much more grown up now than when she left us ... whatever it was, I could easily feel it but I didn't know exactly what had happened to bring about the sudden maturity.

After Lexi and Gale departed, I asked Charlotte Ann to spend some time with me, I needed to be alone with her and talk. We found a quiet place at the back of the property and we settled beneath a tree and began talking.

"Charlotte Ann, I think something is wrong with me … and I don't know what it is," I began, "I feel strange … inside."

"Can you tell me exactly what it is that you feel," she asked seriously.

"I'm not completely sure," I began, "the best way to describe it is that I feel empty … it's almost like a gnawing hunger of some kind … a craving deep inside for something I'm missing and I don't how to satisfy it."

"And you haven't figured out yet what that 'something' is, have you," she asked, now smiling at me.

"I think maybe it has something to do with my growing and maturing, maybe it's because of all the rapid changes in my life since I came here. But at this point I just really don't understand what's going on," I answered.

"Oh it has a lot to do with your growing and maturing," she chuckled, then looking seriously at me she continued, "I know exactly what's going on inside you."

"Then please tell me what it is," I said, "and tell me how to fix it so that I can feel normal again."

"Dale, I told you this day would come … you've met your mate … and what you are feeling – that persistent tugging inside – is her nature reaching out to you and your nature answering her … calling back to her … missing her … and I assure you that whatever part of the world she is in right now, she is also experiencing that same empty tugging inside her … and until the two of you are brought together for good, both of you will have that empty feeling inside."

I was shocked at what she said and not sure what if anything to say in return. She just stood there smiling at me.

"But ... who ... where and how would I have met her," I asked.

"Okay, let's work it out the same as any other problem," she began, "let's start with the humans you've met, here and in the city ... do any of those come to mind?"

"Well, there is Colleen ... but she's part Fae ... and the girl at the club in New York ... but neither of them just don't seem to fit here," I said tapping my chest.

"That's a good beginning, now, what about immortals," she asked, "how many of those do you know?"

I thought quietly for a moment before continuing, "I've spent nearly all of my time since you found me with the four of you either in the city or here at Whitehall."

"That's correct, you have spent most of your 'newly discovered' life almost exclusively around us ... so, do you think it could be one of the four of us ... and if so, which one," she was almost bursting with a smile.

"It certainly can't be James because ... well, just because ... besides that would be against nature and it's just not normal!"

She snickered at my comment, "Then I suppose that only leaves three doesn't it?"

"It can't be Katelyn because she and James are mated," I said, "so that only leaves you and Lexi ..."

"Yes it does," she said, her smile growing larger.

I was suddenly staggered at what I had just said and the realization of it began to sink in.

"... and ... and you already have a mate ... somewhere," I stammered out.

"Yes, I do," she grinned, "which of course leaves only ... Lexi."

I was silent for several minutes as I thought about what she said, trying to make it fit.

"But I thought you said I would know when I met my mate," I finally spoke slowly.

"I said that you would begin to develop *feelings* for your mate," she corrected me, "I've thought and suspected for a while that Lexi would be your eventual mate. However, I never said anything because nature didn't need me playing matchmaker, it's able to take its own course without my help."

I actually knew deep inside that what she was saying was true but the impact of it being said aloud still rocked me back. I began to think about what Charlotte Ann had just said, allowing my memory to spiral backwards to the first time I had seen Lexi. She had still been a human ... frail, delicate, and so easily broken ... when she and Katelyn had come to the city for the weekend. Among my first thoughts of her was that I liked her, and I couldn't explain why.

I had never looked at a human the way I looked at Lexi. Everything about her ... the childish innocence ... the radiant aura and delicate scent ... had combined together and became a strong pulling force on my nature. In spite of my natural reaction to want to feed from her I remembered feeling that she was likable and I had a strong sense of protectiveness toward her. Then for some mysterious reason I had sensed inside me that she was worth protecting.

"You're remembering," Charlotte Ann said as she examined my face, "that's good ... keep thinking ... you've found when the seed was planted ... now keep looking ... delve deeper into your heart ... and don't be afraid to open some new doors ... or of what you might find waiting behind them."

I remembered the sadness and hurt I had felt for Lexi

when Charlotte Ann had told me that Katelyn had changed her ... the sorrow that her young life had ended much the same as my own had. I smiled at the memory of the out-and-out confusion on her face and then how pitiful she had looked when she had first seen Charlotte Ann and me ... and realized that we were immortals, too. I recalled how her new immortal scent, that of rose petals, had enhanced her soft bath powder human scent. My thoughts moved forward to the enjoyment and happiness I had felt when she and I were together as I helped teach her different methods of hunting.

I smiled as I looked up at Charlotte Ann and the recollections of those scenes.

"Keep going ... a little deeper," Charlotte Ann whispered to me, "you're almost there."

Then I remembered her funeral and how she had clung to me, crying like a lost and hurt child as she watched the final connections to her human life being severed. Even more importantly, I recalled how I had felt that day ... as I held Lexi, comforting her while she cried. I thought it had evoked long buried memories of Becky, but now I realized that what it had brought to the surface were not so much memories of Becky ... but memories of being in love. I ached at the recollection of her own pain cutting through me like a dull knife when she was rejected by a human boyfriend and then standing over her coffin begging her to come back, offering my help and guidance.

I felt Charlotte Ann's eyes on me again and I looked up at her ... she smiled and nodded at me without saying a word as once again I sank back into the past. Suddenly my own loneliness and hurt flowed through me like a river as I was again forced to recall the day Lexi had left Whitehall bound for Savannah. I had held her close to me in a final hug, feeling the strength of her immortality but at the same time thinking how tiny and vulnerable she seemed. Then the world had stopped when I looked into her soft brown eyes. That's the moment that I knew something shifted inside me and what I had thought was a picture of me had in reality actually been a picture of Lexi … as a part of me.

"It's all true," I whispered as I looked back up at Charlotte Ann, "it's been there all along … right out in the open … I've felt it several times and never recognized it for what it was."

"It often takes time … something we have plenty of," she smiled, "for us to find and recognize our mate. It's an important part of our lives because like us, it's forever."

"But what about us Charlotte Ann … you and me," I asked, "I love you!"

"Dale … dear, dear boy," she began, "I love you too, but the love we share is different. The love that will develop and grow between you and Lexi is something so much deeper than what you and I have shared. The love for a mate, whether you are together or not, is fathomless and everlasting."

"But what about the relationship we have …" I started to ask.

"I want you to think back now … about us and our beginning," she began soothingly, "I told you then this day would likely come and now it has. The same Fate that brought us together will keep us together, even though it is about to take our lives in vastly differing directions. Our current relationship is about to change … and while we may no longer be lovers, we will still love each other … only now it will be different. It will be something better … something stronger and deeper … an enduring eternal friendship."

"But Charlotte Ann, what if … what if Lexi doesn't

know or feel what I do," I asked fearfully, "I don't want to be alone again."

"You will not be alone, dear boy," she said as she reached and took my hand in hers, then with the other hand softly stroked my cheek, "nature, my child … trust it to do what it is supposed to do."

"What about the others, James and Katelyn, do they already know," I asked.

"They only know that a change is coming, but when it happens, they will know," she answered, "and now that you've had your time of self-discovery, let's you and I go hunting and then we shall return to the house."

or the next three months after the shocking realization of what I had been feeling was made clear to me, I continued to search my inner self. The deeper I searched the more I became convinced that Charlotte Ann had been correct about Lexi. Every memory I had of her, every look, every moment, every touch now fit into place and formed a complete picture in my mind. I was amazed that I couldn't have seen it sooner but at the same time I still wondered if Lexi had seen or felt the same things that I did.

Charlotte Ann and I began spending more time than ever together. She said that she needed to prepare me for what lay ahead. While we frequently hunted together, she began to have me feed from her more often, and as a result I quickly noticed my own strength building. I spent countless hours with her teaching me new things and showing me the operation of different gifts and powers that I had no idea that she had and many of which she taught me how to use.

During this time Katelyn and James began to spend more time together. They hunted together, took several short trips together, and most of their days and nights were spent together. They began to keep a wider and wider distance between themselves and Charlotte Ann and me, often leaving us to ourselves for several days at a time.

"It's really nothing," Charlotte Ann assured me when I asked about their new behavior, "it's because both of them have sensed that something is happening in our lives. They just haven't realized yet that the 'something' is actually happening in your life. They are giving us some space, allowing us to have as much time together as possible, and waiting on whatever is going to happen to happen."

Then late one evening, when James and Katelyn had gone to Miami for a couple of days to hunt, Charlotte Ann came to me in the parlor.

"Since we came into each other's lives, I have taught you and shown you many things," she began, "and Dale, there are many more talents still lying dormant inside you. They will develop over time and be there for you when you need them the most. Dale, I will always be your friend and your teacher and as such I have one last very important gift to give you … I want you to drink from me again. The blood I have shared with you in the past only awakened 'the gift' within you. Now it's time to share more than my blood, I want to share the essence of my life with you. What I am giving you tonight will stir up even more powers and gifts than you already possess … it will make you a stronger and more independent immortal."

"This will very likely be the last immortal blood you drink until you and Lexi consummate your becoming mates by sharing each other's blood. So please drink deeply and allow my life to do wonderful things in you. The two of you, although young in immortality, both carry within you very, very powerful bloodlines. You are going to make an incredibly formidable pair and I pity anything or anyone that attempts to cross you."

Then without another word she opened the artery in the side of her neck and drew me to her. I took her in my arms as I had done many times since our first night together, and pulled her close, bending my head to her neck. I began to drink, just as I had done many times before. I felt her life flooding into me, surging into every part of me, filling me, but this time it was different. It was as if she had unlocked a previously hidden door and flung it wide open to me. I sensed when we merged into one … it was almost as if we were making love, tangled together, and I tightened my grip on her, drawing her closer as I sucked hungrily at her neck. I closed my eyes in the pure sensuality that I felt.

"Drink me in," she whispered to me, "take my strengths, my powers and let them operate in you … be strong as I am strong … be powerful as I am powerful …"

Her blood tasted different than it had in the past, it seemed to be stronger, if that was possible, and I luxuriated in her. Then she did something she had never done … she opened her mind and shared her entire life with me. I witnessed a life that had been lived over nearly four centuries … everything … she held nothing back. She revealed a life of genuine happiness … she showed me Ferdinand and her love for him … James and how they had met … then she showed me a picture of myself the night we met. It was a picture of someone full of darkness, desperation and lost hope … a person I would not have recognized now. Finally she explained to me, mind to mind, the full meaning of having a mate. When I had drank my fill I raised my head from her neck. I watched as her throat healed, her skin becoming soft and smooth as ever. I looked into her eyes, deep and bottomless, as the strength and power of her blood tore like a dynamo through my veins. I smiled and leaned in to kiss her.

"No Dale, not now," she whispered softly, smiling and looking into my eyes, "save your love for your new mate. After tonight, you'll begin to see me in a different light … you'll look at me differently from now on. You and I are becoming former lovers … we no longer love as lovers … we love as friends … immortal friends who have a special bond that connects us forever … something deeper than mere lovers could ever hope to have."

The remainder of the night was spent with her continuing to teach me new things, explaining powers and gifts to me. Then just as dawn was coming, bringing a new day she left me, explaining that she had to go and hunt … she needed to feed and replenish herself.

After Charlotte Ann left me I sat there, all alone in the huge house, thinking about how my life had changed and was about to change – again. I recalled perfectly everything that she had ever shared with me. Finally, as the sun was coming up, I decided that I would go out to the little stream at the back of the property … I had a special place there that I often went to when I needed to be alone and think.

I slowly walked across the back garden, my head down, still lost in thought. I had just started into the tree line when I looked up and saw Lexi … she was standing in a small clearing, literally bathed in the early morning sunbeams and she looked as radiant as an angel. Her eyes shone brightly in the morning sun and she was looking at me, smiling shyly, lightly biting her bottom lip the way she did whenever she was uncertain about something.

"Lexi … I thought you were in Europe," I began slowly, unable to hold back a smile, "how long have you been back … what are you doing here?"

"I was … not long … and I simply couldn't stay away any longer," she replied uncertainly, "the longer I was gone the more restless I became. I felt empty inside and I began to search my soul trying to explain the hollow feeling. I felt like I had a desire for something … a driving hunger … something I was missing … and no matter where I went or what I did, I couldn't satisfy it. Finally, Gale explained everything to me, she told me what I was feeling … she said it wasn't my soul but my heart that was missing something … someone … so I had to come home … I had to see for myself if it really was what she said it was."

I reached and took her hand in mine, looked into her eyes and once again the world stood still, everything vanished except her.

"It was … and is … everything she told you. I've been experiencing the same emptiness, the same longing as you. I didn't know what it was either, until Charlotte Ann explained it all to me. Now, I know what … and who … I was missing … and more importantly, she's here now and she's everything to me," I replied looking into her eyes, "Lexi, I'm so happy that you came back to me."

I opened my arms and she easily folded into them. I held her close, enjoying the unexpected new feeling of how we both just seemed to so suddenly fit together. I breathed in the wonderful elegance of her soft scent, the rose petals and bath powder filling my nostrils.

"Lexi …" I spoke softly into her hair, "I love you … and I want to fill that empty place in your heart … I want you to fill that same place in my heart … I want you to be my mate … and I will be your mate … please, let's don't ever leave each other again."

"I was so hoping you would say that," she whispered and I felt her small body relax even more against me, "Gale said that you would be waiting for me and that you would fill the hollow place in my heart and make it disappear forever."

Then looking up at me she smiled and continued, "I love you too Dale, and I think I've loved you for a long time I just didn't realize it. Now that I do, I'll be here for you forever."

The two of us shared our first kiss, a mate's kiss, standing there just inside the tree line. It was a kiss that was lingering and overpoweringly sexual. She crushed her body against me, our mouths hungrily tasting the other. I had never experienced a kiss that powerful or that erotic. The longer we clung to each other the more excited I became. Although physical, my excitement was different than ever before. I wanted her … I wanted to drink from her … to experience her … to take her inside me … but more than that … I wanted to give … to have her drink from me … to experience me.

When we broke the kiss, she stepped back and looked at me with the most beautiful smile I had ever seen. Her eyes, now bright amber in the sunlight, sparkled as she searched deep into my own eyes. She silently reached out her hand and placed it on the side of my face. Then with her finger she began tracing my cheek, the outline of my lips, across my chin and down to my throat.

"I want you Dale," she whispered softly, "physically, yes … and I can't wait to share my body with you, for us to be lovers … I want to give you my body … but more than that I want to give you my blood … and pledge my life to you … right here … right now."

She moved back close to me, lifting and tilting her head, "I offer you more than my body Dale … I offer you my life … take me … drink from me … make me your mate."

I placed my lips on her neck, lightly kissing it, searching for and then finding her artery. My fangs slid into place and I carefully bit into her, holding them inside her for just an extra moment. She stiffened just the tiniest bit in my arms as I began taking her blood from her neck. Then she relaxed, wrapping her arms around me and crushing her body against me as I held her protectively in my arms.

Her blood was a sweet mixture of young and old, strength and weakness, not at all what I would have expected from one of her youth. It filled my mouth over and over as I drank long and deep from her. I swallowed over and over and felt her inside me, flowing through and becoming a part of me … I felt the empty, void place that had been inside me suddenly fill to overflowing. She pressed her body closer against me, holding me tightly in her arms while I continued to drink. I felt her body arch against me, every muscle locking in place as she was swept up in the throes of an orgasm, her moans and groans of happiness filling me just as her blood was filling me. I raised my head and watched as her beautifully soft skin returned to normal, her neck once again smooth and unblemished.

I kissed her, our lips lightly touching, then quickly becoming more intense. Her tongue was probing and searching; I hungrily took it in my mouth and sucked greedily on it. She took me in her mouth and pulled on my tongue, sucking at it. When I could take no more I gently broke the kiss and still holding her in my arms whispered into her ear, "Lexi, I pledge my life to you forever … take me now my eternal love … take my blood … my life … and my love … I give it freely to you … let me become as much a part of you as you are a part of me."

Her lips were like satin, soft and sensuous as she moved them on my neck tenderly kissing me. She quickly and expertly found the place just under my left ear. I felt the tips of her small sharp fangs against my skin and I groaned with pure unconcealed delight when I felt them penetrate my skin and slip easily into the artery there. I had never experienced anything as powerfully stimulating as when her fangs sank slowly into my neck.

I tightened my hold on her when she withdrew her fangs and began to suck hungrily at my neck. I sensed my life flowing into her, filling her, like she had filled me. I was inside her and she was inside me and we were blending together, two becoming one. I knew the moment that our minds linked, our hearts united, our souls connected … bonding the two of us into one … forever … and at that moment the most intense orgasm I have ever experienced tore through me like the winds of a screaming Banshee. It began in my stomach and flashed outward to my arms and legs … and back again … again and again it washed through me. It was so powerful that it rocked all that I am and my body convulsed as Lexi continued to hold me tight against her. The more she pulled at my neck the stronger and more powerful it became ripping over and over through every nerve and muscle in my body. Finally it began to recede back to the center of my being leaving me so physically weak that I had to concentrate on remaining standing.

I felt the tip of her tongue when she lightly touched it to the two small holes her fangs had left. Then she gently passed it over the area, slowly licking at my neck, and raised her head, again looking into my eyes. But, now it seemed that I was looking through her eyes, seeing what she was seeing. I wondered if she could see through my eyes the same way. Was she seeing the beautiful, sweet but tender little girl that I saw or did she feel the immortal strength that I sensed flowing out of her? We stood silently for several minutes in each other's arms, looking and searching into the other, our bond tightening as we did.

"Would you walk with me," I asked as I took her hand in mine.

"Always and forever," she answered with a sweet smile.

She walked with me the rest of the way to the stream and we sat down together. She cuddled close against me, the happiness shining on her face. Then we kissed again, long and passionately, cementing our new relationship. Our soft tender kisses soon turned more sensual, growing more suggestive and carnal by the minute. While we kissed, I sensed the new change continuing inside me as she settled securely into my heart, filling me and making me complete. There was something inside each of us confirming that while we remained family we were now more ... so much more than ever before. I was her mate and she was mine ... together we would mature and protect each other ... we would develop into one ... and together we would face eternity as one.

We sat together for several hours talking about and comparing what we had felt and how we had discovered what it meant. We laughed like a couple of kids as we compared feelings, looks and touches that we had shared in the past as we had grown to know one another. She told me with a smile that the very first time she had met me she felt something on the inside, but she was only four days old, and had no idea then what it was. She said that every time since then, she had always felt comfortable when I was with her and that deep inside she had known she was safe and protected when she was with me.

Finally, in late afternoon, we stood and began walking along the stream, our arms around the other, chatting and laughing together as we strolled. Our path eventually meandered around the property and led us back to the house. I took her hand in mine and interlacing our fingers we crossed through the garden. We entered the rear door and walking hand in hand we went to the parlor where we found James, Katelyn and Charlotte Ann all standing together and talking.

Chapter Twenty~Seven

ook who I found while I was out wandering around," I said, trying to contain a happy grin, as the two of us walked into the parlor holding hands, our fingers loosely interlaced. Katelyn turned and saw Lexi and broke into a huge smile, "Lexi you're back," she almost shouted, "and I didn't know …"

She stopped short and I saw a flash of sudden amazement mixed with curious interest cross her face. She silently examined each of us, her eyes taking in every detail about us from our faces all the way down. Then she saw that we were holding hands … and how we were holding hands … and that Lexi was cuddling close up against me … and her eyes lit up brightly as she slowly smiled.

"I actually found more than just Lexi," I answered her questioning bewilderment with my own smile, "I … she … well, both of us … found our mate."

Katelyn looked inquisitively at Charlotte Ann who shrugged and chuckled as she answered her, "Sometimes it's just meant to be."

"You mean you knew about this," Katelyn asked smiling, looking at Charlotte Ann and back at the two of us.

"Of course I did," she nodded her head and chuckled, "I've known about it for several months and suspected it even longer than that."

"Why didn't you tell me about it," Katelyn asked, "I didn't have any idea it was happening."

"They didn't anything about it either until about three months ago," Charlotte Ann laughed again, "and I didn't share it with you because nature works its own course and didn't need any extra help from either one of us ... and you know that both of us would have wanted to get involved and help make it happen, which is exactly why I didn't mention it."

"So this is the change that everybody has felt coming," James laughed quietly to himself and continued, "that's interesting ... even I didn't suspect that ... although by now Charlotte Ann I should know to expect the unexpected with you."

"After all we've been through together, you really should," Charlotte Ann laughed and agreed with him, "especially in matters of the heart."

"Lexi ..." Katelyn asked, the smile now spreading across her face, "really ... is it true?"

"Yeah ... it really is," she answered her, looking up at her and a huge smile bursting across her face.

Katelyn stepped over to us and looking at me then at Lexi, and back at me said, "Alright then ... if you'll let her go for a minute ... it's my turn for a hug ... I'll give her back though, I promise."

She took Lexi and wrapped her in a hug, holding her close, then with a sudden girlie giggle she burst out, "Oh wow, Lexi … I'm so happy for you … you've got to tell me all about how this happened!"

"I will … I promise … we'll talk," Lexi laughed, her eyes sparkling again, "Katelyn, this is just too cool … I've never felt anything like this in my life. And have I got a story to tell you … you are not going to believe how all this came about!"

We all found seats and settled in to talk. Lexi and I shared a love seat, cuddled in close together, with my arm rested around her shoulders. We really did look like a couple of newlyweds which sparked the next conversation.

"James, you are the head of the family, and kind of my immortal father now," Lexi began slowly, "so what exactly do Dale and I need to do next … you know … to be … mates?"

"I can think of at least one thing," Katelyn interjected with a naughty little laugh.

"Katelyn … stop that!" Lexi said pretending to be shocked.

"Well, she is right you know," Charlotte Ann laughed, "and now as mates, it will be better than either of you've ever known."

"Really," Lexi smiled hugely, "like rainbows and pink unicorns good?"

"Lots and lots of rainbows and pink unicorns," Katelyn joined in the laughter at what I knew had to be some kind of inside joke between the three of them.

"So, do you really need us to tell you 'exactly' what to do next," Charlotte Ann asked around her own happy laughter, "I'm sure that we can break it down step by step and tell you exactly how to do it if you really want us to!"

"I think I can handle it, Charlotte Ann," Lexi answered, trying her best to keep from laughing, "James …

please … be the adult in the room … give me a little help here."

"You know that our world is a bit different from the mortal world," he replied smiling at the sexy innuendo, "both of you have acknowledged that you are mates, and from the look of your faces you have obviously exchanged blood. So in actuality, it's done … you're mated … and may I be the first to offer my sincerest congratulations."

"Oh no … no, no, no …" Lexi quickly replied, sitting up, "not good enough … I might be really new to the immortal world but I'm still a girl … and when it comes to girlie things like this … I'm a real girlie girl! I want a wedding … or at least some kind of a ceremony … with all of you present so you can watch us exchange our vows."

She was so adamant, and her words so strong that everybody was looking right at her.

"Please …" she added softly, her eyes pleading when she looked up at me, "this is really kind of important to me."

"Then you shall have what you want," I answered her, "one way or another."

"Oh don't you worry Lexi, if it's that important to you then you will have a wedding. We can see to that," Katelyn laughed, "can't we Charlotte Ann … we'll have flowers everywhere … and music … and we'll dance!"

"I don't really know that I would want all of that … well … maybe just a few flowers … and some dance music," Lexi giggled.

The three of them chatted happily for the next hour or so while James and I sat back and listened. They planned the entire event from start to finish in less than an hour. Finally they agreed that it would be a simple gathering of all of us while Lexi and I exchanged our vows with each other. James would officiate since he was the head of the family. Once they had reached their decision they invited me and James back into the conversation.

"Now that our ceremony is settled," Lexi began, "I have one more request to make … it's really kind of big … and I think it will require the approval of all of us as a family."

She reached and took my hand then looking at each one of us in turn continued, "I would like to have my human parents attend … and please let me explain … you all know that I spent months in Savannah with them. They know and have accepted what I am … and how and why I came to be. Katelyn, they know you're my maker … and James, they met you briefly at my memorial service. I would really like for them to meet you Dale, since we are going to be together. And Charlotte Ann, they just have to meet you."

Everyone fell silent at her request. I knew we were all thinking about it and how such a request could affect all of us.

"Since I left Savannah I have had no contact with my parents," Lexi continued after a few moments of silence, "and if you would prefer that the ceremony remains just us then I promise, I will understand, and I will abide by your verdict. It's just that my dad expressed a desire to one day meet the rest of my immortal family, if it were possible. He only wanted to know who his daughter's new family was and this seems like it would be a great opportunity. But again, I'll leave that decision completely up to all of you."

After several moments of silence, James quietly spoke up, "I believe that what you are asking for might not be out of the realm of possibility … your parents are comfortable with your immortality Lexi, and as you noted they already know Katelyn and myself. Therefore, I believe the final decision should be up to Dale and Charlotte Ann."

"Dale," he asked looking at me, "what are your thoughts on the matter?"

I looked around at everyone, then at Lexi and smiled, "You're my mate, I love you and I trust your judgment … so I want whatever you want."

"Charlotte Ann," James nodded to her, "your thoughts?"

"It certainly appears that you are going to have to learn to expect the unexpected from someone besides myself," she chuckled slowly, "and while I don't make a practice of revealing myself to mortals, I don't see a problem in this case, because I suspect this may very likely be the first and last time they will ever see me."

"Very well," James said smiling and turning to Lexi with a nod, "you may invite your parents. Please tell them they are welcome at Whitehall, and they shall have the master suite for their entire visit."

"Thank you so much, James," Lexi smiled and hugged him.

"You're very welcome little one," James replied.

"And thanks to all of you," she beamed, "you don't know what this will mean to me."

"I think we do," Katelyn and Charlotte Ann both spoke up at the same time. They looked at each other and laughed.

"You're a girl … and it's your wedding," Katelyn continued, "so it's supposed to be special."

"If I may get serious for just a moment," James spoke up, "you know of course that your parents' safety is ensured while they are here with us. Still, we are what we are, so may I suggest that we remember we are all immortals and there will be mortals sharing our home …"

"Yeah … I've been there done that," Lexi grimaced,

"only the other way around."

"Then you know firsthand how difficult a situation that can be," he continued, "so after you make your call and extend the invitation perhaps it would be wise for all of us to take time to go hunt and feed. It would be extremely rude of any of us to have to take leave of our guests because we did not prepare in advance."

I walked with Lexi out to the rear veranda and listened as she made the call to her parents. Her dad picked up on the second ring.

"Hi Dad … how are you?"

"Little Bit," he said, "it's so good to hear your voice again … are you back in Savannah?"

"No, I'm still in Charleston, but I have some great news for you, dad."

She paused for just a moment before continuing.

"I've taken a mate … and I would love for you and mom to come up to Whitehall to witness our vowing ceremony."

There was absolute silence on the call for the next few moments.

"A vowing ceremony," her dad asked slowly, "is that like a … a wedding?"

"Yeah, dad," she laughed happily, "it is … only different."

There was more silence on the call.

"You said 'taken a mate' … past tense … as in already done," he asked slowly.

"You know my world is a little different to yours dad … but I still wanted the ceremony anyway."

"Okay … when," he asked.

"Day after tomorrow," she answered quickly, "you and mom can come up tomorrow afternoon. You can spend the night at Whitehall, and then you'll be here for my ceremony the next day."

"That doesn't even give me time to get a tux ... and you know your mom will have to dress shop," he protested.

"Don't worry about it, nobody is dressing up, it's just the family," she laughed, "actually the ceremony is not even necessary ... but I wanted to do something special ... and I wanted both of you here to watch."

"When would you like us to arrive?"

"Anytime tomorrow afternoon is great," she answered him smiling.

"Alright, we'll be there," he said, then added quickly, "oh, by the way, who is the lucky boy?"

"His name is Dale and he's standing right here beside me," she laughed and held the phone out, "say 'Hi' to my dad, Dale."

"Good afternoon, Mr. Gordon," I said into the speaker.

"Okay, that's enough, you can talk tomorrow," she laughed taking the phone back, "we have to go now dad, have a safe trip and I'll see you tomorrow, bye now!"

She hit the end button on her phone, turned and hugged close to me and laughed, "See ... that was easy!"

"Yeah, I still have to *meet* your dad," I answered smiling, "you may be an immortal, and my mate, but you're still your daddy's little girl ... his *only* little girl."

"It's no big deal," she looked at me and with a mischievous grin added, "he won't bite, I promise!"

Then she grabbed my hand and happily danced and skipped her way back into the house to the parlor and told everyone that her parents would be there the next afternoon. She went over the conversation with Katelyn and Charlotte Ann covering details of their arrival. When she finished all five of us quickly separated and departed in various directions to take care of nature and nature's requirements before our visitors arrived.

Chapter Twenty-Eight

 everal hours later we began to return to the house after hunting. I was the first one to return and was quickly followed by Lexi, then Charlotte Ann, Katelyn and finally James. Shortly after we had all gotten back we had another guest, Gale, to join us. Charlotte Ann had called her and asked if she wanted to attend since she had already played such a large part in Lexi's life.

I had met Gale briefly when she and Lexi had passed through on their way to Europe several months previous. The only thing I really knew about Gale was that she was one of the 'Ancients' and had earned that title by having lived across at least one millennium and in her case nearly two – a fact that was nearly incomprehensible to me. I just could not fathom a life of almost two thousand years. I have to admit I was in awe of her, but even more so because of the part she has played in Lexi's life. Lexi had told me about how Gale had entered her life and helped her while she was in Savannah and I appreciated her to no end for being there.

However, with the arrival of Gale, Katelyn and Charlotte Ann began to fill her in on all the plans for the vowing ceremony. As Gale listened to their ideas she began to interject some comments into the already – I thought – established plans. As a result, the more the three of them talked, the more the plans began to change, again. Soon Lexi, unable to contain her happiness, joined in with them and suddenly it seemed that we had four girls working on the vowing ceremony that I thought was already settled but which suddenly seemed to take on a whole new life of its own and begin growing once again.

James and I were left with nothing to do except watch and listen as what, only a couple of hours before, had been completed plans. Slowly the ceremony began to grow bigger and bigger ... the longer they planned and talked the more and bigger it grew. Finally, when the ceremony had grown from the parlor of the house to a historic downtown leased ballroom, complete with a one hundred piece symphony orchestra, I joined Lexi in her struggle with the other girls to try to keep the ceremony simple.

The four of them finally compromised and were able to reach an agreement that pleased everybody ... the ceremony would be small – and restricted to the parlor ... with only a few flowers ... which Katelyn, Charlotte Ann and Gale would furnish ... Lexi got to select the dress and color of her choice ... Katelyn and Charlotte Ann got to dress her and Gale got do her hair ... and all I had to do was stand beside her for the ceremony ... it seemed they were all finally happy.

Later that afternoon Lexi's parents arrived and she and I met them in the drive by the fountain. Her dad was taller than me with a medium build and graying hair at the temples. Her mom on the other hand looked to be a slightly older, but still very pretty, version of Lexi. She hugged and kissed them and grabbed my hand and pulled me over to meet them.

"Dale, this is my Daddy," she said beaming all over and with a happy laugh.

"Good afternoon, Mr. Gordon," I said politely and extended my hand to him.

"It's a real pleasure to meet you Dale," he said, shaking my hand and smiling, "I understand that we are family now, so please call me Bill, not Mr. Gordon."

Then it was her mom's turn, she lightly hugged me and said, "My name is Kathy … and you're my new … is son-in-law the proper term to use?"

"I think that will work perfectly if you are comfortable with it," I answered her with a smile.

The four of us started up the front steps just as the door swung open and James and Katelyn stepped out followed closely by Charlotte Ann and Gale. Lexi was just bursting with happiness at having all of us standing there together.

"Mom, Dad, I'd like you to meet my immortal family," she said as she began to formally introduce her parents to all of them before we walked inside, "you already know James, my immortal father … and Katelyn, my maker … this is Charlotte Ann, my teacher and mentor … and this is Gale, she and I have spent the last several months together in Europe."

This was followed by handshakes for the men and hugs for the ladies and everyone speaking greetings to each other. James and I reached and took their bags, while Katelyn and Lexi escorted them upstairs to the master suite where they would be sleeping. Lexi stayed with them for about half an hour while they settled into their room.

When they had returned from upstairs we gathered in the parlor to chat and give them a chance to get to know and begin to feel more comfortable around all of us. I'm sure it was one thing to know your daughter is an immortal and have her living in your home with you. But it had to be a completely other experience, no matter how safe you felt, to be two mortals walking into a house with six vampires ... even if one of them was your daughter.

Lexi and I sat cuddled on one of the love seats and watched as two families, one mortal and one immortal, began to blend together. I noted before long that James and Bill, like the elder statesmen of the two families, stood to one side smiling and talking quietly to each other. It seemed in no time that Kathy was just as comfortable as Katelyn played the perfect hostess. Soon the two of them, joined by Charlotte Ann and Gale were laughing and talking like old friends.

"This house is huge, Lexi ... do all of you live here," her mom asked, looking around the parlor.

"For the time being, yes, but Whitehall is actually James and Katelyn's home, Charlotte Ann lives in New York City, and Gale lives in ..." she stopped suddenly as she considered what she was about say.

"Savannah," Gale continued with a smile and a nod, "I live in Savannah."

"Wait a minute ..." Lexi's dad interjected, "I think I know you ... aren't you that friendly young lady that owns and runs that glamorous antiques shop that's downtown in the historic area."

"Indeed I am ... and by the way, I sincerely appreciate your use of 'young' ... more than you could possibly know," Gale answered smiling, "I wondered if you would remember."

"Of course I remember, Kathy and I have purchased several beautiful pieces from your shop," he answered and slowly added, "but I would never have thought that you were ... well, you know."

"It's not exactly common knowledge," Gale chuckled, "but you may find it interesting to know that it was I who watched over and protected Lexi the entire time she was visiting your home."

"Thank you for helping take care of my daughter," he nodded.

"And now, back to where we all live," Lexi seized the chance to cut in, "Dale and I haven't decided just where we are going to live yet."

"You will continue to live right here as long as you wish," Katelyn spoke up smiling, "Whitehall will always be your home whether you happen to be staying here at the time or not."

After a while the ladies decided that it was time for them to go into Charleston to shop for Lexi's dress. When they were about to leave Bill hugged and kissed Kathy on the cheek saying, "Drive safely, have fun and be careful."

"I assure you, Bill," James chuckled softly as we watched them drive down the allee, "with the four of those ladies watching over your lady, she is safer than the President ... and now that it's just the three of us, would you like to go to the rear veranda for brandy and cigars?"

"That sounds like a wonderful idea," Bill quickly agreed with a smile.

When we had retreated to the rear veranda James poured three snifters of brandy and passed out cigars to each of us. When he handed Bill his brandy, he said, "Marquis de Montesquieu, 1904 Vintage, a special brandy for a very special occasion."

"And a Cohiba Esplendido ... a very special cigar too," Bill commented happily as he examined the cigar, cut it, lit it, and taking a long draw breathed out, "Ahhh ... that is sooo good ... I haven't had a Cuban cigar in many years, my compliments on your taste in fine brandies and superb cigars. I could get used to these very easily."

I noticed that although James continued to hold his cigar it remained unlit and he only took very small sips of his brandy so I did likewise. The three of us were soon comfortable with each other's company and we spent the remainder of the afternoon and evening talking.

Over the course of our conversation I discovered that Bill was an accountant. However, he was also a hobby historian and had a love of all things history. Once that was known, James treated him to a full history of Whitehall from its founding in 1690 by his grandfather until the present. Bill took great pleasure in hearing its history from a firsthand accounting.

"Thank you James for that window into your world," he said when James had finished his story, "Whitehall is such an amazing place."

"May I ask a favor, please," he continued, "until now, the only thing I've really known about your world is what Lil Bit ... uh, Lexi ... and I have talked about. So if I happen to say or ask something I shouldn't please let me know. I don't wish to be an embarrassment to my daughter."

"Your concern is admirable Bill," James answered, "and I'm sure that being introduced to an entirely new world can be a very unsettling thing. However, don't overly concern yourself with what you should or shouldn't say. We live our daily lives, for the most part, much the same as you do yours and there is very little difference in the social norms of both worlds."

"I suppose after having had Lexi back home that I should have known that."

"Even so, it still requires some adjusting," James said, "but please, all of us want you and Kathy, while you are visiting our home, to be comfortable, feel relaxed, and at right at home."

"Dale," Bill spoke after a while, "I know from talking to Lexi that it's impossible to judge the age of an immortal and so I'm pretty sure that you are older than the innocent teenager you look like. Do you mind if I ask how old you really are?"

"I don't mind at all," I chuckled, "I was born, the first time in 1962, and the second time in 1978, both times in Renton Junction, Pennsylvania, so I'm either fifty-one or thirty-five, whichever you prefer and makes you feel better."

"If Lexi were still aging she would be almost twenty-four, so I think I'll go with the thirty-five," he laughed.

Not long after, the ladies returned from shopping and we spent the next three hours listening to them and talking about the ceremony the next day. Finally, around midnight, Lexi's parents said that they needed to rest and would like to go to their room. Lexi went with them and stayed for another hour before returning to join us in the parlor.

"Are your parents alright," I asked, hugging and kissing her when she returned.

"They're incredibly happy ... for me and for you ... and awfully excited about tomorrow. But for now they're both resting and will sleep peacefully through the night," then she winked at me, kissed my cheek, and added, "I made sure of it."

The next morning all of us gathered in the hallway in preparation for our vowing ceremony. Lexi was absolutely glowing with happiness and looked more stunningly beautiful than ever, if that was even possible, in her new dress.

She had chosen a cocktail dress in her favorite color, pale lemon yellow. The softness of the color highlighted the blond in her hair making it seem to shine even brighter. It was strapless with a half back and the tailor had cut it close to really show off her small body. The dress itself was covered in a layer of floral patterned almond lace, accented with a creamy yellow sash and a satin and lace rose in the back with two streamers hanging to the hemline. It ended at mid-thigh in front and just below her knees in the back. She had completed the whole with a pair of light cream spike heels that would make her seem a little taller standing next to me.

Gale had already asked to be allowed to do Lexi's hair for the occasion, and had created a masterpiece of hair sculpture. She had made two braids starting on each side at the temples, flowing down and back to become one that rested at the bottom of Lexi's neck. Then she had made two more braids just above the first two and brought them around to the back of Lexi's head where she coiled them to look like two roses. When Gale finished she told Lexi that it had been a very popular style when she had been a young girl in Rome. I was more than impressed.

Lexi twirled like a tiny coryphée in front of me and with a happy giggle she looked up into my eyes and in her little tinkling wind chime voice asked, "How do I look?"

"You look absolutely adorable," I whispered as I melted into her soft brown eyes, "and I love you more than life iteself!"

I opened my arms to her and she stepped into my hug and I whispered into her ear, "Lexi, you are the most beautiful young lady I have ever seen!"

I pulled her close and holding her tight, we shared a quick kiss, just a peck on the lips, while everyone clapped.

"Now, if the two of you will please turn each other loose, we can begin," Charlotte Ann laughed as she took over and began putting everyone where she wanted us.

"Dale and Lexi, I need you right here in front ... perfect ... now, Bill and Kathy, would you please come behind them."

Once she had arranged us just the way she wanted, she turned and said, "Gale, would you escort James please?"

Finally satisfied that she had everyone just where she wanted them she excitedly motioned for us to follow her and Katelyn to the parlor. Then with huge mischievous smiles and their eyes twinkling brightly, the two of them swung open the big double doors and ushered us in. They had decorated, just as they had agreed, using only flowers ... hundreds and hundreds of them.

They had set two enormous vases on either side of the double doors leading into the parlor and filled both of them with morning glories and purple orchids, Lexi's favorite flowers. Then, right in the center of the room, and taking up a large part of it, was a giant arrangement made completely of roses. It consisted of one immense rainbow made up of several smaller rainbows constructed of tiny multi colored rosebuds. Then underneath the rainbow were two life size unicorns, one pink and one white, raring up on their hind legs.

Lexi gasped in surprise and covered her mouth with both hands when she saw it sitting there. Then she burst out laughing and was quickly joined by Katelyn and Charlotte

Ann; their laughter filling the room with even more happiness.

"Awww ... that is just too funny," she said her laughter echoing off the walls and high ceiling, "rainbows and unicorns ... and they're beautiful ... whose idea was that?"

Katelyn and Charlotte Ann both joined in her laughter and pointed at each other and all three of them burst out with another round of laughter. I looked questioningly at Lexi, and wondering once again at what the joke about unicorns and rainbows between the three of them was all about.

"I promise, I'll explain the whole thing to you ... later ... when we're alone," she said still giggling at the sight of the unicorns.

After the laughter had subsided, James spoke up, "Lexi and Dale, if you would join me here and everyone would please gather around them we can proceed."

We took up our places, both of us holding hands, where James had indicated and everyone took up places in a loose circle around us as he began.

"Dale and Lexi, it is my pleasure to be able to take part in your vowing ceremony. While I sired neither of you, both of you carry my blood in your veins and I consider you to be my children. The two of you have faced and overcome huge trials and obstacles in your lives, both mortal and immortal, and I am extremely proud of you. I'm greatly honored that you would ask that I oversee this special event. Now, if you would please allow me a moment of liberty ..."

Then he looked over at Lexi's parents and began speaking to them, "Mr. and Mrs. Gordon, as head of this family and immortal father to both Lexi and Dale, I would like to thank you for being here today. It is not too often that we can have both mortal and immortal parents in the same room, so this is indeed a very special occasion. Please understand that Dale and Lexi have already taken part in the customs and mating rites of the immortal world and as such are already recognized as eternal mates. We are here today at Lexi's request. She wanted something in addition to the traditions of our world. She specifically requested a ceremony so that you, her mortal parents, could attend and take part in the occasion. Her desire is to honor you, the ones who gave her first life, by publicly exchanging mating vows with Dale."

"Lexi and Dale," he continued looking back at us, "I know that your vows today are special, because they come from the heart and soul to the heart and soul ... Dale, you may begin."

Lexi and I turned to face each other and I took both her small hands in mine, looking into her eyes as I began to speak, "Lexi, I pledge to you today and forever to be your mate. You are my life, my love, and my heart. Our love is an eternal love and nothing can or will ever separate us. We are united by blood ... your blood flows in me and my blood flows in you ... it is a bond that is stronger than any spoken words can ever describe. I promise to share my powers and gifts with you, but more importantly, I promise to be with you and love you forever as we travel through eternity together."

Lexi closed her eyes and bowed her head, then I felt her squeeze my hands as she looked back up into my eyes and her tiny little musical voice filled the emotional silence of the room, "Dale, I pledge to you today and forever to be your mate. Each of us in our own way has cheated death ... and because of that, Fate has brought our paths together ... it gave each of us a new life and a new family ... and now it has given us something more important … it has given us each other. I promise to share my gifts, my powers and my life with you. You are my partner, my equal and I willingly share my blood and my body with you that we may become stronger as we face eternity together."

We both bowed our heads for just a moment then looked up at James. He reached out, taking both our joined hands between his and began to speak, "Dale and Lexi, in the conventions of the immortal world you have exchanged blood with each other, and in the traditions of the mortal world you have spoken vows to each other … now with these witnesses to attest and as your immortal father and head of this family, I formally declare you mates … now and forever."

At that I took Lexi in my arms and she folded against me, wrapping her arms around me and we shared a very long, deep and intimate kiss.

he next day after the ceremony all of us gathered in the main hall to see Lexi's parents off. They had spent two nights at Whitehall and became very comfortable and felt right at home with all of us. James and I had enjoyed Bill's company and grew to like him very much. Although in the beginning Charlotte Ann had been a little averse to meeting and socializing with Lexi's parents, she quickly overcame her lack of enthusiasm and was soon as comfortable with them as the rest of us.

When it came to Bill spending time with Charlotte Ann and Gale they found him to be very charming and the two of them spent extra hours sitting together and talking with him. It didn't take long for Gale to disclose that she had been raised during the time of the Roman Empire and had witnessed the fall of that great city. Then Charlotte Ann had shared with him how she had grown up during the period of discovery and great exploration in the seventeenth century. He had been staggered to find out when they had been born and grew up. The realization of their ages had left him speechless. When it came to the history they knew he was like a man dying of thirst and they were a drink of water. Needless to say, he didn't get much sleep that final night while each one of them shared a portion of their lives with him.

"Bill, perhaps after I return to Savannah, I could visit you sometime," Gale said with a smile, "and perhaps over drinks share more of my travels across time with you."

"That's a very gracious offer," he replied, "Kathy and I would look forward to your visits and would love to have you in our home anytime you wish."

"Perhaps I might even have you write a book about my sixteen hundred years as an immortal, of course it would have to be purely fiction since everyone knows there's no such thing as vampires," Gale laughed and all of us joined in laughing at her comment.

After the laughter faded away Bill turned to Katelyn and reaching out his hand, taking hers, as a tear began to roll down his cheek, he spoke softly, "Katelyn, thank you for making all of this possible … you loved our Lexi like your own sister … and when she needed you most, you gave her second life … our daughter became your daughter … and Kathy and I owe you a debt of gratitude that can never be repaid."

Katelyn opened her arms and took him in a hug and softly whispered, "It was my pleasure to give my best friend the gift of life … I couldn't not do it … I just could not allow her to die and leave me."

Then drawing in a ragged breath he turned to me, "Dale, I have no doubt that you love my daughter very much. I can see that in the way you look at her and the way you gently touch her. I know that you'll take very good care of her. I want you to know that I'm proud to call you my son, even if I can't do it publically in my world, it's here in my heart."

"While I don't presume to know all the workings of the preternatural world, I would assume that you and she would appreciate some time alone, as mates, to get to better know each other," and reaching inside his coat he withdrew an envelope and handed it to me, "so in honor of your vows to each other, and your now shared lives, Kathy and I would like to give you both a gift. Inside you'll find two, open ended, round trip tickets to any destination of your choice and five thousand dollars in cash for whatever you may desire. We hope the two of you have an enjoyable trip."

I watched with a huge smile as Kathy leaned in and put her arm around him. She beamed happily at him and then at me and Lexi as we stood there with our arms around each other. I was amazed at how Lexi was so similar to her in looks and ways. I suddenly felt more alive than I had in years. I smiled at the irony of having a family that now stretched across two worlds.

"I appreciate all of you opening your hearts and your home to me and Kathy," he continued, "and I would like to extend a reciprocal invitation to any and all of you. Our home will always be open … we will welcome you in as family and be honored to have you as our guests. I'm happy to know that my little girl, the love of mine and Kathy's lives, is in good hands and that she is well taken care of too. I want to express my most sincere thanks to all of you for what you've done in her life … and ours."

Lexi stepped over and hugged her parents and kissed both on their cheeks and with a huge smile she said, "I'm so happy that you were here for me, this was special and something I'm glad I could share with you."

"James, there's one other thing before we go," Bill said, "it's something important and I would like to ask your advice. There's an issue that I'm not quite sure how to take care of …"

"How can I help you, Bill," James asked curiously.

"I've been thinking about something for the last couple of days and I'm sure that you may have encountered a similar situation at some point in the past. The only real asset that Kathy and I have is our home and the property that surrounds it. Currently there's almost five acres including the lot the house is located on and I try to purchase every piece of property around it that comes available. Although it's in an older neighborhood, and the house itself may not be worth much, I suspect with the current rate of growth in Savannah that will change. I believe that in the next few years the part of Savannah it's located in will become prime commercial real estate. As you know Lexi is our only child, and Kathy and I are both getting older …"

"And you would like to see that Lexi gets it," James asked smiling.

"I've worked hard to get what we have," he continued, "and my plans all along was to leave it to her so she would have some kind of a nest egg … however, since Lexi no long lives in our world it seems to present a bit of a conundrum."

"That's no problem at all," James chuckled, "in fact it's something very simple …"

"James, if I may," Gale spoke up, then turning to Bill said, "I know an attorney in Savannah, in fact I'm his only client, and he is very skilled in handling the transfer of property and other kinds of … shall we say … sensitive issues. If you like I will set up a meeting for the two of you?"

"That would be wonderful," he nodded, "where is his office located?"

"He will call on you at your home," she smiled, "his name is Abercrombie … F. Bailey Abercrombie. He will handle all the details, paperwork, any necessary filings and insure that the property transfer is taken care of for you. He will also make arrangements at the same time to assist you in purchasing any other surrounding properties that you may have had your eyes on. Does Wednesday around noon suit you?"

"I'll be waiting and have my plat map ready, too," Bill answered her smiling.

"Excellent," she said with a chuckle, "you see problem solved …"

"Thank you so much, Gale," Bill said, "I had no idea how to handle that issue."

"As always Bill, you just have to know the right people … in the right places," Gale laughed softly.

"In addition to Mr. Abercrombie's visit, you should also receive a package in the next couple of days, Bill," James smiled at him, "I'm having a bottle of that brandy and a box of those cigars delivered to you."

"Thank you again so much," Bill laughed, "I would like for you to be able to join me to share the experience on my rear deck, but either way, when I open it, I shall lift a toast to you!"

Soon afterwards Bill and Kathy departed for their home and once again life began to return to normal at Whitehall. The six of us gathered in the parlor for some special family time and as I listened and watched everyone I marveled at how my life had become so much like theirs. I thought back for a moment to that night so long ago of how my journey had begun ... and remembered my frightened, but simple prayer ... *Please God, show me a way out of this ... I don't want to have to kill again.* I looked around me once more and smiled as I realized I was standing in the middle of, and surrounded by, the answer to that prayer.

Charlotte Ann had been my lifesaver when I needed one the most. I had lived in a spiraling descent for so long and she had reached into the darkness and pulled me out at just the right time. She kept me from descending any further and saved me from final destruction. She steadied me, filled my life with light, and began to show me that I wasn't as lost as I had thought. She taught me that my life was exceptional, and what it was really all about and how to live in the preternatural world. She prepared me to be genuinely immortal and began leading me once again toward having a happy life.

Lexi was now my anchor in this life, the one who would prevent the darkness from ever overtaking the light again. She and I would learn, grow and mature as we travel through eternity enjoying a full and happy life ... together. I held her close to me as we stood there surrounded by family. When she tilted her face toward me and smiled, I couldn't imagine my life without her. I pulled her closer and lightly kissed her soft lips again. My lonely dark life was forever behind me and now my new life, my happiness, and my light was standing beside me.

I had been yanked against my will into the darkness in Renton Junction, Pennsylvania ... becoming a lost boy, filled with fear and having no guidance, one that no one knew or cared about for thirty-five years ... I had finally emerged back into the light of day in Charleston, South Carolina ... surrounded by a new family, who taught me how to live a successful immortal life, and now, I had an eternal mate. After all the years of darkness, the wandering, and the desperation of being unknown and unloved I once again knew what it felt like to be happy … to be loved … and to be in love.

The End

Don't Miss Book Two of

The Epic Saga of

The Master of Whitehall

Lexi's Legacy: The Epic Saga Continues

'Lexi's Legacy' is the exciting sequel to 'Katelyn's Chronicles'. After being diagnosed with terminal cancer, Lexi discovers an unexpected cure from an unlikely source and two best friends become eternal friends. Lexi tells her tale of life and love, lost and found. She relates her experiences as she leaves behind her human life and begins her journey into a new immortal life. No longer the shy, sheltered young girl from book one, Lexi radiates strength and power in her new life as she grows into her own woman.

Don't miss the intriguing conclusion

The Epic Saga of

The Master of Whitehall

James' Journey: The Interlude

In this highly anticipated final installment, James Thomas Dubois, The Master of Whitehall himself, narrates his tale and brings the classic love story of the epic saga full circle. Travel with him across the centuries as his transformation from human to vampire; untrained fledgling to powerful immortal unfolds. The story of James' life, both mortal and immortal, illustrates the role Fate plays as it guides him toward that one special day in the twenty-first century that will forever change his life, and finally fulfill his destiny.

Meet a brand new member of the family in

Hannah's Heartache

A Master of Whitehall Novelette

Hannah Richards has her life all planned out, she was born and raised in tiny little Waycross, Georgia, and she wants nothing more than to spread her wings and fly away. She wants to experience life and find out what the world outside of Waycross holds in store for her. All her plans are about to come together … until she goes to the State wide cheerleading finals in Savannah. After arriving in Savannah, she wakes to find herself thrust headlong into a new world … and it's anything but the world she expected …

Jennifer's Ghost
A Tale of Ghostly Love

Set on the South Carolina coast

Meet Jennifer, an almost thirty single girl who suddenly finds herself summoned to an attorney's office in Beaufort, South Carolina. Once there she discovers that she is the sole heir to her Aunt's estate, a beautiful nineteenth century cottage that sits atop a bluff overlooking the beach on a small coastal island. She is thrilled at her inheritance but soon dismayed when she finds that the cottage comes complete with its original owner … who died in 1864. Find out what happens when the two of them come face to face …

~ About the Author ~

The author was born in the upstate of South Carolina and has spent the majority of his life there. He joined the Navy immediately out of high school. During a six year tour of duty he had the pleasure of visiting some eighteen different countries. After returning home he attended The University of South Carolina graduating with a double Associates Degree with Honors. He completed his education at Presbyterian College in Clinton, South Carolina where he earned a Bachelor's Degree in History. He has since worked in the education field as a teacher and in various management positions in industry. He currently lives alone with his one daughter, a six year old Tuxedo cat, who graciously allows him to think he actually owns the house.

His current works include the award winning *Epic Saga of The Master of Whitehall*, a sweeping six volume narrative set primarily in historic Charleston and the surrounding Low Country of South Carolina.

His short stories include *Jennifer's Ghost*, set in beautiful Beaufort, South Carolina and *Hannah's Heartache*, a Master of Whitehall novelette, set in Savannah, Georgia.

All of the books, *Katelyn's Chronicles, Lexi's Legacy, Dale's Descent, Charlotte Ann's Coven, James' Journey, Behind the Scenes, Jennifer's Ghost* and *Hannah's Heartache* are available on Amazon.com in both print and e-book formats.

Should you wish to receive a personally inscribed and signed copy of any of the books please contact the author directly via e-mail at author@prtcnet.com, Rick H. Veal on Facebook, or via the website, TheMasterOfWhitehall.com.